It was mid-afternoon when they woke again.

They woke simultaneously and that seemed like a small, private, wonderful miracle. They opened their eyes slowly and were looking straight at each other. They laughed a little.

"I love you," Rinie said softly.

He kissed her for a long time until she lay tense against him, breathing quickly.

"Carl?"

"Don't bother me. I'm kissin' my girl."

After a while she said, a little distrustful of the utter happiness, "I was so scared about you last night. Carl, if anything ever happened to you, I—"

"Rinie." His arms were warm and she was safe. "Rinie, don't always think you got to look over your shoulder for the booger man. He's not there, honey. Honest. Here we are, right here, together, an' we'll be like this, or somethin' like, for a long, long time. You're afraid of good things. I know you've had reason before, but don't be any more. Please don't. If you can git at somethin' good, grab it with both hands and hang on for all you're worth."

"I want to," she whispered, hiding her face against his neck. She pressed against him, strangely, violently passionate . . .

Also by Frances Casey Kerns

The Winter Heart
Cana and Wine
The Edges of Love
The Errand
Savage
This Land Is Mine

Published by
WARNER BOOKS

The Stinsons

FRANCES CASEY KERNS

WARNER BOOKS

A Warner Communications Company

WARNER BOOKS EDITION

This Warner Books Edition is published by arrangement
with the author.

Cover art by Elaine Duillo

Warner Books, Inc., 75 Rockefeller Plaza, New York, N.Y. 10019

A Warner Communications Company

Printed in the United States of America

First Printing: July, 1982

10 9 8 7 6 5 4 3 2 1

To my parents who gave me
the background for this book and
to Jack and Alan
who also stand and wait.

1

Rinie looked at the man sitting beside her and out of the train window at the mountains with their gray-green mantle of trees, at the country nearer at hand—harsh, dry, and dusty under the summer sun—and she felt so many emotions that she was a little dizzy and caught a quick gasp of breath. This was the country she had heard of for the past six years, heard of from all the points of view and prejudices of Mrs. Hicks and the Stinson boys, and now she was here, to see and judge it for herself, to live with Carl and his country.

She guessed they were still at least fifty miles from the ranch but the country from here on was pretty much the same, Carl said. There was the valley of the East Fork of the Hayes River. It was a foreboding country, indomitable, unyielding; these things came to her from the feel of the hot, dry air and the smell of it as well as from the look of it. But Carl had told her all that at one time or another. He truly loved the country but he had tried hard to be unbiased, not to lead her to expect anything more than was there. For himself, he expected nothing more than that it be, changeless yet constantly changing, for him to love and contend with and respect. Not rarely, an awe of it was in his voice and in his eyes.

"There used to be volcanoes," he had said·once, "and what they call the necks—the cores of 'em—are still there, big black stumps of rocks, sticking up like—like snags in a giant's wood lot. An' there's floes where the lava ran down, dark swatches spreading out. There's mountains with good timber an' good streams comin' out of them, but most of it's desert." He grinned shyly. "I don't much like sayin' that. We mostly call it high flats, but it's mighty dry an' windy an'—harsh but, Rinie, it's—well, I guess maybe you'll know when you see it. . . . When you see the sunset the way it is sometimes, or a storm push off the mountains, or a spell of cold weather buildin' up—

1

I hope you'll know." His eyes shone, his voice was vibrant with enthusiasm. "I want you to see it. I want to be with you when you see it."

He looked at her now as she looked out at the country. He wanted to ask her what she thought, but that would be unfair. He had been born here, it was home, but he could see that for anyone from outside it would take some getting used to.

"It's so different from around Denver," she said rather lamely, turning and catching his look. "I—I mean the mountains."

"I think you'll like it when you know it," he said softly.

"Oh, I like it, Carl! It's—it's sort of—beautiful. Only it's so big and so empty and so, well, kind of lonesome."

She was saying it all wrong. She was going to hurt him, disappoint him.

"I've not seen anything, really, but right around Denver. That's all I can compare things with. That's what I meant."

He took her hand, smiling. "God, I'm glad you're here."

"When will we be in Belford?"

He looked away from her, out of the open coach window. "Just about ten minutes now, I guess. See the range across the southwest that looks like clouds? That's where Red Bear is. . . . We'll stay in Belford tonight."

"How will we get to the ranch?"

"Well," he said with his shy grin, "I rode down, of course, but I can rent a rig for us and bring it back, or maybe git somebody goin' to town to bring it for me."

"I'll learn to ride," she said stoutly. "Couldn't we just borrow a horse for me?"

"Not this time, honey. You wouldn't want to ride forty miles your first time in the saddle. But I do wish I had a car. It's a long trip for a buggy."

"Carl," she said hesitantly, "do they know about us?"

He looked away uneasily. "I didn't ever exactly spell it out, Rinie, but I guess they won't be real surprised."

"Oh." She felt a little hurt and afraid. He had been planning. He had told her three months ago that when the work eased up in late summer, he'd come for her, and yet he hadn't "spelled it out" for them at the ranch. She had never met old A. J. or Travis, or Travis's wife Ellie or their children. It didn't make much difference about Troy or Doyle, she knew them and they

2

didn't worry her, but she was afraid of A. J. and worried about Ellie. It was terribly important, what the only other woman at the ranch would think of her. She thought it might have made things a lot easier if Ellie, at least, had known she was coming.

Fearing she might be feeling hurt, Carl said teasingly, "I guess really the reason I didn' want to say anything for certain was because I wasn' sure about that Haskell—what's his name?"

She blushed. "You're so silly."

"Aunt Minna seemed to think he was a dam' good idea, not a bit silly."

Rinie didn't like to recall the unpleasant scene with Minna Hicks, but she said, "Anyway, you never even heard of Sid Haskell until this morning, so how could you have been thinking about him? Besides, you know she was just making up excuses. She'd have used you for an excuse if Sid Haskell ever wanted to marry me. No," she said thoughtfully, "I guess she wouldn't. She was awfully shocked, Carl."

He grinned wryly. "Aunt Minna's life—a good bit of it —has been made up of shocks from one Stinson or another."

After a little, she asked timidly, "But where do they think you are?"

"I don't know. I just told A. J. I'd be back in a week or less and left, before Troy got in an' beat me to it."

"Do you do that very often?"

"Ever' chance I git, but there's not many chances."

"And do you go and see girls?"

"Sure, an' sometimes I marry 'em."

Just for a moment, safe in his nearness, Rinie tried whimsically to think what it might have been like, married to Sidney Haskell or anyone else, but it was beyond imagining. Almost since she was old enough to think much about marriage, there had been Carl.

Rinie had been twelve when she came to live with Bill and Minna Hicks, and Carl had been seventeen. The age difference had seemed great, almost as if they moved in different worlds, but she had liked him from the first and there was always a lift of joy in her on the rare occasions when he came to visit the Hicks. By the time she was sixteen and he twenty-one, the age gulf had narrowed almost into nonexistence. There was never, for either of them, an earth-shaking realization of love of the type portrayed in

3

romantic novels. Simply, love was there, warm and quiet between them. There was no reason for upsetting the lives of others with demonstrations and premature declarations. The two of them knew and, until the time was right, that was enough.

Last May, then, Carl had come to Denver. He had arrived at the Hickses' house in the twilight of a spring evening and found Rinie standing on the porch, watching the last of a spectacular sunset fading over the mountains. He came up on the porch and stood beside her.

"Hello, Rinie."

"Hi, Carl."

"Where's Aunt Minna?"

"In the house. Do you want some dinner? We ate a while ago."

"No. Not now."

It was very quiet. The neighborhood streets were empty. Lights brightened in houses where people were together, having their dinners. A moment before, Rinie had been lonely. All those people in all those houses were parts of families, only she was not. She didn't think of it often, and even less often did it make her really unhappy. That was the way things were and always had been, from the beginning. "We'll raise her like our own daughter," Minna Hicks had said effusively at the orphanage. When she occasionally recalled those words, Rinie guessed, a little sardonically, that twelve was too old to become anybody's daughter, even if they really wanted you to. Usually, it didn't bother her. She practiced not being bothered, only sometimes, mostly at this time of day, she thought wistfully how everyone around her belonged with and to someone else, and she was lonely, practice or no practice. But now it was all right, because what she had been lonely for, without quite realizing it, was Carl, and he was standing beside her.

"Mr. Hicks is in the house, too." she said into the stillness, making Carl start a little. "I've just noticed lately how nobody even mentions him—you know, asks where he is and things. It's kind of sad. Why is it like that, I wonder, Carl?"

"Well," he said absently, "I guess because, with somebody like Aunt Minna around, you can't notice or even think much about Uncle Bill. . . . Rinie?"

"What?"

He put his hands on her shoulders and turned her to

face him, though it was too dark now to see each other clearly.

"Do you want to marry me?"

"Yes."

He sighed, relieved that the question and answer were done with, then he said eagerly, "I'll come back in the late summer, when work slacks off at the ranch, and we'll get married."

"Carl? Couldn't I—come with you now?"

He kissed her then, for the first time, holding her hard against him for a moment. Then he let her go and stepped back almost as though he were a little afraid of her—or of himself. Rinie felt strange and Carl seemed strange to her. The kiss had not been as pleasant as she had imagined it would be. For one thing, she had never quite imagined Carl kissing her. In any dreams about love, waking or sleeping, the man had looked like Carl and sounded like Carl when he spoke to her, but she had never let herself say consciously that it *was* Carl. Other boys had kissed her—a few—quickly, a little sheepishly, not with that sort of fierce, holding-back feeling. No, she hadn't liked it much. She was a little sorry and even sad that it had happened, and yet . . . his arms had felt wonderful, warm and protecting, and her body remembered deliciously the feel of him against her. Why had it ended so quickly?

"Couldn't I come with you?" she asked again a little breathlessly. It was odd that she was suddenly so frightened of being parted from this man who now seemed half a stranger.

"No," he said and cleared the huskiness from his throat. "I wish you could, but we've waited this long, we can wait that much more. . . . God, Rinie, sometimes it seemed like you'd never grow up, an' then I'd see you again an' you'd be changed and growin', an' . . . standin' there like you were a while ago, with the light from the mountains showin' up your face. I never saw anything so pretty."

And he reached out and she came and leaned against him lightly and his arms were warm. She felt so mixed up and happy it frightened her.

"Carl, I don't want to be away from you any more, not for even a minute. Let me go with you."

"No. Listen, you're not through with school yet. There's two more weeks—"

"I don't care about that," she broke in pleadingly.

5

"Well, but graduate anyway. There ought to at least be one other Stinson with some kind of diploma besides Doyle."

"But I—"

"Rinie, honey, listen. You're not eighteen yet. You will be next month and then, no matter how loud she yells, Minna can't do anything to stop us. I can't come back until toward the end of August. I thought it all out before I came . . . I guess I've been thinkin' about it a long time. We want it to be right, Rinie, as right as we can make it."

"Did you really think about it a long time?"

He kissed her and they were quiet for a little, the only people in the world, but then she remembered.

"But, Carl, what will I do if your aunt—"

"Don't say anything to 'er—to anybody till I come back. I'll be all right."

She knew it was—even through the tirade from Minna Hicks—she knew. Carl didn't argue or deny or protest. He came while Minna and Bill were still at the breakfast table on that warm August morning, and said that he and Rinie were being married and going to live at the ranch. Then he was silent, frustrating Minna dreadfully.

Minna went all the way back to the beginning, to his parents' marriage and how she had known from the beginning it would be disastrous, up through how she had tried her hardest to help her poor dead sister's children, give them some semblance of a decent upbringing, but A. J. and that terrible country had ruined them all, except Doyle, for whom there still seemed hope. Then Minna went on, in considerable detail, about her kindness and solicitude for Rinie, taking her in, treating her like a daughter of the house, and what had it got them?

"Free work." Carl broke his silence.

"What?" demanded his aunt, wheezing a little, her plump face flushed and perspiring.

"Six years of free work," he said calmly, and then to Rinie, "Why don't you go ahead and get your things? Do you need some help?"

She shook her head, dazedly. Displays of violent emotions always left her a little stunned and frightened. If Carl had not been there to stand between her and Minna's vituperation . . . but he was there.

She went upstairs to get the few things she had decided to take. Justifiably, she could have taken all the clothes;

there weren't so many and she had earned them. In her practicality in choosing a girl, Minna had even thought to select one who hadn't much growing left to do, so that Rinie hadn't even wasted clothing by outgrowing it. But she took only a few things. She wanted to be reminded as little as possible of the past six years. Now Carl would take care of her, give her what he could. She would never again be a charity child.

As she came back to the top of the stairs, Rinie heard Minna saying bitingly,

"Has she bothered to tell you about the Haskell boy?"

"What about him?" asked Carl easily.

"He wants to marry her, that's what about him. A fine boy, his father owns a jewelry store. We've all but agreed to the marriage. She's not likely to do any better."

Carl said slowly, and Rinie could imagine that the corner of his mouth was quirking a little as he tried not to grin, "Well, Aunt Minna, Rinie an' me *have* agreed. I guess these jewelry people will have to look for somebody else."

Minna was furious. "Just tell me this, Carl Stinson, how long have you and that girl been carrying on? I don't suppose I have the right to expect it, but right under my own roof! After all we've done for both of you! You're not the first, you know."

"The first what?" Carl's voice was casual. His aunt found him maddening.

"The first boy she's carried on with," Minna said viciously. "You'd do well to give a little thought to what you're getting into. I wonder if you're worth giving good advice to, but I can't forget you're Jenny's child. Carl, you don't know what this girl is. Her parents were the lowest kind of trash. What other sort of people leave a baby on the steps of an orphanage with nothing but a piece of paper with her name? She may turn out to be—"

Carl had turned to the stairs. Rinie had come halfway down and stood there frozen and sick. He came up and took the bundle from her and led her down.

She was crying as they left the house, partly from anger and shame that she had let Minna hurt her.

"Carl," she began brokenly when they had turned the corner, "there weren't any boys. I never—"

"I know," he said and his voice was rough with the anger he hadn't shown before. His fingers tightened on hers. "Don't bother about it, Rinie. I love you."

7

They didn't have to hire a buggy in Belford the next morning to get to the ranch. A man from Webber named Sutter Keane was in town and he drove them home. Sutter had a lot of questions to ask about this surprise bride, but he also had his mother-in-law, whom he had come to Belford to fetch, and her presence made it necessary for Carl and Rinie to ride in the back of the pickup.

"The little lady ought to ride up here," Sutter offered insistently. He knew how most any Stinson could slide out of answering questions, but the girl, alone, could be queried as to the entire situation.

"This'll be fine, Sutter," Carl said blandly, helping her up, "an' we sure do appreciate the ride."

"It looks like some a yore folks would've been down to pick you up."

"Well, they didn' know exac'ly when we'd be back."

"Had a long trip did you?"

"Not today, no."

Piqued, Sutter got in with his mother-in-law and started the engine.

"Quieter back here," Carl said, above the rattling of the truck and rushing of the wind.

They stood just behind the cab, in comparative shelter, she nearest the center; his arm was warm around her, warm and strong. She felt a sort of detachment, a delicious drowsiness, as though she were watching all this happiness being heaped on someone else. Her thoughts kept straying back, a little guiltily, to touch ecstatically on last night. . . . It must be wrong—immodest, abnormal—for a girl to feel as she had, and did, about that, but, oh surely it was right with Carl! She made herself concentrate on the words he had just said, though, for now, the sound of his voice seemed the important thing, that and the feel of his arm around her.

"Is he a friend?" She indicated the back of Sutter's bald head through the back window of the cab.

"Sutter? Oh, sure. He's been around Webber a long time. He's a sort of part-time preacher an' a good-enough neighbor when he's needed, only he's got some kind of idea the world owes him things, like part of a beef or a hog when somebody butchers, or all the information he wants about people's personal business. I like to let him guess a little."

"But what will he think of me if you won't tell him anything?"

8

"Oh, all kinds a things maybe, but ever'body's used to Sutter."

The road crossed the valley of the Hayes River lazily, its course determined by the location of scattered ranch houses. The breeze, dry and hot, was out of the west and the dust was not bad in the back of the pickup except for when they occasionally met another vehicle.

"I wish I could've brought Skeeter," Carl said.

He had showed her his little mare at the livery stable before they left Belford. Then and now, Rinie felt a prick of jealousy. Sutter's mother-in-law had brought a lot of her things; otherwise, they would have had the mare with them in the truck now.

Restlessly, Carl craned his neck around the side of the cab and drew back.

"At least with a buggy you could see ahead."

"Well, you could ride with Sutter," she said teasingly.

"No, I mean *you*. I want you to see the country. All I want to look at is you."

She snuggled her hand in his. "How will you get Skeeter home?" For now, instead of jealousy, she felt sympathy for the mare, having to be so long away from the one she loved.

"I'll go git 'er if nobody else is goin' down in the next few days."

The day grew hotter. Jar flies dinned in the bushes along a stream they followed and left and followed again. The land, a little way back from the stream, looked parched, almost dead, but there were a few cattle browsing here and there. The houses were farther and farther apart now, until Rinie again felt the emptiness and loneliness of the country.

"How far to the nearest neighbor? From the ranch, I mean?"

" 'bout five miles."

"So far?"

"That's not far, Rinie. Where grazin's no better than it is around here, ranches can't be very close together."

After a while the valley began to narrow and they followed the stream more closely, the West Fork, Carl said, West Fork of the Hayes River. As they rounded a curve, Rinie saw the mountains and drew back a little at their unexpected nearness—the Hayes Mountains, the range Carl had pointed out to her from the train yesterday. They were not so high and abrupt as the Front Range west of Denver at which she had looked all her life, but there was a look and a feel of brooding and total indifference about them that she found awesome and frightening. They're old, she thought reverently, older than anything, and they don't care about anything. We two, standing here, aren't anything to them. She drew close to Carl, finding the mountains a little dreadful.

The road was narrower now, full of rocks and very rough. Carl pointed out two more volcanic necks. She thought them strange and obtrusive, almost obscene things, in a land full of awesome ugliness, but she'd never say that to Carl. He must never know she even thought it. He showed the country as he had shown his mare, saying simply, "That one's Skeeter," and standing back a little complacently, knowing that anyone with half an eye could see the merits without having them explained.

I don't know about horses, Rinie thought, and I don't know about different kinds of country, either. Maybe I'll come to think as much of it as he does in time. She smiled into his eyes, thinking of how much time there would be . . . all that time for them—together. But, for now, it seemed such a hard unyielding country and she wondered what Carl's mother had thought of it the first time she had seen it.

Rinie had heard a great deal about Virginia Carlisle Stinson from Virginia's sister, Minna Hicks: that Jenny was a saint if one ever walked the earth, putting up all those years with A. J. Stinson's foolishness—living out in the middle of nowhere, doing all that rough work, giving birth to her children with no one to assist her but a dirty Indian woman, claiming to believe, with A. J., that there was something to be made out of that heathen country, staying at home, seeing to all the work, worrying to give her sons some kind of proper upbringing—while A. J. ranted over the country without a thought for his family or the propriety of things. Jenny had died in the flu epidemic, though Minna couldn't see to this day how an epidemic spread where there were no people to carry it, but her death was probably a blessing in disguise. It would have been more than even Jenny, saint and martyr that she was, could bear, to see that her boys, for the most part, had turned out no better than you'd expect of A. J. Stinson's sons. Jenny had surely done her best while she lived, but there was only so much a person could do as Minna knew all too well. . . .

But Rinie hoped that Jenny was not the kind of person Minna described. She wondered if perhaps Jenny hadn't had some of the same feelings as she, Rinie, was now experiencing the first time A. J. brought Jenny here: fear and apprehension about whether she would be acceptable to the country and the life it would give her, but, overall, a contentment and love with the man beside her as vast and all-encompassing as the country itself. . . . They would have come in a wagon, A. J. and Jenny, or perhaps on horseback. Maybe there wasn't even enough of a road for a wagon then.

Webber was a scatter of houses along the West Fork. A store and a school were the only public buildings. There wasn't even a flag to indicate a post office. No one was willing to contract to bring mail regularly over this road. The greater part of the buildings in the community were in a state of collapse. On one, Rinie made out, on a faded sign, "Silver Spur Saloon".

"There were several hundred people here durin' the mining boom," Carl explained. "That was nearly forty years ago. About all of 'em went someplace else when the veins turned out to be pockets. There is quite a lot of low-grade ore, but they were mostly lookin' for big bonanzas an' those don't happen too much."

"But what are they doing with the ore that's here? Are there mines?"

"No, not any more. A. J. tried it a couple of times an' some others did, but the bottom fell out of silver prices an' this stuff's not worth the cost of shippin', this far from the railroad."

She was glad there was ore, however low-grade it might be. Minna had never bothered to mention that any actually existed.

"Silver!" Rinie remembered Minna saying caustically as she sat by to see that Rinie ironed curtains properly. "A. J. would go out hunting for the pot of gold at the end of the rainbow. Any excuse at all to be off running around. I told Jenny there wasn't a thing to it right from the first, but that man could twist her around his finger. She'd have believed day was night if he told her, or she'd have tried to anyway."

Minna always talked freely to Rinie. She couldn't very well discuss such things as this with her friends, for it might give them wrong ideas about the family. And Bill, good provider and businessman that he was, was no bet-

11

ter than talking to a post. Not only did he fail to join in a conversation, most of the time he didn't even listen. The girl was, in a way, part of the family. She knew better than to carry tales to other folks, and she was usually an interested listener. She didn't butt in with a lot of silly questions, but seemed eager to hear when Minna felt like talking. There were times when Minna feared she'd said too much, like the time she'd been so upset about Bill staying downtown late every night, and then she became unusually impatient and harsh with Rinie, but the girl never broached a subject again once Minna was through with it. So talking to her was a relief, no more of a worry than talking to oneself about family matters, but with the added gratification of watching the changing expressions on the face of another.

Minna had been looking through the paper that day while Rinie ironed curtains. There was an editorial about silver prices. She didn't read it. She wasn't the least bit interested in that sort of thing, but it got her thinking again of her poor sister's family.

"A. J. bought up hundreds and hundreds of acres of that worthless land." she went on. "*He* was going to have his silver *and* a bit of a cattle ranch. Oh, yes, I'm sure! Like his papa's big place in Texas. He was always telling about that when he courted Jenny, how his papa didn't have a cent after the Civil War and got to be a rich man from selling cattle that didn't even belong to him—a no-good Rebel and a cattle thief into the bargain! And if he was so rich, he certainly didn't give his boy any money, or if he did, A. J. threw it all away before he ever got to Denver. That wouldn't be any surprise either, seeing the way he threw away every chance he had that made any sense after that.

"Bill would have gladly helped him invest his money safe and proper. Bill's not any expert himself on stocks and such, but he knows men that are. Why, the fact that we weren't wiped out in the stock-market crash proves that. Heaven knows, we lost more than we could stand, but there was something left. Those men would have advised A. J. and his money would have gone to work for him at something sure. They could have lived here in Denver like civilized human beings. Jenny would be living now and her boys would have had a decent upbringing, but no! A. J. never thought about a soul but

12

himself. He bought up all that worthless land and never found enough silver on it to make himself one thin dime. And finally, after he'd thrown away every cent, there wasn't anything for them to do but go and live there. That worthless place was all they had and he didn't even seem to care. You'd think he'd have some shame, but he was as brassy as you please and Jenny stood for it. We would have taken Jenny in any time, Jenny and the boys, though it would have upset our lives—the way we live—but she said they'd do all right, that A. J. could always raise cattle if there wasn't any silver. Well, anybody in their senses knows there's no money in cattle. Not that Jenny wasn't smart. She just had a big blind spot where anything about A. J. was concerned. I'll never think that, deep in her heart, she believed all he said, but Jenny was a proud girl, pride is a trait of the Carlisle family, and the poor thing was determined to lie in the bed she'd made."

Passing through Webber now, Rinie thought maybe Jenny had believed. Anyway, she hoped so.

"There were twenty-eight saloons at one time," Carl said as the pickup came to a stop before the Keane house. "Tents and shacks all over the place. A. J. likes to talk about it sometimes. You'll hear about how it was."

He jumped lightly to the ground and held up his arms for her, but Rinie, too conscious of Sutter and his mother-in-law and of other eyes from the house, took his hands sedately and stepped down.

Sutter began heartily, "Well, now, I hope it wasn' too dusty an' windy back there. Li'l Miz Stinson still looks like she just stepped out of a bandbox, don't she, mama? An' here's Essie."

His wife had come from the house and was embracing her mother, casting quick curious glances at the girl.

"What do you think, Essie? Carl's went an' got hisself a wife, an' not a prettier girl around, I'll lay."

Carl conquered a grin. Sutter had some dam' funny expressions for a preacher to use.

Essie shook hands a little coolly. She had three girls of her own of an age for marriage—stouter, healthier-looking girls than this one. Not that she'd fancy a Stinson for a son-in-law, but a mother had to think of her own and there wasn't an awful lot to choose from, back in here. Anyway, Sutter always made such a fuss, especially if there was another woman around to take notice of. She,

13

Essie, though, was not one to shirk or seem unneighborly so she said with a small, persimmony smile, "Come on in, Carl, you an' Miz Stinson. Dinner's ready to be set on the table."

No matter what they thought of her, Rinie now looked on Sutter and Essie Keane with a prejudiced eye. They had been the very first to call her "Miz Stinson" and she always remembered.

"We better go on home, I guess," Carl said. "I'll help you unload this stuff, Sutter, an' then—"

"No, no," protested Sutter. "We won't worry about that now. You two come on in an' eat an' then I'll ride you up to the ranch."

"Thanks," Carl said, "but we'll go on now. Thanks for askin' us to dinner, Miss Essie, but we kind of want to git home."

He picked up their things and, Rinie shyly smiling her thanks, they turned to go.

"No, now wait," protested Sutter. "I'll ride you up there right now. They can wait dinner. It won't take but a few minutes."

"That's all right," Carl said, over his shoulder. "Anyway, I'm afraid you'd git your truck stuck. Our upper ford washed bad in that high water last month an' we haven' got it fixed up yet."

"But that's a long ways for your wife to have to walk, a hot day like—"

"Oh, hush up, Sutter!" hissed Essie, too low for the young people to hear. "Can't you tell when you ain't wanted?"

"Well, daggone it!" he cried in frustration. "I want to know where she come from."

Carl and Rinie, hearing this last, began to walk faster so the Keanes wouldn't hear them laughing.

"But," said Rinie, sobering, "do you think we hurt their feelings? I wouldn't do that for anything."

Looking back as they rounded a curve, they saw that the Keanes' front yard was empty.

"I don't know," Carl said as the house disappeared from sight, "but I can't help it if we did. I couldn't stay there any longer. All I been wantin' all day is for us to be by ourselves."

He put down the things he carried by the roadside and

took her in his arms. Both their lips tasted dusty and neither of them cared.

At Webber their way had left the West Fork, though a road followed up that stream for some distance, to scattered ranches and deserted mining claims. The road to the Lazy S, or Red Bear Ranch as it was mostly called, went up Red Bear Creek, running south for two miles or so, past a few houses, then turning abruptly west into a dark narrow slit of a canyon where the creek had worked its way through a ridge of dark granite. Out in the valley, where Red Bear Creek went to join the West Fork, the stream had seemed insignificant. It had a big channel but there wasn't much water. It seemed tired and thready and retiring, as if it wasn't sure it belonged there in the bottom of that big channel out in the open country. But in the canyon, with its steep descent, it was a different stream, low though the water might be. It rushed and roared and foamed over and around the big dark boulders that choked its way. About halfway up the canyon, there was a twenty-foot waterfall. The water dropped with a crashing roar and rushed foaming to smash through several cramped channels in a ledge of particularly stubborn granite, and then fell again in separate jets into a pool where it swirled dizzily to find an outlet. Rinie felt a little sad about the stream. It seemed to be driven and frustrated and tormented.

Carl wanted to cross on the ledge in the middle of the falls and she was terrified, though she assured him she thought it would be fun. What he called the lower ford was upstream a hundred yards or so at a place of relative quiet, but he always liked crossing at the falls. He was rarely here on foot, but sometimes, with a horse he could trust like Skeeter, he let her go the way she wanted and himself crossed on the rock just for the fun of it. Some might think it a dangerous thing, he guessed. Even in low water, if a person lost his footing, he could get pretty skinned up before he got out, but if you were careful there was nothing to it. If you crossed on foot at the lower ford, you had to take your boots off and the coarse gravel of the bottom hurt your feet like anything. Here you kept your boots on, stepping easily across the separate little channels and getting just enough spray from the falls to feel good on a hot day. This was one of his favorite places and he had thought often about show-ing it to Rinie.

Stepping gingerly onto the ledge, Rinie felt sick. It wasn't far down, not much farther than she was tall, but she couldn't bear to look down at the water dashing so frenziedly among the dark boulders in the pool below. The rock they stood on, what she would have thought of a moment ago as solid rock, trembled with the force of the falling water. It was slippery with spray and moss and she wanted to shut her eyes, to sit down and crawl back, any-thing but to be here where she was. Carl held her hand, and then he stood between her and the lower side of the ledge. What if he should fall? She was fighting tears. His arm was around her and all she could do was inch cau-tiously forward, able to think only of getting across as quickly as possible so that he wouldn't be there on the edge above that battering water.

At last they were across and Carl grinned at her with pleasure and then looked quizzical. She was pale and trembling and he thought there were tears on her lashes, though she wouldn't look at him.

"Rinie? Honey, are you cryin'?"

"It's—it's just the spray," she said shakily, wiping her face.

He led her away from the stream, small rocks rolling and clattering as they climbed up the bank into the sun-light.

"I'm sorry, honey," he said with tender contrition, tak-ing her chin gently in his hand and tilting her face up. "I'm so sorry. I didn' think of scarin' you. I just wanted you to see it. I ought to of thought, you're not used to things like that. I—"

She smiled, a little wanly. "It's all right, Carl. It's not anything. I—I liked it. It's just—well, I was afraid you'd slip, walking so close to the edge."

He laughed uncertainly. "It wouldn' be the first time if I had."

"You mean—you fell? In there?'

"Me an' Troy were crossin' there when I was—oh, eleven, I guess. We'd been fightin' off an' on through the day about somethin'. I can't remember what, an' comin' home from school we tried to ambush each other. Down the canyon there a little, we got off our horses to have it

16

out an' Doyle come along an' run off our horses an' went on home. We were so dam' mad an' we couldn' git at Doyle right then, so we started walkin', thinkin' up all the dirty words we could, an' by the time we come to cross the creek, we was really worked up so we started scufflin' an' we both fell, pretty close to this side. Troy hit his head. I was scraped up some an' didn' pay much attention to him for a while, but pretty soon I wondered why he wasn' cussin'. He was just sorta sittin' there in the edge a the water—it was lower than now—with his head leaned back against a rock an' blood runnin down. God! I was scared!"

He smiled ruefully at the recollection, but Rinie was grave.

"Was he hurt bad?"

"Well, pretty bad. He was knocked out an' bleedin' a lot. It took me a while to drag him outa the water, limp like he was, an' then I didn' know what to do. I was afraid to leave him to git help, an' afraid not to, so finally I started for the house.

"Doyle had got home an' so had our horses an' Travis an' A. J. had come in for supper. Doyle told 'em we just had a little ways to walk an' ought to be right along. When I got there, they'd started to eat, figgerin' we was just foolin' around. A. J. an' Travis and Doyle went back after Troy, but Ellie wouldn' let me go. I was pretty bloody from all them scrapes an' scratches an' she thought I was hurt more'n I was. Kirby was a little baby then. I remember because Ellie had some kinda ointment for him that she used on me an' it felt good.

"Troy hadn' come to when they got him home an' he didn' till nearly midnight. Then he had a high fever an' was out of his head most of the time for a couple of days. A. J. was so worried about him that first night an' couldn' do nothin' about it, so he beat the devil outa me'n Doyle. A. J.'s not one that can just wait around."

"Oh!' she said angrily. "Why did he, though? You didn't mean it to happen."

"Well, no, but I thought I did by the time he got through with me. Me an' Troy was fightin'."

"But you were scared, so worried about him," she said, outraged. "It wasn't fair to beat you."

Carl kissed her, picked up their things, and took her

hand. She wasn't shaky any more. She had forgotten about being scared of the crossing.

He said, "Well, that was a long time ago an' it's nothin' to git mad about now. What I was tryin' to tell you is that there's nothin' to be afraid of about crossin' back there."

She laughed and his heart skipped. It was such a pretty, light little laugh, mixed in with the sound of the water. She said, "You've got a funny way of putting a person's mind at ease."

"It's a new thing to me," he said earnestly. "I hope I'll git better at it."

They walked in silence for a while. The canyon opened abruptly into a broad valley, the stream slanting south-westerly, away from the ridge that so grudgingly gave it an exit from the mountains. A covey of quail flew up from some high dusty weeds by the road and Carl wished aloud for his shotgun. The road itself had fairly high dusty weeds growing between the wheel ruts.

Carl pointed out some cattle, small dark spots across the valley. "They're ours."

"You mean all this is part of the ranch?" she asked, impressed.

"Honey, you've got to have a lot of acres to feed one steer in country like this. It's not as much as it seems like to you."

He looked thoughtfully across the semidesert land-scape.

"I'd like to put a dam higher up on the creek someday. We could irrigate quite a lot an' raise a lot of hay an' grain an' stuff. I read about some irrigated land—in south Texas, I think it was—where two acres will feed a cow an' calf. Course, I can't believe any land is *that* good, but we could make this here a lot better, usin' some a this water that's just runnin' away, doin' nobody good."

"Why don't you, then?" she asked with eager interest.

He shrugged. "The others don't think much of it. Only, Doyle'll talk, but that's all. Troy figgers it's a lot of work leadin' to a lot more work, an' A. J. feels pretty much the same. A. J. says ranchin' is a man an' his stock livin' off the land, an' when you start doin' things to change how the land is, then you're a farmer. Travis wouldn' want to spend the money—if we had it. I guess it don't matter much. We get some hay and grain from the beaver meadows up above. It's enough to feed a little when the winter's bad. That's all we need, really. . . .

"Are you tired, Rinie? It's awful hot."

"No," she said absently "It's not far now, is it?"

"Less than a mile. Here's the upper ford."

The stream was wide here and normally shallow, but the sandy bottom was unstable and washed badly in high water. They took off their shoes and waded across, the deepest water not halfway to Rinie's knees.

"I like this," she said, smiling up at him. "Only the water's so cold. How can it be, I wonder, when the sun's so hot?"

By wordless agreement, they sat down in the shade of a cottonwood.

"Can you swim?" he asked.

"I don't know," she said, putting her feet back in the water. "To tell you the truth I never was in any water except in a bathtub before this."

He was surprised. It seemed he knew her so well and yet how could anyone he knew have passed their eighteenth birthday without ever having been in a running stream?

"I'll teach you to swim. We've got a good place up above the house a little."

"What did you mean about what you said to Mr. Keane about the upper ford? Were you just making it up?"

"No. It's a funny place. The bottom's sandy with some gravel and it washes in high water an' there's apt to be holes, nothin' to bother walkin' across or ridin' a horse, but enough to git a wagon or a car stuck. There were several holes when I left the other day, but I guess Troy filled 'em so he could git his car out. They're gone and so's the car."

"How do you know that? About the car?"

"On the other side there, it's gone up outa the water, but it hasn' come back on this side." He yawned and stretched. "We oughta do somethin' about this ford, but nobody knows what."

She felt inspired. "Why don't you get together with everyone who uses the road and build a bridge?"

His eyes had been half-closed but now they widened. "Honey, nobody uses this road but us an' people comin' to see us. It don't go no place but our house."

"Oh."

It had seemed like such a good idea and now he must think she was silly because she couldn't seem to stop thinking about neighbors and community projects.

"We could move it," he said indolently. "There's a place less than a quarter mile below here that would prob'ly be better but that would take a good bit of road work. Anyway, you can see this place from the house. A. J. says that's handy sometimes, though I can't see it's exac'ly necessary. It's not like we have to keep a lookout for Indians or revenuers or things like that."

Rinie was immediately uneasy. "Can we see the house?" She felt as if she were under the scrutiny of unseen eyes. "Do you think they've seen us?"

Carl laughed. "Not likely. This time of day, people mostly have somethin' more to do than watch for somebody comin'."

She was frightened. It all came to the surface now, the tension and apprehension that her joy in being with Carl, in knowing she would always be with him, had kept veiled. But now the time was almost upon her and it didn't much matter how Carl felt. She knew he loved her, but she knew enough of the Stinsons to know that each made his own decisions, regardless of the feelings of the others. What if they didn't like her? Oh, what would she do, marooned here among them, if they didn't like her?

Minna had said that A. J. was crude and rude and vulgar and many other things. Carl had said once, with admiration, that if A. J. had something to say, he got it said the fastest way. Well, what could she do if he didn't like her or want her here? He was the boss at the ranch. She had even heard the tempestuous, wayward Troy admit that. Carl would stand by her, of course, she hadn't a minute's concern about that, but this place was Carl's life. She sensed that he couldn't be himself and happy away from it, any more than she could be happy away from him. But nobody could have any peace if A. J. was displeased.

Travis, as the eldest son, was next to A. J. in authority. What if he didn't want Carl to marry? Maybe he'd think Carl would work more, better, single. Maybe he'd think she, Rinie, would be lazy and not earn her keep. Maybe Ellie wouldn't like the way she did things, and it was, after all, Ellie's house, she being Travis's wife. And what about

20

their three children? For as long as she could remember, Rinie had yearned over the thought of brothers and sisters and, through the summer while she waited for Carl, she had dreamed happily that Kirby and Jeff and Helen might be like little brothers and sister to her, that they would be friends on sight, always congenial . . . but now she knew with sickening clarity that they might not be friends at all.

There was no concern about Troy and Doyle. She knew them. Doyle had lived in his aunt's house during three high-school years since Rinie had come to live there. They were reasonably good friends, though they had never been close in any respect. Troy had come for a few brief visits. She had found him fun and he inclined mostly to a good nature, even about the times he tried to kiss her in his aunt's kitchen and failed. But, even counting Troy and Doyle as allies, her trepidations about the rest of the family were still more than enough to make her wish they were not quite so near the house.

Carl thought maybe her feelings were hurt about the bridge or because of what he had said about people not having time to watch for them. He probably had sounded a little short, though he hadn't meant to. She had had enough short answers and long-winded criticisms from Minna to last her for life. He raised his eyelids and peeked at her.

She had taken her feet out of the water and sat with her arms around her drawn-up knees and her head down, looking small and forlorn. A sunbeam came down through the leaves and touched the heavy brown braids wound round her small head. She had such pretty hair, thick and rich. He liked it best loose, the way she'd toss her head and shrug a shoulder to get it back out of her way. But, of course, she couldn't wear it loose to go riding around in the backs of pickups. Thinking of her wearing her hair loose brought back the memory of last night, warm and enveloping. He lay very still, feeling as if everything inside him were melting.

"Rinie?"

She raised her head quickly and smiled a little but her eyes were sad. She had warm brown eyes and a pretty little face. He wanted badly to kiss her, but he wasn't sure if she wanted him to.

"I love you, Rinie."

She moved over and lay in his arms, but she was crying. "What's wrong, little girl? Please don't cry."

"I—I just want to be *right* for you," she sobbed.

"Right?" he said. "If you weren't just what I want, do you think I'd of waited around all this time for you to grow up?"

"Don't make me sound like such an awful baby," she said, trying not to cry. Then, her voice muffled against his shirt she said, "I've wanted a family all my life and now I've got one, I—I don't know what to do."

He held her close. What was he doing to her anyway? She was so sweet, so gentle and considerate. He was all but throwing her into a lion's den. Stinsons were not known for tact and thoughtfulness, particularly A. J. Carl paid no attention to barbs and small derisions—that was just the way people talked at home—but, now he came to think of it, Rinie, so eager to be loved, to be a part of a family, was so vulnerable and defenseless. He should have told them before he left that he was going to be married. Then, at least, they could have got a good part of their speculating and discussing done without Rinie's being there. If they made her unhappy. . . . But she can handle them, he thought proudly. She'll like them when she's used to the kind of people we are. Anyone who had been able to maintain a good-natured equilibrium under the badgering of Minna Hicks could take on the Stinsons, even A. J.

"Carl?" her voice was small. "What will I do? I want everything to be just right."

"Don't worry about it, that's what you'll do. Why don't we just go on up there? If a thing bothers you, puttin' it off don't help any."

It was very still. The stream made only a few rippling sounds here. The cottonwood rustled quietly in the warm breeze. A few leaves fell, drifting lazily on little eddies of air. A grasshopper made his dry song to the sun and autumn.

Rinie wasn't crying. She sat up and looked at her husband. Now he was worried over her and that was not at all what she wanted. She smiled and, despite the tears that still hung on her lashes, the smile was authentic.

"I'll wash off some of the dust," she said with decision, "and then we'll go."

She bathed her face and arms in the cold water and

pulled on her stockings and shoes while Carl watched, full of love and pride. It was this resiliance in Rinie that had from the first exasperated Minna Hicks and attracted Carl. She was sensitive, yet rarely sullen or vengeful over hurts, tractible, but with a streak of stubborn self-sufficiency that could stand up under the most determined onslaughts.

2

The house sat back a little from the edge of a bank above the creek, facing south. In front of it, across the creek, the valley was wide, its soil coarse and sandy, growing sparse vegetation and scattered with dark boulders. From the far ridge, a volcanic neck towered somberly above the scrub trees. Behind the house the land rose in dark plateaus, the lowest and the next above much like the land across the creek, but the third level was dotted with pinion and juniper and a few scrub oak, the one above that showed a good cover of small trees, and the next supported some big ponderosa pine and showed the lighter green of aspen. Above that, it was all green and cool-looking and distant —until the eye was led up to where a gray spine of rock stood bare and exposed, light patches of snow in its weathered crevices, gleaming in the sunlight against the dark, brooding rock.

"You can see Utah from up there," Carl said, his voice lowered for reasons he could not have explained. "Not that Utah's any dif'rent from Colorado around here."

They were still a little distance from the house, standing there so that Rinie could look.

"I'd like to see it," she said, "whether it's different or not. I've never looked at another state."

"We'll go up there sometime," he said. "It's a hard climb after you come out of the trees, but it's kind of a—special place."

The house was log and it looked big and substantial. Originally, it had been two large, square rooms and these.

the front room and the kitchen, were still the center of the house and of the family's life. Along the west side, four bedrooms had been built in a row, the foremost extending some feet beyond the front wall of the front room, and in this ell was a porch. The porch went round the corner and more than halfway along the east side of the front room to where two more rooms had been added. There were two chimneys and smoke drifted wispily from the back one. It was not a pretty house, nor striking in any way. Its only digression from the solid, unadorned rectangle was the ell-shaped porch. The windows were small and dusty-paned, their curtains made of flour sacks with the printing bleached out and now grayed by time. There was a sunken strip across the front of the house which had, perhaps, once been a flower bed, but which now contained only spindly weeds, some rocks, and a few rusty cans.

A rusty old pickup sat near the porch on the east side, the right front tire going flat. The yard was unkept, not fenced off at all, and, as they looked, a yearling heifer came lazily out of the shade of a cottonwood at the top of the bank, snuffing the air. When she perceived them, she bolted off the bank, snorting in fear. A few other cattle, resting in the shade along the creek, caught her fright and ran with her off across the flats.

"I haven't seen a cow that close to the house in a long time," Carl said, "not even the milk cow."

"I guess they learn to stay out of the yard," Rinie said hopefully, and he grinned. He couldn't help it.

"They're wild," he said, trying not to laugh. "They don't learn anything; they just don't like to git close to people."

"Oh."

Unkempt and ungarnished as it was, the house had a personality. It was stolid and solid, more a part of the country than something built on its surface. It was where it was to stay and it had a feeling about it of complacency and sureness in its belonging.

The outbuildings were behind the house and to the east: a good-sized barn in need of repair, a small chicken house looking raw in its newness—it was scarcely weathered yet—and surrounded by a fence of chicken wire that gleamed in the sun. There were several sheds in different states of disrepair. There was a complex of corrals, empty and silent in the sun.

Carl felt as if he were seeing the place for the first time.

24

He had never really thought about it before; it had always been just home. But how did it look to Rinie? About all she had seen besides the orphanage—which she had described to him once as "bare and awfully clean"—was that neighborhood around the Hickses' place with well-kept lawns and houses with fancy ironwork and stone things across the fronts of them; a neighborhood where every leaf was raked up and people watered their grass and pruned things and painted when they didn't need to, just because the neighbors had. Carl's gaze moved critically along the pole corrals, the outbuildings, to the house. Never mind about those in Denver. This was a place where people *lived*, not just something for show. Maybe Rinie didn't see that now, but she'd come to. This was a place where people were born, where they laughed and cried and grew. He had been born here, he and Troy and Doyle. Their mother had died here. Ellie had had four children here. One of them had died. This was not a place that you fixed up for company and fussed over and nobody could touch; it was a place where you worked and fought and learned and played and lived. Only . . . what if Rinie didn't like it? He hadn't considered that before. Now that she was here, looking around, taking it all in, so silent and sober and he couldn't tell what was in her mind and was afraid to ask, it seemed possible that she didn't think much of it.

"Troy's gone, all right," he said, to be saying something. "Prob'ly Doyle too. I wonder how long."

Rinie thought that it looked like a good solid house with a purpose in being, but she wondered, a little guilty about questioning, why Ellie didn't fix it up a little. There could be flowers there, maybe, and those chairs on the porch could be painted. But, of course, that was up to Ellie. She wondered eagerly what was in the outbuildings, what they were for. She wondered why there wasn't a fence around the yard. She didn't ask questions because she was beginning to think it was better to keep quiet if you didn't know something. If Carl couldn't help laughing at her, what would the others do? And he'd be embarrassed, surely, if she seemed stupid in front of people. She wondered apprehensively when they would see someone or someone would see them, who it would be, what they and Carl and she would say. Perhaps no one was around the house now. It was so quiet. Maybe they could look inside alone, before anyone came. She'd like that, but then her eye caught a movement on the porch and at the same instant great grizzly looking dogs came boiling from beneath the porch, frantically loud and fierce with their belated barking. Recognizing Carl, they changed from warning to greeting, but were no less noisy. Trying to pet all of them at once as they quieted to whines and jealous rumblings, he said, "Jethro an' Sheba an' Sport an' Nero an' Christmas an' Pup."

Rinie acknowledged the introduction with a tentative smile. She was a little afraid of dogs and these sniffed at her so heartily and there were so many of them and they were so big. Feeling that something more was expected, she said, "What—what kind are they?"

"Oh, all kinds," Carl said carelessly. Here dogs were judged on individual merit, not pedigrees. "Mostly one kind of hound or another, except Nero's got some mastiff or something an' Sport's mostly shepherd."

"Carl? What you doin? Who's that you got with you?"

Rinie looked apprehensively toward the porch. She didn't have to be told that it was A. J. Stinson standing there. He looked bigger than life, raised a few feet above them as he was, but he would have looked that way to Rinie, standing on a level. She had heard so much about him that he was like a legend come alive, a fearsome legend. He was a big man, tall and growing heavy as he approached seventy. His hair was gray and in disarray, rather fiercely so, retaining all the strength and vigor of youth with only the color changed. His face, though the muscles were beginning to play him false, was still handsome, the skin ruddy under a three-day stubble. His eyebrows were thick and fierce like his hair and they were raised a little now, quizzically, as Carl and Rinie came forward.

"A. J., this is Rinie . . . she's—my wife."

There was a moment of rather dreadful silence. Rinie kept her eyes down.

"Your *what?*" the old man exploded.

"We got married yesterday in Denver."

Carl sounded calm enough. She looked at him and he was grinning shyly. She got her eyes as high as A. J.'s chest and then had to look away. His shirt was unbuttoned, exposing a great hairy expanse of his midsection.

"I'll be goddamned," A. J. rumbled. "Well, come on up here. an' le's have a look at 'er. What'd you do, boy? See 'er walkin' down the street an' drag 'er to the church? I

26

didn't know you had it in you. How fer behind's her pa an' the posse?"

"I've known her a long time, A. J. It's Rinie—Irene—that lived at Aunt Minna's."

"Minnie's girl!" roared A. J., astounded. "Jesus Christ, Carl! What you been up to?"

"Nothin'," Carl said easily. "I been figgerin' to marry her a long time."

"You have, have you?" A. J. laughed rumblingly. "An' what's Minnie been figgerin'?"

"Well, she didn' know anything about it till yesterday, an' now I guess she figgers . . ." Carl let the words trail away. Maybe it would be the wrong thing to say them, but A. J. finished the thought.

"Another pore defenseless woman that she spent her time an' patience an' lovin' care on's been drug off to feed the wolves. God almighty! She musta been fit to be tied. You shore this come as a surprise to 'er?" His voice was full of diabolical glee and Rinie could easily see why Minna hated him so, but, for herself, she couldn't help smiling a little.

"Oh, yes sir," Carl assured him. "It was a definite surprise."

A. J. snorted with laughter. "Wish I coulda seen her face."

Rinie started to raise her eyes again and then looked away, blushing. The thought had come to her that she was glad Carl wasn't all hairy like that and it made her hot with embarrassment. She was half-convinced A. J. could see what she was thinking and that he would mention it.

"Well, come on up an' set down," said the old man brusquely. "Where'd you walk from? Where's Skeeter at?"

Carl explained as they came up the last step and sat down on dusty, rickety chairs.

"Ellie!" yelled A. J. "Ellie."

"I guess she's outside," Carl said when there was no answer.

"Well, go find 'er," said his father.

Carl got up reluctantly, not quite meeting Rinie's eyes. She wanted to say "Don't leave me," or to get up and follow him through the house, but she couldn't. She felt A. J.'s eyes on her as the silence lengthened. Flies buzzed loudly. A cow bawled, off across the creek.

"You talk, I expect," he said stiffly and cleared

27

his throat. "I can't feature Buck marryin' somebody that don't."

"Yes sir, I do," she said diffidently.

His eyes were blue, the deepest, most piercing blue she'd ever seen in eyes, not much like Troy's at all, and Mrs. Hicks had always said Troy was the image of A. J. She thought he could see a lot of things, but somehow she wasn't afraid of him any more. One corner of his mouth was curving up the least bit, the way Carl's did, though A. J. seemed to feel this was a time for seriousness.

"I expect you been told I'm the devil hissel'," he said solemnly. "Minnie don't care fer me a bit, nor this place, though she's never seen it."

She thought how Mrs. Hicks loathed being called "Minnie." She said softly, "Carl told me different."

"Did, did he? Well, now you can't believe him either, ever' time. Carl's apt to be full of a lot of—stuff at times. . . . You like the boy, do you?"

"Yes sir, I do." She was blushing, but she didn't look away.

He nodded soberly, clearing his throat. "You're a kinda little thing, frail an' skinny-lookin'. This ain't no easy life. Did he tell you that?"

"Oh, I'm strong," she said eagerly.

His eyes softened and he let the grin come. "Yes, I expect you are. Minnie wouldn't 've had you around if you wasn'."

Carl came around the corner of the house with a little black-haired girl on his shoulder and a boy following shyly behind.

"Here's Helen, Rinie, an' Jeff. Ellie'll be here in a minute."

"Are you married to Carl?" the little girl asked. Her eyes were dark and bold, not shy at all.

Rinie nodded.

"Are you gonna live here?"

"Yes."

"Where you gonna sleep?"

A. J. gave his snort of laughter. "Helen ain't bashful, are you, Puss?"

"How come you're not in school?" Carl asked her, putting her down and taking a chair close to Rinie.

"Cause I didn' want to. Kirby didn' so I couldn' go by myself, could I? Kirby's helpin' daddy, but they wouldn' let me."

28

"That wild stallion's been after the mares again," A. J. explained to his son. "Travis an' Kirby went after 'em." He looked irritated and a little embarrassed and felt it necessary to say, "I wouldn' been no help fer I can't ride but mighty little right now. I'm still stiff in the joints from some cause. Troy an' Doyle pulled out the day after you left. You didn' see 'em in Belford, did you?"

Carl shook his head.

"I don't expect you was lookin' fer 'em," A. J. said dryly. "You goddam' kids. Cut a little hay an' pull out. I admit, hayin' ain't decent work fer a man, but that ain't no call fer all of you to go off at once. I don't aim fer it to happen agin."

Rinie kept glancing at Jeff. Helen was leaning against Carl's chair and staring at her with curious interest, but Jeff had given her one swift glance and no more. He didn't come onto the porch and he looked utterly bereft. It was so terribly important to her to be friends with Jeff because he was so special to Carl.

"Maybe I better go see if I can help 'em," Carl said in reluctant obedience to his father's hint.

"Oh, hell, no," said A. J., satisfied. "They been gone since sunup. They either got the mares or give 'em up by now."

Ellie came shyly out of the house and Carl introduced the two women.

"Did you know anything about this, Sal?" A. J. asked Ellie, indicating the newlyweds.

"Not till Carl come an' tole me a minute ago," said Ellie, a small, stiff smile on her lips. She was completely miserable. Carl had no business bringing this fresh, pretty, delicate-looking little girl in here without a word of warning. The house was a mess and Ellie herself was, too, after washing all day in the heat. She had run in the back door when Carl told her and washed herself a little, slipped on a clean dress and apron, twisted her black hair into a more tidy knot, but she could feel the sweat on her body, looking at this Rinie, so cool and fresh, and she thought hopelessly of strewn rooms and unmade beds. Maybe Rinie was just a charity child of Minna Hicks's but she couldn't but have Minna's high-toned notions. She *was* a city girl. . . . Carl bringing her in here like this without a word to anybody! Ellie wanted to go off by herself and cry, and she hadn't cried for a long, long time.

"I expect these young'uns is hungry, Ellie," prompted A. J. What was wrong with her, anyway? It wasn't often you caught ole Sal without nothin' to say. "I don't know but what they're fixin' to live on love, but I guess they ain't had no dinner."

"I can fix somethin'," said Ellie, trying to sound hospitable, thinking dismally of cold biscuits, two pieces of gristly meat and one fried pie that were the sum total of leftovers from noontime. Why there wasn't even a fire in the kitchen stove. She'd let it go out because she was washing.

"Oh, no, don't bother about that," Rinie said quickly. "It's not long till suppertime."

"I'm half-starved," Carl said frankly.

"Then I'll help you," said Rinie, getting up to follow as Ellie went inside.

Oh, Lordie, thought Ellie, without hope. Well, if she's gonna live here, she's got to come in sometime.

Rinie followed through the front room, with papers and boots and a half-mended bridle, among other things, strewn over furniture and floor, into a kitchen in even greater disorder. Enough dirty levis for another tubful lay on the table. Ellie hadn't got to those yet. She threw them aside, distraught.

All these years Ellie'd waited for the time one of the boys would marry, when there'd be another woman to help with all this work and to talk to, and then it had to be like this . . . a city girl from Denver with her brown braids so neat and tidy and her cool-looking green-sprigged dress.

"Helen," Ellie said and her voice was curt and cross and not really steady, "go tell Jeff I want him."

She could fix some ham, that wouldn't take long, and fried potatoes and biscuits and some canned stuff. May as well fix supper for all and have it done with. Travis ought to be back soon. She kindled the fire.

"Whyn't you just set down?" she demanded, looking round at Rinie. "There ain't all that much to do. . . . Jeff, take this knife an' go git some ham—enough for supper— and watch that fire out there. May as well put it out when you've brought the meat."

Rinie looked away as the boy went out with his painful limp. And Ellie noticed. Just as she had supposed, the girl was chicken-hearted as could be. Surely, if Carl had seen and talked to her those times he went to his Aunt Minna's, he'd told her Jeff was crippled. Well, she needn't pity the child. Pity did no good for anybody.

"Couldn't I finish the washing while you're doing this?" asked Rinie shyly, noting the fire in the backyard with the wash kettle.

"Jest set down," said Ellie a little desperately, "unless maybe you want to change your dress or somethin'. That's Carl's room there."

Rinie said she was fine and sat down resignedly. Obviously, Ellie was angry. She could easily understand why —a stranger coming in like this without any warning— but she wished it wasn't so.

"Mama," said Helen in a whisper audible all through the kitchen, "she can't use Carl's room, can she? I don't think he'll like it one bit."

Tears of frustration and embarrassment stung Ellie's eyes.

"Git on outside outa my way," she said fiercely to her daughter, "an' don't be botherin' around here till you hear that supper's ready."

Ellie cleared her throat. She had to say something to cover the awkwardness. "I'da been done washin' before noon—I generally always am—but I had to quit an' hunt Helen up. She sneaked off after her daddy an' Kirby. Jeff can't ride an' A. J.'s so stove up with his rheumatiz lately, so I had to go. Musta took two hours. . . . I don't know what's to become of the child. It ain't hardly natural, one little girl raised off here with just men an' boys. They spoil her rotten." She had excused Helen's rudeness a little and now she said with a hint of pride, "First Stinson girl in four generations, accordin' to A. J."

"She's such a pretty little girl," murmured Rinie shyly. Ellie said everything in such a belligerent, unequivocal tone that Rinie wasn't sure if she wanted replies or not.

Ellie was peeling potatoes with great dispatch.

"She don't look much like the Stinsons, more like my people, like my baby sister Bess."

There had been times when Ellie had thought that perhaps Bess and Carl. . . . Admittedly, this girl was prettier, in her way, but Bess knew how to do in a kitchen and about housework and all without a lot of electricity and modern things, and Bess was sweet on Carl, nobody had to tell Ellie that.

"Do your folks live around here?" Rinie asked awkwardly.

31

"Other side a Belford. Used to live at Webber when me'n Travis married, but they bought over there right after. Land's a whole lot better, an' close to the railroad."

Now she didn't see her folks, any of them, as often as once a year. She couldn't very well leave here except in case of some dire emergency. Why the last time she had seen Bess was—nearly two years back when she'd lost the baby and Bess had come to see after things till she was on her feet again. Bess had been eighteen then and Ellie had thought how nice it would be if Carl married her and she just stayed on. Some sisters couldn't get along in the same house for more than a day or two, but Ellie and Bess had always been real easy together. Ellie wouldn't much wish a sister of hers married to Troy. He was too much to run around and not take anything serious or think of anybody but himself, and Doyle, well, she hadn't even thought about him, but Carl and Bess. . . .

Ellie guessed this girl was younger than Bess. She wondered if Carl could have been thinking about her as much as two years back. She said abruptly, "How old are you?"

"Eighteen."

Bess would be twenty now. They could have had a baby by this time.

Jeff came in with the ham and Ellie said she'd be back in a minute; she was just going to the cellar to get the canned stuff.

Rinie jumped to her feet. She saw flour, butter, milk, salt, baking powder—all she needed for making biscuits. She wasn't "company" here, she was Carl's wife and she wanted to be treated like it. She would be glad to do things the way Ellie wanted them done, if Ellie would tell her what she wanted, that was the way it should be, but she had to *do* something. What if Carl had come in and found her just sitting there, doing nothing, while Ellie cooked for all of them? She'd have been ashamed, that's what.

She mixed the batter, a lot of it, in a big crock and, looking up, found that Jeff was still there, watching her gravely. He turned his eyes away.

"How old are you, Jeff?" she asked awkwardly.

No answer.

She tried again. "Carl has told me, but I forgot."

"Ten."

Jeff was painfully shy and this girl was a shock. Carl

32

was . . . well, special. Carl would listen and talk to him like another grownup. Carl could think farther than crooked legs and a back that hurt. Now how would it be for them? Now that she was here?

"Do you know which pan your mother uses for biscuits?" she asked with a conspiratorial smile.

"Yes'm. I'll git it."

She hurried to roll out the dough, but at the same time she must take advantage of the opportunity for making a start toward friendship.

"Do you know I've never been out in the country like this in my whole life before?"

After a moment he said, very softly, his eyes on the floor, "Once I was in Denver, but it was before I can remember."

Rinie was starting to cut the biscuits when Ellie came back. Ellie stopped and looked at her, dismayed. She put her cans on the table.

"You ought not to 've done that," she said crossly.

"But I wanted to so much, Ellie. Shall I put them in now, or wait a while, do you think?"

"Well, wait'll I cook the meat some, I guess. Here. If you've got to fuss around, put this apr'n on."

She hoped the men wouldn't make remarks if these biscuits weren't what they were used to. Maybe the girl did know something about cooking, making fancy dishes like Minna would have, but she wasn't anyway used to cooking for five grown men and three growing children. Provided Troy and Doyle didn't get back, there might be enough bread for supper.

"There comes Kirby and your daddy, Jeff. Go tell 'em we got—we got supper nearly ready."

"Rinie?" Carl was at the back door. "Come see the mares."

She went out, vastly relieved to be with him again. He put an arm about her and they stood shading their eyes against the low sun.

Two riders came down the bench, the mares straggling in front of them. All the horses walked with a shambling gait, their heads down.

"They've had a hell of a run," Carl said softly. It bothered him to see horses that worn out.

"What happened? she asked soberly. "I don't understand."

"They're our brood mares," he said. "We've got a big

33

fence pasture for 'em up the creek, but this wild herd comes down off the ridges sometimes an' the stallion breaks the fence, or the mares do, or all of 'em together an' they're gone. Our stallion was killed last month, but the mares are all bred. We can't afford to lose any of 'em."

She was embarrassed. She had never before heard anyone utter words such as stallion and bred. Carl said them so easily.

"How was he killed?"

"Who? Oh, Rowdy? Lightning."

He was watching the mares. They had reached the creek and stuck their muzzles in the water, but they weren't drinking, just standing there with their sides heaving, tails moving languidly against the flies.

Carl said, "I'll help git 'em back in the pasture. We'll be back in a few minutes."

"You mean he was struck by lightning?"

"What? Oh. We loose a few head of stock every year to lightning. Well, don't look like that, honey. There's worse ways to die."

3

Rinie woke and lay tense. There had been—something that wakened her. There had been many things through the past weeks. The coyotes. She had heard them that first night, startled and appalled by their frantic yapping from the flats across the creek.

"Never heard coyotes before," surmised A. J. as her eyes widened.

They hadn't yet finished supper.

"No," she said, awed.

"They're after the chickens," said Kirby, smirking.

Kirby was tall and heavy for twelve, with dark red hair and blue eyes. He was handsome in the bold way that his Uncle Troy was handsome, the way his grandfather had been. He had been talking a good deal through supper about the chase after the mares.

"They're not either," said Helen fiercely. "You always say somethin's after the chickens. They got a fence an' a house to live in, an' the dogs wouldn't let no coyotes around."

"Chickens!" muttered A. J. "A decent ranch ain't no place for chickens. That's one a your husband's fancy ideas, missy."

He was speaking to Rinie. She remembered Doyle's saying once that when A. J. started to call you by a name that bore repeating but wasn't your real name, you had made it with him.

"It was Jeff's idea," Carl said placidly. "I notice you seem to eat the eggs all right."

"Them eggs is good to have," agreed Travis, "an' them fryers was all right, too. I don't know how they'll winter, but up to now, it's been a dam' good idea."

Travis was tall and thin with a narrow face shaped like his mother's. He always looked tired and worried, though he was good-natured and even-tempered as a rule.

Jeff had cast one quick look of gratitude at his father and dropped his eyes to his plate. He was smiling.

Travis said, "Got any more biscuits in the oven Ellie? Them's real good."

"They're all gone," she said curtly. "Rinie made 'em."

"Well, Carl, you got yourself a cook, looks like," Travis said, giving the girl a shy smile.

"Man don't live on biscuits alone," said A. J. sagely. "Has to have other stuff, don't he, Buck?"

Carl frowned a little and Rinie, blushing, said quickly, "Could I pour you some more coffee, Mr. Stinson?"

"Hell, call me A. J.," he said mellowly. "All my kids do. It ain't very respectful of 'em, but it is my name."

Rinie insisted on helping Ellie with the dishes. She thought the kitchen was rather a wonderful place, with everything bigger than life, the wood range, the table that normally accommodated ten but could seat more. Most of the staples—flour, sugar, salt—were bought by the barrel. Coffee beans came in a big sack and were ground fresh every morning. Most of the pots and pans were bigger than any at Mrs. Hicks's and there were stacks and stacks of dishes, mostly ill-matched and chipped, but more than sufficient. She was eager to look into all the cupboards. She felt like a little girl waiting to be set free in a toy shop. She had guilty feelings about the unfinished

35

washing and made herself a vow to do it in the morning unless Ellie was absolutely outraged by the idea.

By the time they had the kitchen in order, A. J. had gone to bed, after a few choice words of advice to Carl who didn't need them and said so. Kirby was in bed, too, tired out after chasing the horses all day. Travis, looking exhausted, was trying to keep his eyes open by reading an outdated newspaper. Carl was sitting by the table where Jeff and Helen were putting together a jigsaw puzzle. Rinie came and stood by him, resting her hand on the table. He looked up at her, his eyes darkening.

"Here's what it'll look like," said Helen, offering Rinie the box lid. "Miss Johnson give it to Jeff."

"It's pretty," said Rinie. "Who's Miss Johnson?"

"Our teacher," said Helen importantly, only Jeff can't go to school 'cause it hurts his back."

"Helen, it's bedtime for you an' Jeff both," said Ellie.

Travis yawned. "I hate to, but I believe I'm gonna have to go to bed. I'm kinda tired tonight."

"I expect Rinie's used to stayin' up late in town," said Ellie, a little apologetically, "but it don't do around here. A. J. goes to bed at dark an' gits up at sunup, rain or shine, winter or summer, an' they ain't no sleepin' when A. J. gits up."

"The men always sleep till you make 'em git up," said Helen primly.

"Well, the men ain't got to cook breakfast," said her mother. "Now you git on to bed."

Rinie had sat down near Carl and was looking at the room. She hadn't had a chance to pay much attention to it before now. It was big and square. There were several doors and three windows and a big fireplace, but still enough wall space so that it didn't look too chopped up. She had read in Mrs. Hicks's ladies' magazines how rooms shouldn't be "too much intruded upon by doors, windows, etc.," but she guessed the decorators who wrote the columns hadn't thought much about a living room that had to give access to a porch, kitchen, and three bedrooms. The ceiling was beamed with huge heavy logs and the log walls were hung with many things: Indian rugs and blankets, a patchwork quilt that Jenny had made in the wedding-ring pattern and that Ellie, when she and Travis were first married, had rescued from the bottom of an old trunk where the mice had already got at it a little. There were some pictures from magazines, chosen by

Ellie, pictures of little girls with kittens or of primly dressed children in a flower garden. At irregular intervals and heights, there were pegs to hold a variety of guns. Ellie didn't like that. It seemed to her each of the men could keep his weapons in his own room as he did the pictures that were of particular interest to him, but with A. J. as stubborn and contrary as he was, there was no chance of doing much to change the boys' habits. Why, they had a good big barn and all kinds of sheds around the corrals and A. J. still insisted on having his saddle and bridle hanging on the front porch just outside his bedroom door and on having his horse brought up to the steps to be saddled.

The fireplace and hearth and chimney were of the rough granite rock of the country. The mantel was littered with many things: fish hooks, screws, nails, a piece of chalk, a sash weight, a can of tobacco, playing cards, some cartridges for a .30-.30 and a cleaning rod, two books—*A History of America for the Seventh Grade* and a pulp novel entitled *Ma Brown's House*—a cup with a little coffee dark in the bottom over crystallized sugar, a harness bit, a china dog with a broken leg, a small rubber doll with no clothes on, some other things that Rinie couldn't identify, and a great deal of dust. But in the mantel's approximate center were two objects which looked strange and incongruous among the other things—a gold picture frame and a handsomely inlaid mantel clock. The frame contained a picture of A. J. and Jenny Stinson, shortly after their wedding.

Rinie and Carl were alone in the front room for the moment and she got up, took down the picture, and brought it closer to the lamp.

"A. J. looks like a peacock, don't he?" Carl said, grinning.

"Your mother was so pretty," said Rinie. They spoke in hushed voices, glad of being alone. "I saw several pictures of her at Mrs. Hicks's, but she wasn't this pretty in any of them. I think she was so happy in this one."

She replaced the picture tenderly and looked up at the cobweb-hung rack of elk antlers above the mantel.

"A. J. shot him up in the edge of the scrub timber the first year they stayed here through the winter," Carl supplied.

The room's furniture was a potpourri, ranging from split-bottomed chairs to a massive horsehair sofa. One of the oil lamps that was lighted tonight was a complicated affair with dusty pendants hanging from the ornate shade. It was placed on a rickety table toward the rear of the room, near where Travis had been reading. The other lamp burning in the room, placed on the big inlaid, scarred center table where the puzzle was spread, was a cheap, heavy, red glass base with a cracked chimney and no shade. A big yellow tomcat lay cleaning his paws daintily on a faded, brocade slipper chair, and Carl sat comfortably in a rickety-caned rocker with his feet up on the arm of a black Morris chair whose stuffing was visible in several places. Against the back wall of the room on a scarred library table was a large radio, the battery for its power supply on the shelf beneath the table, the wire to the aerial fastened loosely between logs till it reached the front door and disappeared outside. Beside the table stood a relatively new Victrola. On a small table in a corner was a huge old Bible with a heavy gold clasp, almost covered by a copy of a stockman's magazine.

"Mother brought these things," Carl said a little sadly, "the good things, the chairs and tables and sofa, some bedroom things that Travis an' Ellie have got. I guess they really did have some money then, though sometimes I . . . Rinie, would you like to have a lot of money?"

"Oh, Carl, no!" she said positively. To her, money meant Minna and Bill Hicks—their friends, their pretensions, their misery.

Carl laughed. "Well, you don't have to look scared. I don't think it's a thing we'll ever have to worry about much." He stretched and took his feet down from the arm of the chair. "Sleepy, little girl?"

"Mm-hmm."

He got up and opened the front door to let out one of the dogs. They blew out the lamps and went into the kitchen where Ellie was setting bread dough for the morning.

"Night," she muttered and then, compulsively, to Rinie, "don't you bother 'bout gittin' up so early as we do. You ain't used to it."

Carl had opened the door to his room when Helen came running, barefoot and in a floor-sweeping night-gown, from her room across the kitchen.

"No, wait, Rinie! I want you to sleep with me an' tell me a story."

38

"Well, Helen," began Rinie, flushing, "I-I—"

"Don't sleep with *Carl!* He pulls out his covers an' grits his teeth an' don't know hardly any stories."

Ellie swept down upon her child. "You git to bed young lady, without another sound, or I'll wear you out."

"But, mama, tell her not to—"

She was borne away ahead of her mother, her feet barely skimming the floor, her wailing protests loud in the quiet house.

Shyly, without looking at him, Rinie walked through the door Carl had opened. There was no light in the room but that of a heavy full moon. The windows were bare. Carl didn't like curtains. The only furniture was an iron bedstead with a tattered patchwork quilt for counterpane, a dusty, dome-topped trunk, a teetery kitchen chair, and a small battered dresser with a cracked mirror.

There was a moment of awkward silence as they stood alone in their room, and then, glancing covertly at Carl, Rinie thought his shoulders were shaking and, turning from the window, she found him convulsed with laughter he was trying to stifle.

She had heard the coyotes again on that first night after Carl was asleep, and she crept very close to him, reveling in the chill of fear mingled deliciously with the sure knowledge of safety.

It was not coyotes that troubled her sleep on this night, though. She had been at the ranch nearly two months now and there were times when she didn't even notice the coyotes. But this other thing . . . she had drifted into sleep and it had wakened her again . . . a horrible sound, but she couldn't quite recall it, fully awake. She lay taut again, straining to hear. Had it been something inside the house? She didn't think so. She tried to see the windows, but it was a dark night, heavy with clouds. The men had been terse and uneasy at supper, fearful of snow before they got the cattle down to Belford for shipping. The roundup had been late this year because they had waited for Troy.

Doyle had returned to Red Bear the next day after Carl and Rinie came home to report that Troy and two of his friends in Belford had decided to go to California.

"Californy!" roared A. J. "What in the bloody, goddam' hell for?"

"Because they hadn't been there, I guess," said Doyle unruffled. "They want to see what it's like, what's going on out there, get a look at the Okies and all. He said he'd be back."

Rinie had, inconspicuously, gone out on the porch because she was so embarrassed by A. J.'s language. No father should call his own son those things, but the others didn't seem to mind.

"Well," A. J. finished, finally, "why didn' you go with 'em?"

"I've got to get my things together to go back to school," said Doyle.

Travis drove him down to Belford two days later to get the train for Denver. He was beginning his third year of college—"an' no Goddam' good for anything," A. J. said—but the Hickses were paying for the education.

They couldn't round up with just four hands counting Kirby, so they waited. Not idly. They repaired a holding pen they had used last year up on the tableland and built a new one over on the flats. They did some repair work on the outbuildings, brought down wood, and reshod their horses. Travis and Carl hired out to some of their neighbors to help with their roundups.

One day Carl went off up to the ridges by himself and only Rinie knew he was looking for the wild stallion. He dreamed of catching the big sorrel as stud for the Lazy S.

And then, finally, Troy came home. It was in the night and the dogs set up a terrific din as the old Model T rattled up to the house.

"It's Troy," Carl said as Rinie sat up, wide-eyed.

They heard A. J.'s bare feet thudding across the front room before Troy got the door open, and whoever was awake in the house heard the torrent of abuse that was unlashed about the ears of the returning son.

Finally, when A. J. had to pause for an apoplectic breath, Troy said loudly and pleasantly, "Hey, ever'-body! I'm home."

He came to the kitchen, A. J. subsiding to a muffled roar and stomping back to bed. Troy opened Carl's door. He had a small oil lamp in his hand.

"Carl? You here? *Carl!*"

The light had fallen on Rinie. Troy stared and then withdrew.

Carl got up and went into the kitchen.

"I'm tired," Troy said a little dazedly, "because we drove a long way today an' had flats an' all like that, but I—I thought there was a girl in your bed."

"It's Rinie," Carl said calmly. "We got married."

"Rinie! From Hickses? Well, I'll be dam'ed!"

"Listen, Troy, you better git some sleep because we got to go to work in the mornin'."

"I'll be goddamned . . ."

"Ever'body else, just about, is holdin' in the pens at Webber, waitin' for us to be ready to drive, an' they won't wait much longer 'cause—"

"I'll be double-dam'ed for a dew-lapped dog."

"—it's gonna snow soon."

"Oh, hell, didn' you hear me git all that from A. J.'s welcome home? An' I knew it anyway, before I got here. What I want to know is, is there any coffee? An' how come you to marry Rinie? An' why don't she come out an' take notice of her brother-in-law that's hungrier'n a bitch bear?"

Rinie got up, dressed, and cooked breakfast, though it wasn't much after midnight when she got started. The three of them sat around the table, talking and laughing, Carl and Troy eating plates of hotcakes and all of them drinking coffee. After a while they heard A. J.'s heavy tread again. Clad only in his "longhandlies," he joined them, ate, and was as gay as any and most boisterous of all. He even had a number of questions about California. Before long, Travis was up, too. Ellie had a bad headache, he said, but she sent word to call her if Rinie needed help.

When the men finally went to bed it was by the light of the morning star. Rinie washed the dishes and went back to bed. She did hope Ellie wasn't sick, was sleeping peacefully, but she, Rinie, was so happy and contented just now, because at last she had, for that one prolonged meal, been the only woman at the stove.

Rinie snuggled close to Carl now in the chill of the October night, forgetful of the frightening sound. She smiled happily, thinking that even in this blackness she knew exactly how he looked because of other nights when she had been wakeful and the moon had shown through the uncurtained windows. For then she had looked her fill at her husband without anyone, even Carl, to notice. His hair was red-blond and thick and wild. Ellie gave the haircuts at Red Bear and Carl missed every one he could. His face was not square and stubborn-looking like A. J.'s, but narrower, finer-featured. His eyes were brown-gold and expressive. There was an innocence, a kind of purity, about

41

his face in repose that made Rinie feel funny inside and smile tenderly. His hair and exposed skin were burned by the sun and wind, otherwise, his complexion was quite fair, lacking the Stinson ruddiness. His hands were thin, but strong and not large. Travis said it was Carl's hands that made him so good at breaking horses. A. J. said, with perhaps more logic, but less romance, that he was good at breaking horses because he could "pretty well stay on the goddam' things."

And then it came again, the terrifying sound ripping and moaning through the night.

"Carl!" her voice was not audible, but her fingers bit into his arm.

"What?" He was instantly wide awake, trying to loosen her grip.

"Oh." This time she had really heard it when she was fully awake. She was shaking and helpless, frightened tears ran down her cheeks. "Oh! A noise! An awful—awful—"

"Shhh, Rinie. Sweetheart, don't cry. It couldn' be anything so bad. What did it sound like?"

"A—a scream," she whispered.

"A lion, maybe."

"No. You said they scream, but this was a woman, Carl. A long scream and then this awful moan." She shuddered violently.

The tension went out of him and he stroked her hair gently.

"It's the elk, Rinie. It's rutting season."

"What—what's wrong with them?" she said dubiously.

"Nothing. They call and threaten and challenge."

"But—"

"It's the time when they mate," he said softly.

"Oh."

She lay very still in his arms. It didn't bother her much now to have Carl see how stupid she could be. It didn't seem to make any difference in the way he felt about her and he never reminded her later of her ignorances. It was all kept between the two of them and she was so grateful for his tactfulness and understanding.

But it was a strange, terrible noise to make . . . at that kind of time. . . . She turned in his arms to kiss him, but he was already half-asleep, worn out by the roundup, badly needing this few hours of rest before the drive.

In the morning, when Carl and Troy and Travis had left with the cattle, the house seemed very lonely and very still. Travis would be back in the afternoon, but Carl and Troy would go on with the men and their combined herds from the upper West Fork to the shipping pens at Belford. They would be gone three days at least, probably four, more if the weather turned really bad. Today it was heavily cloudy with a little breeze that blew fitfully, first from one direction, then another. At times the sun shone briefly, but there was a feeling of deception to its heat and brightness.

Helen and Kirby went off to school, Kirby's handsome face petulant because he had not been allowed to go with the cattle. He had worked hard in the roundup, done a man's share of branding, vaccinating, castrating, dehorning, sorting, all of it; now he had to go to school while Carl and Troy went to Belford.

Travis had thought it would be all right for Kirby to go on the drive. Troy and A. J. had been vociferous in their agreement at the supper table last night, but, when it really mattered, Ellie could be as stubborn as any Stinson.

"He's already missed too much school as it is," she said with dour finality.

"Aw, mama, it ain't worth botherin' about," Kirby said pleadingly. "Gosh, this don't happen but once a year. If I'm old enough to do all that work, I oughta git to have some fun."

"I didn' want you doin' all that work," she retorted and, glancing around, made it a reminder to the table in general. "You ought to a been in school then, too. You got just this year to finish what schoolin' Webber's got, an' then I got no say about what you do for more education, but you're gonna have this."

"Hell, Ellie, let 'em go. A kid's got to bust out once in a while." A. J.'s tone was stiffly placating.

"Christ, yes. What's so all-fired important about a few days of school?" Troy asked. "He can learn a hell of a lot more on a drive."

"Of some things, I don't doubt, but he ain't goin'," she said with compressed lips and put more peas on Helen's plate.

"I ought to go, too," meditated Helen. "I opened gates an' things. How come I have to eat more peas just 'cause you're mad at Kirby? I don't like peas."

"Come on, mama," said Kirby, near tears. The general knowledge and discussion of his problem, the fact that the others agreed with him, made it hard for him to accept defeat. He could easily imagine the fun of riding with the big herd, the companionship of the other men and boys, the camp at night. "Jess Corbett's goin'."

Travis looked at his wife, wanting the boy to go.

Ellie said, to her husband, "He's been outa school half the time this year, an' when he's out, Helen's got to miss, too. She just ain't big enough to ride that far by 'erself. Now winter's gonna set in an' they'll be a lotta days when it's too bad for them to go. The first thing you know, he just won't be goin' atall. He can go on the drive next year an' all the years after that, but I want him in school now."

"He makes good grades," Troy argued. "He won't have no trouble makin' up what he misses."

"Hell, what difference does it make if he makes it up or not," put in the grandfather.

A private discussion in this house was practically impossible and Rinie admired Ellie, wondering how she, Rinie, would manage, standing against all the others.

Encouraged by his uncle and his grandfather, Kirby said stoutly, "Well, I'm goin'. I ain't no baby."

"Don't talk that way to your mama," Travis ordered. "You're gonna do what she says." He threw a look around the table meant to indicate that the subject was to be dropped.

"Ah, for Chrisake, Travis," Troy began, but Carl said softly,

"Keep out, Bo. It's not your affair."

"Well, don't come all over high-handed now Carlisle," Troy said mockingly. Carl hated his full name and no one used it except in anger or, on rare occasions, to tease him. Troy said, "Just 'cause you're a married man don't give you call to start tellin' people where to head out an' where to head in." His face looked mean and he sounded mean. Rinie was tense.

"Go to hell," said Carl placidly, buttering himself another piece of cornbread.

Through the rest of the evening, Ellie had gone about her chores stolid and mostly silent, her lips compressed, a fortress prepared for siege. In the morning, Kirby had opened the gates and watched the three men drive the small bunch of cattle down the valley and, later, sullenly,

44

had saddled horses for his sister and himself and gone to school.

A. J. hadn't gone on the drive, either. After the work of roundup, his joints were so stiff and swollen that it was torture to move. He had missed other drives for other reasons, but never because of his health, and he felt, miserably, that his body was betraying him—he was old. The pain he suffered, and more than that, the frustration and chagrin of it, made him irascible. Up to the last minute, he had intimated he was going. The boys had conferred about it briefly while they washed up for supper on the back porch the night before the drive.

"I wish A. J. wouldn' go," Travis said worriedly. "Much more ridin' an' he ain't gonna be able to move."

Carl nodded with a rueful grin. "But I wouldn' like to be the one that made him that suggestion."

Shortly before, wondering why A. J.'s horse had not come to the corral, Carl had ridden to the house to see about him, but he didn't mention that to the others. The shame and pain and bewilderment that had been in the old man's eyes hurt him too much. He guessed that was the first time A. J. had had help getting off a horse, ever. When Carl caught sight of him, he was just sitting there in the saddle, then, knowing he was being watched, he had started easing his right leg over and with pain wrenching his face and a few lurid curses, he had given up and lifted the leg over with his hands. Carl looked away, his eyes stinging. When he glanced back, A. J. was sitting sideways on the saddle but his legs wouldn't seem to straighten out right; he couldn't trust them to hold if he got down. The horse A. J. was riding was skittish, and Carl was afraid it might spook and cause him to fall.

Cautiously, he dismounted from his own horse and went to the gelding's head, taking hold of the bridle. He anticipated being driven away with curses and, not unlikely, the end of the old man's lariat, but instead A. J., looking apologetic and portentious at the same time, leaned on the boy's shoulder and eased himself gingerly to the ground. He swayed a little, but after a moment, he took a step and released his hold. Moving with aching slowness, he crossed the porch and went into the house. No word passed between them, but as he got hold of the door, A. J. threw his son one blistering look that said with

45

indubitable clarity, "You say anything about this, goddam' you, an' it'll be the sorriest day you ever lived."

Carl unsaddled the gelding, hung up A. J.'s gear and went on about his business.

Now, as they stood outside the kitchen, about to go in to supper, Troy, vigorously rubbing his face and hair with a towel, said carelessly, "Ah, hell, don't worry about A. J. He's a tough ole buzzard an', like he says, ridin' prob'ly keeps him more limbered up than settin' around the house."

But when the morning came and A. J. eased himself miserably out of bed, he knew he couldn't make it. At breakfast, he said with elaborate carelessness that he guessed he'd stay at home where it was dry and warm. He was sure a snow was coming. What did a man have kids for, if not to do the work in bad weather and such? He was unusually short-tempered, cursing Rinie because she didn't warm up his coffee when his cup was still three-quarters full and he gave the boys detailed instructions about everything they already knew. He freely berated the weather, cattle buyers, the railroad, some of his neighbors, and, not least of all, his sons. As soon as they were out of sight, he crept miserably back to bed.

4
_____

So the house was quiet and lonely. There were so many things missing, the bawling cattle that had been in the corral, the pressure to have a big dinner ready. Rinie felt desolate. She knew it was silly and tried not to think about it, but knowing that Carl wouldn't be home for dinner or supper or when it was time for bed, or when she woke in the morning, or if she woke in the night, made it hard to keep back tears if she thought about it too long at a time. It seemed such a long time ago, almost like something from someone else's life, that time when she had been alone, without Carl. What had she done all

46

that time? What had been the purpose of sleeping and waking and working—of living?

Ellie had had Kirby help fill the wash kettle and start the fire before he left and, while Rinie did the dishes and put the kitchen to rights, she started the washing. More than likely, this would be the last day for a long while fit to wash outside. Ellie did hate having the tubs and all the mess of washing in the kitchen. With no one here but Jeff and A. J. and Rinie and herself to worry about till suppertime, it was a good chance to wash about everything in the house, a proper way to get ready for bad weather.

When she had finished in the kitchen, Rinie went outside and began taking clothes from the rinse water, wringing them and hanging them on the line. The air was chilly, but there was the fire to keep the kettle boiling for the white clothes, and washing this way was work to keep one warm.

Rinie said hesitantly, "I was thinking, in the kitchen, a hot water bottle might help A. J. some. Do you think we ought to fix him one?"

Ellie was punching sheets down in the boiling water with a stick she kept for the purpose This punching stick was completely smooth all over and the wood had a soft patina from long friction with hands, clothes, and boiling water

"A. J.'s best left alone," she said. "If he wants anything, we'll know it. You can be easy about that. There's nothin' worse'n a man sick, an' A. J.'s worst of 'em all, but I expect he's some better now. He's taken the whiskey to bed with 'im"

"Oh," said Rinie, beginning to scrub shirts on the washboard.

Ellie still spoke tersely, but Rinie realized now that that was just her way. The more deeply Ellie was moved, whether by anger or gentleness, the more curt became her conversation.

Ellie had accepted Rinie, after a fashion. The girl did try and she was good-tempered and eager to learn and biddable enough. In fact, Rinie's eagerness to please put Ellie off a little, that and the calf's eyes she and Carl made at one another all the time. Rinie was so painfully young, so wide open to all the hurts life had. This morning now she was mooning because Carl was gone for those few days, and Ellie didn't doubt Carl was in the same condition of depression. Soon enough, though, he'd likely be looking around for reasons to be gone from home, leaving Rinie with his children and his family and the dreary lonely sameness.

Ellie guessed she'd been a little like Rinie once, but, Lord knows, it hadn't lasted long. All that hoping and excitement and eagerness would die hard in Rinie and Ellie couldn't help feeling sorry for her. She also felt impatient because the girl didn't see how it was going to be and harden herself to it, and Ellie felt a little responsible and guilty because she ought to be able to tell Rinie or let her know someway how life was, but she guessed nobody ever could tell anybody else.

And Rinie was still a city girl, brought up in Minna's house. Ellie doubted that she could ever feel really easy with someone like that. Still, there were a lot of things she wondered, about Minna and Bill, their friends, their possessions, and about Rinie herself. Cutting another chunk of lie soap into the tub where levis were soaking, Ellie said crisply, "I expect washin' wasn' anything like this much work at Minna's."

"Well, no. There were only three people, and not much work that would get clothes really dirty but, well—I like it better here." She was scrubbing Carl's shirt. The soap was harsh and the rubboard left her knuckles scraped and stinging, but never, at the Hickses', had she washed a shirt of Carl's.

Ellie put more wood on the fire under the wash kettle.

"I guess Minna's washin' ain't done over no woodfire in the backyard."

"No." Rinie spoke absently, then she realized that for almost the first time, Ellie, not she, was making conversation. "There's a washhouse out in back with a flagstone walk to it. There's a stable, too, or what was a stable. Mr. Hicks keeps his car in there now."

"The times I was there," Ellie said, looking into the rinse water, "I wasn't showed around the place none. Minna never had much likin' fer Travis, said he let A. J. run over him, ruin his life, stuff like that, because Travis was satisfied to stay here on the place an' work the way he always has. Minna wanted all the boys to better theirselves, go to school in Denver, git into some kinda business, let her run things, an' Travis wouldn' even go so far as to try high school. I reckon he never wanted nothin' much but to be right around here. He won't even go to Belford if he can possibly help it.

"Troy went to high school, was about ready to graduate when he got in that trouble, an' Minna sent him home. Carl went, one year, an' then Doyle was old enough an' they couldn' do without both boys at once here. I guess Carl didn't care. An' a course, Doyle's gone on an' on, but I don't think Minna ever got over Travis not even tryin', him being Jennys oldest an' all. An' then," Ellie showed a grim little smile, "I know she never thought of me as bein' somethin' better for him . . . anyway, we was there for a night three times the first years we was married. She give us a room an' fed us an' was civil. I never had such miserable times in my life. What sort of things does she use to wash with? She's got one a them machines, I guess."

Rinie has stopped scrubbing in amazed pleasure. She had tried to resign herself to the fact that Ellie would never utter more than two or three brief sentences at a time. Now she had to make an effort not to stare.

"Yes," she said, beginning to scrub again, "it's run by electricity and it's got a wringer and everything."

Ellie nodded. "I seen 'em in the catalog. What about ironin'?"

"There's a room in the basement where the ironing board's always set up, and the iron's electric." She dropped the last shirt into the rinse water. "I'll get the other things from the kitchen."

When she came back, Ellie was hanging the recently finished load of clothes on the lines.

"Punch them sheets down, Rinie," she called companionably, "an' I'll take a turn with the board."

Back at the tubs, Ellie said, "I guess she's got a icebox." Rinie nodded.

"An the man comes around an' brings the ice?"

"Yes. Every day."

"An' what kind's her stove?"

"It's oil."

"I just can't hardly think of a house without no wood to be got in. How do they heat that big place?"

"With coal. A truck brings it and dumps it down a chute to the cellar. The furnace is down there with pipes going all over the house."

"Who puts the coal in the furnace?"

"Well, Mr. Hicks did most of the time when he was home, and I did, other times. It only has to be done about twice a day."

"Did you cook? I mean, all the time?"

"No. A Swedish lady who didn't understand much English came in to cook dinner—I—I mean supper." Rinie corrected herself, blushing. Ellie would think she was putting on airs. "I fixed breakfast, and dinner at noon if I wasn't in school."

"I expect Minna's pretty fussy about her food."

"Well, she—yes, I guess she is."

Ellie scrubbed at the dirty seat of Kirby's levis. She would like to know so many things about Rinie, the orphanage, if the girl had been treated as one of the Hickses, sitting with Bill and Minna at table, meeting their friends, going places with them, or if she had been treated as a servant, always keeping out of the way, not speaking up, coming into Minna's fancy parlor only when sent for. Ellie guessed Minna would take a lot of pleasure in ordering someone like Rinie around, somebody that would listen. It seemed she'd wasted a lot of breath in orders and advice to the Stinsons. But Ellie couldn't just come out and ask the girl about things like that.

Rinie was uneasy, sensing Ellies speculations. She couldn't have said exactly what her position had been. Minna had harried and badgered her, often to secret tears; she had spent large amounts of time, in a sort of counseling about the dangers of the world for a young girl—counseling that never quite said anything but was full of lurid hints and gruesome stories about what had happened to someone or other that Minna had heard of. Sometimes, Rinie had had nightmares along the lines of these reports. Minna talked to her almost constantly when they were alone in the house, always on a negative note about her family, her friends, her husband and about Rinie herself. But Rinie supposed, when she couldn't help thinking about it, that Minna would have treated a daughter similarly. Minna insisted that Rinie be "in company," but when there were guests in the house and Rinie was with them, Minna spent most of the time either in correcting some fault or mistake of the girl's—often imaginary—or in elaborating on the Hickses' largess in taking the child into their home and "looking after her as if she were our own."

Bill Hicks, for the most part, was silent at home. He was always kind to Rinie, but, on the whole, ignored her. In the beginning, he had shown fondness for her, pleasure at having her in the house, in little ways, by asking if she'd like to walk down to the drugstore with him of an evening to have some ice cream while he bought cigars, by bringing home an occasional bag of jelly beans, but such small attentions upset Minna. She said he was spoiling the girl and she became almost viciously critical of Rinie.

Rinie had no real friends. The girls at school were never cruel to her as children often are, they liked her, but there was no possibility of her becoming a member of any of their cliques; she was not allowed time or freedom to go out except to school and on errands and Minna would not tolerate other young people in her house. As she grew up, boys became increasingly interested. At first she was terribly shy and fearful because of Minna's oblique warnings, but even when she was less so —chiefly due to association with Doyle and other visiting Stinson boys—there was no hope that Minna would allow her to go out with young people and the boys eventually gave up.

Life at the orphanage had been, of necessity, somewhat barren and institutional and sometimes, even as a very small child, Rinie could remember a wistful yearning for something more—her own room, her own things and, most of all, someone who would care about her and not have to divide their love and attentions among dozens of girls, but she had had friends in the orphanage, many of them, and the house mother had been kind and loving and understanding.

Rinie's life at the Hickses' had been miserable, but she tried to make the best of it, not from any sense of martyrdom, but because it seemed the only thing to do. And, when she knew Carl, there was always the brightness of his last visit, the anticipation of the one to come, the happy time spent in surmises about what he might be doing, thinking, saying, just at that very minute. But even to Carl, she had never tried to speak of her unhappiness at the Hickses'. Rinie was unused to talking about things that were so much a part of her. It seemed as if it would be good, now, to confide in Ellie. Ellie knew about Minna and would, in her gruff way, be sympathetic to Rinie, but she couldn't do it. She wouldn't know how to begin. It was

over now, and done with, though the hurt, the bewilderment, and frustration of those six years were still with her
when she let herself think about it. But why talk? Talking
couldn't change a minute of it. Maybe, someday, when it
didn't make her feel so much like crying, she would tell
Carl some of it, a little at a time.

But Ellie was being so kind and friendly today. She
should say something and not just stand here, staring into
the wash fire. With the punching stick she began lifting
sheets from the kettle and dropping them into the rinse
water. She said brightly, "I guess the thing I liked to do
best at Mrs. Hicks's was sewing and knitting and things
like that. She had a little sewing room upstairs at the back
of the house. It was so nice and cozy. I liked to be up there
on winter days."

She didn't mention that the window gave a view of a
hill where she could watch the neighborhood children
playing with their sleds.

Ellie was troubled by the girl's big, wistful eyes. That
Minna! she thought fiercely. I don't believe the child ever
had a chance to play, not in that house. She said crossly,
"You much of a hand at sewin'?"

"Well," Rinie said shyly, "I made all my own things
and some things for Mrs. Hicks the last two years or so,
and I knitted most of the sweaters and socks. Mrs. Hicks
didn't like doing that kind of thing."

Ellie expected Mrs. Hicks didn't like doing much of
anything but bossing.

Rinie went back and forth to the kitchen, replenishing
the water in the wash kettle, putting in more white clothes
and soap. When she stayed to wring things out of the rinse
water, Ellie said, "We got a sewin' machine. It was Miz
Stinson's. It's in mine an' Travis's room. I keep the rips
sewed up an' the patchin' done an' make somethin' or
other once in a while, when I have to, but I just never was
no hand to sew. Seems like I can't set still long enough.
Makes me jittery."

She scrubbed angrily at a pair of Troy's levis. Troy always got the bloodiest when they altered calves. Ellie
guessed he enjoyed it. She said casually, "I got some real
nice print feed sacks. My mama sent 'em last Christmas.
I been meanin' to make Helen some dresses but can't sit
myself down to it. She needs 'em, too, growin' like she is."

Rinie put more wood under the kettle. She said softly,

a little breathlessly, "Ellie, would you let me try making them—sometime?"

"Why I reckon so, if you want to," said Ellie matter-of-factly, swooshing the levis in the suds.

A. J.'s room was quiet at noontime. Ellie told Rinie to go and see if he wanted any dinner and, after a timid knock, she cautiously opened the bedroom door. The old man lay on his side, his face toward the door, asleep. His whiskey bottle was on the floor by the bed. He looked old and completely harmless. His face was lax, his mouth slightly open, and he snored a little. He's not mean, Rinie thought tenderly. I don't see how I could ever have been afraid of him. It's important to him to keep up appearances, make people think he's tough, but he's not, not really.

And then, as she softly closed the door, the thought came, surprising and disconcerting: What was my daddy like? She used to muse over such questions often, dreaming, awake and asleep, of what her parents might have been like, making long, complicated, beautiful stories about why they had been forced to abandon her, but she had stopped that years ago.

Well, she thought with a little defiant toss of her head because sadness of one kind or another seemed determined to come on her today when there was no reason at all for it, I've got a husband now, and a daddy and brothers and nephews and a niece and a sister. She felt warm and good about Ellie. Surely things would be easy between them from now on.

The two women and Jeff had a lunch of leftovers from last night's supper. All that was necessary was to warm them up and make a pot of coffee.

"I feel like I'm havin' a vacation," said Ellie, almost gayly, running her hand over Jeff's rough, fair hair in passing. "You want some coffee, Mr. Stinson?"

Jeff grinned and nodded.

'I wonder if it'll snow?" said Rinie. She couldn't help thinking of how long it would be before Carl was home.

When they had eaten and washed the few dishes, she said tentatively, "I could maybe start a dress for Helen, there's not much of anything else to do."

It seemed to Rinie that this was the perfect opportunity to give the house a thorough cleaning, but she couldn't think how to suggest it without the possibility of offending Ellie.

"Well, I ain't got no pattern." Ellie said dubiously, "nothin' that's big enough for her now."

Rinie went into the front room and came back with the catalog.

"Maybe we can find something in here."

"Can you cut it out just from a picture? Without her even here to measure by?"

"I think so. I can measure a little by one of her old dresses."

Ellie got out the sacks. There were a lot of them and Rinie was delighted with the number and variety of prints. There was one, a light brown-gold, that she yearned for. It was almost the color of Carl's eyes and would make him such a pretty shirt.

Ellie settled on three pictures of little-girls' dresses that were especially appealing to her and, happily, Rinie began to cut a dress, spreading her materials on the big kitchen table.

Ellie sat watching and leafing through the catalog. Abruptly, she laughed and Rinie was startled and delighted.

"I can't remember when I've just set this-a-way, not doin' a thing. I don't feel atall right about it."

"Why not? Everybody ought to have a rest sometimes."

"Well, I'll go out direc'ly and git some a the clothes. They ought to be about dry enough to iron . . . I guess about the last time I set this way was when I was sick after I lost the baby. I got right tired of setting then, though. It ain't a good thing to do for long at a time."

"Was—the baby a little girl?"

"No, a boy. He just never did breathe. I don't know why. Heddie was here an' she done all she could. She's a real good hand, but he just didn't. He came early, I guess was the reason." She sighed sadly. "He was blond like Travis an' Jeff. . . it was just meant to be, I reckon, but it ain't never easy."

"I guess there's not any—doctor?" asked Rinie hesitantly.

Ellie shook her head. "Heddie's right good with all kinds a sickness. People all around here generally gits her if somebody's bad or if a baby's comin'. She's part Indian, kinda queer some ways, but she knows more about herbs an' remedies n' anybody I ever heard of. Some say she works charms an' such. I couldn't say about that part of it, but it seems to me like, if a body's bad sick, it don't hurt to try anything that might any way do good."

She leafed through the catalog.

"My sister Bess come an' stayed nearly two months that time. She was about the age you are now an' she couldn' do ever'thing just the way the men was used to, but she done a good job an' me'n her spent a lot of time talkin'. Up to then, I hadn' seen none a my folks for more'n a day or two at a time since they moved away from Webber."

"Did you have a lot of sisters and brothers?"

"Seven of us." Ellie looked wistful. "All married an scattered out now but Bess an' my brother John. John's married, but him an' his family's got a house on my folks' place. They're startin' to raise a lot of dairy cattle, John an' daddy. The train stops just a mile from their place ever' mornin' an' carries the milk to Belford. That's how mama come to have all them sacks, from feed they buy for the cows."

Rinie put down the scissors and poured coffee for both of them. Ellie looked around guiltily, as if someone would come and find her shirking.

"Where's Jeff at, I wonder."

"I saw him gong toward the barn a few minutes ago."

Ellie sighed. "I wisht we could do more for Jeff."

Rinie had wanted to talk about Jeff for a long time. Trying to sound casual, she said, "I've wondered, Ellie, if one of the men couldn't drive him to school and go pick him up. Wouldn't he like to go?"

"We talked about that. Carl wanted to do it, but the pickup's always in such bad shape. It's got to be saved for real needs."

"But Troy's car—"

Ellie made a little gesture of dismissal. "Troy don't like for nobody else to use his car mostly. He's gone a lot anyway . . . besides, Jeff's learned as much as he would have in school. Miss Johnson says he's as far along as Kirby is. Carl's taught him a lot. He's the one mostly taught him readin' an' figgerin'. None a the rest of us ever seemed to have the time—or we didn' make it. Carl's always been foolish over Jeff, even before he got sick. Carl was about fourteen when Jeff was born, an' when Carl come back from livin' that school year at Minna's, Jeff was just walkin' good. He used to follow Carl like a puppy dog. Still does only—"

She looked away out of the window, blinking her eyes quickly to clear away the blur that came between her and the clothes blowing out there in the wind.

"Ellie? Do you know what it was?"

Ellie shook her head. "I forgit the name. It was the winter he was three, just a little while before Helen was born. He had a sort of sniffly cold for a day or two an' then, in the middle of the night, he woke up screamin'. His head hurt him and at first he couldn' move his neck without screamin', an' then he just sort of—drawed all over. It was a awful time. For days, we thought ever' minute that he couldn' live . . . but he got better . . . only his back still hurts him, an' his legs. . . ."

Rinie couldn't help tears. Ellie's face was taut with misery, but she didn't cry. Crying, she had found long ago, was no use. Rinie would learn that, too, soon enough, she thought wearily. The girl would have to toughen up.

After a while, Rinie said timidly, "Did a doctor ever look at him?"

"Yes," said Ellie shortly. "I knowed it wasn't no use, but Travis had to have it, Travis an' the other boys, too, till we took him to Belford an' the doctor there sent us to a doctor in Denver an' we took him there. That was about the time you come to Minna's. I wouldn' stay at her house that time. My boy can git along without her false pity."

She picked up her coffee cup and held it tight till her hands stopped shaking.

"The doctor says it's a disease they don't know much about. President Roosevelt had the same thing, but it mostly hits children. He said if they'da had Jeff in the hospital when he was sick, they'da put a cast on him, all over, from the neck down an maybe he wouldn' been crippled so bad. But, Rinie, he'da had to stay like that for months, like—like a corpse. I can't hardly bear to think about it . . . an' still he'da been crippled.

"There wasn't nothin' they could do after the sickness was over. Oh, the doctor in Denver talked some about a special hospital off someplace, where they might still coulda put him in a cast, even broke his bones an' tried to make 'em grow straighter, but I couldn' stand that an'

Travis couldn' either. Travis . . . I never seen him cry but when Jeff was so sick, not even when the baby didn't live."

She brushed some crumbs off the table.

"But I knowed a doctor wouldn't be no good. I don't set no store by 'em an' the sickness was over anyway. We done all we could. Heddie come then an' stayed days. The Stinsons ain't no way religious, but I was raised a Christian, an' I never did pray as much as then. Some things is just the willa God. That's the only answer there is for 'em an' it don't make no difference whether they make sense to us or not. We ain't give to know anyways near ever'thing."

Rinie thought fleetingly that Heddie seemed an interesting topic for conversation, vague questions crossed her mind, but she felt too sad now to ask them or talk about anything.

After a few moments, Ellie stood up briskly.

"Well, I've set as long as I can, longer'n I ought to. I'm goin' out an git them clothes an' start ironin'. Why, Rinie, you're near done cuttin'! My land! I'll go git stuff offa the sewin' machine."

"No, I'll help iron. Sewing is play. I'll help with the work first."

Ellie grunted. "Sewin' ain't play fer me. You just go on with that. Why Helen'll be tickled to death."

Rinie stopped working on the dress to fix supper while Ellie went on with the ironing. Helen, when she arrived from school, was delighted with the new dress and insisted that it must be finished in time for her to wear it to school tomorrow. A. J. got up, feeling somewhat better physically and in a much better mental state. Jeff and Kirby had the chores almost done by the time Travis got home. Travis had some news of Webber and someone had brought up everyone's mail from Belford. The mail reminded Rinie that she had intended writing a note to the Hickses. She didn't want to, she didn't want to think of them any more, but the little courtesy could be spared from all her vast happiness.

There was a new catalog, a note from Doyle, and a letter for Ellie from her mother.

"Well," said Ellie with pleasure, "an' just when I been talkin' about 'em."

Travis guessed he'd have a cup of coffee, waiting for supper to be ready.

"Maybe the weather'll hold," he said, optimistically for him. "If it was gonna git real bad, I believe it woulda started to show by now.

"Snow by tomorrow night," stated A. J. unequivocally. "I believe that's what's wrong with my goddam' joints. Did the drive git off all right?"

Travis rolled himself a cigarette, a luxury in which he rarely indulged.

"Yeah. The cattle was pretty frisky, bein' held down there so long, but I guess they won't have no real trouble."

"Dam' Troy," A. J. muttered, but he was grinning. "Californy!"

"Carl went off on a half-wild bronc," Travis reported. "Said he'd save Skeeter, her bein' in foal."

"Christ, the kid's more a fool about that mare'n he is about missy there. Ain't that right, missy?"

"Oh, I don't think so, A. J., I hope not." She couldn't help blushing, but she didn't much mind being teased any more.

"Well, maybe not in one or two ways," commented the old man, "but I didn't see him takin' you along on the drive."

" 'Stead a ridin' any a them good cow horses they took," Travis continued, "nothin' would do him but to ride a ole piebald gelding that Mr. Corbett had just got in out a the hills a few weeks back. Corbett says it acts like a good cow horse but for some reason don't like bein' worked in with other horses, so Carl's got to try."

Rinie opened the stove to put in a stick of wood to hurry the bread and A. J. spat adroitly in, past her hand.

"I expect that's how come Corbett to bring the horse," he said, "so Carl'd work 'im over."

"What's your mama say, Ellie?" Travis asked.

Ellie looked up from the letter, which she was reading for a second time, and smiled wistfully.

"W'y, Mamie's comin' home. My sister Mamie that married a Mormon boy from over in Utah an' ain't been home since—well, not long after me'n Travis married," she explained to Rinie, and, to the room in general, "an Bess is gittin' married this Saturday, an' she's marryin' Larry Treadwell."

"Who's that?" asked Travis.

"W'y, Larry's mother," Ellie explained triumphantly, "was daughter to ole man Clint Bell that this county's named after, an' Belford, too."

"Well!" said Travis, impressed, and Rinie smiled because Ellie was so pleased. But A. J. said disparagingly, "Clint Bell wasn' nothin' to brag about. I remember when I first come out to this part a the country, a bunch of us was foolin' round one night after a little rodeo we'd had an', not havin' much to do, we had us a wettin' contest Ole Clint didn't even git across the fire an it wasn' no big un neither."

Travis was grinning broadly. "Well, in spite a that, one a his sons is in the state legislature an' some think he'll run fer gov'ner some time. It's nice for Bess to be marryin' into a family like that. What else do they say, hon?"

"Oh, not much," said Ellie, helping to dish up the supper. "Just about ever'body's health an' how are we, an' how mama wishes she could see the kids an' why don't we go for the weddin' an' to see Mamie an' about John an' daddy buyin' a bull of some fancy breed. I guess the dairy business is right good. Helen, where's your brothers at? Tell 'em to come on to supper."

They sat around the table and filled their plates and Travis was still loquacious.

"Alva Tippitt's fixin' to marry Miss Johnson."

"He is?" said Ellie. "Well, course that ain't no real big surprise, but I'm kinda sorry to see her marry. She's a good teacher an' has taught here longer'n anyone I can remember."

"They say she ain't aimin' to quit teachin'," said Travis. "She likes it so much."

"If she quit," said Kirby, without much hope, "they'd have to close school till they got somebody else."

Helen said thoughtfully, "Who teaches teachers?"

"Other teachers," answered her father.

"Well, who teaches *them?*"

"Theorn McLean says a lion killed one a their colts last week," said Travis. "They was too busy to hunt it. If it shows again, we'll have to go after it."

"Travis?" Rinie was hesitant, but she had to ask. "Was it awfully wild? The horse Carl was riding?"

A. J. laughed. "Missy, that Buck a yours' been ridin'

59

anything with four feet since before he could walk. You ain't gonna fret about it now, are you?"

"It wasn' much wild," Travis said reassuringly, "just kinda ringy. It'll be all right. Carl's got a way, a real hand with horses."

"Daddy, can I go after the lion with you?" asked Kirby eagerly.

"I reckon you can."

"Christ, I'd like to see a lion bayed."

"Kirby Stinson, you better watch your mouth," said his mother sternly.

"I bet they ain't no better huntin' dogs in the country than ole Christmas an' Jethro," said Kirby, little daunted.

"Ole Christmas the only one that's any good after lions," said A. J., "an' she's gittin' about too old, only she don't know it. We ought to try Pup this time. He's a big brassy sonofabitch. Not that that means much of anything."

"Sutter wants one a Sheba's pups when she has some," Travis said.

A. J. grunted. "Sutter wants a lot a things, I'll lay. He bred that bitch of his to ole Nero, tryin' to git hisself some bear dogs, an' I ain't seen hide ner hair of a stud fee pup. That's been—le's see—nine, ten months ago. I reckon she musta whelped by now. Not that I give a dam' about a pup, but it galls me when people don't stand by their word."

"Ellie," said Rinie on a sudden impulse, her eyes sparkling with pleasure, "Why couldn't you and Travis go over to your folks for your sister's wedding and all? Why not?"—as Ellie began to shake her head—"There's not that much to do here. I can look after the kids. Oh, please do! It's been so long since you've seen your sister Mamie. You'd have such a good time. Please take her, Travis."

"Oh, I don't think so, Rinie," said Travis regretfully. "I got a lot to do around here. I couldn' hardly . . . I'd like to. Ellie don't hardly ever git to see her folks or go nowheres but I guess we can't. . . ."

Ellie wished Rinie hadn't said anything. Putting it in words like that made it hard to bear not going.

"No," she said, "we can't."

"But just for a few days," Rinie begged eagerly. "You both ought to have a little fun sometimes."

"The weather's apt to turn bad any day," Travis said glumly. "If the roads was to git bad. . . ."

"Oh, hell!" said A. J. explosively. "Go on! Both a you got a notion this place can't git along without you. Me an' missy an' the young uns can more than manage things, can't we?"

Jeff and Kirby nodded readily, but Helen said, "I want to go."

"Oh, but you have to be here so you can wear your new dress to school tomorrow," Rinie reminded her persuasively.

"I'm obliged to you for thinkin' of it, Rinie," said Travis uncertainly, "but I don't see how I could be gone—"

"Listen, Prunes," said his father forcefully, "you're about to be in-law to a in-law of somebody that might be gov'ner, even if his pa couldn' piss over a medium-sized fire. You better git on over an git Stinsons on the good side a that bunch."

Ellie looked shyly at Travis. A little hope made the wish so strong it hurt. Travis looked embarrassed. He was feeling trapped. There was so much to do here and, on top of everything else, he disliked staying long in another man's house, but Ellie did deserve to go. He said, "The ole truck's in such bad shape. Troy's gonna look for a generator in town, but—"

"Go ahead an' take Bojack's car," cut in A. J. "It won't hurt him none an' if it does, he can tell me about his pain. Now quit tryin' to git out of it, both of you. I believe you're afraid to be off by yourselves."

"Travis?" Ellie's voice was small and breathless. They were all looking at him and Travis was seeing Ellie, the way she had looked—Jesus! It was nearly fourteen years ago when they'd married and she'd taken on the care of the place, his father, his three young brothers.

"All right!" he said, suddenly very happy and Rinie jumped up to get the coffeepot.

Ellie looked at Travis for a moment and, to her chagrin, her mouth began to tremble. She got up abruptly and hurried into the bedroom.

Travis looked bewilderedly at the closed door and A. J. said loudly, "Ole Sal's not a half-bad woman, but she don't want nobody to find it out."

When the dishes were done and the kitchen set to rights, Ellie went on with the ironing, "doin' up" the things she and Travis would take with them. She was mostly silent, coming out now and then with a sharp reminder of something the children or Rinie mustn't forget to see to while she was away.

Rinie was doing the hand stitching on Helen's dress. It was a simple dress but Rinie felt proud of it because it had turned out so well. She couldn't help thinking wistfully that she would have to go to bed soon, alone. She felt the emptiness of the house all the time, no matter if they were sitting in the kitchen, warm and talking and happy. What was he doing? Sitting in the light of the big campfire laughing and talking with the other men? Riding night-herd on that half-wild horse Travis had been talking about or another like it? Thinking of her?

Travis was finishing mending the bridle that had been lying in the front room for weeks. A. J. was cleaning his old rifle for no particular reason other than that talk of lions had made him think about the gun. Kirby, with sighs, was working arithmetic problems and Jeff was avidly reading his brothers geography book. Helen stood close beside Rinie, interestedly watching the needlework.

"I could sew," she said a little dubiously.

"I don't see why not," agreed Rinie.

"But not tonight," said Ellie. "It's bedtime."

"Rinie, can I sleep with you?" asked the little girl shyly, leaning against her.

"Yes," said Rinie, giving her a quick hug. She would be glad not to be entirely alone. "Go to bed and I'll be there when I've finished hemming your dress."

The men talked sporadically, A. J. yawning often. It was well past dark and past bedtime, no matter if he had slept a good part of the day. His legs ached from sitting around too much, but he felt drowsy and rather mellow. This missy was a good, thoughtful little girl. Buck was lucky to have her. It was good to see how the two of them were about each other, only . . . it did seem to make him feel his age, goddammit to hell. . . .

Rinie looked up, startled and pleased. Under the men's talk about cattle prices, Ellie had hummed a bit of song. Her voice was low and true and pretty. It sounded so right here in the kitchen with the dark outside and the wood making warm companionable noises in the stove. In a moment, she sang a line or two, very softly, not thinking about it.

Travis and A. J. exchanged quick glances. They hadn't heard Ellie sing since before her baby died and very little then. She had sung almost constantly at her work when she was a young girl; they used to tease her about it. But after a while the days of endless toil mounted up and up and she was tired in the morning as well as at night and then came the terrible time of Jeff's sickness, and since then, she had sung only to soothe a child or on the occasions when she could go down to Webber to church.

Now she sang most of the verse of the hymn, breaking off almost at the end to concentrate on ironing the bosom of the white shirt she had hunted up for Travis to wear at Bess's wedding.

"Hon," Travis said huskily, not looking at her, "I ain't heard that in a long time, Sing it all, will you?"

Ellie was embarrassed. She hadn't realized she was singing. "I don't know that I can remember all the words." But she did and the kitchen was hushed when she finished.

"Gosh, mama," came Jeff's awed voice from the bedroom, "that was so pretty."

"Well," said A. J., hoisting himself up painfully, "I'm goin' to bed. Now you recollect, Sal, to find out how many more wives this Mormon husband of your sister Mamie's has got, for I always did mean to look into that business."

5

The last thing Ellie said to Rinie as they were ready to drive away in the morning was, "If they's any a them sacks you want to use for somethin', use 'em. I'll likely bring back a bunch more."

Rinie was tempted, but she had other plans to carry out first. It has been hard to sleep last night and, to keep her mind from dwelling on loneliness, she had thought just how she would do it: begin with the bedrooms, then the front room, the kitchen last.

When the car had driven away, she hurried back inside to wash the dishes, eager to get started.

"Well, missy, you aimin' to spend your time stitchin'?" asked A. J., coming in from the barn. He liked to see a woman sewing. It made a place homey, provided she wasn't too fussy about it.

"I'm going to clean the house, A. J.," she said happily, "wash the windows, mop the floors, all that."

"Lord God! I knowed you'd picked up a bunch a foolishness from Minnie. The last time that was done, nobody couldn' find nothin', from a shotgun to a pair a drawers for a month."

"Well, I won't lose anything," she promised, undaunted. "I just want to have it all cleaned up at once."

"You mean for when Buck gits back. Well, that's all well an' good, I guess. A man likes to know he's got a woman that's a good hand to work, but lemme tell you, ain't none of 'em likes a woman that puts a goddam' clean floor before a husband. That'n a yourn, he's about as foolish over you as I ever hope to see anybody be—he always was easy carried away over some little thing or other—but he's a little odd some ways. I expect he'd ruther have hisself somebody that'll run out to watch the sun go down with 'im than one that all the time worries about keepin' the house done up to a fair-thee-well. Now then, before this ruckus starts, do you reckon I could have me one more cup a coffee? Then I believe I'll go down to Webber an' set around the store a while. I ain't done that in a long time an' I'm wore out, stayin' around the house. Besides, I purely an' teetotally can't stand to be around a woman with the cleans."

The housecleaning involved two days of hard work. Rinie barely sat down for meals; she was too engrossed and eager to stop for anything. For the moment, this was her house, no Minna to correct and criticize, not even Ellie to wonder about pleasing. She wouldn't really have minded Ellie, now that they were getting used to each other, but it was more fun, having it all to herself for this little time. She was glad, too, that A. J. kept out of the way. A man around made so much more work—except Carl. Only when Carl was around, it was hard for her to concentrate on going on with anything.

On the first day, after she had swept down the cobwebs

and was washing windows, Jeff came and said timidly,

"I could help you—Rinie."

It was the first time he had called her by name and she was delighted.

"Oh, good, Jeff! There's plenty to do and I sure could use some help."

"What'll I do?"

"Well . . . there's all the furniture in the whole house to be dusted. Maybe you'd want to do some of that. You know a lot more about where things belong than I do. I'd like to put things away, especially some of the stuff in the front room, but I wouldn't want to put them where people can't find them. You'd be a lot of help with that."

At the time, she was washing the windows in Ellie and Travis's bedroom, and she was pleased when he brought the dustcloth and started his work where she was.

Sport, on the porch, put his paws on the window and whined. Jeff gestured for him to go away.

"Are you gonna wash the outsides, too?" he asked.

"I don't know," she said. "If there's time and it doesn't get too cold. Sport's a nice dog. He's mostly yours, isn't he?"

Jeff nodded. "Troy brought him to me when he was a puppy, not old enough to eat except out of a bottle."

"He's so smart," she said, "the way he goes and hunts the cow when you get down the bucket. I never knew a dog could learn things like that."

Jeff said shyly, but positively, "I think he's the only dog on the place that's worth anything. The others are friends an' all, but I don't care about huntin' dogs."

A. J. had been mistaken about the weather. It didn't snow. It cleared, reluctantly, and Friday, the second day of Rinie's housecleaning, was cold and fine. Rinie thought they managed very nicely. Helen helped with the dishes and other little things in the evening. Jeff took care of the chickens and the milk cow, his regular chores, besides being helpful with the house. Kirby did most of the other outside chores and chopped wood in the evening for the next day's use. A. J. found a few things to do around barns and corrals. He mentioned that he ought to ride out and hunt up the two calves they had doctored for screwworms and make sure they were getting along all right, but he knew he wasn't ready to ride again yet.

Rinie was pleased most of all about her companionship

65

with Jeff. As they worked together in the front room, she said, "Did you really think of getting the chickens?"

"Well," he said diffidently, "a thing came in the mail last winter from a hatchery. Me'n Carl talked about it a lot, an' then, when the weather got a little warmer, we built the chickenhouse an' ordered 'em, some hens an' a rooster an' some baby chicks to raise for fryers. Carl paid for the lumber an' wire an' chickens with money he made at the rodeo last fall, but I'm the one, mostly, that took care of 'em an' raised 'em."

"You really like animals, don't you?"

"Yes," he said soberly, "but wild ones are best. We've raised a lot."

"Oh, I wish I'd seen them," she said softly. "Almost the only animals I'd seen till I came here, besides dogs and cats, I mean, were the ones at the zoo and I always felt sort of—sorry for them."

Jeff looked closely at her face. She meant it. He guessed maybe she really was all right, like Carl said.

"We had chipmunks an' all kinds a squirrels an' two foxes an' a coyote an' rabbits, all baby ones that we raised, an' one year Doyle found a fawn that somebody had shot its mother. We always let 'em go when they git grown an' want to leave, 'cause they wouldn' be happy to stay here, but I like to watch 'em grow, see 'em real close up. Most people don't git a chance to do that even if they can—" He flushed and broke off. He had almost said "even if they can walk good."

Rinie said, "Have you ever had a mountain lion?"

"No," Jeff said earnestly, "but I wish I could . . . once Carl tried to git a baby eagle but the mama an' daddy bird came back. The nest was 'way up in a tree an' they tried to knock him down an' peck out his eyes an' ever'thing. He's got a scar on the back of his hand where one bit him when he was climbin' down."

Rinie shivered. She had noticed the scar once and had asked Carl what it was. He said casually that it was an eagle bite. She had thought he was teasing and had let it go. It seemed that almost every time anyone talked about her husband it gave her something new to worry about. She wondered fearfully if he'd go climbing after baby eagles now and she guessed he would if he took the notion.

Jeff said proudly, "Not many people have been bit by a eagle."

66

"No," she agreed, readily enough, "I guess not."

Rinie found much of interest in the house as she worked, the heavy, dark, inlaid bedroom furniture in Travis and Ellie's room, as good or better than anything the Hickses had, a cache of whiskey under A. J.'s bed and a few bottles in a drawer of Troy's dresser, numerous figurines and other small keepsakes, left in odd places, some of the things delicate and beautiful, a big box of books in fine bindings, mildewing a little. Jeff said he had read some of the books and that no one would mind if Rinie read them whenever she felt like it. They had belonged to his grandma. He said Doyle had read them all and Carl had read some, but that Carl said there was more to see and learn outside than in books.

Late Friday afternoon when Rinie was getting supper, the housework almost finished, Jeff came in from the barn, hurrying as fast as he could, sloshing a little milk out of the pail in his haste.

"Rinie, come 'ere," he said eagerly, "I want to show you somethin'."

"In just a minute, Jeff. I have to keep stirring this or it'll boil over."

He was disappointed and said with shy urgency, "If you don't come now, you can't. I can't show you after Kirby an' Helen git home."

She set the pot off the stove and went with him.

"One a the hens gits out," he explained, limping along in painful haste. "We'll have to clip her wing. She flies over the fence. But I was lookin' for her nest an' I found the—what I want to show you."

They came into the barn and Jeff said they must go up into the loft. Rinie wanted to cry when he climbed up the ladder. It was obvious from one quick glance at his face that it was so painful for him, but he took it as a matter of course.

In the far corner of the loft, nesting in some old hay, was the barn cat Lucky and four kittens—two yellow like the tomcat, one black like Lucky, and one a combination. They were the tiniest live things Rinie had ever seen close up. Lucky was concerned and uneasy about intruders, but, speaking to her reassuringly, Jeff picked up the yellow and black kitten and give it to Rinie.

"Oh," she breathed, "it's the softest thing I ever saw. Oh, Jeff, look at its cute little face, but," she felt sick, "there's something wrong. Look at its eyes. . . ."

"Don't you know," he said incredulously, "that kittens and puppies an' a lot of baby things don't git their eyes open for a week or two after they're born?"

"Oh," she said, vastly relieved, "no, I didn't know that."

She was very still, feeling a strange tender thrill as the kitten moved in her hands, butting his little head blindly in quest of food.

"But don't tell anybody," Jeff said urgently. "They'll kill 'em."

"Oh, *why?*" She was horrified.

" 'Cause there'd be too many cats if we kep' 'em all, only I never tell an' Lucky knows I don't. We better go now, before Kirby an' Helen gits her."

"Jeff," she said softly as they walked back to the house, "thank you for showing me."

And then it was Saturday and Rinie was full of excitement. Surely Carl would be home tonight. It was clouding up again and A. J. was predicting snow, but the cattle would be safe in the shipping pens.

Rinie spent most of the morning in the kitchen. She baked a huge chocolate cake, four pies and two kinds of cookies.

"Good Christ," said A. J., helping himself to a cookie, "anybody'd think they was a weddin' here instead a over to Ellie's folks—or a funeral."

A shiver ran down Rinie's back. He shouldn't say that, even in fun.

"Now, listen, missy," he warned, looking over his shoulder as he was going out the back door, "don't you count too much on him bein' in tonight. Even a married man's got a right to a Saturday night in town onct a year."

When lunch was done and the kitchen in order, she barricaded its doors, took a bath and washed her hair. She put some stew meat on to cook for supper and then she was ready to relax and wait.

Last night she had cut out two shirts from Ellie's sacks. She had had to pass up the gold-brown again because there was only enough of that for one. She used a dark blue because she wanted to make matching shirts for Carl and Jeff. She hoped Kirby wouldn't mind. He didn't seem to care about things like that, but she planned to make shirts alike for him and Travis as soon as she had time.

By suppertime, she had the machine work done on the shirts. It grew dark early, the sky heavy with clouds.

When A. J. came in, he reported with satisfaction that the wind was around to the northwest and picking up fast.

Jeff and Helen volunteered to wash the supper dishes and Rinie carried wood into the front room to start a fire in the fireplace. She thought it would be nice to sit in there for a change and she was so proud of the way the house looked. As she was bringing in a final armload of wood, a few flakes of snow came cold and fresh against her face.

Oh, Carl, please be close. Please get home tonight. I don't care if it snows from now on, if only you're home.

She brought the shirts in to do the hand work on them, sitting at one end of the huge horsehair sofa, her feet barely touching the floor. The wind moaned around the sturdy corners of the house and across the chimney top.

Kirby turned on the radio and it made Rinie nervous. She was straining to hear above the wind and the sounds in the room, the hooves of a horse, the greeting whines and barks of the dogs, steps on the porch.

After a while, Kirby grew disinterested, turned off the radio—there was too much static anyway—and he and Jeff started a game of checkers.

They had some more of the fresh-baked cookies and some apples.

Helen fell asleep, curled up on the sofa by Rinie.

A. J. looked outside.

"More'n a inch a snow already. I'm goin' to bed."

"Tell about the blizzard, grandaddy," urged Jeff and Kirby joined him.

Standing with his back to the fire, A. J. told about when he'd first come out here, looking for land and silver, and a spring blizzard had struck, taking everybody unawares. The few people in the West Fork country then were living in thrown-together shacks or tents, and two men, each living alone, had frozen to death.

Rinie wished he'd gone to bed without telling the story. A. J. was never one to leave out details and it frightened her. What if Carl—? To stop her thoughts, she said, "But there is silver here, isn't there?"

"Goddam' right," he said heartily, "plenty of it. If the gover'ment'd keep a decent price an' the goddam' railroad men had the good sense to run their line up the West Fork, we'd be rich. There's coal, too. Not the best kind, but as good as they're gittin' outta them mines east a Belford.

This here land's worth holdin' onto." And he stomped off to bed.

Rinie carried Helen to bed and the boys went after a while. She sat on by the dying fire, working on the shirts until her fingers were stiff with cold. The wind was fierce now and there was nothing but whirling, white-blurred darkness when she tried to see outside. It was hard to believe how swiftly the temperature was falling. She put a stick of wood on the coals in the kitchen stove so it wouldn't be so numbingly cold to get up in the morning. The mantle clock struck one as she went sadly into the empty bedroom.

This room, being at the northwest corner of the house, was loudest of all with the moaning, howling, indomitable wind. Carl must be safe and warm somewhere in Belford. Surely, he was not out in this. If he had started home today he would have had plenty of time to get here before the storm got so bad. She was very tired, but it was hard to go to sleep. She couldn't seem to get warm or to stop listening.

But she did sleep because the sound of the back door, slammed shut by the wind, startled her violently. She jumped up, pulling a blanket around her shoulders, lit the lamp on the dresser, and looked into the kitchen.

Carl looked up from where he had dropped into a chair close to the stove and tried to smile. He looked frozen.

"Oh, Carl—?"

"I'm all right, Rinie," he said curtly. "I'm all right. I—I'm just cold."

"Some coffee," she moved to put the pot on.

"No. I don't want it." He stood up shakily. "I'll just get to bed."

His fingers were stiff and unmanageable. She helped him undress and got more blankets to cover him with. She lay close beside him, chafing his hands, trying to give him her own warmth. He was only half-conscious.

"I wanted to git home," he said, the words slurring together. "Bo stayed in Belford . . . this storm . . . I couldn' even tell it was comin' till I was halfway here . . . mmm, you're warm, Rinie. I knew you would be. I didn' have anything but a slicker, they're not very warm . . . a slicker an' a brush jacket . . . just after we come into the canyon down there, Skeeter slipped on a snowy rock, pulled a tendon, I think . . . I hope to God that's all. My fault . . .

70

shouldn've been ridin'. I couldn' see anything. . . . She had to rest a lot, then, comin' the rest of the way home. . . . God, Rinie, it's so cold out there."

"Let me get some coffee, Carl."

"No, I'm too tired. Just stay here with me."

His violent shuddering shook the bed unceasingly. Rinie was frightened. She'd have to go and ask A. J. what ought to be done, but then she heard the heavy treading around her again.

"Did you give him coffee?" demanded the old man.

"He didn't want it. I—"

"I didn' ask what he wanted," A. J. said curtly. "Here, Buck, swaller some a this."

He half-lifted Carl to a sitting position and held a cup of whiskey to his lips.

"No, I—"

But A. J. poured the whiskey into his mouth, a good deal of it spilling.

"You dam' kid! You ain't got the sense of a ign'rant houn' dog, out till three o'clock in zero weather. What the bloody hell do you think you are? Somethin' God or the devil's got a special watch on? Open you mouth, goddammit!"

"Skeeter," Carl said, angrily trying to push the cup away. "I gave her grain an' put a blanket on 'er, but. . . ."

A. J. refilled the cup from the bottle he had brought along.

Rinie was in the kitchen, heating water for the hot-water bottle and rocks to wrap in rags and put in the bed for extra heat. She was shaking with apprehension. Pneumonia or. . . .

A. J. heaved Carl's shoulders up again and offered the cup roughly.

"It burns," Carl choked pleadingly.

"It ought to. Quit spillin' it, dam' you, it costs money. Quit shakin'."

"I'm cold," he said, outraged.

"You are! Well, I'll just be goddamned for a dewlapped dog! Shut up an' drink."

Some color was coming back into his face. Rinie put the wrapped rocks and the hot-water bottle around his feet and legs.

"You ain't frost-bit, I guess," said A. J. resentfully, "which is more'n you deserve."

"A. J., Skeeter—"

"I'll tend to 'er, Carlisle, for God sake!" He screwed the lid on his bottle. "Well, here he is, missy. You wanted him home, there he is, half-froze, full of whiskey an' I hope you're satisfied."

After a little, Rinie got back into bed, grimacing at the reek of whiskey. Carl lay inert except for sporadic shivering. She took his hand and it was warmer. She heard A. J. tramp back in from the barn and go to his room.

Carl roused. "Rinie?"

"What, sweetheart?"

He spoke thickly, groggily. "Rinie, before that cattle drive, I never did know what it felt like to be really lonesome. Honey?"

"What, Carl?"

The words were almost unintelligible as he drifted into sleep. "I love you, Rinie . . . you're warm."

It seemed such a brief time before Rinie was wakened by the rattling of wood being put into the stove and A. J.'s heavy tread in the kitchen. She got up and dressed quickly. The room was frigid. Carl was sleeping heavily. His face was a little flushed, but he didn't seem feverish. The smell of whiskey was strong. She'd have to wash all the blankets to get rid of it. One of his hands hung limply over the edge of the bed. Tenderly, she put it under the covers and went into the kitchen.

A. J. had the coffee on. He had slept little after going back to bed, the aching in his joints having been increased by going out in the cold to look after the mare.

"Cleared up," he said, by way of greeting. "That wind's colder'n hell, but pretty near all the snow's blowed off somewheres. Buck all right?"

"He's sleeping," she said, getting out a piece of ham to slice, "but I—I'm afraid he'll be sick."

A. J. snorted contemptuously. "He's all right. A man can't stand a little cold in this country ain't worth a hoot."

Jeff and Kirby came in, shivering, to put on their boots in the warmth from the stove.

"Did Carl come?" Jeff asked. "I thought I heard somebody in the night."

A. J. and Rinie said he had.

"How come he was so late?" asked Kirby.

"Skeeter slipped an' hurt herself a little," A. J. said unsympathetically. "He had to make it easy on her."

"Troy didn' come," said Kirby. It wasn't a question. He knew how Troy liked Saturday nights in Belford. He wished he could have gone on the drive. You wouldn' catch him riding home in any storm.

Jeff put on his coat and got the milk bucket.

"Wait till after breakfast," Rine urged him. "It's so cold out there."

The sun was only now showing up the tops of the ridges.

"The cold don't hurt," Jeff said, and Kirby, grumbling, got his own coat and went to see to the rest of the chores.

"Jeff's got to see to the mare," said A. J., with a hint of pride. "If anything, he's more a fool about a critter'n Carl is."

Before the boys got back, Helen was up and dressed by the stove. All of them were so inured to getting up with or before the sun that they couldn't seem to help it. Helen said she had got cold, anyway, sleeping by herself.

Rinie cooked ham and eggs and biscuits, yawning often as she worked. She was worried about Carl, despite A. J.'s rough reassurance. As she got out plates, she said, trying to sound casual, "People talk about that Indian woman, Heddie. Where does she live?"

It was so terribly far to a doctor if one should ever be needed.

A. J. looked at her sharply. "Why, Heddie lives just the other side a Webber a little ways. Why?"

"I—I just got to thinking about her."

When the boys came in, Jeff put the milk on a shelf by the sink and opened the door again. Reaching out, he took a dog by the scruff of the neck and gently coaxed it inside. It was old Christmas and she was reluctant to come in. The other dogs were kept out forcibly, if at all, but some time in her past, Christmas had been taught or had decided that the house was no place for her.

"You better git that dog outta here, Jeff Stinson," said Helen primly. "Rinie just got the house all cleaned up nice."

Rinie nodded at Jeff's wistful look and he shut the door.

"She was out in the barn," he said. "The cold hurts her."

The old dog moved with painful stiffness.

73

"Come an' set down,' said A. J. "She ain't gonna hurt nothin'."

Kirby came in from the front room and they sat around the table as Rinie served up the eggs, cooked to individual preference. Kirby said, I guess I'll go rabbit huntin' when I eat. I was lookin' for my game sack."

"Where'd you leave it?" asked his sister wearily. "You can't never find anything."

"Ah, Helen, quit try'n to act like mama," he said impatiently. "You're a little short yet. I left it in the front room. I remember for sure. The last time I had it was when I went quail huntin' an' I put it in there when I put the shotgun up."

A. J. glanced at Rinie, the corner of his mouth quirking. She said, "I—I guess I picked it up, Kirby."

He frowned. "Well, gosh, Rinie, I got to have it."

"I'll help you find it after breakfast," she said contritely.

"Anyway, Kirby," said Helen, "I couldn' find my crayolas yesterday, or my gum I left on the dresser. I just chewed it a little while, but Rinie throwed it away."

Carl came in from the bedroom, his eyes bloodshot, his face haggard.

"Your woman's had the cleans while you been gone," A. J. reported, "an' they ain't a one here ain't loss somethin'."

Carl pumped cold water and washed his face.

"I don't want to eat, Rinie," he said as she started for the stove, "an' I'll tell you one thing for dam' sure— somebody that poured whiskey all over the bed ain't got no cleans."

"Set down, Buck. Drink some coffee. A man with a hangover always feels a little ringy. No use fussin' at missy."

"I'm not fussin' at missy," Carl said shortly. "I'm goin' to see about Skeeter."

"I looked at her, Carl," Jeff said quickly. "Her leg's swelled a little, but I don't think it's hurt much. She eat her grain real good an' acted like she wanted out, but I thought you'd want to keep 'er in a while longer."

Carl hesitated and finally came to the table.

"Thanks," he said gruffly.

Rinie brought him coffee, touching his shoulder with shy tenderness.

"You should've slept longer. How do you feel?"

"My head hurts an' it stinks too much in there to sleep. If I'm gonna be drunk, I'd like to do it on my own."

"Listen here, young Buck," said his father angrily. "The next time you pull a fool thing like you done last night, won't nobody catch me wastin' good whiskey on you."

To break the awkward silence, Rinie began to tell him about where Ellie and Travis were and why.

"They'll be back sometime tonight," said Helen. "I expect they'll bring some presents."

"Troy comin' back today?" asked Kirby.

Carl, drinking the coffee, felt a little better. He said, "He said so, but he may not, cold as it is."

"Did you git there all right?" asked A. J. "How'd Corbett's horse work out?"

"Which horse was that?"

"The piebald Travis was tellin' us you went off on?"

"Oh, he's all right. Real good horse in time."

"Have any trouble with the drive?"

"Billy Barnhart got hurt some," Carl said, rubbing his eyes. "When we was puttin' 'em through the chute for the brand inspector, an ole steer crowded him into the fence. Cracked a couple ribs, I guess."

"Barnharts never did have much cow sense. What the hell was he doin' on foot?"

"Standin' there," said Carl.

A. J. snorted. After a moment, he said, "You put the money in the bank?"

"Troy did."

"You seen 'im, did you?"

"Yessir, I did."

Proceeds from the sale of cattle were almost the only cash the ranch provided. The bank account was accessible only to Travis and A. J. Normally, Carl didn't care. He didn't need any money and it wasn't as if the cattle money was ever spent selfishly. It all went for necessities for the ranch. It had to. He didn't particularly want money now. He had worked for three other ranchers while waiting for Troy to come back from California, and he and Rinie had chosen a few clothes they needed from the catalog and paid for the order with the wages he had earned. But Carl was resenting things this morning and he didn't like A. J.'s questioning him about the cattle money.

A. J. reached down to scratch the ear of old Christmas who had been all this time easing over to him. She was afraid somebody would notice her and make her go out in the cold again. A. J. didn't feel easy when the boy got ringy like this. If it had been Troy or Doyle, it wouldn't mean anything, and Travis had always been touchy, not to get mad and raise hell, but just get his feelings hurt, but if old Buck stayed cranky like this, maybe missy had reason to worry. Maybe he was sick; it wouldn't be any wonder. A. J. said tentatively, "We had a letter from your brother Doyle."

Rinie poured Carl more coffee. She was so pretty, prettier than he remembered, even. He smiled at her and felt better.

A. J. immediately felt better, seeing the smile and the look of the kid's eyes. He might not be in the best shape, but he wasn't very sick. A. J. said with a touch of derision, "Says he aims to be a lawyer, Doyle does. He finally decided how he's gonna employ all this education he's been soppin' up."

"Well, it won't hurt to have a lawyer in the family," Carl said, taking a hot biscuit to butter.

A. J. grunted. "Means more schoolin'. Course I can't say too much about that. It kinda does me good to think about Minnie turnin' loose all that money, but it looks to me like your brother's just huntin' excuses to do anything besides go to work. It just ain't natural for a grown man to set in school till his behind's all flattened out. Eat some a this here ham."

Carl didn't want the ham. He accepted the platter and set it down out of A. J.'s reach without taking any.

"Doyle claims," A. J. went on, "that a man's got to have that much schoolin' 'fore he can make money worth a dam', but hell, I didn't have no schoolin' to speak of an' there's times I had more money'n he'll see, prob'ly."

"Maybe," Carl said, and his mouth looked like A. J.'s when it quirked a little at the corner, "all that learnin' teaches a man to hold on to it."

A shadow of anger passed over the old man's face, but then his mouth quirked, too.

"You can't take your whiskey any too well, can you,

Buck-snort? A kid as old as you are oughtn't to git so waspy over a little hangover."

Rinie stood up and said to Carl, "I'm finished now. I'll put clean things on the bed. Maybe you ought to rest some more when you're through."

"Now then," said A. J. quietly when she had gone into the bedroom, "what, exactly, come off last night?"

"I did, for one thing," Carl said, grinning ruefully. "Skeeter fell . . . God it scared me—I mean about Skeeter."

"Lord a-mighty, boy, you'd think there never had been another mare in foal. How come your clothes like they was?"

Carl flushed. He had hoped A. J. hadn't noticed, but he should have known better.

"You young-uns go on about your business," said the grandfather curtly.

Kirby and Jeff went in search of the game pouch, but Helen said smugly, "I got to git these dishes washed," and began stacking them.

"You got to do like you're told, Miss Puss," A. J. said, " 'fore I bust your runnit."

Helen went after Rinie, deflated a little.

A. J. spat accurately at the slop bucket and looked at his son, waiting.

Carl turned his coffee cup on the oil cloth and looked out the window. He said sheepishly, "I fell in the creek."

A. J. kept his face straight, but his voice shook a little. "Was it cold?"

"Godam' right."

A snort of laughter escaped the still almost sober face. "But you don't mean that's where Skeeter slipped? She wasn' all iced up when I seen 'er, like them clothes a yourn."

Carl shook his head sulkily. "Where she fell was just this side of the lower ford. By the time we come to the upper ford, she was favorin' her leg so much I was afraid to ride her across. I'd been leadin' 'er, thinkin' she'd be all right to cross the creek on, but then I thought, limpin' like she was, she might fall an' git us both in the water, so I . . . dam' it, A. J., go ahead an' laugh if you got to!"

He did.

"So you fell in the water all by yourself?"

"Yessir, Mr. Stinson, I did."

"You're the damdest fool kid I ever seen," said the father, and went off again in snorts of guffaws.

Carl stood up, not laughing.

"I'm goin' to see about Skeeter."

"All right," said A. J., choking a little, wiping his eyes on his shirt sleeve. "An', Buck—?"

Carl looked back, his hand on the door.

"That little gal a yours, she's been right handy, waitin' on the place."

"That's good," he said cautiously. It wasn't like A. J. to hand out straight compliments. This must be leading up to something.

A. J. cleared his throat, squelching another burst of mirth.

"When you git all done seein' to the horse, whyn't you go back to bed a while? You ain't had much sleep for a feller that's tooka soakin' like that, an—uh—missy, she's worked right hard while you been gone. I expect she needs restin', too."

It was mid-afternoon when they woke again. They woke simultaneously and that seemed like a small, private, wonderful miracle. They opened their eyes slowly and were looking straight at each other. They laughed a little.

"I love you," Rinie said softly.

He kissed her for a long time until she lay tense against him, breathing quickly.

"Carl?"

"Don't bother me. I'm kissin' my girl."

"Are you really all right?"

"My God! Do you doubt it?"

"Well, I don't doubt you're a little conceited."

"All right, now shut up. I have to kiss her some more. I haven't seen her for—oh, a long time an' I missed her like anything."

After a while she said, a little distrustful of the utter happiness, "I was so scared about you last night. Carl, if anything ever happened to you, I—"

"Rinie." His arms were warm and she was safe. "Rinie, don't always think you got to look over your shoulder for the booger man. He's not there, honey. Honest. Here we are, right here, together, an we'll be like this, or somethin' like, for a long, long time. You're afraid of

78

good things. I know you've had reason before, but don't be any more. Please don't. If you can git at some- thin' good, grab it with both hands and hang on for all you're worth."

"I want to," she whispered, hiding her face against his neck. She didn't know how she'd managed to get through those days and nights when he was gone. "Only I can't help thinking . . . I thought a lot of times about having somebody to—to love me, how it would be to be—special for somebody, but even dreaming about it it wasn't like this."

"You're somebody special," he said gently. "You're so dam' special I nearly ruint the best mare in the county because I had to git back to you. I kept thinkin' all the time I was gone an' especially walkin' that last part of the way home, how it would be, here with you, an' then I had to go an' pass out that way. I'm awful sorry about that, honey."

"She'll be all right, won't she? Skeeter?"

"Looks like she'll be fine. I guess you think I'm kinda silly about her."

"Oh, no, Carl," but her eyes were a little wistful.

"She's the best cow horse in the country," he said irre- pressibly. "Mostly, you favor gelding for a workin' horse. There're problems, usin' a mare, but she's way too good to waste. She's seven now an' never been bred be- fore this, an' I didn' mean for it to happen now. I wanted to enter her in some of the cuttin' contests this fall if I had the money. But last winter the wild bunch come through. She was here, in the corral. I kep' 'er up so there wouldn' be any chance of Rowdy gittin' to 'er It takes time to git a horse trained right, even one with all the natural sense she's got an' I didn't want to take time out for colts. But that goddam' wild stallion got 'er. She jumped the fence after 'im. The weather was real bad an' it was a while be- fore I could go look for 'er."

She pressed against him, strangely, violently passion- ate.

"I'm glad!" she whispered fiercely. "I'm glad he wanted her and came after her and she wanted him and got out to him."

She couldn't breathe in the sudden fierce clasp of his arms, but it didn't matter; she didn't want breathing.

When the violence was spent, there was a time of long sweet lethargy. Finally, Rinie stirred reluctantly.

"I ought to get up," she murmured. Her voice was small and hushed. She was still deep under the spell of the awesome, wild beauty of what had happened to them.

"Why?" he said drowsily.

"They must be hungry. Look how late it is."

The sun, far down the western sky, was warm across the foot of their bed. From where they lay, they could look straight through the north window and up to the barren rock ridge.

The other boys had never had much preference as to a room, but Carl wanted this one because he wanted to be able to lie here, times when he didn't have to do or think anything, and let his eyes move slowly up the benches and the woods to the ridge and the sky.

Rinie didn't like to look at the ridge. It was so stark, so harsh, so alone with no need for anything. No trees grew on it. The wind swept it and the sun and rain and hail and snow beat on it and the clouds covered it and moved on, and it was there—unchanged, aloof, indomitable, indifferent, alone. Now she found Carl's hand, warm and limp in his drowsy completion, and they looked up to the ridge together.

He liked the lonely things though, she thought. The thought had come often before and always it had left her lonely. She had felt left out, unable to share with him the things he valued most. But now she was beginning to feel differently. She couldn't appreciate or, in many cases, even begin to understand the other things he loved but now she was certain that above everything, he loved her, that she need not feel jealousy or resentment or loneliness again. Some things could not be shared, but that didn't diminish love.

"There'll be more time now," he said dreamily. "How'd you like to start learnin' to ride?"

"I'd like it," she said contentedly.

"All right. Tomorrow, if it's not too cold."

"I ought to go fix supper."

"They had somethin' a while ago," he said, "I heard 'em in there. Besides it won't hurt 'em to do without you a while. Anyway, if they wanted anything bad, they'd let us know—A. J. would."

"Carl?"

He turned his eyes to her and they were silent for a moment with the wonder of looking at each other. She said shyly, "Would you like for us to have a baby?"

He smiled. "Well, not just right now, no."

"But you would like one, wouldn't you—sometime? You do like babies, don't you?"

He looked uneasy. "I don't know, they're—odd, but they generally grow out of it, I guess."

"I never held a little baby," she said reverently. "At the orphanage we helped out with the little children as we got bigger, but they kept the babies at another place till they were about two. Oh, Carl. . . ." Her eyes were suddenly full of tears. "I'll love a baby so much! I can just feel how it would be in my arms and it'd be ours, that you gave to me and I gave back to you. You wouldn't mind having a baby, would you?"

"No, Rinie," he said gently. "I'd like it."

"Because," she said eagerly, "it wouldn't take any of our love away from each other. It would just make love deeper and bigger and—and fuller."

Carl stroked her hair. He was thinking fiercely. What kind of bastards were they to go and leave her on the steps of a goddam' orphanage? Rinie, that's got so much love and couldn't hurt anybody if she tried. A baby, just a little helpless baby, that's wanted loving so much all her life and never asked for anything. The goddam' sonsabitches! His teeth were gritting and he didn't know it. She raised her head and was frightened by his face. He shook his head slightly and tried for a smile.

"What's the matter?" she asked fearfully.

"Nothin', honey. I was just thinkin' about something that made me mad—once."

"Carl?"

"Hmm?"

"Is it—is it you don't want—a baby?"

"No, Rinie, it's not that at all." He drew her close. "I want a baby just as quick as one feels like comin' along. Then I'll have me two babies to love."

After a while of close, warm silence, she thrust a foot tentatively out from under the covers and drew it back quickly.

"Ooo, it's cold out there," she said, snuggling against him.

"Then don't be pokin' things out," he said, stretching luxuriously.

"Carl?"

"What you want, missy?"

She smiled. "If you could have anything in the whole world, what would you wish for?"

He looked at her and sighed with deep contentment.

"Nothin', Rinie, not one dam' thing."

Kirby had shot three rabbits. He had them cleaned and soaking in salt water for supper. Jeff had sent Sport after the cow and was putting on his coat to go milk. Helen, with great care and pride and not too much waste, had peeled potatoes for supper.

"We had dried peaches for dinner," she told Rinie. Rinie felt guilty, but Helen said with pleasure, "We eat 'em in the front room so we wouldn' wake up you an' Carl. Granddaddy let us toast 'em in the fire. Kirby says you bloat up an' bust if you don't eat nothin, but dried peaches, but nobody didn't."

"Listen, Missy," A. J. said seriously as she fried the rabbits, "I can't find the cleanin' rod for my .30-30 nowheres. Now I tole you, cleanin' up the place is all right, but it's easy overdone."

"I'm sorry," she said contritely. "I'll help you find it. What's it look like?"

"Oh, Lord, let it go," he muttered. "Don't even know what a cleanin' rod looks like." He went irascibly toward the front room to make another search.

Looking apologetically after him, she called softly, "I am awfully sorry—daddy."

A. J.'s heart did a funny thing. He didn't understand it at all, so he said shortly, "Well, see it don't happen again."

Before Carl and the boys had finished the chores, Troy arrived, surprising them all a little.

"I was told to come home," he said smugly, "an' I did. I nearly always do, only I come after my car an' where's it at?"

Through supper, they told him about Travis and Ellie's trip and about part of Carl's adventure of the night before.

A. J. kept smirking at Carl and grinning broadly from time to time and Carl knew it was only a matter of time until the whole of it was general knowledge, but that A.

82

J. would savor the full enjoyment of having something on him before he told. Carl would have told it himself to have it done with, except he knew it would scare Rinie. Besides, he didn't relish the idea of looking a fool in front of her.

Troy had had a fine time in Belford last night. He told them some of it. Carl and A. J. could pretty well fill in the rest. His eyes were red-rimmed and he looked tired, but he was in a fine, expansive mood.

"I guess you heard about that lion over at McLean's," he said, passing his plate for more pie. "I sure would like to git me a lion. That's good pie, Rinie, real good."

He got up and went into the front room and after a moment he called, "Hey, you kids been messin' with my stuff agin? I'da swore I had a can a tobacco in here."

Rinie flushed helplessly and the others laughed.

"Rinie's had the cleans," Carl told his brother. "Pretty bad case, looks like."

"The tobacco," she called defiantly, "is on your dresser. At least I know what that looks like."

Troy came back, rolling himself a cigarette. Rinie began to stack the dishes and Carl poured more coffee.

"You know what?" he said, putting the pot back on the stove. "We ought to do somethin'. Have us a party or somethin'."

He went into the front room to turn on the radio.

"Not that," Troy called. "They talk to much. Play some records."

Carl wound the phonograph and put one on.

"Oh, goody, a party!" squealed Helen.

"No, you have to go to bed," Carl told her.

"Oh, Carl." She couldn't believe it. He was always such fun to play with and have parties with.

"Say, you're feelin' pretty good, huh, Buckshot?" said Troy, grinning. "Just what kinda party you got in mind?"

"Well, one without kids. One where A. J. lets us kill off a couple a bottles a that stuff under his bed—that kind."

"I thought you didn' like drinkin'," A. J. grunted.

"I never said that. It's takin' a bath in whiskey that I don't care about."

"Ruther have your baths in cold water, I expect," surmised his father with a little snort of laughter.

"Rinie, do you know how to dance?" asked Carl undaunted. "It's funny I don't know that about you."

"No," she said regretfully, "and I don't know how to drink either."

"Good God, Buck, you ought to know your Aunt Minnie wouldn' have that kinda goings-on."

"Well," said Troy, getting up eagerly, "leave the dishes alone. Come on. We'll teach you fast enough."

"*I'll* teach 'er," Carl said ungraciously. "You'll have to git your own somebody to teach."

"Well, goddam'," said Troy, offended. "You sure are selfish. She's married to you, ain't she? I ain't gonna ruin 'er from just dancin' with 'er. I thought we was buddies that shared."

"I don't know how you ever come to think that," replied his brother. "You go git your own girl while we git the place squared away."

Troy got his coat but he said dubiously, "The radiator on that ole pickup may have busted. I ain't sure there was enough antifreeze in there for as cold as it got last night."

Carl grinned. "I feel sorry about it if anything busted last night, but if it did, you'll just have to go to bed with the rest of the kids."

"For Chrissake," muttered Troy, slamming the door.

Carl made the children go to bed. Helen cried and A. J. opined that they ought to be let to stay up for a while, but Carl was adamant.

"I reckon the next thing, you'll be tryin' to git rid a me," said the old man hotly.

Carl was drying the dishes, awkwardly, and putting them where Rinie told him they belonged. He said calmly, "No, we need your whiskey."

Troy returned with another young man and two girls. The man, Theorn McLean, was tall with black hair and bold black eyes and a loud laugh. One of the girls, Vanda Forrester, was slender and quiet with greenish eyes and dark brown hair. She spoke in a soft slurring voice and moved with a beautiful feline grace. The other girl, Doxy Keane, old Sutter's daughter, was short and plump with a full, almost overripe figure. Her face was round and childish, her blue eyes sparkling but shallow and a little vague.

"I picked 'em up in front a the store," Troy reported. "Ole man Putney run 'em out for bad conduct."

"Oh, Troy Stinson, he didn' neither," said Doxy, giggling. "He was closin'."

"How come your daddy lets you run around like this on Sundays, Doxy?" Carl asked.

She gave him what she considered to be a melting glance.

"W'y, daddy knows I ain't gonna do nothin' wrong, Carl, an' how'm I ever gonna git married if I don't never go nowhere? Daddy says he can't last much longer with three of us girls at a age to marry. The place just swarms with boys."

"I'll lay," muttered Carl.

"Which girl is Troy's?" Rinie asked him privately.

"Both of 'em. Either one. He don't care. I guess Theorn is goin' around some with Vanda, but he ain't no more serious than Bo is. Come on, le's dance."

She was shy about trying to learn in front of the others, but it wasn't so very hard, not in Carl's arms. She was also hesitant about drinking, but he gave her some whiskey weakened with a lot of water and she drank it. It was about the worst thing she'd ever tasted, but it felt good in her throat and farther down.

A. J. went to bed, but first he came to Rinie while she was putting cookies on a plate and said, trying not to grin, "Now it's up to you, Miz Stinson, to see that these kids behaves theirselves. You're the married woman around here an' that Buck a yourn ain't no chaperonin' material. Why, he's worse'n the rest of 'em an' he'll git drunker'n seven hundred dollars if you don't watch him."

"I've got a bunch of new records that I bought in Denver this summer," remarked Vanda as Troy wound the Victrola. "Tommy Dorsey and Guy Lombardo and some others. I wish I'd known I was comin' to a party. I'd have brought them."

After a while Rinie danced with Troy. He'd had quite a lot to drink—he and Carl and Theorn were mostly drinking straight out of the bottle—and he held her close. Guiltily, she liked it, a little. Liking it a little didn't take anything away from the way she felt about Carl. It gave her grounds for comparison and made Carl even better, but she oughtn't to like it.

She saw Carl dancing with Doxy Keane and she didn't like that a bit. Why the shameless little snip was just about wrapping herself around him and he was grinning.

"I think I'll sit down," Rinie said shortly to Troy.

He laughed. "You poor little kid. Don't git all het up about that. Don't you reckon he ever danced with any body else? Just because Aunt Minna never let you out of sight, don't mean Buck's been settin' home. He was quite a boy on the West Fork, I can tell you. After all, he had a long time to wait." He leaned down and rubbed his cheek against her hair. "I don't know but what it was worth it, though, I sorta wish I'd thought of it first."

When the record was over, she sat on the sofa. Vanda Forrester was there already, her feet tucked under her, curled up and sleek like a cat.

"I guess it's pretty dull for you after Denver," Vanda said. "I lived there with my married sister while I went to high school and it was awful hard to have to come back around Webber again."

They talked for a while—Rinie shyly, Vanda with ease —about Denver; where each had lived, what they'd seen in common. Vanda knew a good deal more about the city than Rinie did. Rinie thought she liked Vanda, but she was a little awed by the other girl's ease and grace.

Their eyes were attracted to Troy and Doxy, dancing. Carl and Theorn had momentarily retired to a corner with the bottle to discuss horses. Doxy leaned against Troy, looking up at him with what she supposed to be languishing eyes, and Troy leaned down and kissed her, a long slow kiss while their bodies swayed together.

Rinie looked away, embarrassed.

"She's the awfulest little flirt," murmured Vanda. "They sure named her right, though I don't guess they know what doxie means. Mr. Keane's supposed to be a preacher so it looks extra bad for her to act like she does, but they don't seem to care. I don't think she knows half what she's doin'. She's just sixteen and Troy ought to be ashamed, carryin' on that way an' I'm gonna tell him so."

Rinie danced with Theorn. He stamped around a lot in his boots and she worried about her toes being stepped on, but she thought he was nice.

She was glad to be with Carl again. It was wonderful how good it always was just to be near him.

"How do you like your first party, little girl?"

"Oh, Carl, I like it. I keep finding out more and more things I missed and never even knew about."

"I want to make 'em all up to you, Rinie, all that I can. Do you want another drink?"

"I—I guess so. Carl? You won't—get drunk?"

"Why not?"

"Well, I—wouldn't know what to do."

He laughed. "I never get drunk," he said blithely.

He mixed her drink and they sat on an ornate little loveseat at the back of the front room. His arm was warm around her.

"Carl, did you—have lots of girls?"

"I went around with some."

"Did you—did you ever—" she felt like crying at the thought.

"Rinie, before was before. Now it's now an' I love you just—well, just so goddam' much I could set right here an' eat you, all of you, you're not very big. When you leave your hair down like that, it's just about more that I can stand." He pulled her on to his lap and kissed her.

"Carl, they'll—they'll see," she said, blushing and laughing.

"Hell, let 'em look. I don't care if they see that I love the prettiest, sweetest little girl around."

"A. J. said to set a good example, or something like that," she said, smiling into his eyes.

"A. J. don't know a good example from a sour apple," he said, kissing her again.

Amid the music and talk and laughter, all of which grew louder as A. J.'s whiskey disappeared, the front door opened, admitting cold air and Travis and Ellie.

"Well, my land! What in the world?" demanded Ellie. "I never heard such a racket."

"We had you a welcome-home party," Troy told her. "You're a little late, but welcome, anyway." And he grabbed her and danced her across the room.

Travis had shut the door and stood there grinning.

"Now quit, Troy," ordered Ellie. "I'm tired."

But Carl had her now and was making her dance. He said, "We heard about the gov'ner, Miss Ellie. Did you bring him with you?"

"You silly thing! You're drunk, Carlisle Stinson. Ever' one of you is drunk."

"It's scan'lous," Troy agreed, leering.

"W'y, you know we wouldn' git drunk, Ellie," Carl

said reprovingly. "My God, you've got a dirty mind. The next thing you'll be sayin' we—"

"You hush up."

"See, I told you it was dirty. Here, you talk to Rinie, or whatever this lady's name is. She's not drunk a bit, an' we'll git you an' Travis somethin' so you will be."

"My land," said Ellie, smiling in spite of herself. "I ain't even been able to git my coat off. Are the kids all right? Did you have any trouble while we was gone? W'y, Rinie, you've cleaned the house up. It looks real nice. Lord, what a racket."

It was very late when they got to bed. The house seemed very still after the music and dancing and laughter stopped. The thin moon made their room a little light and Carl and Rinie smiled at each other, shivering and snuggling close in the cold. Rinie felt dizzy and she couldn't seem to stop smiling.

"Travis and Ellie were sweet," she said drowsily. "I like to see them dancing together."

Carl said thoughtfully, "They've not had much chance for fun, only I never knew it till lately. When they married, Troy was twelve, I was eleven, an' Doyle was eight. That was a hell of a thing for them, bein' stuck with us to raise when they were just married, us an' A. J., too. It's funny I never thought about it before."

They were silent for a while, drifting close to sleep, then he started a little, remembering.

"What's wrong?" she said sleepily.

"Nothin', only I ought to've seen about Skeeter agin. Her leg's swollen. It ought to be rubbed several times a day."

Rinie sighed resignedly and kept on smiling. Whiskey made her feel so silly and she didn't even care. She said, "I guess I oughtn't to worry about you and other girls. For the last seven years, anyhow, you've had Skeeter."

6

The morning was clear, it was cold but the wind was down. Rinie and Carl had to put off their ride because at breakfast Travis announced that they ought to butcher the two pigs today. It might be bad again anytime and this seemed like the day. The men built up a big fire down by the sheds and took the wash kettle to scald the carcasses in. They carried up the meat as it was ready and Ellie, full of talk about her family, began to initiate Rinie into the secrets of preserving meat.

"I just can't feature goin' to the store ever' day or two after meat," she said incredulously. "W'y, for one thing, how can you be sure it won't be ruint, passin' through so many hands and layin' around like that."

Rinie didn't care for butchering time at all. The kitchen was hot and steamy, the air heavy with the smell of meat with the blood recently drained out, and she couldn't help thinking of the two bristly, good-natured pigs she had watched so often, eating with such tremendous gusto. For what? Just to get fat so they could be—like this. Why last night, even this morning, they had been alive, completely blithe and unaware that so soon they would be— just meat. She thought of all the ham she had eaten for breakfasts lately, and she thought she wouldn't ever want to eat any more.

A good deal of the meat was put down in salt. Travis would sugar-cure the hams and the best bacon and he would smoke two hams. He was a real good hand at curing meat, Ellie said proudly.

"Most boys raised up on a ranch never gits the hang of it, but ever'body in the country talks about our hams and bacon."

Travis had bought hickory chips in Belford for the smoking, there being no local wood suitable to the purpose. A. J. complained that it was a waste of money, buying wood and Troy and Carl went on facetiously about how cottonwood or sagebrush smoke ought to give an interesting flavor, different anyhow. Travis, with his accustomed sober intensity, went on with his business, paying them no mind.

They would can some of the meat that had less keeping quality. Some that was not good for anything else was to be rendered into lard, and Ellie said she'd be glad of a good big supply of grease for she needed to make soap. All the usable meat scraps were ground and mixed with spices for sausage. The men cooked the heads outside for head cheese. Ellie said she guessed she was a little bit squeamish but she couldn't help it; she just couldn't abide cooking heads in the house.

"Some ranches eats nothin' but beef for meat from one year's end to the next," she told Rinie, putting some ribs and backbone in a big pot to cook for dinner. "That's all they used to have here till me an Travis married an' daddy give us that first sow for a weddin' present. But I don't think it's good for people's health, eatin' so much of the same thing without hardly no change. I was right glad when Carl fixed up an' got them chickens for Jeff. A. J. didn' like it much. He always says a ranch is a place for men an' stock, but I notice he don't mind bein' done for by the womenfolks an' he eats what's set before him. Anyway, he's always got to say somethin', it's just his nature. W'y, we could use twict as many eggs as we git. I just hope the chickens winters all right."

Rinie smiled a little to herself as she ground sausage meat, thinking how much more Ellie had come to talk lately. This was the way she'd dreamed—well, not quite; her dream hadn't included fresh meat sitting all over the kitchen in nearly every pot and pan in the house—but two women, working together, talking, or with companionable silences.

Carl came in for coffee and said he was going to cure the pigskins. He liked things made of that kind of leather.

"How'd you like some gloves, lady, maybe a pair of slippers or somethin'?"

Rinie shrank inwardly. The poor pigs! She thought she'd seen about all she could stand of what could be done with their various parts, but she said, "Can you make things like that?"

"Well, no, not much, but when the skins are ready, I'll

take 'em down to Heddie. She's a real master hand with leather stuff. She taught me a little when I was a kid an' when she was here that time to stay with Ellie till Ellie's sister come, she showed Jeff some about it an' he caught on real fast. . . . You know what, Ellie? This coffee tastes like lard."

"Well, that ought not to be no real big surprise. Ever'-thing in the house is gonna taste an' smell like it for a while, I expect, an' they ain't no law says you got to drink the coffee." She was washing jars to can meat in. She said, "Jeff made me them deerskin moccasins that time after Heddie showed him. I wore 'em plumb out."

"Where is Jeff?" Rinie asked, realizing she hadn't seen him since breakfast time.

"Jeff don't like butcherin'," said Ellie gently. "Some-times I think he'd be better off if he wasn't so tender-hearted."

"He's up the creek by that rock he likes," Carl said, "readin' a book."

"Is he wrapped up warm?"

"He's all right. It's not cold in the sun."

The dogs began a great commotion and Troy burst in at the back door.

"You couldn' guess," he said breathlessly, "who's comin' up the road."

"Sutter," said Carl and Ellie together, with resigned grins.

"How in the *hell* does he know?" Troy marveled. "I believe he can smell fresh meat all that way. He ought to be hell on wheels in the woods with a nose like that, only he's too goddam' lazy."

He got a cup and poured himself some coffee.

"I see you got all bloodied up again," said Ellie shortly. "You ain't got a pair a levis to your name but what's got bloodstains in 'em."

"Well, I don't know why they don't git washed out," he said carelessly. "Listen, Buck, le's go after some game this week."

"It'd be better to wait till it snows agin."

"Ah, hell, I want to go huntin'. What you gonna do? Set around till stuff comes down where you can shoot it from the house?"

"Well, that don't seem like such a bad idea."

"You git, say, a deer an' a elk, an' with that fatnin' calf, we ought to be fixed for meat for the winter," said Ellie.

Rinie felt sick at the thought of all that meat.

Carl said musingly, "Wonder if A. J.'s goin' round front to call off his dogs so Sutter can git out of his truck?"

Troy frowned. "How come this coffee tastes like lard?"

It was the end of the week before they went riding. Carl went up on the benchland and found old Jim, a gentle, slow, bay gelding that nobody rode much. Jim was a loner and it took most of the morning to find him. Carl rode him back to the ranch to make sure he wouldn't have any kinks to straighten out when Rinie got on. They were washing the dinner dishes when he got back. He ate quickly and he and Rinie went to the corrals.

Skeeter cantered around, nickering eagerly, but Carl wouldn't ride her. He had decided not to, again, until she'd foaled. He gave her a little grain and Rinie hesitantly followed him into the corral where she was. The blocky little black mare put her ears back and looked mean. She's jealous of me, too, Rinie thought a little grimly.

Carl saddled Daylight for himself. Daylight was a little, dappled-gray gelding, young, but with the makings of a good horse. He had a mind of his own and got hard to handle sometimes, but Carl liked that in a horse.

Rinie petted old Jim cautiously. He wanted to lip her hand, just by way of getting acquainted, but that made her nervous. She had been looking forward to this moment— and dreading it—for a long time. Horses were so big. She was only now getting used to the dogs. But if she wanted to have any time at all alone with Carl, she'd have to learn to ride.

"Ready?" he said, smiling.

Carl had about the same feelings as Rinie about this moment. Riding together, he could show her so much of the country, share the only things he knew with her, just be with her, away from other people, with just the sky and the big empty land and the two of them, only . . . what if she didn't take to it? He thought she looked a little pale, and the way she was smiling, he thought maybe she didn't feel much like smiling. He guessed it wouldn't be so easy for a person, after they were grown, to start riding horses.

She said, trying to sound playful, "Why is mine bigger than yours?"

Carl was surprised. "Well, that don't make any difference. Ole Jim's got a real easy gait an' you have to kick hell out of 'im to make him go faster than a good walk. Come on."

He helped her up, holding the reins, though he knew there was no need to.

"Helen used to ride Jim some, but she thinks she needs somethin' with a little more spirit now. Do you want me to lead him to begin with?"

She did, but she wouldn't say so. She didn't like his talking as if Helen, seven years old, had already graduated from a horse that she, maybe, couldn't be trusted to rein for herself.

He put the reins over Jim's head and gave them to her.

Daylight sidestepped as Carl came around to mount. "You sonofabitch," he muttered. He has to pick this time to act up; Carl could see it in his eyes.

"Just set easy, Rinie, till he straightens out," he said, untying the reins and mounting with a quick jump.

Rinie wondered how he thought she could sit easy. He had cautioned her so strictly against overreining a horse —"They know what you mean with just a touch on the neck if they've had decent trainin'; go jerkin' 'em around, they git jumpy an' they're apt to act up"—that she was afraid to put any pressure at all on the reins, though she gripped them and the saddle horn so hard that her hands hurt. Jim wasn't tied or anything now. What if he decided to go somewhere? But old Jim didn't move anything but his ears as Daylight unlimbered.

Carl rarely lost his temper with a horse, but he was mad now. If he'd had his spurs on, he'd have given the little devil something worth bucking about.

Ellie and Travis were in Helen's room, looking out the window.

"Don't you let Rinie see," Ellie warned. "She's scared about this, an' bashful. An' wouldn' you know he'd have to ride that bloomin' Daylight."

Travis grinned. "Daylight ain't bucked like that since the day he was broke. He shore needs the han'lin'. Look at Carl! God, he's mad! We're always tellin' him to wear his spurs all time. Reckon I ought to run out there an' take 'im a gun? I believe he'd use it."

"Oh, quit your laughin'. It ain't nothin' funny. He's just doin' it to show off."

93

"Daylight maybe, but Carl ain't."

"Rinie's scared to death," said Ellie, outraged. "He ought to be ashamed of hisself."

It didn't last long. Carl brought the horse up beside Jim and held him. Daylight was chewing the bit and snuffing, but Carl wouldn't even let him throw his head. He wasn't hurting him any, but he wanted to.

"I'm sorry, honey."

He was afraid she was going to cry. Her hands were white from holding on so tight.

"He'll be all right now. Some horses just never git over actin' that way once in a while. It's like a game."

Rinie's lip was bleeding inside where she'd bitten it. She felt weak and dizzy but she swallowed hard, determined not to disappoint him any more than she could help. She smiled feebly.

"Well, anyway, I'm glad you weren't leading Jim."

They went up the creek to the southwest, riding back away from the stream where the ground was level and easy. It was hard at first, but Carl held Daylight to a walk. Old Jim went along soberly, pleased at being ridden again. He never had been much of a cow horse, but he liked people in his grave, stolid way, and seemed to have real consideration for his rider. Rinie began to relax a little. Maybe it would be fun, once she got really used to it. She still felt shaky. She had been so scared about Carl back there at the corral.

"You needn' hang on like that, Rinie," he said mildly. "The saddle horn's not for hangin' onto."

"What's it for, then?' she demanded, nervous and piqued. She had thought she was doing so well.

"Well, it—it's for a rope, but . . . I didn't mean . . . It's not anything that matters."

After a stiff little silence in which she held her hands carefully away from the pommel, she said, "What's that, Carl?"

A pole fence enclosed a scattered bunch of junipers and willows on a knoll that rose between them and the creek.

"That's our graveyard," he said.

He couldn't help feeling a little surprised each time there was something she didn't know about the place. He knew it all so well and, almost without his being conscious of it, she had been a part of his thoughts so long and so constantly that it seemed she ought to know about everything, whether she had actually seen it or not.

"Is your mother buried there?" she asked softly.

He nodded. "We'll stop on the way back if you want to."

Daylight was just now giving indication that Carl could ease the reins a little and Carl didn't want to stop and have to start up again just yet.

They rode up as far as the mares' pasture, a mile and a half above the house. There were good patches of woods for shelter, scattered through the fenced area, Carl pointed out, good grass and plenty of water.

"If we rode through here an' on up the creek, we'd git to where the hay meadow is." He frowned. "It's dam' silly to have to haul hay so far, an' wild hay at that. We could put a dam up there with a flume an' have all that flat from just below the house down past the upper ford for any kinda fields we wanted."

He shook his head a little, feeling itchy and frustrated, but no use fussing at Rinie about it. He said eagerly, "Above the meadows it's pine woods, ponderosa and aspen—oh, some of the prettiest places in the world up there! We'll go up sometime, but you don't want to git tired, this first ride."

"Oh, I'm not," she assured him quickly, but her knees were beginning to ache from being forced to try to bend the wrong way. "Where does the creek start?"

" 'Way to the southwest," he said, gesturing grandly.

She gasped, fearing that Daylight would be upset by the motion, but he seemed as imperturbable now as old Jim.

"Up in the lodgepoles," Carl said. "The top of the ridge isn' bare rock down there. Trees grow all over it. First there's just a little draw an' then a seep spring comes up out of some rocks an' that's the start of Red Bear. It was named Red Bear because Mr. Rigby, the first white man that owned this land, the one that built the old part of the house an' that A. J. bought from, killed a red bear up in the beaver meadows when he was first lookin' the land over. There's currants an' chokeberries an' stuff up there an' the bears like it a lot."

"Are there still bears around?"

"Sure. I saw a bear sign this mornin' when I was huntin' Jim. They come after the pinion nuts this time of year, up on the benches."

She was about to ask if they weren't dangerous to people and stock, but he was so matter-of-fact about them that she supposed he would think she was being silly. She said instead, "I never heard of a red bear before."

"Well, no. They're black bears, really, but they're all shades. What they call red is a kind of cinnamon color, I guess."

"Like your hair?"

"No. Darker an' prob'ly not really much red."

"Anyway," she said smiling, "I could call you my cinnamon bear. I like that."

He grinned a little sheepishly. "I guess you can call me about anything you want to."

They only saw one of the mares, Fancy, a blue roan, who snorted, threw her head up and galloped away at sight of them.

They turned back toward the ranch. Carl didn't like to. He wished they could ride all day. He wished they had brought an outfit for sleeping out, that they could stay away a long time. He was proud of Rinie. He guessed she was doing better than most women that had never ridden before, but she was probably getting tired.

Daylight was all right now, the sonofabitch, and Carl let the reins lie loose and made himself a cigarette. He didn't smoke often, only when he was relaxed with nothing else to do. It wasn't as if he had to drop everything for a smoke every few minutes like Troy and a lot of men did, but once in a while, he enjoyed smoking. Ordinarily, he didn't even carry the makings with him, but he'd been down to Putney's store at Webber yesterday to buy some rivets and he'd got a little sack of Bull Durham and some papers.

Rinie said uneasily, "Can you just let him go like that?"

"I'm not," he said, leaning down a little to strike a light on his boot. "You don't really need reins with a good horse. You train 'em to answer to the way you move your legs, your thighs mostly. There's a lot of times, workin' cattle an' times like that, when you got to use both hands an' can't be bothered with reins. You could lay Jim's reins down if you want to. He wouldn' even think about doin' anything he oughtn' to."

She was beginning to feel a little trust and liking for

good old Jim, and she did wish she didn't look such a coward to Carl, but she couldn't bring herself to let go the reins and she said uneasily, "But if he's trained to answer to the way I move, what if I move wrong, without meaning to, and he does something I don't expect, or don't want him to do?"

"Well," Carl said quizzically, "just don't do nothin'."

At the little cemetery fence he helped her down and told her about ground tying. She thought it was amazing and wonderful that horses would just stand like that, only because their reins were trailing. Carl doubted that Daylight was all that remarkable and tied him to a post.

There were four graves in the little grove, each with one of the rough, dark boulders for a stone, and a wooden cross, rough and weathered, bearing names and dates. The graves were clean and neat. Carl said Ellie came up sometimes to take care of them and that they repainted the crosses so that the lettering wouldn't fade out and be lost. They were all sere and withered now from the cold, but there were wild roses and iris and daisies and columbine and asters and gentian planted around the graves.

Rinie knelt down to look at the crosses. Her legs were stiff but she didn't think about it.

"Virginia Carlisle Stinson, 1880-1919."

"Do you remember her very much?" she asked gently, looking up at him.

"Not a lot. I was six when she died . . . I remember she used to sing songs to us and sometimes she'd laugh like anything at A. J. I don't know what about, but he'd laugh too. We used to laugh because they were. It was nice to hear. She liked to look at the snag." He meant the volcanic neck on the edge of the mesa across the valley. "I remember once she was workin' in the flowerbed that she had across the front of the house, an' she just stopped an' looked up at it an' said 'That's the proudest thing I ever saw.' An' A. J. was sittin' on the porch an' he said, 'It ain't nothin' compared to you.'

"She picked this place for the graveyard when Arnold died because you can see the snag, for one reason."

They raised their eyes to the great grim plug standing stark in the westering sun.

"I remember enough to know that most of what Minna

97

says about her isn't true. She was a hell of a lot more woman than Minna makes out."

Rinie looked at the grave of the baby "Arnold Wallace Stinson, 1909-1910."

"He was the first one born here at Red Bear," Carl said. "A. J. said he was always sickly an' they never thought he had much chance to live. They had a little girl, too, two or three years younger than Travis, but she just lived a few days. That was when they were still in Denver."

And there was the grave of Travis and Ellie's baby who had never really lived.

Rinie moved to the last grave and Carl stood a little apart, waiting. What would she think? How would she take this? Minna had probably told her something about it, all the wrong things. But could he tell her right? So she'd see how it was and understand?

She knelt reverently by the grave and looked at the cross. "Aaron James Stinson, 1920-1922." Another child of Jenny and A. J.? But, no, Jenny had died before that. . . . That Travis and Ellie—? They weren't married until 1923. She stood up slowly.

"Carl. . . ."

He came and took her hand and led her to a sunny spot by the fence. It was warm and drowsy in the sun today. He drew her down to sit beside him and his arm was around her.

"Rinie," he said slowly, "when mama died, Heddie was here—you know, Heddie that takes care of the sick and all—and she—she stayed on to take care of us. A. J. couldn' wash an' cook an' all that for four kids. Doyle wasn' but three when she died. Heddie stayed till Travis an' Ellie married."

Rinie was silent. Minna had hinted at it, but she'd been too inexperienced to understand. "Boys brought up by a filthy Indian woman! What kind of thing was that to do to my poor, dead sister's children? Oh, that vile, selfish, unfeeling man! Jenny not cold in her grave."

Rinie felt tears starting, hot with disappointment and disillusionment and hurt. Carl said gently, "Rinie, a man can't hardly live by himself, not when he's been used to a wife, not when he's got kids that need somebody."

"Oh, Carl," she cried bitterly. "I thought he loved her. I know he was kind of wild, but I thought he *loved* her!

I thought it was kind of—of special, a little like the way we . . . but he didn't care about her at all."

"Yes, he did, Rinie," he said vehemently.

"No, he didn't," she cried, choking on sobs. "As soon as she was dead—maybe before. . . ."

"Rinie, for God sake, I know it's hard for you, but don't act like Aunt Minna."

She pulled away from him, covering her face, sobbing wretchedly. A. J. had come to mean so much to her, but now. . . .

Carl looked up to the snag and to the bare ridge on the opposite horizon and made himself breathe slowly. He had no business being angry with her. She was so young, she didn't know anything, not really . . . except about loneliness and needing love. She ought to understand about that. He said quietly, "Heddie was good to us. She loved us in her way an' we loved her. It didn' take anything away from lovin' our mother—not for us, nor for A. J. either. It's just . . . when somebody's gone—mourning—doin' without—don't do any good, really. You can't help doin' it, but they can't come back, an' kids, little kids, don't pay a lot of attention to death. I mean, when somebody's gone, they—they just go on with livin' an' thinkin' about livin'. Think how it'd be for Helen, for instance. Rinie?"

"Oh, Carl, I know that. You boys needed a woman to take care of you. You can't be blamed. I guess it was a good thing for you . . . but for him." She was shaking with the vehemence of her emotions. "For him to just put her in the ground and go to bed with another woman—"

"Don't you talk like a bitch," he cried fiercely, gritting his teeth. "It's not a filthy thing like you're makin' it. A. J. loved my mother. He was as good to her as it was in him to be. She loved him and she was happy with him. He didn' give her cause not to be."

She was hurt by his words to her and by the violence with which they'd been spoken, more hurt than she'd ever been by anything in her life. All the wonderful, impossible happiness lay in ruins. Her tears had stopped. She was too miserable to cry.

Softening his tone, Carl went on desperately. He had to.

"But A. J. wasn' quite fifty years old then. He was a strong healthy man an' a man needs a woman. It's nature, an' anybody that thinks it's not is foolin' themselves or they're goddam' unnatural"

She was silent, feeling numb and cold and broken.

"They had the little boy," Carl said pleadingly, touching her hair. "He was the cutest little kid I ever saw. Heddie was a good-lookin' woman, still is, though she's over fifty now. She's half French and half Snake Indian."

Rinie shuddered. He moved close to her, but he didn't think she wanted his arms around her. He said, "Aaron was named after A. J. He had black eyes, quick, snappy black eyes that laughed and dark red hair like A. J.'s. He died of diphtheria. All of us had it and were real sick."

Rinie said brokenly, "Why isn't she still here? If she was so good and A. J. had to have a woman? Did he find another one, or what?"

"No," he said, putting down his anger. "Travis—well, he was nearly sixteen when mama died an' he felt—somethin' like the way you do, I guess. When a person's that age, it seems like he sees things all in black an' white—no gray or anything in between—an' Travis an' A. J. had some trouble about it. Travis liked Heddie all right, but he just couldn' feel like she ought to . . . anyway, when he wanted to marry Ellie, he talked to them about it, an' after she'd thought about it an' talked about it with A. J., Heddie left."

"But why?" Rinie cried. It was all incredible. "If she was all that good and they loved each other some way, why didn't they build another house, for them, or for Travis and Ellie? How could he treat people that way? She took care of all of you, had his baby and it died. Being married to him, how could she just let him. . . ."

Carl swallowed, drawing a deep slow breath. She might as well know every bit of it now because she'd hear about it sometime. It hadn't been a big scandal around here, not the way it would have been in Denver, probably, because people in this country mostly understood that humans were not a lot different from other animals in the things they needed most, but people did still talk about it some. Thank God, Minna didn't know it all, just that Heddie had lived at Red Bear, not about the little boy or the rest of it.

"They weren't married, Rinie. Heddie was raised a Catholic. She married a man that came out here prospectin' an' he went off an' left her with three little kids to raise. He used to come back sometimes, they say, to see if she had any money or things he could take to sell. He quit comin' before she lived at Red Bear, but there's no divorce in the Catholic Church so she's married to him yet if he's still alive."

Rinie was filled with sick loathing. "And yet she lived with your daddy and he let her raise his children! No wonder Travis . . . I don't see how he could stand to stay here."

"Honey, please, just think about it later. You'll see, sometime, that—"

"And what about her children?" she cried vehemently.

"They were grown and gone away when she came here. She'd raised 'em by herself."

"You mean she was a whore to make money to raise them?"

Carl felt sick. His words came slow and hard.

"I never thought I'd feel ashamed of you, Rinie."

There was a long silence. Old Jim nickered questioningly. It was getting chilly, just standing, ground-tied.

"Rinie, you can't just—just assume a thing like that about another person, an' it's not like you to do it. Heddie took care of people when they were sick, did housework if a woman wasn't able to, made leather goods to sell, the same kind of things she does now. She's a good woman."

"A good woman wouldn't live with a man if she couldn't be married to him."

Carl made an angry gesture. "Nobody's got the right to say what's good in another person—or bad—an' marriage is not that important."

She stared at him, wide-eyed and hurt beyond speaking.

"Listen," he pleaded desperately, "I don't mean that exactly. But marriage is—more for other people than for the couple that gets married. It's for the law and the church if you're married by a preacher, but if the people—the couple—feel that—that the way they're doin' is right— then—that's what really counts, don't you think? Rinie?"

She said dully, "I want to go home. I can't stand it here. Please don't talk about it."

When she was about to mount the horse, he wanted to hold her close in his arms and make it all right somehow. She looked so small and hurt and forlorn. He'd said all the wrong things in the wrong ways. She was so young. Just now, she looked like a little girl who had had a most precious dream cruelly, deliberately destroyed by someone she had come to trust. More important than her actual age, though, was the incredibly small amount of exposure she had had to human nature and to living. Her only standards for measuring behavior were the warped, prudish morals Minna had tried to instill and Rinie's own beautiful, idealistic, humanly impossible dreams.

She drew away from Carl when he would have taken her in his arms, and he helped her up on Jim. She didn't think of being frightened or of what he might think of the way she was riding. She didn't think of much of anything. She just felt crushed and numb and sick.

After a little Carl said,

"Yesterday, when I was down at the store, I saw Mr. Forrester—you remember Vanda?—well, her daddy. He's talkin' about gittin' some men together to go after some wild horses. Not my—not the ones that live up yonder in the ridges, but a good-sized herd that stays mostly around on the mesa to the south of Forrester's place."

She didn't say anything.

The house was in sight now, just the roof and smoke coming out of the kitchen chimney.

"Rinie? Want to see if you can kick ole Jim up to a trot to go home on? Show 'em how well you're doin'?"

"All right," she said dully.

He could barely hear her voice, though he rode close. He tried to smile, as if he didn't see the pathetic, crumpled look of her face, but his heart ached so bad, he thought he'd cry if he didn't do something.

"It's rougher ridin' to trot," he warned her gently, "but nothin' to worry about. Just reach back a little with your heels an' sorta dig in—we're gonna have to git you some decent boots—kick hard, ole Jim's kinda numb."

They came down past the back of the house at a good, brisk trot, and Kirby, just going in at the back door, turned and gave them an Indian yell by way of salute. Daylight thought the yell might be a good excuse to bolt, but Carl held him. Rinie was holding the reins in a tight fist though they lay loose on Jim's neck, and she was only gripping the saddle horn a little.

On the third Sunday of each month, the Reverend Mark Turner came up from Belford to preach at the

Webber church. Actually, Webber had no church. The school was used; as it was used for meetings of the stockmen's association, occasional Saturday night dances, gatherings of a town-meeting type—for any reason that the community had for gathering.

The third Sunday was Reverend Turner's Sunday to preach, to marry, to baptize, and perform any other duties for which an ordained minister was required. The other Sundays, Sutter Keane preached if anyone came to listen.

On Reverend Turner's Sunday in November, there was a good crowd, in fact, the biggest crowd a church service had drawn since old man Arliss Butler's funeral happened to come handy to a third Sunday. Old man Arliss Butler, some said, was the meanest man in Bell County and he'd been gored to death by a bull, which, some said, was just about his due.

But on this November Sunday, the congregation was larger than usual because Alva Tippitt, whose family owned a good ranch just up the West Fork from Webber, was marrying June Johnson, the schoolteacher. Miss Johnson's people lived clear back down in Georgia, and most of the women, all of them who had children in school, felt a proprietary air toward her. She needed folks at her wedding. Well, here they were.

There were no flowers at this time of year, but some of the women had decorated the room prettily with evergreens and their own specially prized house plants. It seemed fitting and touching that Miss Johnson be married in the schoolroom where she'd taught the past three years.

A. J. didn't go to church. He didn't care about being preached at and weddings didn't effect him much, but all the rest of the Stinsons, including Jeff, were there. Ellie went every third Sunday if she could and she took Helen with her. Rinie had gone with them once before this, but none of the men had been since old man Arliss Butler's funeral and even A. J. had gone then.

It was a nice wedding. Rinie cried, hearing the words again that she and Carl had heard for themselves three months before. During a prayer, Carl's hand found hers and then she could scarcely keep from sobbing aloud. Things were different now, changed, since that day they'd gone to the cemetery. She couldn't feel the same about anybody in the family. They all knew about and more or less condoned those years when A. J. and that woman. . . . She didn't blame any of them, of course, except A. J., but

103

she couldn't stop thinking of the wrongness of it and it seemed they couldn't help knowing what she was thinking.

Carl looked nice, she thought, stealing a glance at him, her heart aching. He looked right in a white shirt and tie, not awkward and sheepish the way some of the men did, but she knew town clothes made him uneasy and he disliked wearing shoes instead of boots.

Neither she nor Carl had mentioned the subject again, but it hurt dreadfully, remembering how angry he had been with her that day: "Don't talk like a bitch." "I never thought I'd be ashamed of you, Rinie."

None of those things that had happened had anything to do with him, really, the thing she couldn't understand, that hurt so much, was his arguing so hotly that they had been right: Carl who was so good and clean and honest. She supposed that eventually she'd be able to think about it without feeling anger and shame and betrayal and pain, but still things would never be as they had been before that day.

Back home, they hurried to get dinner on the table. Most of it had been prepared before they went to church. The men were hungry and relaxed and loquacious, as soon as they got out of their town clothes.

"It was a right nice weddin'," Ellie reported to her father-in-law.

"Women always thinks that," he said ungraciously. "When you gonna take the jump, Bojack?"

Troy grunted. "Not any time soon that I know about. Why? You want to see all your kids roped?"

"Well, it don't hurt. I ain't had but three grandkids for some while now." He looked at Carl, but Carl had nothing to say.

Carl knew Rinie's troubles and he couldn't help her. Everything he said seemed to come out wrong because they were both so constantly aware of that afternoon at the cemetery and what it meant to her. He supposed it was a thing that only a lot of time and some learning and growing could make right, but he wasn't about to join in any discussion of weddings and children just now.

"Who was that boy with the Keanes?" Travis wondered.

"He's from Greenfield," Troy said. "They say he's been comin' over real often to see Supina."

"Who?" asked Rinie, finding the name incredible.

"Supina Keane. Sutter's oldest girl."

"But a subpoena, that's something you get to make you appear in court."

"Well, I don't know how they come up with the names, but that's hers."

"Sutter got one a them things," surmised A. J., "an' had to go to court an' marry Essie so they named the kid that, I'll lay."

The others laughed, but Rinie looked away miserably. What right had he to make jokes about other people's morals?

"Maybe Doyle ought to have married her if she's somethin' legal," said Travis.

"Anyway," Troy said, "it looks like Sutter may git rid of one of his girls of a marryin' age."

"My Lord," said Ellie, "I believe I might be as worried as Sutter if I had six girls."

"Four boys ain't no easy bunch," muttered A. J.

"Granddaddy," said Helen thoughtfully, "if I'm the first girl in this family for four—four—"

"Generations," supplied Jeff.

She nodded. "Yeah, well, then where did all the boys come from?"

A. J. looked to Travis.

"Well," explained the father, "the Stinson boys married an' the women they married was the mothers of more Stinson boys."

"Oh," said Helen, meditating. "Then when I marry, I can have Stinson girls."

"No," said her mother. "When you marry, you change your last name to what your husband's is. Like Miss Johnson ain't Miss Johnson now, she's Miz Tippitt."

"Well, I won't do it," Helen said indignantly. "I ain't gonna have no other name."

"You have to," Jeff said.

"I don't neither."

"Well, that's enough about it now," Travis said. "It ain't a thing you've got to worry about any time soon. I wonder how long this weather'll hold. I hope we can git done with that fence."

Troy sighed. "It's gittin' so the whole world looks full a post holes. I got to work on my car sometime. I guess I can do it after dinner."

"Carl," said Travis, "you want to go to Belford in the

mornin' to pick up the rest of the wire? Maybe Rinie'd want to go along."

All of them had noticed the change. Rinie had always been quiet and Carl, too, at times, but something was wrong. Travis was trying to help. He knew Troy would be the one who would want to go to Belford, but maybe if Carl and Rinie went off together. . . .

Carl wished Travis hadn't mentioned tomorrow. He wanted to talk to Rinie about it first. He said awkwardly, "I don't know if I can or not."

"Well, hell, I can," Troy said quickly. "Do you mean you'd ruther work on the fence than go to town with a pretty girl?"

"I don't know what you're buildin' that goddam' fence for anyway," muttered A. J. "Waste a money."

"Because, like you know," said Travis, "half the time we have to hunt clear to the head of the creek after the horses. We've wasted days of time doin' that."

"So now you're wastin' it on a fence."

"You can come to town with me, Rinie," Troy said exuberantly. "What you say?"

"Anyway," said A. J. "it'll snow by Tuesday."

"You always say it's gonna snow," said Travis glumly.

Kirby shook his head. "In the summer he says it's gonna rain."

"Just when it is," averred the old man.

"Carl don't want to go to town 'cause he's goin' after horses," Kirby said. He had overheard the talk outside the schoolhouse.

They all looked at him, waiting. He had meant to talk to Rinie first. He said, "Mr. Forrester wants me to go with his hands after that wild bunch up on Buffalo Mesa."

"That's a big bunch," Travis said. "Van'd make a good bit a money."

"He gonna pay you?" Troy asked.

"If I go."

"Good, Rinie. You come on to town with me an' we'll spend his money while he's makin' it."

"I expect he wants you to snap the broncs for 'im," said A. J. "Or does he aim to sell 'em raw?"

Carl frowned. All right, he might as well tell it all.

"He wants 'em broke," he said a little irritably. "He wants me to break 'em an' take 'em to Belford. He's got a buyer in Nebraska for as many as twenty an' he'd like to git a few to keep."

"Well, I'm gonna fix my car," said Troy. "You can peel broncs if you want to, but I aim to have a little fun. Somebody said this was the slow season."

Rinie had begun to stack the dishes. Carl said unhappily, "Come for a ride, Rinie?"

"After I help with the dishes."

"Please, Rinie, I—"

"Go on," ordered Ellie shortly.

"I will," offered Helen.

"No, you won't neither. You got to help with these here dishes."

Carl saddled quickly while she stood by the fence. Jeff opened the gate for them and waved as they rode away.

"He'd like to go," Rinie said sadly. "Can't he ride at all?"

"He does a little sometimes, but—I can't watch. He's so used to hurtin', I guess he don't much think about it, but . . . I used to hold him an' he'd go with me some. Bein' held up off the saddle, it wasn' so hard on him, but he's gittin' heavier now, an' old enough that it bothers him to have to ride with somebody. Once in a while, he wants ole Rifle saddled—he's gentle an' easy as a kitten—an' he rides off for a little while, but he can't mount or git down by himself. Ellie don't like him to ride an' I guess it's not the safest thing, but, hell, the kid's got to do somethin'."

They were riding up across the benchland, angling northwest. There had been another bit of snow, but it was gone now except for spots under the trees and in rock shadows.

"It's dry," he said stiffly after a long silence. "We need snow for next year's grass."

"Look what a lot of magpies," she said bleakly.

They had ridden together several times now and she was beginning to be able to think about other things and ride at the same time. She felt desolate. He was going away again. The cattle drive had been a lonely time, but if he went with the tension between them, it would be so much worse. She was the one responsible for it. She knew that, but she couldn't help it.

"I didn' mean this to come out at the dinner table," he blurted suddenly. "Mr. Forrester asked me this mornin'. I told you before we'd talked about it."

She didn't remember. She'd been too upset that other time.

"How long would you be gone?" she asked unhappily.

"Well, I—quite a while, Rinie, off'n on. I'd come home for Sundays and when the weather was bad."

"It sounds like you'd be going away to live."

"No, I wouldn't. You know better than that. If we caught the horses right away, in two or three days, an' I think we could, then I'd work with 'em for—oh, maybe three weeks altogether. Say till pretty close to Christmas."

"Oh."

"He'll pay me day wages while we're huntin' 'em, an' then, for everyone I break, he'll pay ten dollars. Rinie, that's the only way I can make any cash money. It's the only way I ever have. I've been doin' it for other people since I was sixteen, an' I can put a rein on a horse. I don't mean to brag, but I can, an' I like to. I like to see 'em done right if they got to be caught an' broke, an' that's what I can do. A man's got to be able to do somethin', one thing, that he does better than most. If I start turnin' down jobs, people'll look for somebody else. Bo's not half-bad, though he's a little rough and don't really like it much. Theorn McLean's a real good hand. This is the biggest job I ever been offered. I'd make at least two hundred dollars."

"But, Carl, I don't care about the money. You could get hurt so easy and—"

"People can git hurt any place, Rinie, but the main reason I wanted to be able to talk to you about this first, just to you, was because, if you say so, I won't go."

This shocked her a little and made the hard desperation go out of her. She hadn't thought of his asking her. Did men really do things like that—Stinson men? Yes, she thought with a flood of tenderness, Carl did, and she could see by his eyes that he meant it. If she asked him to, he'd tell Mr. Forrester he wouldn't come. It would be so easy for her and yet—he'd still want to. He'd not hold it against her or sulk. He meant for her to have the choice or he wouldn't have given it to her, and yet she'd always known that he wished he had gone. On the other hand, she thought with a little wry smile, maybe he wasn't being so good to her after all.

He was looking off up at the ridge, his face quiet, his reins lying loose, leaning a little forward with his hands resting lightly on his thighs. Nobody in the movies is as good-looking as he is, she thought proudly, and none of them knows anything at all about horses.

"Carl?"

He turned his head and his eyes were quiet, waiting.

"Will Vanda be there?"

"What?"

"Vanda Forrester."

"You silly little kid." He began to grin.

"I bet she will," she said petulantly. "I bet she'll come out and watch you all the time."

"You won't hardly have time to worry about that," he said, reaching for her hand. "You'll be at Belford and around with your brother-in-law."

7

Rinie didn't go to town with Troy. She persuaded Ellie to go. They hadn't really laid in supplies for the house for the winter and she insisted that she'd have no more knowledge of what ought to be bought than Troy would. She'd have enjoyed the trip except that she felt strange about being alone with Troy. Not that he'd get out of line —well, not much anyway—and not that she couldn't handle him if he did, but she oughtn't to feel drawn to him the way she had that night when they were dancing together, and she didn't believe, no matter what he said, that Carl really wanted her to go. She thought he must feel about her and Troy the way she did about him and Vanda Forrester. Vanda was pretty, smooth and sure and easy, and she and Carl had known each other all their lives, gone to school together. Rinie had seen Vanda several times since that night after the boys got back from the cattle drive, and she liked her. Vanda was steady and sensible with a quick humor, good to talk to, only, around Carl, Rinie couldn't like her so much. Her green eyes had a way of getting warmer when she looked at him and she'd just sit quiet with a little, soft smile on her pretty mouth. Maybe she did that with other boys, too, but Rinie didn't have any reason to notice about them.

Vanda could ride a horse better than a lot of men

could. Shortly after the party, she had ridden up to Red Bear on a wild-eyed red-roan gelding that was tricky to handle even after coming all that way from her folks' ranch. Ellie said privately to Rinie that Vanda was a showoff about horses, but it looked to Rinie as if she just enjoyed them—something like the way Carl did.

With some help from Jeff, Rinie did the washing while Ellie was gone to town. It was warm and sunny. They all kept saying how the weather just couldn't stay like this, with it right at the first of December. If it turned bad, Carl would come home.

"I wonder if they've got sight of 'em yet," Jeff said dreamily.

They were sitting on an old bench in the sun to rest, the last of the clothes hung on the lines. Rinie had stew cooking for dinner. Travis and A. J. would be in to eat soon.

"Do you think they'll be hard to find?" she asked.

She knew immediately, of course, that he was talking about the herd of wild horses Carl was looking for.

"Carl can find 'em all right," Jeff said quietly. "He tracks better'n Troy, an', anyway, a bunch of horses don't take trackin'. All you got to do is know their ways."

Rinie wanted to ask him if he thought Vanda Forrester had gone on the hunt with the men—Vanda would probably be a help—but she couldn't think how to put the question. It wasn't that she was really jealous or had any doubts at all about Carl. It was just that he"d be around Vanda so much for the next few weeks. It made Rinie feel extra lonesome, thinking about that.

In the middle of the night on Thursday, they heard the mountain lion scream. To Rinie, it sounded fearfully close, though the men said it was back up in the trees. It screamed several times, and by the time it was done, everyone but Helen was awake and out of bed.

"Fix some breakfast, gals," ordered A. J. excitedly. "It'll be breakin' light in not much more'n an hour."

There was a great hurrying to check over guns and get supplies together.

"Now, A. J.," said Ellie mildly, as she ground coffee, "hadn' you best not go? The way your joints been—"

"Jesus Christ, woman! You ain't got no more sense'n a cross-eyed cow."

Ellie took no umbrage. She had done her best.

"Dam'! Wish Carl was here," said Troy, pushing a rag through the barrel of his rifle.

"Which horse you want to ride, A. J.?" asked Travis. "We got Persimmon an' Spot an' Booger an' Flinty an' Nimrod an'—what else, boys?"

Kirby said, "I ain't sure, but, daddy—"

"Mac an' Rose an' Dan an' Juber," supplied Jeff.

"Daddy," said Kirby urgently.

"I reckon ole Dan," A. J. said.

"I'll have Cracker," said Troy. "You forgot about him. Best dam' horse we got for gittin' through the woods."

"I'll take Spot," Travis told his elder son. "You go on out and be saddlin' up while we're gittin' this stuff ready. Maybe Jeff can help you some."

"Yessir, but daddy, I—"

"I want Jeff," broke in A. J., "to take ole Christman an' shut 'er in the barn. God a-mighty! Did you hear that ole gal cut loose when that lion squalled? I hate to leave 'er, but it's li'ble to be the last of her if she tries to go."

"We just take Pup an' Jethro an' Sheba, then," said Troy.

"Won't hurt for ole Nero to go along."

Travis looked up impatiently. "Well, Kirby, don't just stand there, son. Git on about your business."

Kirby was in a terrible state of apprehension. "Daddy, I—I ain't got to stay here an' go to school, have I?"

"With a lion to go after?" said Travis in amazement. "I thought you'd have more sense than that."

When they were finally gone, the house was remarkably peaceful. Ellie drew a deep sigh.

"It's the Lord's mercy to be rid of 'em when they're wrought up that way. They's nothin' more cranky an' fidgety an' hard to git along with than a man fixin' to go huntin'—well, unless it's a man housed up too long in the winter time. You know, Rinie, we ought to just go back to bed an' loll around. This is li'ble to be the most peaceful day we'll have for some while." She yawned. "I don't expect I could go back to sleep though, could you? It's funny how strong habits gits."

She poured out the dish water.

"Anyway, le's set around an' drink coffee a while. I ain't in no humor to do nothin'."

"Do you think they'll get him?" Rinie asked, hanging the dish towel near the stove to dry.

"Oh, I expect they may, but lions travel a lot an' he

111

had a good start before it got light. I just hope he didn' kill none a the stuff. But, anyhow, it's the huntin' that counts with men, as much as the gittin'. W'y, you wouldn' see no little kids worked up over a thing any more'n them grown men was. If they don't git 'im, they'll be some disappointed, but, then agin, it'll mean maybe they can hunt 'im agin, don't you see?"

Carl got home just at suppertime on Saturday, riding a wild, beautiful, white mare with a black mane and tail. He had ridden away on a good, trusty, chestnut named Buddy, but now he was riding some of the wild stuff any time he rode, to give them the handling.

Rinie ran out to the corral and into his arms.

"Oh, Carl! It's been the longest week in the world."

Carl kissed her a long time and Kirby and Jeff, coming out of the barn, poked each other and snickered.

"Are you all right?" Rinie asked softly. She knew he didn't like being asked, but she couldn't help it.

"Sure," he said exuberantly and picked her up and swung her off her feet. His shoulder was stiff and sore as anything, but it needed the limbering up. "How's my lady? An' what's been goin' on around here?"

She had no chance to answer. Kirby was clamoring, "We went after the lion yesterday."

"Did you git 'im?" asked Carl eagerly.

It took most of supper for A. J. and Travis and Troy and Kirby, all trying to talk at once, to tell about the lion hunt, how each had heard him squall, what their individual thoughts and actions had been in those first moments, which horses they had ridden, how the dogs had behaved.

"Ole Jethro got his scent right south a that blasted ponderosa," said Troy, getting the floor temporarily.

"That Pup might make a hunter," put in A. J. "He come off right well, considerin' his age."

A. J. was sick. Carl thought he looked real bad, haggard, as if he hadn't been sleeping. He guessed the chase had been nearly too much, A. J.'s rheumatism like it was, but he didn't mention that.

"Ole Christmas nearly went wild 'cause she couldn' go," Jeff said. "I shut 'er in the barn, but she jumped an' scratched an' whined an' howled so much, I brought 'er in my room."

Carl was eating hungrily while they talked. There was steak and fried potatoes and homemade light bread and a lot of other things. The chuck wasn't nearly this good at

112

Forrester's. He wished he could have been with them after the lion.

"An' Sheba," Travis said, "she near went crazy when she got the scent. I believe she'll be as good as her mama when she's had some more workin'."

A. J. shook his head. He wasn't eating much. It just seemed like he couldn't relish his food with this aching in his bones. He said unequivocally, "Pup'll make a better lion dog than Sheba ever will. That is, if there's enough lions to practice on. They used to be thick as fleas around here an' now you don't hear one more'n onct or twict a year. Anyway, Sheba's got a two years' start on Pup an' he's about up with her already."

"Well, for Chrissake," said Carl impatiently, taking another steak from the platter Rinie offered, "where's the lion? Tell me about that."

"Ain't that what we're doin'?" snapped his father.

They went on with a detailed description of which way the lion had gone, how the dogs had followed, gaining on him some, they thought. Up in the rocks, at the foot of the bare ridge, Troy's horse had thrown a shoe.

They thought, when he headed straight for the rock ridge, that they'd lost the lion sure. The dogs might make it, but it would take a long, slow time to pick a way for horses to get over that spine of rock, if it could be done at all. But, surprisingly, and to their joy, he turned south.

"He'd killed somethin', sometime in the night," Troy said. "He didn' want the trouble of climbin' that rock, either."

Troy had kept riding old Cracker, slowing up and picking the easiest way. He ought to have turned back, but that was too much to expect of a man.

"Long about noon," Travis took up the story, "the ole cat treed. Way up at the head of the creek in a big ole birch, great big tree."

"With a lightning blaze down the side," Carl said smugly.

They looked at him, surprised, and Kirby said, "How'd you know?"

"I remember the tree an' that's where I'da gone if I was anywheres close an' was a cat that felt like climbin'."

"Well, they wasn't no reason fer him to tree," said Travis. "He still had a good lead on the dogs. Just seemed like he thought he'd wait around, rest awhile, make things more excitin'."

113

"I expect Buck'd do that, too," muttered A. J. wryly.

"But when he heard the horses," Travis went on, "before we could git any kind of chance for a good shot, he jumped an' run."

"We seen 'im," Kirby said softly, awed by the memory. "Granddaddy shot, an' Troy did, too, but it just seem' like that ole thing floated out a the way."

"Them dogs was wild," Travis said, "an' we run 'way on to the south, down in where Deer Creek heads. He just kep' out of the way was all, the sonofabitch, an' finally, the dogs an' horses was so wore out, there wasn' nothin' we could do but come home."

They were all a little disappointed, but it had been the most fun and excitement they'd had in a long time.

"If he ever comes back through here agin, we'll git 'im," Kirby said defiantly.

"Well, now I wisht you'd eat your suppers," said Ellie. "It takes somethin' mighty important for the bunch a you to let your food lay on your plates till it gits cold an' greasy."

Carl and Rinie had finished eating and were holding hands under the table. Disappointment over not having been on the hunt stung Carl a little, but he was so glad to be with her again that nothing else mattered much. She looked better. Some of the sadness and bewilderment had gone out of her eyes. They couldn't stop stealing glances at each other and smiling.

"Tell us about the horses," said Jeff.

"We got 'em," Carl said simply, "thirty-four head for Mr. Forrester, countin' colts."

He didn't much want to talk. Going after the wild bunch seemed pretty tame after chasing a mountain lion, and besides, he wanted to look at Rinie, to be alone with her.

"Here, eat some more meat an' taters," encouraged Ellie.

"Hell, he et half the supper already, while we was talkin' to 'im," said Kirby.

Travis said sternly, "By God, Kirby, I want you to quit your cussin'."

They all laughed, except Travis, who looked embarrassed.

"I don't think they fed you much at the Forresters'," Rinie said softly.

And A. J. said with a smirk, "It don't look to me like chuck's what he's been missin' so much."

"That's a real pretty white horse you brought home," said Helen.

She had finished eating and come around the table to lean against Carl's shoulder. She would have liked to stand between him and Rinie, to be close to both of them, but Carl wouldn't let her.

"Did Mr. Forrester give you that horse?"

Carl grinned wryly. "No, he didn't, an' I wouldn' take her on a bet. You kids stay out of there where she is. She's meaner'n hell."

"Did you have much trouble gittin' 'em?" asked Troy.

"No. We got sight of 'em Monday ev'nin' just at sundown. I thought we could git around 'em, head 'em toward the ranch the next day, but it took a while. It was Wednesday night when we got 'em in to the ranch. The ole boss stud an' a few others got away, but I—well, that don't hurt anything."

Travis said, "What kinda stallion is that one?"

"A black. A great big sonofagun, but I think he's gittin' kinda old. He looks like he might have some Morgan or somethin' in 'im, big an' built the way he is."

A. J. said innocently, "If you was close enough up to 'im to reckon his age an' bloodiness, how come you not to catch 'im?"

"There was forty-two horses altogether that we brought down," said Carl, ignoring the question. "But six was branded mares from other ranches, an' two a the mares had little colts. Two of 'em was McLeans an' two was Tippitts. One belonged to Mr. Randall on down the valley an' he hadn' seen 'er in eight years. The other brand, nobody could recognize, but Mr. Forrester found out just this mornin' it's from a ranch 'way to hell an' gone down south. He showed me on the map. It's more'n a hundred miles across country."

"Any good stuff?" Troy asked.

Carl nodded enthusiastically. "Eleven two- an' three-year olds that ought to make real good horses, five yearlin's an' three little colts. The rest're ole mares that won't be good for nothin' but breedin' stock."

"What's that one you brought home?" asked Ellie. Carl grimaced. "That's Mr. Forrester's pick of the bunch."

"She don't look like much to me," said Troy. "I thought he was supposed to be some judge of horses."

"Well, he does know horses," Carl said, "but he's not just interested in cow horses. He likes this ole thing for her looks." He frowned contemptuously and A. J. snorted.

"Too big for a good cow horse, anyway," Travis said.

"Yes, she is," Carl agreed, "an' I never could abide a white horse, but he says she's the prettiest thing ever come off the mesa. God! She's the the meanest ole thing I ever saw."

"How old is she?"

"Four, I guess, maybe five."

"*I* think she's pretty, too," said Helen importantly.

"What's Forrester aim to do with her, besides look at her?" asked Troy.

"He aims to race 'er," Carl said grimly, "an' she can dam' well run. Mr. Forrester seen 'er when we was roundin' up the bunch up there, an' he said to go git 'er, whether we got the others or not. Me an' Theorn went after her, but I had ole Buddy an' he ain't awful fast so I went to head some others. She 'bout run Theorn out of a horse, an' when he roped 'er finally, he couldn' do nothin' but set there an' hold 'er. She ought to've been tied an' left a while, but there wasn' a goddam' thing up there to tie 'er to that woulda held 'er, so Mr. Forrester come up to help 'im, an' it took them two men to bring in that one ole thing while the other five of us got the rest."

Rinie was serving up the cobbler, made with dried peaches and topped with cream. Rounding up the horses sounded beautiful and exciting to her. She wished she could have been there to watch. She was wondering, though . . . she said hesitantly,

"Why—who all went along?"

"Mr. Forrester an' his three hands," Carl said, beginning to eat again, "an' Theorn and Bud Corbett an' me."

Yes, that made seven. He had said two men with the white mare and five others. She was relieved.

"How many have you snapped?" Kirby asked.

"I've had saddles on five," Carl said. "I'd like to take more time, let 'em git used to seein' people up close. That's what I'd do if they were ours, but he can't wait. He wants to ship the ones to Nebraska as soon as he can, an' he keeps sayin' to hurry up because he wants to see what kinda horses they're all gonna make, but hell, you can't tell nothin' this soon."

"But you know about the white one?" said Rinie, with a little, teasing smile.

"She might make a race horse," Carl conceded, "but that's all she'll ever be good for. She kicks, she strikes with her front feet, she bites. . . ."

"An' she throws people," opined A. J. quietly.

There was a little silence, the men grinning into their cobbler.

"Well, yes," Carl said reluctantly, "she does that, too."

Rinie was looking at him, questioningly, fearfully, but at least she was learning not to ask about his health and she might as well know how it was.

"Tell us about it, bronc peeler," encouraged Troy, his face sober, his blue eyes averted.

"She bucks like a sonofabitch," Carl said simply, "an' when that don't git her nowhere, she goes over backwards."

"Oh, Carl!" Rinie gasped. She couldn't help it. "And you rode her home?"

"She only did it twice," he said by way of reassurance, "the first day I tried her, but she like to ruined my saddle."

Helen said truculently, "You ought to've killed the Chrissakin' ole bastard."

There was an instant's silence of absolute astonishment, spoons poised, jaws stopped working and then they, all of them but Ellie and Helen, went into convulsions of laughter, made more convulsive because they tried not to laugh. A. J. spewed most of a mouthful of cobbler down the front of his shirt. Carl choked and turned red and finally had to go outside and lose part of his supper from coughing so much.

"You just come right on over here, young lady," said Ellie with immediate and terrible authority, "an' git your smart mouth washed out with soap."

The men and boys withdrew hastily to the front room. The process of cleansing entailed first pleading and threats, then a lot of screaming. Rinie stacked the dishes with her back to the sink where retribution was taking place. She felt sorry for Helen, but Carl kept looking at her around the front-room door with one eye and then drawing back hurriedly, so that she had to repress little spasms of laughter in spite of herself.

When the purification was completed, Ellie sent Helen, crying and outraged, to bed. Then she went and stood in the front-room door, her hands on her hips and stared until all of them were compelled to look at her.

"You think it was so bloomin' funny," she said, low and angry, "but what are you gonna think when she's—say, sixteen an' spews out stuff like that all the time? She don't know what she's sayin' now, I know that, but the good Lord knows she's got plenty a chance to pick it up around here an' can't hardly help it. It ain't no way for a girl to talk an' I ain't gonna have it. When you laugh, it's that much harder on her."

"Yeah, but, Ellie, that lye soap," began Troy, a little outraged by his niece's punishment.

"Don't you fuss at me, Troy Dean Stinson!" she ordered fiercely. "You'da been better off if somebody'da done the same for you when you was her age, an' it wouldn't hurt you one little bit right now."

She went back to the kitchen.

"Whew!" Troy breathed softly. "Fire was comin' right outa her eyes."

"She was right pretty," murmured Travis with a little smile of pride.

"Havin' missy around here's ruinin' 'er," stated A. J. "Two women together always gits to thinkin' they can run things."

Carl snorted. "Chrissakin' ole bastard," he muttered brokenly and the four of them were off again.

Rinie spent a lot of time knitting the next weeks. Carl had brought home his pay and given it to her. She was surprised and touched and uncertain.

"What'll I do with it?"

"I don't know," he said magnanimously. "Spend it."

"But I don't want anything, or need anything."

"Well, it'll be Christmas before long. Buy presents."

On Sunday afternoon, he went with her down to the store at Webber to look around. Mr. Putney opened his store on Sundays for the benefit of those who came to church and wanted to take advantage of being in town to make some purchases. There were usually several people sitting around on the porch in summer, inside, by the stove, in winter. They saw Doxy Keane and Bud

Corbett, among others Rinie knew. Doxy was telling everyone she saw that her sister Supina was going to marry the boy from Greenfield.

There wasn't a lot to choose from in the way of gifts. Mr. Putney's stock was mostly of a utilitarian sort, but he did carry a fair variety of yarns. Rinie thought that she could make matching socks and scarves for the menfolks. Carl said that would be fine. His eyes showed his pride that she was so handy at making things.

They had looked through the catalog a little during the morning and had decided to buy a doll for Helen.

"The more dolls, the more she ought to feel like a little girl," Rinie said tenderly, remembering Helen's punishment of the night before. "She really doesn't have much chance around here to be—well, feminine—to do feminine things."

"You manage pretty well," he said, touching her hand on the page. "You do girl things pretty well."

She blushed. "Oh, Carl, you know what I'm talking about."

"An' you know what I'm talkin' about," he said, laughing at her embarrassment.

She made as if to slap him and he caught her hand and held it. It was such a little, pretty hand, not yet too much roughened by water and strong soap and hard work. It made his hands feel rough and hard, just touching it, and he held it very gently. He decided to buy her some of the things women in town used; lotions and creams and perfumes, things like that, if only he could find what would be right for her.

At Putney's, Rinie said she could knit things for Helen's doll from what was left over of the yarn and she found some maroon broadcloth that Carl agreed would make nice Sunday dresses to match for Ellie and Helen.

"And out of the scraps," Rinie said happily, "I can make a doll dress to match theirs."

So they bought material and thread and buttons and a pattern and the yarn.

While they paid for the things, Theorn and Vanda came in.

"Well, Carl, you never told me you could knit," said Theorn.

"I took it up just lately," he said with his crooked grin.

"My goodness, Rinie, you got married to the best horse

catcher in seven states," said Theorn lightly, but he wasn't teasing, really. His black eyes were full of admiration. "I bet they wasn' never no Indian any better."

"How's your shoulder, Carl?" asked Vanda in her soft, purry voice.

Carl flushed a little. He didn't like being reminded.

"Ah, it wasn' anything. It's all right."

Rinie felt angry. She resented Vanda's knowing about the injury. She had no business knowing about it and mentioning it and embarrassing him.

Rinie had seen the shoulder last night and he told her briefly that he'd hurt it when the white mare reared and went over backward. She had cried, but she hadn't let him see. The whole shoulder was a mottled purple from deep bruising. Once, in the night, when he'd turned on it in his sleep, he'd made a little, whimpering moan and then muttered a few curses. Vanda shouldn't even know about it. She had no right.

The round trip from ranch to store and back again was the longest ride Rinie had had so far. It was past mid-afternoon when they started home, and very cold, though the sky was clear.

"It don't look like we'll ever have real snow," Carl mused.

"Maybe ther'll be some for Christmas," she said. And then, she couldn't help it, "I wish you didn't have to go back."

He reached out and took her hand. She didn't hold onto the saddle much at all now, though she still wouldn't let the reins lie.

"I'll have to leave as soon as we get there," he said regretfully. "As it is, it'll be dark before I git to Forrester's."

"I hate for you to ride that wild horse," she said fearfully.

"You mean the Chrissakin' ole bastard? She'll be all right. The more I can ride her an' the rest of 'em the better off they'll be an' the sooner I'll be done down there. . . . Some people think breakin' broncs is just settin' on 'em once—the first time they been rode—for a little while. But there's a lot more to it than that if you want to do it right."

"I want you to take those cookies I made with you. Do you think the mare will mind?"

She felt pleased with herself because she was not begging him to be careful, though she worried so desperately.

"I won't ask 'er," he said, leaning over and giving her a quick, light kiss.

"Do they have good food—at the Forresters'?" She was afraid she was going to cry. He was still here, beside her, but she could feel the week, stretching out, long and bleak and empty.

"It's not bad," he said absently.

He wished he knew what she'd like and that he could give it to her; anything in the world, just walk into a store and lay down the money and bring it to her. He'd never cared about having money before, but now he wanted so badly to give her something really fine, really beautiful, like she was.

She said, "Mrs. Forrester's not as good a cook as Ellie, then? I guess not many people are."

"Miz Forrester? Oh, well, I wouldn' know what kind of a cook she is. They've got a Mexican woman that cooks for the hands. The Circle F is a real nice, big ranch with year-round hands an' a bunkhouse an' all that."

"You mean," she said with relief, "you don't eat with them or sleep in the house?"

He shook his head.

"But—the Mexican woman—what's she like?"

Carl grinned. "She's about ninety-five years old an' she don't speak any English."

"Are you sure she's so old?"

"Well, not exac'ly, an' I can't ask er 'cause we don't understand each other."

"Well, if she's old, it's all right, but speaking English doesn't matter because you don't need to talk . . . to understand each other . . . to. . . ."

He was laughing at her and her face felt hot.

"It seems to me, some people talk too much for their own good an' git into places that they can't talk out of," he said happily "If you want to know, I didn' see Vanda all week. You could've just asked me."

"Then how did she know about—" she broke off guiltily. Even at Red Bear, she was the only one who knew about his shoulder. He hadn't asked it of her, but he didn't have to. She knew he didn't like it mentioned.

"Mr. Forrester stays around the corrals a lot," he said irritably. "I wish he wouldn'. It bothers me, an' a horse that's bein' broke ought to have just the man that's doin'

121

it to think about. But it's his corrals an' I can't very well ask him to leave."

Rinie smiled a little, thinking that he probably came awfully close to it. Then her eyes were warm and soft, looking into his, thinking how well she was getting to know him. She had really known him so little those times in Denver and when he first brought her home, but now she was coming to know how he thought and felt about things—some things—what she shouldn't mention, what it meant when his eyes darkened the way they were now and looked strange and mysterious and almost frighteningly sensual.

"Rinie?"

"Hmm?"

"What would you like? If you could have a wish, what would you wish for?"

She almost said she'd wish he'd stay at Red Bear and not go back to the Forresters', but that would be unfair. She wouldn't say it.

"I don't know of anything," she said tenderly. "Carl, I love you."

"But in the catalog," he persisted after a moment, "wasn't there anything you'd really wish for?"

"Not that I can think of," she said, trying hard. "A lot of the things in there would be nice to have . . . Carl?"

"What?"

"The only thing I keep thinking of sometimes that I'd like to have. . . ."

"Well? What, honey?"

"Is a—a baby. . . ."

His eyes kept darkening and she felt weak and shivery.

"Do somethin' for me, will you?"

She nodded soberly.

"While I'm gone this week, think up somethin' I can buy you. A baby's fine, but we may not can manage one by Christmas an'—Rinie?—When I come home next Saturday night, wear your hair loose, all down around your shoulders an'. . . . Oh God! I love you."

Thinking how he had looked and what he had said that afternoon gave her a tender warm feeling all through the week, whatever she was doing, whenever she happened to think of it. She and Ellie decided to do some special baking for Christmas. Ellie hadn't done much of that sort

122

of thing in years, but now, with another woman to share the work and the pleasure of creating special things, she looked forward to it. They bought some extra spices and candied fruits and a big bag of nuts in the shell. Jeff liked to crack the nuts and sit by the table and pick them out and A. J. liked to happen by and take a handful from the bowl.

The old man was unable to walk more than a few steps at a time since the lion hunt and he spent a good deal of time making broad hints about how selfish and silly it was to have all "them nuts and goodies an' cook all that stuff that got the house so scented up, an' then just put it back for some other time."

They made two fruitcakes, several kinds of cookies and candies, mince pies, and they hid it all before Travis and Troy and Helen and Kirby came to the house. Jeff was in the secret, but he was the only one besides the women. They put all the good things in boxes under Rinie's bed and giggled together about her having to stay awake nights to make sure the mice didn't get at them.

"We'll have bowls of nuts and candy an' cookies all over the place," exulted Ellie, "but not any earlier'n Christmas Eve. When somebody goes to Belford to git Doyle, they can git a bunch a apples an' oranges an' like that."

"Only they won't ever get home with them," said Rinie, laughing.

Jeff, licking the last bit of batter from a bowl in which Rinie had been making cookies, stopped smiling abruptly.

"Gosh, I just thought of somethin'. What'll we do with all that stuff when Carl's home? He'll smell it."

"Well," said Rinie slowly, "maybe I can convince him. . . ."

"You know better than that," said Ellie sensibly.

"He'd sneak some while you're asleep, prob'ly," said Jeff a little sadly.

After two days and a good deal of consternation, Ellie remembered that there used to be a key to the big trunk in Helen's room where they kept blankets in summer. She finally found the key in a drawer of her dresser and the problem was solved.

"We might even have Reverend Turner to dinner," Ellie said happily. "Third Sunday's right before Christmas."

"Oh, yeah," said Troy bitterly. "Plan on havin' the preacher. Have the whole dang community. Whyn't you write Minna an' ask her? But don't give us one bite! Not one dam', lousy taste! We just git the smell is all. Ever' time I come in here, somethin' smells just like heaven an' Rinie's runnin' off to hide another plate or pan or somethin'. What good's food if you can't eat it? Save it for Christmas! My God! The next thing, you'll be wantin' to hold the biscuits over till Valentine's Day."

"I think you sound a lot like your daddy," said Ellie sweetly.

"An' I think women—ever' one of 'em—is more'n a little touched in the head. Christmas! I'm *hungry!*"

"Well, don't yell like that," said Rinie reprovingly. "You'll make the cake fall."

She worked on socks and scarves every spare minute. Getting all that knitting finished by Christmas would take some doing, but she could manage it. What bothered her was getting a chance to make the dress for Ellie in secret. She showed Ellie some of the material, telling her it was for Helen, which was true.

"Oh, it's so pretty," Ellie said softly, fingering it. "Won't that look good with her black hair?"

And Rinie couldn't think what to give Carl. She had thought of ordering yarn, really good, soft wool, as near the color of his eyes as she could find, and making him a sweater, but when she had pointed out a picture of a man in the catalog wearing the sort of sweater she had in mind, and said, "Do you think Troy might like something like that? Or Doyle?"

He had said, "Well, Doyle might, but I don't think Troy'd feel right, wearin' something like that." Which meant, she knew, that Carl wouldn't either.

She laid her problem before the family, and they had suggestions—a new knife, boots, a rifle, levis, but nothing really special.

On Friday afternoon it began to snow—A. J. had said it would—and Rinie was glad because it meant Carl would be home. She kept looking out to make sure it hadn't stopped. She was in the front room, sitting close by the fire, knitting rapidly on a blue scarf for A. J.

A. J. was sleeping on the sofa, snoring lightly. He never paid any attention to the women's handiwork, none of

124

the men did, otherwise it would have been impossible for her to get anything done, they were around so much.

Ellie was churning in the kitchen and Jeff was in there, talking a little sometimes. It was warm and peaceful. Troy and Travis would be back soon and Kirby and Helen home from school. They'd all be here safe together tonight. It made her feel so good.

Fleetingly, she thought of Vanda Forrester. Vanda was a nice girl. She'd been silly and childish ever to think of her in any but a friendly way. Of course Carl liked her. Carl liked nearly everybody. His liking other girls didn't take away from his love for her. . . . He had said almost those same words to her, that day up at the cemetery, about A. J. "It didn't take anything away from his love for my mother."

Tears welled into her eyes. Carl would never, never . . . no, that was about A. J. and that woman. She thought of the graves up there on the knoll in the snow, mostly of the one where the cross said "Aaron James Stinson."

A. J.'s lips pushed out gently as he exhaled, lying there on the sofa. He was an old man, and sick. Carl loved him so much. Maybe that was why Carl couldn't see how wrong it had been. Only, when you loved somebody, truly loved them, it didn't mean you were blind to their faults and the things they did wrong. It meant that, even seeing those things, you loved them and tried to understand . . . but that was what Carl was doing, of course. Carl was so good. He could do that kind of thing and she couldn't. She just couldn't. It was wrong. Maybe, because he was a man, it seemed less wrong to Carl, she didn't know how that would be. It was wrong. Only . . . it was all so long ago. . . .

"Got somethin' in your eye, missy?" A. J.'s drowsy voice startled her.

"Oh! Oh, no," she said, sniffling, and wiping hurriedly at her eyes with the half-finished scarf.

A. J. sat up and lowered his feet with aching slowness. It hurt Rinie to see. He grunted a little as he stood up and came to put wood on the fire and poke at it a while. He didn't straighten up completely till he was through with that; he gave his dam' joints that much. Then he stood by the window near her and said, yawning, "I expect Buck'll be home direc'ly. Looks like it might snow two, three days."

A. J. didn't know when it had happened, or why, but some time back missy had got odd with him. Just when she was beginning to show a little spunk, she'd turned standoffish and quiet. Not bashful, more like she'd just got her first real good look at him and didn't much like what she saw. He was sorry about it. He liked missy. He'd expected her to act that way in the beginning, coming straight from Minnie's, but she hadn't. This had come on just lately. Well, he guessed she'd come out of it. Women acted funny sometimes. He looked down. She was a pretty little thing, curled up there in that big chair with her hair all over the place and the firelight shining on it and the side of her face, sitting where she could look up and see out the window, down the road, watching for Buck.

Then A. J. thought about what she was doing. She'd been at that a lot lately, he remembered now, sitting around, quiet. His heart gave a funny kind of lift and he looked out at the snow again.

They had supper on the table when Carl came. He let out a wild whoop when he sighted the house. The dogs ran out, baying and barking joyfully, and the gray horse he was gentling for Mr. Forrester threw a wall-eyed fit, which was what Carl had expected he'd do. He hadn't let Rinie watch when he left on the white mare Sunday, because he didn't feel at all easy about the white mare, but this gray was all right. Oh, he could turn it on, all right, but he'd give up after a little while, not throw himself over backward when there wasn't anything else left to do.

They all ran out on the porch and stood there with the snow sifting in on them a little, the men and children yelling, Ellie murmuring "My Lord a-mercy," Rinie holding her breath.

The gray got close to the edge of the creek bank and A. J. bawled, "Watch out, Buckshot! You're fixin' to git wet again." He slapped his thigh, the one that pained him most, and doubled over with laughter and the pain of what he'd done to himself.

Before the gray was ready to bring his head up, Carl forced him up next to the porch and swung off, taking a quick hitch around a post with the reins while the exasperated animal still had his back bowed. In one stride,

Carl had Rinie in his arms. She had her hair down, as he had known she would, and he nuzzled his snowy face into it.

"Jee-zus Christ," muttered Troy in a mixture of incredulity, contempt, and envy.

"Git in the house, ever' one of you," ordered Ellie, " 'fore you catch your deaths in this cold. Here we all come out without coats."

"Whyn't you ride 'im right in the front room, Buck?" asked Travis.

"I could," offered Carl exuberantly, turning toward the horse.

"I'll betcha five dollars you couldn' git him up the steps, let alone in the door," said Troy.

"I'll take it." Carl had his hand on the reins.

"You won't do no such of a thing," snapped Ellie. "You go put that horse up an' be quick about it if you want any supper. It's on the table now. That pore thing's scared to death."

"Ellie always feels sorry for the underdog," Travis explained.

When they had finished supper and were just sitting around the table, drinking coffee, Helen got up and came to stand by Carl.

"What you been doin', Miss Puss?" he said, putting his arm around her.

"I'm gonna speak a piece in the Christmas program," she said smugly.

Kirby and Jeff groaned. She'd been speaking the piece all week long.

"It's at church the day before Christmas Eve. Will you come?"

"Oh, yeah."

"Will you be done at Mr. Forrester's?"

"That ought to be about the day after I git through over there."

"How many," A. J. began to ask, but Helen was saying confidentially to her uncle, "Rinie likes for me to sleep with her."

"She does, does she? Well, that's good to know."

"She says I'm good an' warm."

"Mm-hmm."

Rinie felt her face getting hot. The others were starting to grin.

"Helen," Ellie said warningly.

127

"An' I don't pull out the covers an' things."

Troy snorted.

"Helen, you better help your mama with the dishes," said Travis, but he only said it because Ellie was looking at him like he better say something.

"An' I don't grit my teeth, either. Rinie said so."

"Well, Helen, I'm glad about that, but what is it we're gettin' to?"

"Well," she said importantly, "I think Rinie'd be better off if I slep' with her all the time. You can have my room."

"All right, Buck. What you say to that?"

"Well, I—Helen, Rinie's my girl an' I like 'er somethin' awful. I'd be pretty lonesome. . . ."

"I thought I was your girl. You said I was, sometimes."

"Well, you're both my girls, but—"

He looked around the table for help, but none was forthcoming. Then Helen was inspired. She said, delightedly, "Then we could take turns! Or all three of us—"

Ellie got up. "If you don't quit pesterin' you can't even sleep with Rinie when Carl's gone. Now you git busy helpin' with these dishes."

Helen, sad and sullen, moved slowly away.

"Pull your lip in, Puss, 'fore you step on it," said her grandfather placatingly. "You ain't sorry Buck come home, now, are you?"

"No," she said reluctantly, "but I want somebody to sleep with."

A little later, as A. J. was about to go to bed, he said casually to Carl, "You know what missy's been doin' lately? Knittin' is what."

"Has she?"

A. J. was disappointed. The boy wasn't blushing or anything. Missy was, though. She looked real pretty.

"I always heard tell that when a woman starts all that stitchin', you might can start expectin' somethin'."

"I expect it's about bedtime," Carl said blandly.

Troy was interested. He said, "You mean A. J., like they talk about in the movies, the patter of little feet?"

A. J. nodded, grinning. "You reckon, missy—?"

Rinie was thinking about the way A. J. stomped around the house barefoot, and about the warm blue socks, and despite her embarrassment, she began laughing.

"Oh, well, some feet may patter, A. J., you never can tell."

8

Rinie went with Troy to Belford to meet Doyle that next week. There had been almost a foot of snow that weekend but, by Thursday, it was mostly off the roads, at least after they got through Red Bear Canyon and out to Webber.

Carl had said he and Mr. Forrester's hands would take the horses to Belford for shipment on Friday or Saturday and he'd be home to stay by Sunday at the latest. Because of the snow, he hadn't gone back to Forrester's until late Monday, and they had spent a good deal of time cutting wood. They didn't so much mind cutting the logs and bringing them down, but the cutting to length and splitting they put off as long as possible, usually keeping not more than a day ahead of the needs. However, there came a time each year when it was reluctantly agreed that, with bad weather upon them, they ought to get up a good woodpile. They had a cross-cut saw for cutting to length and Troy, once he got started, was "a master hand" with an ax.

A. J. said that cutting wood wasn't a fit job for ranching men, and Travis said what did A. J. want them to do? Leave it for the women? Maybe it wasn't a fit job, but it had to be done.

A. J. sat in the kitchen and watched through the window as they worked. Ellie and Rinie were in there, too, ironing and cooking. A. J. recollected a lot of incidents he had heard of or knew about firsthand, where a man had had a tree fall on him, or his foot or hand or things cut off by an ax, and it seemed like an appropriate time to recall them aloud.

Rinie thought that if Ellie would go to Belford when it was time to pick up Doyle, she could use the opportunity to make Ellie's dress, but Ellie insisted that she wasn't going. She had too much to do, and besides, she'd been to Belford twice in two months.

Rinie had quite a list of commissions. Besides things

129

she was to buy or see about on behalf of others, she and Carl had decided on gifts for Jeff and Kirby that she'd have to find, and that would take care of their Christmas list—except that she still had no gift for Carl and no good ideas as to what she might get him.

As they drove along, she told Troy about the problem of getting Ellie's dress made.

"Well," he said reasonably, "why couldn' you just shut the door an' make her stay out of where the sewin' machine is?"

"A lot of reasons," Rinie said, a little exasperated. Men never seemed to half-think a thing out. "The sewing machine's in her own room for one thing, and besides, it's too cold to work in a room shut off from any heat. And besides that, she'd know I was making something for her. I don't even want her to know there *is* anything."

"Hmm. Well, we'll have to think of somethin'. Oh! What about when she goes to church on Sunday? She'll want to go this time for sure."

"But so do I want to go, Troy. It's the Christmas program that Helen's in."

"Oh, yeah. Well. . . ."

Carl hadn't been any help, either. He hadn't even thought about Ellie's going to church. Well, she had the dress cut out and some of it pinned together. It wouldn't take long if she could just think of some way.

The sun was warm and there was a good, extra fresh smell and taste about the air, the smell and taste of melting snow. Rinie felt good, bumping along in the Model T. Doing something different was nice.

"Carl ought to git him a car," Troy said, rather abruptly.

"I guess he doesn't need one," Rinie said absently. She was thinking about A. J.'s misconception about the knitting and all, wishing it was true.

"He ought to, though. If I had a girl like you, I'd want to take her to Belford to the show a lot, an' to dances an' all like that."

"Well, why don't you get a girl and take her those places?"

"Oh, I don't know. I guess I'm kinda tired a the ones around Webber, Mary Tippitt an' Nell Corbett an' Barbara Hunter an' Perrymans an' Barnharts an' Keanes. I mean, they're all right, mostly, but I just like somethin' different. Besides, I'm gettin' kind of old for most of 'em.

The ones nearer my age are married an' have got a bunch of kids."

"What about Vanda Forrester? I think she's awfully nice."

"Don't you know about Vanda? It's Doyle she's after. Oh, it won't do her any good, but she is. Not that she wouldn't go with me, but she talks about him too much with me or Carl. A guy don't like to go all the time with somebody that just wants to talk about his brother."

Rinie left sorry for Vanda and a little ashamed of her own suspicions.

"Anyway," Troy continued, "the girls around here mostly think about gittin' married."

Troy made himself a cigarette with one hand.

"Doyle meets a lot of different kinds of girls, livin' at school like he does. Maybe I ought to have gone to school. It's a hell of a lot easier on a guy than livin' up at Red Bear. Only I doubt if Minna would have financed me. She feels like I'm a lost cause."

"Well, you did get in that trouble," she said hesitantly. A little while back, she wouldn't have dreamed of mentioning it.

"Oh, hell, Rinie, that wasn' anything much more'n Minna's imagination—hers an' that girl's mother's— Mary, her name was, an' she fooled around with a lot of guys. She just picked on me when she thought she was— in trouble. It turned out she wasn't even."

"You'd've been married over six years now," she said, smiling, "if you'd married her."

Troy grunted. "Well, I didn't. I don't know as I ever will. Marryin's for people that wants to settle down, change diapers, set by the kitchen stove of an ev'nin'— people like Travis. Travis' been a ole settled feller since he was born. I don't know how he got in this family."

"But A. J.'s not been an old settled feller," she said mildly.

"Well, it seems like sometimes a man like A. J. comes across a woman that's just right, an' then marriage ain't a ball an' chain around his neck, chokin' him to death. I guess Buck thinks you're just right—it sure looks that way—an' if I—if I ever found me just that certain one, w'y marryin' wouldn' be bad at all, I guess, but I don't think that I ever will."

He grinned and threw out his cigarette butt. "Ellie was tellin' me, a little while back, how I ought to be ashamed, lettin' Carl git ahead of me, marryin' first, when I'm the oldest. Ellie'd be glad to see the whole world married. I guess most women would. She's likely already got somebody picked out for Kirby an' he's just barely thirteen. Ellie's been hintin' for us boys to git married since we been old enough to—well, a long time. I guess a lot of it was because she was lonesome up there, only I never thought about that till just lately. She sorta had Carl matched up with her sister, an' thought Vanda'd be real good for me. She always said Doyle'd marry some city girl with money. I expect she's right about that, an' it dam' well wouldn't hurt for somebody in this bunch to git hold of some cash."

He smiled with reminiscent wistfulness. "God! Me an' ole Buck used to have some high times. Ellie was always layin' down the law."

"What kind of times?" Rinie asked with eager interest.

Troy laughed, but his blue eyes seemed a little sad as he threw her a glance.

"I guess you better git your ole man to tell you about 'em himself."

"I guess," she said gently, without rancor, "you'd be happier if I hadn' come here. If things were still the way they used to be."

Troy kept his eyes on the road.

"Carl's a pretty special kid," he said slowly. "We always been close, less than a year's difference in our ages an' all, an', like ole man McLean says about somebody he likes, Buck's a good man to ride the river with—or most anything else. . . . No, Rinie, it's good he's happy like he is, an' you are. Sometimes, lookin' at you, I think you're both a little cracked in the head, but I guess that's how it is with the right one. The trouble is, an' I never knew it till it was too late, I wish I—I wish it'd been me that brought you to Red Bear."

There was a long silence. Rinie blinked hard at tears, her face turned to the window. He sounded so lonesome, suddenly. She couldn't bear loneliness in herself or in anyone else.

"Rinie?"

"Troy, I—I wish you hadn't said that."

"I know, Rinie, I oughtn't to. It don't matter. Just act like I didn't, will you?"

He wanted to kiss her so badly that everything inside him ached.

132

After a long time she said, with a brightness that sounded forced, "Look at the kids with sleds."

They were coming into the edge of Belford.

On Saturday it started to snow again. Rinie hoped that Carl would come home, but A. J. stated that he was in Belford with Forrester's horses and wouldn't be home till sometime tomorrow.

"He won't miss the Christmas program," stated Helen with certainty. "He wants to hear my piece. He said so."

"He heard your piece about two million times," said Jeff.

Rinie and Ellie were doing up the family's clothes for church and the Christmas program.

"What if it snows too much for us to get to Webber?" Doyle suggested, teasing Helen, but she was sure it wouldn't.

"Anyway," she said, "there's that old sleigh in the barn we could use."

"That would be fun," said Rinie, delighted.

"It would take a week to fix that old sleigh fit to use," Doyle told her. "Besides, there's no horses on the place that could be trusted in harness."

"W'y, there's Jake an' Trixy," said A. J. reprovingly. "Might be fun at that."

"Jake and Trixy!" cried Doyle incredulously.

"Why, yes. We used 'em hayin' an' to drag logs, Siefog."

"Well, I don't know about dragging logs, since I wasn't here for that," Doyle said dubiously, "but it's a miracle somebody wasn't killed, haying with those old wild horses."

"Hayin's a pretty dull business," A. J. said. "If it's got to be done, it don't hurt to have somethin' to liven it up a little."

"Anyway, granddaddy," said Helen, "what's a siefog?"

Rinie had wondered that, too, and never thought to ask. It was A. J.'s name for his youngest son, and mostly nobody thought about it.

A. J. looked quizzical. "Well, Puss, you recollect how your uncle Doyle does sometimes; lookin' off into the air, not payin' attention to his business, walkin' around like he maybe don't know where he's at? Well, that siefoggin' around, so he's a Siefog."

There was a great stamping at the back door and Travis came in, beating his hat against his leg to knock the snow off. He went straight to Ellie where she was stirring a pot on the stove and kissed her. All of them, including Ellie, were surprised and pleased. Travis was rarely demonstrative.

Troy came in behind him, grinning.

"Right in front of God an' ever'body?" he asked with a raised eyebrow.

"Right over the dinner pot," muttered A. J., with a quirk at the corner of his mouth.

"I guess a feller can kiss his wife out in public two or three days before Christmas if he feels like it," Travis said stoutly. "Right after dinner, we're goin' after a Christmas tree."

"Goody!" squealed Helen. "Can I go?"

"I expect you can. Your mama is."

"Ah, Travis, I can't do that," protested Ellie, touched. "I got so much to do——"

"It'll keep," he said with finality. "You ain't been to help pick out a tree in a long, long time. We got to have an extry special one this year an' it needs a woman to decide."

Troy winked at Rinie. Things had not been easy between them since the day they'd gone to Belford. Not that Troy was any different, or that Rinie was, but their sharing the knowledge of the thing he had told her seemed to make things ambiguous and more significant than they ought to be. Now she realized with gratitude that he had thought of a way to get Ellie out of the house so that the dress could be made, and she smiled her understanding.

"I can be the woman," Helen offered, "if mama don't want to, an' why is it got to be such a special tree."

" 'Cause your daddy wants to git your mama off in the woods," opined the grandfather.

They had a hard time getting through to Webber next morning, but all of them went, even A. J. Carl hadn't come home. With the snow, it took longer to get the horses down, probably. In her excitement, Helen all but forgot him, but Rinie didn't. She looked around at all the families, sitting together, smiling, most of the men sheepishly, but all their faces showing the special happiness of

Christmas and she desperately wanted Carl there beside her.

Mr. and Mrs. Forrester and Vanda came in, and Rinie caught the quick pleasure in Vanda's eyes when she first caught sight of Doyle.

Forrester said that Carl and the men had left with the horses early yesterday.

"They wouldn' of started back till this mornin'," Travis said in the hushed tones all of them used when the school became the church. "He'll be home by dark." But Rinie felt frightened. So many things could have happened with those half-wild horses. He could be lying hurt somewhere and she might not know of it for days, with no telephones or anything.

Reverend Turner had left home before daylight to give himself plenty of time for battling the snowy roads, but he was there, and the time for starting the service came and passed. People grew restless. The children were nervous about the program.

"Where's Miss Johnson—I mean—Miz Tippitt, I wonder," Jeff whispered to Rinie.

A. J. shifted his position, grunting under his breath with pain and impatience. The bench was hard on his joints. If he went to all the trouble of coming out in this weather and sitting here, it seemed like they could get the thing started.

Mrs. Forrester leaned over and said worriedly to Ellie, "Nell Tippitt just come in with 'er folks. They say June's got the flu real bad. Alva stayed at home with her she's so sick. Nell's been helpin' out with the childrens' program an' knows about their parts an' all, but with June not here, they's not a soul to play the piano."

"Ah," said Ellie in deep disappointment, "it just won't be a Christmas service without music."

"Rinie can play," said Doyle loudly.

Rinie gasped. "Oh! Oh, no, I—I can't. I—"

"I remember you did at Aunt Minna's," said Doyle perversely.

Reverend Turner had come over, sensing what might be going on.

"We'd just appreciate it so much, Mrs. Stinson, if you would. We need the piano. Nell can help the children, but all of us sing better with accompaniment."

Rinie's face and neck were burning. She was going to

135

cry. She wished Carl was here. He wouldn't let them do this to her. She wished she had stayed at home.

"I—I don't know the songs," she pled, not raising her eyes to the minister's face.

"You can read music," Doyle said blithely, and she wanted to kick him—hard.

"Here's the book with the special songs the kids do," said Nell Tippitt. "They're real simple."

"Oh, no, but I—"

"Oh, git on up there, Missy," ordered A. J. tersely. "Le's git this business over with."

Rinie was trembling and biting the inside of her lip. If she started crying now and made an even bigger fool of herself, she'd just never get over it.

First they'd sing some Christmas carols from the hymnals that had been passed around, the minister explained in a low voice, then he would make a brief talk, then would come the children's program. Hastily, Nell scribbled the page numbers of the children's songs so Rinie could look them over. They looked fairly easy, and she had played all the traditional carols before, of course.

Minna had had her given piano lessons by way of proving to her friends how generous she was to the little charity girl. Rinie thought miserably of how Minna would call, insipidly, for her to "Come into the living room and show us how well you're doing with your piano." Rinie hardly thought of life at the Hickses' these days and she didn't want to. She was going to cry, sure. The tears were already creeping between her eyelids and now she'd have to open them because Reverend Turner was announcing the number of the first hymn.

She sat in profile to the congregation and she gave a quick, surreptitious dab at her eyes with the back of her hand—she hadn't even brought a handkerchief—while her face was averted and she turned the pages of the hymnal. She felt trapped. Maybe she could play the music all right, but there was a hostility in the room. After all, she was a stranger here to all but the family. Many of these people she'd never met; most of the others she'd been no more than introduced to. They were just waiting, waiting to see how the little city girl from the Stinsons' would do.

The family looked a little tense. They were wondering, too, except for Doyle. His face, as always, was smooth, with a touch of cynicism around the mouth. Well, they were waiting and she'd have to begin.

It went all right, that first carol, and then there was a prayer. As the prayer ended, there was a little noise at the back of the room and Rinie felt cold air against the back of her neck. When she raised her eyes, the family was beaming at her, except Doyle, of course, whose expression hadn't changed.

The next carol was announced. It was "Silent Night," so simple, so well known to Rinie that she dared glance away from the book and over the congregation. Most of the people didn't need to look at their books either, and their faces were happy and friendly. The hostility had been all in her imagination. They were glad she was here. They liked her. She was doing something with and for them. She belonged, not just to Carl, which was the most important thing in the world, or at Red Bear with the family, which still seemed at times too good to be true, but in and to the community of Webber.

And then she saw him, sitting at the very back by the door, uneasy because he hadn't had time or opportunity to change his clothes. He'd stopped at Forrester's to get his few belongings that were there, and to shave, and he'd cut himself twice, trying to hurry. He didn't have any Sunday clothes there, naturally, so about the only other preparation he could make for church was to take the spurs off his boots and comb his hair down a little while it was wet with snow.

It was a shock to see Rinie sitting at the piano, up there in front of everybody. He hadn't even known she could play and she looked pale and half-scared to death. He hoped to God she *could* play.

The preacher was calling out the number of a song and old man Hunter was poking a hymnal back over his shoulder at Carl. He took the book, but didn't open it. About the only times he felt like singing were times when he was out by himself with just big, free emptiness all around. He watched Rinie. She turned the pages of her book and started playing. It was "Silent Night." It sounded just exactly like it. By God, nobody could say she couldn't play, and, on top of that, she was doing it without halfway looking at the music. Carl's face felt strained from grinning so wide. Probably, you weren't supposed to grin like that in church, but God! She was something else.

She saw him and smiled, a little shakily, and looked back at her book. He thought she might feel like he ought to be singing, so he opened his book, but he couldn't do much of anything but watch her, glad he was all the way back here so he could do all of that he felt like. Besides, his book was open to the wrong page.

Ellie asked Reverend Turner for dinner and he said he'd like to, but with the weather like it was, he'd better start right back for Belford.

They had a big dinner and the kitchen was warm and cozy with the curtain of snow outside the window, full of talk and laughter and all of them there together again.

"Three foot deep by mornin'," predicted A. J. His bones felt like they'd like to lie down after sitting on that hard bench so long and after that rough ride in the truck, but he hated to miss out on times like this. To ease himself some, he'd had a little whiskey while the women got dinner on the table. The boys had had one or two snorts apiece, too. It was dam' cold outside.

"I figgered to go huntin' tomorrow," Troy said lazily, "but I guess if there's gonna be that much snow, I'll just let it go."

"We ought to go after an elk," said Carl.

"Ought to've had one before this," said A. J. critically.

"Yeah, but it's been so dry," Troy said, "This would be just right. The meat'd still be real good."

"And we could just dress it and hang it up and let it freeze," added Doyle. "Keeping the meat wouldn't be any problem."

"Maybe we better go after dinner," said Kirby hopefully.

The men were all feeling warm and drowsy and reluctant to move.

"Oh, I don't hardly think so," said Travis luxuriously. He took just one last biscuit to put chokecherry jelly on.

There was a pleasant silence, with just forks on plates and chewing and wood shifting in the stove.

"It really was a good program, wasn't it?" said Helen.

They had all agreed with her previously, a number of times, that it had been.

"Yes, it was right nice," said Ellie, "but that's enough about it now. You ain't to git the big head. They was lots of others in it besides you."

"How's your Aunt Minnie?" A. J. asked Doyle. He

hadn't thought of asking till now, didn't give a dam', really, but he was glad to think of something to ask. It had always been hard for him and Doyle to find things to talk about together.

"Brinda Barnhart forgot hers," said Helen, "right in the middle."

"Aunt Minna's all right," Doyle said. "I saw them about a week ago. They said to wish everybody Merry Christmas."

"I bet she had her fingers crossed when she said it," muttered A. J.

'An' Jerry McLean couldn' even git started with his," Helen recalled.

"Now, A. J.," said Travis reprovingly, "this here's the time of year to be charitable and forgivin' an' all like that."

"Peace on earth, good will to men," added Ellie a little unctuously.

A. J. grunted. "She ain't got no good will for no man, an' there'll not be peace on earth no place Minnie Hicks is at, the ole—"

"I wonder what's wrong with teacher," mused Helen.

"She's sick," snapped Kirby, his voice lowered. "Now will you shut up?"

"I can talk if I want to," she whispered. "It ain't nice, tellin' people to shut up, especially if they're girls and you ain't."

"I guess you didn' have any trouble gittin' the horses down?" Travis asked Carl.

"No, it was fine."

"What would you all think of cuttin' one a them goddam' fruitcakes?" asked Troy hopefully.

Rinie and Ellie had already decided they would. In fact, they had taken one secretly from the trunk while the men were in the front room nipping at the whiskey to drive off the chills. But Ellie said shortly, "It ain't Christmas Eve. We told you an' told you, none of that stuff was comin' out till Christmas Eve."

"Hell, we could all be dead by then," he said sourly.

"Well, you've made it this long. I don't see why you couldn' last one more day."

A. J. said, "Just in case we don't, an' to help us make it, go git that bottle off the mantelpiece, Buck."

"Can't we have some?" asked Jeff hopefully.

"Shore can't," said his mother.

"Ah, come on, Ellie," urged Troy. "It's Christmas—nearly."

She frowned, but got three glasses of water and tipped about four drops of whiskey into each one. The men protested that that wasn't even enough to taste, but she set the glasses firmly before her children.

"I ain't gonna have no three drunk young 'uns on my hands along with ever'thing else."

Rinie was cutting and serving the fruitcake.

Carl said, "Dam', you ought to have warned me. I don't think I got room."

"I bet you have," she said. "I never yet saw you lack for food space."

"Gittin' to sound like Sal, ain't she?" grinned A. J. "You better take 'er down a notch or two, Buck, 'fore she gits plumb outta hand. Woman's got to be kep' in 'er place, ain't she, Prunes?"

"Goddam' right," Travis agreed happily. "Ever' mornin' an' ev'nin'."

"She must be awful sick to miss the program," Helen thought aloud.

"What, ever' mornin' an' ev'nin'?" Troy asked his brother.

"When you git one, you'll catch on to what."

Ellie gave her husband a withering look that only made him grin. She said to Rinie, "The cake turned out real good, didn't it? That candied ginger's the best stuff. I could eat ever' bit of it myself."

"Prob'ly did," muttered Troy, "ever' mornin' an' evenin'."

"I picked out all the nuts," Jeff told Doyle.

"Now wait a minute Joebob," cautioned A. J. "I helped some with that part."

"Helped eat," said Rinie.

"Can I have some more, mama?" asked Kirby.

"W'y, I reckon you can when you finish that piece you got. Oh! Whiskey. No, you shorely can't, an' don't ask agin."

"Know what we ought to do with this place?" asked Doyle expansively, leaning back in his chair. "Something that's getting to be a real big industry in this state?"

They didn't know, but Troy thought maybe it might be moonshining.

"Indians made whiskey outta ever'thing. We could try skunk cabbage or cow parsnip roots or—"

"Indians didn', either," protested Carl. "White men corrupted 'em with firewater."

"Corrupted, hell! Where do you git things like that? You wouldn' know a corrup if one run up an' bit you on the leg."

"I dam' well would."

"What does one look like?"

"It's round an' fuzzy an' you can't tell the head from the tail."

"An' that's what the whites done to the Indians? The dirty sonsabitches! But there's money in moonshinin' anyhow."

"Not moonshining," Doyle said patiently, "raising sheep."

"Sheep!" It was an explosion around the table.

"Well, what's wrong with it?" But Doyle was accustomed to this kind of reaction.

"What ain't?" scoffed A. J. "Sheep."

"I've been reading a little about them," said Doyle placidly. "They don't need so much grazing area, eat more kinds of things—"

"Stink," supplemented Travis.

"I'd like to have a little lamb," murmured Jeff wistfully.

Helen agreed eagerly. "We could name him Jesus."

"What?"

"Jesus is the Lamb of God. It says so. Borned in a manger."

Carl said, "Mr. Forrester's got a lot of peach trees ordered for the spring. He's gonna plant 'em on some of that irrigated land of his. He says over in the Grand Valley, they're startin' to make quite a bit of noney out of orchards."

"I wisht you'd git irrigatin' out a your mind," snapped his father. "I'm tired of hearin' about it—that, an' sheep."

Troy said, "You can make brandy, too, peach brandy. Rinie, cut me just another little sliver, will you?"

"I ruther think some orchard land than sheep," said Travis, "if I was to think change, but puttin' all other things to one side, we ain't got no money for no experimentin' an' foolin' around. Anyhow, this is a ranch."

"Yeah," said Troy, very serious. "Who in hell ever heard of a peach ranch?"

"I bet she's gittin a baby!" cried Helen, everything suddenly clear.

"Who?" asked Doyle.

A. J. looked knowingly at Carl and Rinie.

"Miss Johnson—I mean, Miz Tippitt. I bet that's why she couldn' come for the program. I hope she brings it to school—"

"Helen Marie Stinson, hush up right now an' eat your cake."

"I did, mama."

"Well, then, start in stackin' the dishes they're through with."

Travis said, "Forrester's got the money to fool around with different things. We ain't."

"I didn' say we did;" Carl said, a little irritably, "but I'd like to try somethin' different *if* we had it."

"Well, there never will be any money out of this old range stock," Doyle said. "You ought to upgrade if you've got to run cattle. Sheep, now—"

"We are upgradin'," said Travis disgustedly. "Didn't you ever notice that Hereford bull we bought five years ago?"

"Ma-ry had a lit-tle lamb," Helen sang, as she went around the table, collecting dishes.

"That was Jesus," Kirby whispered to Jeff and they began laughing into their fists.

"I'm gonna git me some money," Troy said.

"I know," said Carl, "from your still."

"No, besides that. I'm goin' to work for Mr. McCarthy at his feed store in Belford. He asked me about it when I was there last time. His son-in-law that works for him has got to have an operation an' can't work for a while. I told him I'd be ready to go to work when I bring Doyle back to go to Denver."

"What's wrong with him?" asked Ellie.

"Who? Doyle? Nothin' that I—"

"Mr. McCarthy's son-in-law," she said patiently. They just kept passing the bottle, but it was nearly Christmas.

"Oh. He's got a hernia."

"You'll git one, Troy," Carl said. "You ought not to go."

"What's a hernia?" asked Jeff.

"It's like bustin' a gusset," Kirby explained, "from liftin' stuff, like feed sacks."

"Yeah, well, I'll be makin' deliveries an' stuff like that," said Troy. "When did you say you have to go back, Si?"

"You trying to get rid of me? I said the second."

"Deliveries, huh," mused Carl.

"Just right," Troy nodded. "Time to do somethin' for New Year's Eve an' sleep it off."

Doyle said, "It seems like men would have hisias and women hernias."

"Doyle better stick to law books an' stay away from sheep," warned the father.

"I haven't been around any sheep."

"Dam' right, you ain't, nor cows, either, but you sure can talk."

"Lit-tle lamb, lit-tle lamb. . . ."

Carl said to Troy, "How come you want to go off, Bojack, just when I'm ready to stay at home. I thought we'd go huntin', all like that."

"I won't go for a week yet. After that, it'll prob'ly be too much snow to git out much. I don't want to be housed up here when that time comes."

"I do," said Carl with anticipation.

"Just have one more little slug, Ellie," coaxed Travis.

"Sure, Ellie, it's Christmas."

"I bet she is," claimed Helen. "It's fleas was white as snow."

"Peach brandy sounds good," Doyle mused.

"Sagebrush wine," said Carl smacking his lips.

"With that certain distinctive flavor," added Doyle.

"Cottonwood essence," murmured Troy dreamily, "whatever the hell that is. I'm not sure you drink a essence."

Rinie couldn't help almost constant, half-suppressed laughter. The three of them were being so completely ridiculous and their faces looked so serious and sober.

"Lit-tle lamb. . . ."

"You all git on out of the way now," Ellie said severely, "so we can git this kitchen cleaned up." But there was a pretty little smile on her lips when Travis put an arm around her.

"Sheep." A. J. just couldn't get over it. "Sheep an' peaches! That's what comes of goin' to church."

"Sheep shower wine," mused Carl.

"Not shower," corrected Troy.

"You have your kind an' I'll have mine."

"It's fleas was—"

"*Fleece*, Helen," said Doyle impatiently.

"Where's that other bottle at, Bojack?" wondered A. J.

"What's fleece then?"

"Other one!" said Ellie, outraged. "It's Sunday."

"Hell, El, it's Christmas," proclaimed Troy. "I know 'cause you let loose a some of your good stuff."

"You better watch your mouth," warned Travis.

"Go git the other bottle for the Chrissakin' ole bastard," Carl whispered and he and Troy were convulsed.

Rinie hurried over to the sink to laugh in private, but Carl came after her and kissed her.

"But what's fleece?" demanded Helen, quite loudly.

"It's the wool of a sheep," said Doyle resignedly.

"Sheep!" exploded A. J. "Why in hell does ever'body keep talkin' about sheep?"

"And peaches," Troy reminded him helpfully, breaking the seal on the other bottle.

"Lit-tle, lit-tle lamb. . . ."

"Helen," said Doyle, exasperated, "don't they ever tell you around here about how children are supposed to be seen and not heard?"

"Yes," she said a little pathetically, "but nobody *listens*."

On Christmas Eve they got out the sleds. There was a good long slope behind the house and, after some coaxing by the others and some grumbling on her part, even Ellie came out to slide and all of them were laughing and shouting and covered with snow.

It was a more wonderful Christmas than Rinie ever imagined. It would never have occurred to her to imagine one like it. At the Hickses', they had had decorations, beautiful ones, but they were all placed with a stiff precision, and the special holiday foods were almost exclusively for when company came. Before that, at the orphanage, there had been gaiety and anticipation and excitement, but the decorations and special foods and gifts were few and had to be meted out with such careful justice that the joy was a little dampened. Then, too, after Rinie was old enough to read, she felt that Christmas was empty, because in the stories it was always such a time of loving and happiness for families, even for those of the poorest children an author could conjure up. Or when, as sometimes happened, the child, or one of the children in a story was an orphan, it always somehow came to find a family at Christmas time.

Well, she had found her own family, and she sometimes thought they were almost more than she had bargained for, but she thought it with a happy smile. She wouldn't have had one of them changed for the world. In her imagination, Christmas with her family had always been a perfect gem of gentleness and love and beauty and tenderness. All those things were at Red Bear, but more in the nature of a rough, just-minded diamond than a perfect gem. Replacing a good deal of gentleness and tenderness was rough housing and harsh half-friendly language. There was hilarity instead of the more refined mirth and gaiety. Ellie said if a person got through Christmas here, they could stand just about anything.

The decorations would have been considered crude and makeshift by many, but, to Rinie, they were all the beauty one could wish for. They had found a nice pinion for a Christmas tree—Doyle said they ought not to cut trees because it let the soil erode—and it was trimmed with many things. There were still a few of the really beautiful, delicate ornaments that had belonged to A. J. and Jenny in the early years of their marriage, but mostly the decorations were things such as strings of popcorn and holly berries and ornaments cut from paper and colored with crayons. They brought mistletoe down from the woods and put it up everywhere and evergreen boughs festooned walls and mantel. The smell was something lovely to remember.

After supper on Christmas Eve, the men, with Travis in charge, made a wassail punch, which they called simply "the Christmas hooch." It took a lot of mixing and tasting and advice and argument and they mulled it in a big blackened kettle in the fireplace.

"It smells awfully strong," Rinie said. "What's in it?"

"I don't know," Carl said happily, "mostly hot whiskey."

"You know what the trouble is around here?" Doyle asked the room in general. "The trouble around here is that there's not enough girls to get kissed under the mistletoe."

Troy, who had been the chief punch taster and was still standing by the fire with a ladle, though he'd been given strict orders by Travis to leave it alone till it was ready, said hilariously, "You better watch where you kiss 'em under, little brother. All the ones around here is took."

Doyle grinned, but he said severely, "Don't be uncouth."

Troy snorted. "Well, now, Lawyer Stinson, I guess I'm about as couth as the next feller around here, prob'ly couther'n some."

Most of the punch was gone by the time they went to bed, so they had to make up some more the next day, because now it was really Christmas and time to celebrate. A. J. said it was dam' hard on the whiskey supply and did they think it grew on trees, but his rheumatism was bothering him a lot less than it had before all this celebrating business had got started.

The presents were opened and Ellie said there'd never been so many or such nice things. She grew very cross when she opened the package with the dress from Carl and Rinie.

A. J. was a little sad about the blue socks and scarf. Not that he wasn't proud to have them, but he guessed he'd been wrong about missy's condition, and he was disappointed. He'd like more grandchildren while he could enjoy them, and a kid of Buck's ought to be some young 'un. Besides, A. J. liked to get in on other people's secrets.

Carl gave Rinie some perfume and lotion and a beautiful little locket with a thin gold chain and tiny seed pearls encrusting the heart. She cried when she opened the little package and said she'd wear it always. He had thought of giving her a ring, her wedding band was thin and cheap, but a fancy ring might get in the way of her work and she'd have to leave it off a good deal of the time. When he saw the locket in the jeweler's window, he forgot about rings. It just looked like Rinie.

He didn't tell her Vanda had chosen the lotion and perfume. She had driven down to Belford on Saturday to do some shopping of her own, and Carl had asked her to. He just couldn't bring himself to go in someplace and ask to smell all that stuff, and no saleswoman knew Rinie, so he couldn't have trusted any of their judgments. He'd tell her, sometime, about Vanda, but he had a feeling it might make her a little less happy if he told her just now.

Rinie gave Carl a watch. She gave him a scarf and

socks, too, but the watch was what she had finally decided on as the something special. Not one Stinson had a watch. They told time by the clocks if they were in the house, or by the sun when they were outside. He didn't need a watch, but that made it all the more special. At first, in the jewelry store, she had thought a wrist watch. They were more fashionable, and one would look nice on his arm, but then she realized it would be completely impractical for someone who rode broncs and threw ropes as much of the time as he could, so she bought a pocket watch with a nice, sturdy chain, and, for a fob, she was delighted to find a tiny gold horse with its legs in the position of a dead run. But she was a little afraid Carl might feel about the watch as he had about the sweater, and she watched with a painful mixture of anticipation and apprehension as he opened the package. This was the first thing she had ever given him, and if he didn't like it . . . Carl wasn't the kind who could conceal things. His face registered almost everything he thought and felt, once you learned to read it, so she watched him closely.

At first he looked quizzical, getting to the box, then excited, incredulous, and finally, completely delighted, like a little boy getting just what he wanted. So it was all right, it was wonderful, and Rinie cried again.

They had a ham, one of the smoked ones, baked with spices and fruit juices, and a great many other things to go with it for Christmas dinner. While Ellie and Rinie worked in the kitchen, the men and children tried out the games that were new. The men started brewing their new batch of Christmas hooch. They all kept eating cookies and fruits and candies and wondering when dinner would be ready.

"Women don't do a thing but cook and wash dishes, times like this," Ellie said a little wearily, but she smiled. "I reckon it's worth it though."

For a period of over an hour, Carl dropped whatever he was doing every ten minues by his new watch, and came to kiss Rinie. When the interval seemed longer than usual and she peeked in to see what he was doing, he had fallen asleep on the floor in front of the fire.

While she stood there, in the doorway, under some mistletoe, Troy kissed her. But it wasn't a mistletoe kiss. He put his arms around her from behind and, pulling her head back, kissed her on the mouth. She pulled away from him, thankful no one had noticed. She felt anger with him, and sorry for him, too, as he walked past her muttering.

"I didn't mean . . . Rinie. . . ."

Carl slept until Doyle poked him somewhere while testing Kirby's new knife. They fought all over the house, with Troy and Kirby and Jeff joining in. Helen was playing in a corner with her doll and a new doll bed and things from Santa, too occupied with sudden motherhood to have time for such nonsense.

The scuffling woke A. J. who'd been dozing on the sofa most of the morning. He got up and tried the hooch and ate an orange and then dinner was ready.

The day after Christmas, the men got a young bull elk, up in the timber and a good way north of the house. A. J. didn't go and it was hard for him. When they had been gone less than two hours, he began pacing the floor as much as his joints would allow, looking covertly out the window to see if he could see them coming back. Jeff asked him to play a game of checkers and he consented, but checkers wasn't A. J.'s game, too much waiting around and figuring. He was so irascible, Ellie told him shortly, he oughtn't to play if he couldn't be a good sport, which made his patience even shorter. But Jeff didn't seem to mind. Rinie thought tenderly that Jeff must understand his grandfather's feelings at a time like this better than anyone else.

The next day, Theorn McLean came by for dinner—they were having elk steaks and told Theorn he was as good a fresh-meat scenter as Sutter Keane, and Theorn said he was even better because he'd had all that snow to contend with. He had come to tell them that the New Year's Eve party would be at the Forresters'.

The day before New Year's Eve, Carl and Troy and Doyle began trying to clear the road, having decided reluctantly that it wasn't going to warm up any and melt the snow. They had an improvised snow plow for the pickup, but it was hard going, particularly in the canyon, where the snow had drifted so badly.

Travis took no part in the road-clearing, saying that it didn't make any difference to him if he didn't leave Red Bear again until spring. But the other three, once it was begun, seemed to enjoy the work and they came in at suppertime ravenous, half-frozen, and laughing.

148

The party at the Forresters' was gay and lusty. Carl told Rinie that all the young people from the upper West Fork were there, except for those from the one or two families with really deep and definite religious convictions, and there were some from Greenfield and even a few from Belford.

"They like to come up here," Carl said smugly, "because there's more boys than girls."

Besides Rinie and Carl, there were two other married couples—June Tippitt, the schoolteacher, and her husband, Alva, and Supina Keane Fletcher with her husband of less than a week.

"I thought the Keanes were religious," Rinie whispered to Carl.

He nodded vigorously.

"But there's Doxy and Becky, besides Supina."

"Well, they can't git husbands by stayin' at home with their lights under bushels, Rinie. Sutter can always find a way of gittin' around things with God, I'll lay. I guess it's not so hard when you've got a real direct line."

The party went on until daylight and then the girls cooked breakfast. Some of the men, by that time, had fallen into deep sleep, induced by the New Year's hooch, which was basically the same as the Christmas hooch, and they refused to be wakened. The three Stinson boys were still awake and becoming a little volatile.

During the late hours of the night, Rinie had seen Doyle kiss Vanda and she was glad he had, but then she wasn't glad because he ignored Vanda for the rest of the time. Vanda's eyes couldn't stay away from him, though she tried not to let it be obvious, and sometimes she looked so miserable.

They had square-danced about half the time. It was Rinie's first experience at square-dancing and she loved it, though it seemed to make her tired faster than just about anything.

"I don't see why," Carl said. "All girls do is get slung from one guy to another. It's us ought to be tired."

Troy offered rides to almost everyone who lived up the valley, and several accepted—Theorn McLean, Doxy and Becky Keane, Bud Corbett—so there were seven to go in the Model T.

Carl said that Troy oughtn't to drive because he'd had too much to drink, and Troy said that if Carl wanted a car to wreck, he'd have to get his own. Rinie thought they were going to fight and she was a little frightened but mostly, she thought it was funny because they were both so deadly serious and said such crazy things, and almost anything seemed funny in the delightful exhaustion after a whole night of dancing.

Finally, Doxy said, "Let him drive, Troy. He's a ole married man now. You come set with me."

So the problem was solved. Troy held her on his lap, the car was crowded, and Theorn commented that things were getting interesting back there by the time they got to his house.

At Keane's, Doxy asked, obviously meaning only Troy, "Whyn't you come in a while? Mama's had to go to our Aunt Ethel's, an' daddy's still asleep." She giggled. "He sleeps real sound."

"Doxy, you're a doxie," said Doyle indolently.

Troy wasn't too steady on his feet, but he was getting happily out of the car with Doxy and Becky.

"Listen, Bo, you better come on home," Carl said. "I won't come back and git you."

"You can dam' well wait. It's my car. Doxy's been tellin' me about somethin' she wants to show me, or I been tellin' her, I forgit which."

"When Sutter wakes up, he'll put you to work."

"Hell with Sutter. Listen, Buck, there's two of 'em, Doxy, Becky, one, two. You come, too."

"You'll have to walk home."

"Oh, yeah. You can't come in. Well, Doyle, then."

"You're crazy," said the younger brother coolly.

"Come on, Troy," said Carl, beginning to get angry as Troy put a familiar hand on Doxy's shoulder and started up the path, paying no attention. "Goddam' it," he muttered and got out of the car.

"Oh, Carl, you ole mean thing," pouted Doxy as he took Troy be the arm.

"You Chrissakin' ole bastard," added Troy, but Carl didn't laugh.

"I dam' well ought to leave you," he said. "I think you've lost what little sense you ever had."

"I want to make love to a girl. What's wrong with that?" demanded Troy peevishly.

Doxy and Becky had retired to their front door, but

150

were listening and watching avidly, poking each other and giggling.

"You're drunk, that's what's wrong with it."

"Well, hellfire, Buck, that ain't no drawback. You're gittin' to act like some prissy ole lady. Just because you git all you want at home, you sonofabitch. . . ."

"Can't you do something?" Rinie pled with Doyle. She was frightened now. "They'll fight."

"Sure they will," said Doyle blandly, getting more comfortable on the seat.

Rinie wished Theorn and Bud hadn't both got out at Theorn's house. But, she thought angrily, they'd just have watched, too. She was on the verge of getting out of the car herself, but she knew Carl wouldn't like it. Besides knowing the way Troy felt about her made it such a delicate business.

Carl was saying reasonably, "You can't go into her house in broad daylight with her daddy and sisters there."

"She needs it," Troy said with conviction. "She's been askin' for it since she quit wearin' di'pers. It ain't as if I'd be the first."

"I didn't say you would, but you come on home an' sober up, an' then see if you can't think up a better arrangement. You'll see what I'm talkin' about when you—"

Troy knocked him down in the snow.

"Will you quit actin' like my keeper, Carlisle! You goddam, smart-alec kid."

Carl got up with blood spurting from his nose. He was mad. His eyes were almost gold with anger. Rinie had never seen him so mad like that. She thought she was going to be sick. The Keane girls squealed.

"Doyle," Rinie begged.

"Relax, missy. They almost always fight on New Year's."

Troy was mad, too. His blue eyes shot sparks.

Sutter Keane came rushing out in underwear and pants.

"Here now! That'll be enough a that. You boys quit."

He couldn't come down into the yard because there was snow and he was barefoot, and besides, he didn't want to.

"What's this about?" he demanded of his daughters.

"Oh, daddy, you know how boys are," simpered Doxy.

No one said anything all the way to Red Bear. Doyle whistled a little between his teeth. Troy drove. He had blood all over his face and his shirt was torn. Carl's nose was bleeding badly, all over the front of the brown-gold shirt Raine had finally made him, and his eyes dared her to say a word.

In the kitchen, Travis and A. J. and the children looked interested and Ellie looked resigned. Troy and Carl stood side by side at the sink, washing off blood, glaring at each other in the small cloudy mirror.

"Well," Travis mused, "it looks like the New Year's off to a good start."

"Them shirts'd better be put to soak," said Ellie.

"Have you a little car wreck, did you?" wondered A. J. with a quirk at the corner of his mouth. "Missy musta been drivin', I expect."

"Oh, hell, I'm goin' to bed," Carl said sullenly. His nose wouldn't seem to stop bleeding. Any minute now, Rinie was going to start making a fuss about it.

Troy said, with equal sullenness, "Well, I'm Christawful glad I don't have to sleep with you."

Carl turned and they glowered for a moment and then Carl's mouth began to quirk at the corner.

"Yeah," he said, "I guess Doxy is more your type."

Troy couldn't help grinning and that made him mad. He went to his room and slammed the door.

"Lord a-mercy," said Ellie, when Carl had gone, too, "I'm glad that's over with. I ought to know better after all this time, but them two scares me half to death the way they look when they're mad."

"You better set down, Rinie, an' drink some coffee," advised Travis. "You look a little peaked. I expect you had too much New Year's hooch for a little gal ain't used to it."

"You young 'uns go on about your business," A. J. ordered shortly.

"I got to wash my baby a dress," explained Helen.

A. J. looked irritably at her mother.

"Ellie, that young 'un argees. She always argees, whatever's said to 'er."

"Go on, Helen," Travis said, and she followed her brothers reluctantly into the front room.

Doyle told them about the fight and Ellie sighed, commending the combatants to the mercy of the Lord. A. J. said, "That dang Bojack ain't got the sense of a cross-eyed cow when he's drunk, not much more when he's sober. If he don't watch out, next thing we know, we'll have ole Sutter up here ready to make the match." He spat in the slop bucket and grinned. "If it was to ever come to that, Travis, you can be the one that han'les it."

Travis looked a little stunned. "Me! W'y, hell, A. J.—"

"Now wait. Listen. You're the oldest son. It's time you taken some real responsibility. You got them three a yourn comin' on, an' practice don't hurt nobody."

"It's a good thing Troy's goin' to Belford for a while, I expect," said Ellie.

A. J. said, "You're mighty quiet about this whole thing, missy. What you think about your man now?"

Rinie smiled a little. "I was just thinking how good his aunt Minna'd feel about this."

They all laughed and Doyle said, "Yes, just the kind of thing she always knew would happen."

When Rinie tiptoed into their room in mid-afternoon, Carl opened his eyes—one was a little swollen—and smiled at her ruefully.

"How is it out there?"

"Clear and sunny.

"You know I don't mean that."

She smiled. "Troy and the others are playing poker."

"He seem all right?"

"Well, his face is black and blue, like yours."

"I don't mean that either, Rinie," he said impatiently, pulling her down beside him, "an, you know it."

"He seems to be in a good mood," she said, when he stopped kissng her. "Why? Are you scared?"

"You know better'n that. It's just—well, he tends to hold a grudge longer'n I do. . . . Did you like the party?"

"Mm-hmm. Carl? Did you know how Vanda—feels about Doyle?"

He nodded.

"But you never said anything?"

"Well, things like that are kinda private, honey. I wouldn' like it talked about if I felt that way about somebody an' they didn' give a dam'."

"Oh," she said and was sorry she had been the one to bring it up. He was right, of course. It involved feelings too deep and important to Vanda for light discussion and speculation among her friends.

Carl said gently, "I didn't mean for you to be scared this mornin', Rinie. I wasn' gonna fight 'im."

"I know."

"Rinie?"

"What?"

"Do you know why he hit me first?"

"Yes." Her voice was small and they didn't look at each other.

"I never knew till I was layin' here thinkin' about it, just before you came in."

"Carl, I—I don't want to make trouble."

"It'll be all right, I guess," he said slowly. "He'll be goin' to Belford tomorrow for a while."

"But you won't be mad? I—I mean there's no reason—"

"No, but I'm glad he's goin' for a while. Now I see, it makes things look different, things I never noticed before. . . . It's kind of odd, too, that I didn' know. Bo always did want ever'thing. He used to want my marbles an' Doyle's, an' his, too . . . an' a bean flip I made once . . . he made one before I did so mine was newer . . . an' when Heddie was here after mama died . . . oh, hell, I better git up."

"Carl?"

"Hmm?"

"I love you."

He had been hurt and lonely sometimes, too. She could see it in his eyes. He held her fiercely.

"I don't blame him for wantin' you," he said vehemently. "I don't see how any man could help it, but all that time I was waitin', he knew about you an' he just never noticed."

"Don't let it make a difference," she said pleadingly. "It doesn't mean anything to me, and it won't last long for him."

After a while, she said, smiling, "Get up, Carl."

"What for?"

"Well, you haven't had anything to eat for one thing, and besides, you ought to look in the mirror at your nose."

9

It was a cold January. After Christmas, not much snow fell—A. J. said it was too goddam' cold to snow—but what was on the ground didn't melt. The eaves of the house dripped a little in the middle of the day when the sun shone, and the paths to barns and sheds and corrals and privy that they tried to keep shoveled were packed hard and slick. Sometimes Kirby was allowed to stay home from school, and Helen did fairly often, because of the severity of the cold.

At the end of January, the weather moderated—A. J. had said that it would—and Carl went out to see how the stock had fared in the cold. Rinie and Ellie were glad of a chance to hang out clothes to dry without having them freeze before they touched the clotheslines. Both women, all three children, and A. J. had colds. A. J. said that's what came of being housed up. He wanted badly to go out with Carl to look things over, but when he thought of the cold and damp creeping into his joints, he just couldn't do it. He had nothing but contempt for his deceitful, traitorous, aging body.

Jeff had been quite ill for several days with a high fever and a bad cough. It was easy for him to catch things, Ellie said, always had been. She made poultices and broths and was cross because she was worried. But Jeff was better now. He sat out in the healing sun, wrapped up in an old coat of Travis's while the women hung their clothes.

Carl didn't come back till the middle of the afternoon. He said things looked good, considering. He had found one cow that had calved before her time. Both she and the calf were skeletons with wolf and coyote tracks all over the place. He had seen deer and elk at several points and had caught a glimpse of three bighorn.

"Didn' you have no rifle?" demanded A. J. petulantly.

155

The boy was so goddam' young and healthy with his face red from riding in the wind. A. J., looking at him, could all but feel the breeze that riding made on a man's face this time of year, cold, but with such a fresh freedom brought down from the high, lonesome country that sometimes, riding all by himself, a man just had to holler or shoot off a gun or something.

"Well, yes, I had my rifle," Carl said thoughtfully, "but I—well, we got plenty of meat."

"A man your age ought to have sense enough to know it'll run out," said A. J. irritably. Carl had become twenty-four a few days ago and A. J. referred often to his age, mostly because the wish came so often that he could be twenty-four again.

Travis came in from the barn.

"Carl, I believe Skeeter's fixin' to foal."

Carl was about to sit down to the dinner Rinie had warmed up for him, but he put his jacket back on and said he'd just go see about her, get some straw down, and put her in a stall.

"I guess she is, all right," he said when he came back. There was a look of awe and anticipation in his eyes. Birth never stopped being a miracle. "I'll eat and then I guess I'll go back out there and keep an eye on her."

"Good God!" scoffed A. J. "You'd think there never was a mare foaled before."

Rinie went out as the sun was going down to take Carl a lantern. He was sitting on a rickety old chair outside Skeeter's stall, reading a book.

"How is she?" Rinie asked softly.

"All right, I guess. Kinda slow, but it usually is, the first time."

"Carl, I've never seen a little baby colt," she said, all but whispering. She stood beside him and his arm was around her. "I've never seen anything that's just been born or that's being born. Let me stay."

Skeeter had been rolling her eyes nervously at Rinie since she'd come in. Carl looked uneasily from his wife to the mare and back again.

"It'll be a good while yet," he said gently. "She's only just started, really. And it—it makes a female—any kind, I guess—jumpy to have people around that they don't know real well, a time like this."

"Oh," she said sadly. But then it was all right; she

156

smiled a little. "I—I guess I'd feel the same way. I could bring you some coffee, though, couldn't I?"

"I'll come in an' git some after a while. You oughtn't to be runnin' around in the cold. It'll make your cold worse. It's a hell of a time for a mare to foal anyway. That goddam' stud."

"I don't think she's sorry," Rinie whispered.

Carl came in after they had finished supper. A. J. and the children had gone to bed. Carl looked worried. He drank his coffee and didn't say much.

"I'll come out with you a while," said Travis when Carl got up and put on his jacket again.

Rinie looked fearfully, questioningly, at Ellie when they had gone out.

"I expect it's turned wrong," Ellie said quietly. "It happens with mares just like with every kind a female."

"Will she . . . will it?"

"They may can straighten it out. If they can't it's apt to go hard . . . We may as well go on to bed."

But they didn't. They sat on by the kitchen stove, not talking much. Ellie was mending and Rinie worked on a sweater she was knitting for Helen. Rinie wanted to go to the barn, but she didn't. Carl had told her not to, and she was afraid of facing the terrible combination of fascination and repulsion that was there.

Travis came in looking grim. He had to refill the lantern. The women waited.

"I don't think we can do it," he said grimly. "We even rigged a block an' tackle an' tried all we dared, but it won't come. Skeeter's bad."

He went away. After a while, Ellie said wonderingly, "You git to thinkin' they're so hard an' rough sometimes, till a thing like this comes along. . . . You know, Rinie, we got us two of the finest men in the world."

The clock in the front room struck two just before Travis came in again. He said harshly, "Where's the meat saw at, Ellie?" He didn't want to say it. "An' I want hot water an' whiskey an' whatever ole blankets you can spare."

Rinie didn't understand at first. She got up to help Ellie get the things together.

"The saw's in that cabinet," she said, "but what do you—"

"The foal's got to come," Travis said and left hurriedly.

"Oh . . . oh, no!" Rinie burst into tears, turning sick and shuddering all over.

After a little Ellie said, "It's like that sometimes. If they don't git the foal Skeeter'll be dead, too."

"But the colt . . . the little baby," pled Rinie, sobbing.

"It's a thing that happens, Rinie. There's no help for it."

"Oh, Carl! Oh, poor Carl! How can he bear it? Being out there. . . ."

"Car'll be all right," said Ellie with quiet firmness. "There's somethin' I wish you'd do, though."

Rinie looked up, through her tears, waiting.

"Go to bed, hon," said Ellie gently. "Course it's hard on Carl, an' he'll know it ain't easy on you, you never knowin' firsthand about things like this. It'll be better for him if he don't have to talk about it right off."

"But I wouldn't—"

"When a man's hurt, Rinie, it's bad on his pride for him to break down, at least for Stinson men. It's a thing they can't hardly git over. The breakin' down sticks in their minds longer'n whatever it was hurt 'em in the first place. Now if you was to be asleep, or play like you was, when he comes in, he wouldn' have to say a word about anything, or even look at anybody for a while, an' then he'd be all right, don't you see?"

After a while, Rinie reluctantly went to bed. Ellie was right, she could see that, but she wanted so desperately to hold Carl close and, just as desperately, she needed to have him hold her. She couldn't stop thinking, and the meat saw was so vivid before her eyes, even when they were closed in the dark bedroom, that she thought she couldn't bear it. It was terribly cold in there. She bunched the cover on top of her, huddled as small as she could. She even pulled Carl's pillow over her head and she cried with a crushing anguish. . . . Ellie's baby that just never did breathe . . . the two other graves of babies, up there on the knoll. The cow and her calf eaten by wolves. Skeeter . . . it was a hard, cruel country. What about her own child, not even conceived yet? What kind of chance did it, did any tiny helpless thing, have in this great, wild, loneliness.

Finally, exhausted by her emotions, Rinie slept a little

and when she woke, it was to the sound of breakfast preparations in the kitchen. She got up hurriedly. Her legs were stiff and aching from the position in which she slept. She felt ashamed that she had been able to sleep at all.

Carl was there in the kitchen, his hands straining on the coffee cup he held between them. Rinie went to him, timidly, and put her hand on his shoulder. He put his arm around her and looked up for just a moment, then away.

"Oh, Carl, I'm so—sorry." She bit her lips hard. She was sorry as much because she was so helpless as about the foal. "Is—is Skeeter all right?"

"No," he said dully. "I don't think she'll live."

He couldn't eat, and in a little while he went back to the barn. Rinie followed him later, but she couldn't bear it for long. That animal lying on the bloody straw wasn't Skeeter, not that lovely, shining black horse that had followed Carl around the corrals, nickering and laying her head over his shoulder.

He had her covered with all the horse blankets, trying to save what meager warmth her body could provide, but even covered like that, it was incredible how emaciated she looked, as though she'd been sick a long, long time. Her coat was dull, her eyes sunken, unseeing. She breathed slowly, shallowly, with a heavy groaning. Now and then, her legs jerked spasmodically.

Carl sat on the straw by her head, staring at nothing, one hand in her mane. He'd done all he knew, all Travis and A. J. knew. They had got her up on her feet, trying to get the colt born, and after they were through with it, they'd got her up again, using the block and tackle because she was too exhausted to stand by herself. He'd tried to give her warm mash but she couldn't eat, so he'd held her head while Travis poured whiskey and warm water into her, and they covered her and kept her on her feet. For a little while, she'd seemed better and he had thought it would be all right for her to lie down. But now. . . .

"I can't leave her," he said to Rinie. She hadn't said a word since she came in. She just stood there, looking small and hurt and scared. "I know she's just a horse an' all the rest of it, but I can't."

"I know, Carl," she said brokenly. "I just wish there was something. . . . "

"It's my fault." The words were a helpless cry. "I waited too long about the foal. I kept thinkin' . . . It was a colt, a sorrel like the stallion, goddam' him to hell."

He flexed his hands, trying to rid them of the feel of the saw. She stood there, helpless. There was nothing to be done, or even said.

Kirby and Helen went to school. Ellie and Rinie started on the ironing. Jeff wanted to go to the barn, but Ellie wouldn't let him. It was the first time Rinie had seen Jeff cry.

A. J. sat in the front room, alone, close up to the fire. He couldn't seem to get warm all the way through, though it was a good deal warmer today than many of the days just past. He remembered a red-roan gelding he'd had once, when he was a boy back in Texas, younger than Buck was now. He hadn't thought of old Chili for a long, long time.

Carl came in just as the sun was dropping behind the barren rock ridge to the west, and they knew that Skeeter was dead. He was haggard and exhausted. He hadn't eaten since the middle of yesterday afternoon. He said, "How long till supper?"

"Oh, thirty minutes, about," said Ellie brusquely. "You must be needin' food, I guess."

"I—could I have the kitchen to myself a few minutes? I want to wash."

They waited in the front room and in a little while he opened the door, dressed in clean clothes, with his hair painstakingly plastered down, though it was already beginning to escape as the water dried.

He sat at the table and filled his plate and talked with A. J. and Travis about how cattle prices might be in the fall. Kirby told them he had heard at school that at Hunters, way up on the West Fork, they'd heard the mountain lion squall three nights ago and the next morning had found a yearling dead. The government hunter wanted to go after the cat, but there was too much snow.

"I hope he don't git 'im," said Kirby fervently. "I want us to."

With his eyes, Carl kept asking Rinie for more coffee and she kept pouring it for him. He felt colder inside than he had that night he'd come home in the storm, soaking wet and icing up from the creek . . . that night Skeeter. . . .

He said, "We ought to clear off some of the creek ice to slide on."

"Yeah, le's do," clamored the children eagerly.

"Tomorrow," he said, "I will."

Helen said that Mary Keane said that Supina and her husband had moved in with the Keanes.

"Well, now that must just tickle Sutter to death," A. J. said gleefully. "He thought he got rid of one, but got two or so instead."

"At least," said Travis, "maybe Miss Essie an' the girls can git the son-in-law to help out with chores. That's more'n Sutter ever done."

"That's all right," Carl said. "Sutter goes out an' brings home the bacon." But he didn't smile. His eyes were bleak.

"Wonder when Troy'll be home," mused Kirby. "Maybe we can go after the lion again then."

"He said not till the end of February," recalled Travis.

A. J. said crossly, "Buck, if you ain't gonna do nothin' but drink, drink somethin' that'll do you some good."

"No, I guess not tonight," Carl said. "I think I'll just go to bed." He stood up slowly. It hurt to move, he was so tired.

Rinie looked miserably at the closed bedroom door.

Ellie said briskly, "There's some a that broth left that I made when the kids was sick. I'll heat it up an' you take some in there to 'im. It's real heart'nin'."

He didn't want the soup. The smell of it sickened him, but her eyes were so pleading. He sipped a little. Somehow, it was hotter than the coffee and it felt good inside him.

"It's good," he said sh ly, feeling ashamed that he was so upset.

She took the bowl when he'd had all he wanted, and stood there, hesitant, wistful.

"Don't got back out there," he said trying to smile. "They'll want you to wash dishes or things like that."

She put the bowl down and came close to him, crying now because he wanted her with him. He was through with the really lonely part now, or most of it.

He was sitting up in bed with a blanket over his shoulders. She put her arms around him, standing there, and held him gently, like a child. He leaned his face against her breast and felt the pain let go a little.

She stayed with him and it was not long before he slept, but all through the night he dreamed, sometimes shuddering and whimpering. Rinie lay close to him. His misery made her cry, but she was thankful he couldn't know how completely he was revealing his hurt.

They cleared snow off the creek ice to skate. It was really only sliding because they had no skates, but it was fun. There was a good place for the sleds, where they could come down a long, regular slope, across the cleared ice and partway up the bank on the other side. They tried to see who could get the farthest up the other side and Kirby almost always won. While he was having another try, Carl grabbed the tow rope of the big toboggan and Rinie's mittened hand.

"Come on," he said and they started plowing uphill, pulling the toboggan with them as fast as they could.

"I wish Jeff could sled," she panted. "It's so hard to see him always just watching."

"We used to pull him around some," Carl said. "It's too hard on him to slide and hit rough places, but he feels like he's too old to be pulled around now. He's not, if he wanted it, but I'm glad he's proud. Do you know what he told me today?"

She shook her head.

"He said he wants to be a veterinarian. He says he decided because of Skeeter an' the colt."

It had been nearly three weeks now since the mare died.

"I don't see why he can't do it, or whatever he might change his mind to later on," Carl said defiantly. "We can all work for the money it would take."

"Maybe your Aunt Minna—"

"Oh, she can go to hell. I hope Jeff's generation won't have to have anything to do with her."

"I always wondered why you lived that year in Denver," she said hesitantly.

"I don't know," he said a little wonderingly. "I've always wondered about that myself. I guess I just wanted to see what it was like. I'd found out more than I wanted to by Christmas time an' I was all set to stay at Red Bear when I came home, only, somehow, I didn't. I guess I couldn't let them, A. J. or Minna or any of them, think I was givin' up."

"Carl?" Climbing through the deep snow, pulling the toboggan, made it hard to talk. "I—I feel sorry for her. I don't think she's ever been happy, not in her whole life. Neither has Mr. Hicks, maybe."

He slipped a little, looking at her face. She looked older and it wasn't a drawback. She looked less vulnerable, less childish, and he felt a little easier about how she was going to deal with life. He said unsympathetically,

"People pretty much make their own lives. It's not hard to see why she's not happy."

"But some time"—she tried hard—"there must have been some time when she could have turned out all—different."

"Well, anyway, about Jeff," he said. "He can go to school as well as anybody if he can just git there. Travis an' Ellie have got to do somethin'."

"Yes," she agreed, panting, "but it's so hard to send him away and he already knows more than he could learn at Webber."

"The doctor in Denver that time told them about a special hospital for crippled children where they might have helped him some. I always wished they'd of let him go, only it wasn't my affair. But if—if he was ours, I'd want it."

She said slowly, "In just a few days we'll be married six months. Carl? You don't think there's—anything wrong. . . ."

"No," he said with finality. "Now, come on. You're not a hell of a lot of help with this thing."

"But where are we going?"

"Just up here a ways."

"It must be clear to the ridge," she said dryly. "I have to get back to help with supper."

"Hell with supper. You have to do what I tell you."

She grabbed a handful of snow to rub in his face. He took it away from her and they went on—after he'd kissed her.

"I ought to teach you to snowshoe," he said. "It makes you sore in all kinds of odd places, but it's fun when you git used to it. I don't know why I haven' even had my snowshoes out this winter. A. J. says it's no way for a ranchin' man to git around, but it beats a horse all kinds a ways in deep snow."

"Carl, don't you think A. J. ought to see a doctor?"

"It wouldn' do him any harm, but he'd dam' sure think it would. He'll be all right, or at least better, I think, when the weather warms up an' dries out. . . .

"Rinie, talkin' 'bout snowhoes made me think of Heddie. She's the one taught us how to make 'em an' use 'em right. . . . One day soon, I'm gonna take those skins down an' ask 'er to make some stuff. Will you come with me? I'd like you to."

"Oh . . . I don't know, Carl. I think. . . ."

"You can tell me what you decide when I'm ready to go down," he said easily. "Now le's git this thing turned around."

She looked back. "All that way?"

He nodded happily.

"But through those trees?"

"Sure, that's the best part. It's real steep there."

"Oh." She stood still, doubtful.

"Listen, you know about this thing. You just lean when I lean. That's all there is to it, an' we'll end up right by the back door. Well, come on! You don't want to walk all that way back."

After the first moment, she kept her eyes closed, clinging to him in wild terror and exhilaration. When the swooping, almost flying, ride ended with an upset because he forgot about the privy path until it was too late to avoid it, they lay in the snow together, half-hilarious with laughter, half-wild with sudden violent desire.

"A. J. keeps tellin' us we don't need that shoveled," he said, laughing, and his voice went husky. "Rinie, Rinie. . . ."

"Carl, they'll see," she whispered, pressing against him.

"What the hell? There's nothin' for anybody to look at. Men and women lay around in the snow a lot. You see 'em all over the place."

He was kissing her, his mouth hard and warm. She made a little whimpering sound, lying against him, and his breath caught harshly.

"I guess we better git up," he said hoarsely. "Somebody might think we're hurt."

"Besides, it's cold here," she said dreamily.

"I never noticed that," he said.

They got up reluctantly and began brushing snow off each other.

"Now I'll tell you," he said, smiling at her proudly, "that me an' Troy used to make that run, but Doyle never would because he was afraid. You're a pretty brave little kid."

Their brushing of one another was getting rougher and rougher.

"Was it as much fun with Troy?"

"Well, this was sort of—different." And she was in his arms again.

"Six months," he said musingly. "I won't git any work done next spring an' summer if we're gonna keep gittin' worse this way."

"Remember what you told me about grabbing good things with both hands?" she said, digging her fingers into his shoulders. "I almost never feel afraid of being happy now."

"I'm glad an' I love you, but dam'! That hurts."

"I'm gittin' right tired of snow," Ellie said. It had been snowing frequently for a week, ever since the day Troy had come home.

The morning of that day had been warm and nearly springlike with snow melting everywhere. Carl came in after some cleaning in the barn and said that he was going to take the skins down to Heddie when he changed clothes. He said it privately to Rinie while she was sweeping in the front room, so that she needn't worry about the others knowing her decision.

"I'll be ready," she said, "when I finish in here and get my clothes changed."

The footing was tricky for the horses, with slush on top of unmelted snow, but Carl said old Jim had never stumbled in his life. Carl rode Daylight. The gelding needed handling, and Carl was beginning to yearn for a little action. Daylight behaved reasonably well, needing a tight rein only about halfway down to Webber, and when he did act up, feigning fear of a snow shower that slid off a boulder as they passed beneath it, bucking a little and flinging up great spurts of slush, Rinie was hardly even apprehensive and Carl felt good.

"I guess I'll have to try an' make a decent cow horse of 'im," he said fondly. "He might be all right if I can ever make him quit playin'."

Rinie smiled a little, wondering who enjoyed the playing most.

Heddie's home was a one-room cabin across the river from most of the other buildings of Webber. There was smoke coming out of the chimney. Rinie was sorry. She had determined to meet the woman with as little prejudice as possible, because it was important to Carl, but she dreaded the meeting.

Heddie stood in the doorway as they rode up, a short, broad woman with a face that was still good-looking in a haunting, secretive way; sharp, piercing black eyes, and gray-streaked black hair in braids wound around her head. Rinie thought her hair must be very long when it was let down.

Heddie didn't smile, but there was a fond look in her eyes when she recognized Carl.

He helped Rinie down.

"Heddie, this is Rinie. Rinie, Heddie St. Claire."

There was frank curiosity in Heddie's eyes as she looked Rinie over. Rinie thought, she's the one that ought to feel uneasy, not me.

Heddie said, "Carl tole me long time back he was married. He never said you was so pretty. You come in." Her voice was deep. She spoke laconically and with authority.

The cabin contained a bed, a stove, a table, two chairs. From hooks on rafters and walls hung bags and bundles of Heddie's herbs. There was a strange but not unpleasant smell. She indicated that her guests were to sit on the chairs.

"I git you coffee."

This was the woman, Rinie thought sadly, who had replaced Jenny. Bright-eyed, blonde, pretty Jenny, whom Carl remembered singing songs and that A. J. said was the proudest thing he'd ever seen, and this cold stolid woman had been the only mother the boys had had for four years. Why when Jenny had died, Carl had been younger than Helen was now. What could this woman have done to comfort him? To compensate for the mother he had lost? Rinie felt stifled in the little cabin. Probably, Heddie had washed, cleaned the house a little sometimes. No doubt, she had kept sufficient food on the table, but love? Perhaps, love of a kind for A. J., but Rinie couldn't imagine her being gay, singing songs, picking up a child and hugging it just for the joy of its being alive.

"I brought an elk hide an' a couple of pigskins, Heddie," Carl was saying, as she gave them coffee. "Troy would like to have a jacket out of the elk an' I'd like some pigskin gloves. You use the rest for whatever you feel like."

She nodded. "Pigskin gloves are good, ridin' horses in cold weather, thin so the reins handle easy, but warm. . . . It's good you come today. Tomorrow I go up to Hunter's to stay awhile."

Why would anyone want her around in sickness? Rinie wondered incredulously. She was so dour and depressing, and she wasn't clean. Why even the coffee cup Rinie held was not clean.

"I'll go put the skins in your shed," Carl said, and Rinie felt angry. She had only come to please him. Why must he leave her alone with this woman?

"He's good," Heddie stated when he was gone. "All of them are good boys, but he's the best. He don't forgit an' not have time."

There was a little silence and Rinie asked awkwardly, "Is—is Mrs. Hunter sick?"

"No," said Heddie carelessly. "She gonna have her ninth baby in a week or two. She sent word for me to come on up there before the snow gits bad agin."

Rinie shivered involuntarily. When I have a baby, she won't touch me, she thought with revulsion.

"How long you an' Carl been married now?"

"Since August."

Heddie looked at her significantly. Rinie flushed with anger and thought she was going to cry and Carl came back.

"We have to go, Heddie," he said, quickly sizing up the situation in the cabin. "We thought we'd stop by the school for a while. I think there's snow comin' by the looks of the clouds."

"How's A. J.? I heard his rheumatism's bad."

"It's pretty bad," Carl said soberly.

She went to a corner and brought back a little bag.

"You make some tea with this, just a spoonful in about a quart of water. Make him drink some, boilin' hot, mornin' an' night."

"*Make* him drink it," Carl laughed. "You know how he is about medicine."

167

She grunted. "Well, put some whiskey with it an' tell him Heddie says."

This last outraged Rinie. It sounded so possessive, so intimate.

She had been looking forward to the visit to school, which they had decided on, riding down, but now she felt as bleak and dismal as the clouds coming over the mountains to the north and west, spoiling the lovely day.

Carl was disappointed. He had hoped to accomplish some sort of understanding, but there was only obstinate outrage in Rinie's eyes. Well, he guessed he'd have to let it go. There wasn't anything else he knew of that could be done.

At school, they were treated to one of the first rehearsals of an Easter play the lower grades were to present, about the Easter Bunny and his family. Helen was Mrs. Bunny. She was pleased with having members of her family present to the point of being obnoxious.

"You an' June had a lot to talk about," Carl said as they rode along. He made himself a cigarette. Daylight was behaving beautifully, almost too well. "I didn' plan on bein' playground supervisor durin' recess."

Rinie had been thoughtfully silent since they'd left the school. He didn't believe she was thinking about Heddie now. Sometimes she looked pleased, sometimes doubtful, sometimes a little scared. She said slowly, "June's going to have a baby in the fall."

Carl grinned. "Helen was right then, just a little previous."

"Carl, she—she asked if I could come and help out with the younger children from Easter till the end of school."

"She did? Well, what did you say?"

"I don't know. I—I mean, I told her I didn't know. Carl, I'd love to but—"

"How would you git there?"

"Well, I hadn't even thought of that, but I could ride Jim, of course. Couldn't I?"

"There'll be a lot of bad weather between now an' the end of school, Rinie."

"Yes, but I . . . you don't want me to do it?"

"I'm just talkin' about the weather. Sure, I want you to do it, if you want to. Do you?"

"I'm afraid to," she said diffidently. "I think I'd like it so much, working with those little kids, but I don't know anything about teaching. She'd help me, of course. She says they're just getting a little too much for her, now that she isn't feeling so well. She even offered to pay me. Carl, I never realized that so few people around here have high-school diplomas. June says that Vanda and I are the only women to have them and aren't too tied down to help, and Vanda's in Denver at her sister's."

"It looks like you better do it, then," he said proudly.

"But I—I ought to be there to help Ellie."

"You ought to quit tryin' to think up excuses, if this is somethin' you want to do. Ellie'll think it's fine. I never thought I was marryin' me a schoolmarm."

"Carl? Please . . . don't say anything at home yet. I told June I'd send word by Friday, what I decided. I have to think about it some more."

Daylight came unstrung then. Carl didn't even know what it was that spooked him—not that it really took anything. He was all but thrown on the first jump because it came as such a surprise.

"You sonofabitch," he said and spurred the horse happily. "You might as well git it out a your system."

When Daylight and Carl were through, Rinie said hesitantly, "Why did you want me to see Heddie?"

He took a long time answering.

"I thought it might be you wondered about her. What she's like."

"What did she mean that you take time and don't forget?"

He looked embarrassed. "Sometimes, I stop by and cut some wood, or take her a quarter of venison. Lots of people do."

"Does Travis?"

"No, but—"

"Does Troy?"

"Well, when he thinks of it, but he's always got other things. . . ."

"Carl, promise me something."

"What?"

"If ever I'm sick, I don't want her near me."

"Rinie, she's—"

"I can't help it," she said, close to tears. "I couldn't stand it."

"She's just an old woman now—an old woman that knows a hell of a lot about takin' care of the sick. Whatever you think about what happened when mama died, remember it was all a long time ago."

"I know that, Carl, but I can't help the way I feel." She was painfully earnest. "Please promise."

"All right, Rinie, but it might be you'll change your mind."

That sounded almost threatening and she was silent, the day seeming bleak and cold again, though the clouds hadn't quite reached Red Bear yet.

And when they came to the upper ford, they found Troy there, the back wheels of his Model T through the ice. They had to hitch Jim and Daylight to the bumper to drag the car out. Both horses were outraged. Troy said irritably they were going to have to do something about the dam' ford, but he was glad to be home. He didn't like being tied down there the way Travis always had and the way Carl didn't seem to mind lately, but he was always glad to get back.

It snowed that night and the next day and intermittently for a week and Ellie was tired of it. School was closed. It wasn't that it was so cold now; it was simply that the roads were so choked with snow. Everyone said how they hadn't seen this much snow on the ground in a long time.

"One thing to be thankful for, though," said Ellie, "is that it ain't real cold. Lord, I hate to think how it'd be if we had them men an' kids right under foot all the time. As it is, you can't sweep or cook or wash or do one bloomin' thing without havin' it poked into by two or three know-it-alls."

"Ah, El," said Troy cajolingly. "You need a little fun an' relaxation. We ought to have us a party or somethin'."

Ellie grunted. "It looks to me like that's what you been havin' all this time."

Rinie didn't mind the snow at all. She was glad of it. Carl was getting restless. He had mentioned that Corbetts', near Webber, Perrymans', way up the West Fork, and Frasers', down the valley, all had horses for him to break, not a lot like Mr. Forrester, just some of their own for their own use. But as long as there was all this snow, he'd stay close to home.

Carl and Troy and Travis and Kirby got out their snowshoes and dragged sleds loaded with hay far enough from the house so that the half-wild cattle and horses would come and eat it. the stock was getting pretty gaunt with all the snow.

They tried to teach Rinie to snowshoe, but she couldn't seem to get the hang of it and kept getting tripped up. None of them had much patience with a slow learner but she didn't mind. There were plenty of other things to do.

They kept clearing the strip along the creek to slide on and the sleds and toboggan got a lot of use.

Once when Troy and Carl and Rinie were tobagganing down the long, steep slope through the trees, they upset somehow and Troy banged his head against a pinion trunk. He lay there dazed for a moment and Rinie came near fainting, it frightened her so badly.

"You're always doin' that," Carl said impatiently, rubbing his brother's face with snow, "hittin' your head on somethin', an' now I've got a girl that turns green at the sight of blood." But it scared him, too. He was white and his hands shook.

"Shut up," Troy mumbled groggily. "You caused the dam' thing to turn over an' quit throwin' snow in my face. Don't you think I had enough snow?" He sat up dazedly, blinking to make things stop spinning.

"You—you better come and get something on your head," Rinie said shakily.

"Yeah," Carl agreed. "You're bleedin' an' gettin' the snow all messed up."

They built a gigantic snowman in the backyard, one so huge they had to have a ladder to stand on to finish his head. Helen named him Jack the Giant, and Ellie said she was half-afraid to go the toilet past that thing. But then Troy and Kirby came down the toboggan slide and smashed into Jack—some said deliberately—and had to have help digging out from under the demolished behemoth.

They made a snow fort to fight behind and that was one game Jeff could join in. He couldn't throw very far because the effort hurt his back, but he had almost perfect aim at closer ranges and patience—lacking in the others—to wait until the foe was near.

"I swear, Rinie, you might a been born a Stinson," Ellie marveled, but it did her good to see the girl so happy.

Carl and Troy and Kirby went hunting on their snowshoes and came back with several rabbits.

"They're about the only things can stay on top a the dam' stuff," Troy said, "besides us. Deer an' elk an' all are yarded up and the meat wouldn't be worth carryin' down anyway."

Rinie and Ellie were getting supper that night when there was a commotion in the front room and Travis, in the doorway, said urgently, "Look here, girls."

Across the creek, out on the flats where they had put some of the hay, there was a big buck deer. They could see him from the front windows. He hadn't come up to the hay, there were three or four cows around, but he stood with one delicate hoof raised as though arrested only momentarily in his progress toward it. He was looking straight at the house, not seeming frightened or worried about it, just looking, and the sun, almost down, glinted off his antlers.

Moving as quickly and cautiously as his joints would allow, A. J. grabbed his .30-30 off the wall, checked it, eased out the door and around to the corner of the front room.

Almost before it came to Rinie what the old man was doing, the shot was fired. The buck raised his head—it wasn't a jerk, just a kind of quizzical gesture—and then he dropped. Rinie gasped, put her hand to her mouth, and ran.

Carl left her alone for a while and then he followed her into the bedroom and put a blanket over her where she lay, crumpled, on the bed.

"Rinie, honey, don't cry like that."

"Oh, Carl, it was so beautiful! And then he—he had to kill it."

He sat on the bed and put his hand on her hair.

"The buck didn't have any pain," he said slowly, "not a bit. He won't ever git old now, an' stiff an' sore. He won't have to go hungry. He won't ever have wolves and coyotes after him when he's sick an' weak. Rinie, it's better to die quick."

She sobbed miserably. "It's so hard and cruel. Everything about this country is so—so—sometimes I can't. . . ."

He drew her up so that she lay in his arms, against his breast, and he laid his cheek on her hair.

"It won't be long till you'll see it soft," he said gently. "When the calves an' the foals are born, an' all the wild things, an' the birds come back, an' ever'thing gits green. Don't hate it. It's not had a chance yet."

She put her arms around him, the pain and horror melting out of her. How could she hate the country? She might never really love it or understand it, or stop being afraid of it, but to hate it would be like hating something about Carl.

He said reluctantly, "Anyway, I'm afraid A. J. may not ever be able to hunt again. This may be his last deer an' it's important to him. He's just a born hunter an' it hurts him so bad to be old. I don't think he ever really believed it could happen to him till just lately."

"Oh," she murmured. She hadn't thought about that, and now Carl looked nearly as troubled as A. J. must feel sometimes.

"Come on," he said, kissing her. "Ellie'll need you to help dish up supper."

Troy had gone out and got the deer and dressed it. He and Carl started reminiscing about a trapline they used to have.

"I wish I could do that," Kirby said.

"Hell, there's no reason why you can't," Troy told him. "The traps are still out there somewhere in one a the sheds."

"It sure wouldn't hurt to git rid a some a the coyotes," said Travis.

"You reckon I could make me a lot of money?" said Kirby, getting excited.

"There's a bounty on coyotes," Carl said.

"No, but I mean *furs*."

"Oh, Kirby, for Chrissake, you know there's not much fur left around here," Troy said impatiently. "You sound like Doyle, all the time dreamin' about stuff that can't be. Quit bein' so lazy an' do what you *can* do. I'll help you fix up the traps if you want to use 'em, an' show you how to take care of any hides you do git that's worth keepin'."

"What would you do, son, if you had a lot of money?" Travis said.

Kirby stared dreamily into the gravy bowl. "I'd git me some boots made outa kangaroo hide."

They stared at him.

"I seen some at a store in Belford," he said reverently. "An' I'd git spurs made outa silver—all the way through— an' a .30-30 that'd be just mine."

There was silence except that A. J. spat into the slop

bucket. These were worthy wishes for a boy of thirteen, the men thought, and needed no comment.

Helen said, "I'd git me a .22 an' shoot it whenever I wanted to, if I had lotsa money."

"Thank God you ain't got a penny. That doll business didn't last long."

"Yes, I have, daddy. Doxy give me a nickel last time we was at church."

"She did? Well, now, what for?"

"Oh, she just said I was a nice little girl."

"You oughtn't to take money that-a-way," reproved her mother.

The men were all looking at Troy, grinning.

"The best way to a man's heart ain't through his niece," he said, eating undisturbed.

"Well, it ain't through his stummick, neither, I don't care what they say," proclaimed A. J. He was feeling good tonight. He was taking the medicine Heddie had sent, though he tried to prepare it secretly, and he couldn't say if it was that or the whiskey he laced it with, but something was loosening his joints up a little. He felt good about the deer, too, even if it was just a yard shot. The meat wasn't worth much of anything this time of year, but the buck had had a good rack on him, something worth keeping, and a man had to do something once in a while to stir up the man in him a little, even when he'd got to be nearly seventy.

"Anyway, Helen," said Ellie, "you are a little girl an' I wish you'd act like one. Why would a little girl want an ole .22 for?"

"To shoot with."

"What would you get, Jeff?" Rinie asked.

"Oh, I don't know. Books, maybe."

"You read all the ones in the box?" asked Carl.

"Well, all but the ones that make you kinda sick, like *Wuthering Heights* an' them. Doyle told me about the library at college. I'd like to see that many books all together."

While the women washed the dishes, A. J. decreed that a bottle should be opened. Whiskey was running low, but he was in a magnanimous humor. If it didn't thaw soon, one of the boys could snowshoe down to Webber—and get some more whiskey. And if it did thaw, somebody could ride down. Maybe he'd do that himself.

Troy sighed restlessly, looking into his whiskey glass. "Le's do somethin', Buck."

Carl yawned. "Like what?"

"Well, hell, I don't know, burn the house down or somethin'. It's too dam' peaceable."

"We wouldn' have any place to sleep," Carl objected soberly.

"Le's see who can stand on our heads longest," suggested Kirby, and they tried, Kirby and Carl and Troy and Helen, and Helen won.

"Le's play poker," said A. J. "You boys ain't never gonna grow up."

So they did that, while Jeff and Kirby played checkers and the women sewed. Helen decided to try making a dress for her doll, but she couldn't abide her own mistakes and gave up shortly.

"Just like a Stinson," muttered Ellie in disgust. "Ain't got the patience of a bobtail bull."

After a while, Rinie fixed popcorn and A. J. consented to another bottle being opened, provided the ladies would drink, too. Helen said she would.

"I believe it's fixin' to thaw," predicted A. J. He was sleepy and fairly comfortable with his boots off and his feet up on a chair by the fire. "We'll not have no more real cold weather, maybe not too much more snow."

"It's not the middle of March yet," Carl pointed out mildly.

"Don't make no difference," snapped the old man curtly. "When you've had as much to do with the weather as I have, you might maybe know somethin' about what it's aimin' to do."

"I've lived in Colorado nearly as long as you have," Carl observed, his mouth quirking.

"You been a smart-alec a good bit a that time, too," said his father. "Do you think 'cause your woman's about to be a schoolmarm it means you got any more sense?"

Rinie still felt shy and hesitant about helping at school, but she had sent word to June Tippitt that she would. The family was full of pride in her and she really looked forward to it, only . . . what if she couldn't? What if the children didn't like her? Or wouldn't mind?

Ellie said, "You kids go on to bed now if you're through with your popcorn. It's late."

"There won't be no school tomorrow," Kirby observed.

"We have to go anyway," Helen said resignedly. "They want to git drunk."

"Right here in the catalog," observed Travis, who was thumbing through it, "they got a popcorn popper that's electric."

"Just what we need," Troy said dryly. "Ellie, when Rinie starts teachin' school, does she have to go to bed early, too?"

"An' a thing to toast bread in," marveled Travis, "an' a mixer to stir up batter."

"Le's say tongue twisters," said Carl. "Like: Betty Botter bought some butter—"

"Who did?"

"Betty Botter, Bo. You remember?"

"Oh, yeah, Betty. What'd she do?"

"Bought some butter to put in her—"

"They got the electric line up as far as Fraser's," Travis said.

"Wouldn' that be somethin'?" mused Ellie, "If we'd ever git it up here."

"Did Minnie have one a them popcorn things?" asked A.J. Rinie said she hadn't.

"We ought to git one then."

"An' invite her over for popcorn," said Troy and Carl said with butter and Troy agreed that it wouldn't be right without that.

Travis got the bottle and replenished everyone's drinks. Troy got up and wound the phonograph.

"What'll it be, Rinie? Bob Wills or Ernie Tubb or Glen Miller?"

"Oh, I don't know," she said happily, but he knew she preferred the dance band to the western group so he chose that. He was about to put the needle on the record when A. J. held up his hand.

"Wait, Bojack! Listen at that."

They all strained to hear.

"What?"

"That wind," said A. J., grinning complacently. He eased his feet down off the chair and trod to the door in his socks. He threw open the door triumphantly, and the wind, developed to a strong breeze, blew straight in upon them.

"Buck, you feel that?"

"Yessir, I do, an' it's goddam' cold."

"Which-a-way's it from?'

"It's from the south, A. J. You win. Just shut the door."

"House'll be drippin' in a hour with a wind like that," said the old man smugly.

"It'll be one Christ-awful mess if alla this melts at onct," said Travis worriedly.

"Well, I'm goin' to bed," said A. J. contentedly. "I guess I know when it's fixin' to thaw, don't I, boy?"

"I guess you caused me to waste a whole paper fulla tobacco, openin' that door like that," muttered Carl.

"Are you gonna leave us this bottle?" asked Troy incredulously.

"Oh, hell, I reckon so," said the old man magnanimously.

"He can afford to be generous," Carl said wryly, "bein' right all the time like he is."

As A. J. trod heavily toward the kitchen, Ellie said solicitously, "Don't forgit your medicine."

"Medicine!" snorted A. J. "I ain't takin' no medicine. I'm just gonna look out the back door, see how the weather is on that side of the house."

"Lord, it's good to see him feelin' pert again," said Ellie fondly.

"He was cheatin' like hell in that poker game," said Troy. "The old son of a sawbuck."

They danced for a while and finished the whiskey.

"I'm ready for bed," said Ellie drowsily. "A. J.'ll be up at four in the mornin' to watch the house drip. . . . Carl, what in the world are you doin'?"

"Puttin' wood on the fire, Miss Ellie."

"Well, you ain't got to burn the house down, have you? My land! Look at that blaze."

"I like it," Carl said with gusto and he and Rinie sat on the floor in front of the fire with their arms around each other. Troy lay on the sofa and Travis and Ellie sat holding hands.

They were all silent for a time, looking at the fire. The wind was picking up. It made the blaze waver and flare.

"It's dam' hot," Travis said, after a time.

"You just ain't the romantic sort," said Ellie.

"Well, El, don't that depend on what he's talkin' about?" asked Carl innocently.

"I remember," said Troy with a happy grin, "I musta been about six. A. J. come home drunker'n a hootowl,

177

him an' Mr. McLean an' ole man Arliss Butler, an' they had 'em a bet on."

"Oh, Lord," groaned Travis, beginning to laugh. He remembered too, vividly.

"An' A. J.," went on Troy with relish, "went out an' roped a calf an' brought it in here. He left his horse on the porch—it was that old Mac, the old one, that would stand for anything—but he drug the calf right in here. Them others had a fire goin' an' they put the old Lazy Ass brand on that calf right there where Carl an' Rinie's settin'."

They were all laughing, but Rinie was incredulous.

"He didn't really, though, did he?"

"I don't know why he wouldn' of."

"But your mother—"

"She'd took Carl and Doyle an' gone to visit in Denver," Travis said.

"She'd ought to a stayed," said Ellie shortly, but she was still smiling.

"Anyway, she wouldn' of stopped him," said Troy reasonably. "They had a bet on. He won some money."

"An' you can't hardly cheat at calf draggin'," added Travis dryly. "I wonder what ever became of that calf. I remember it was a bald-faced heifer an' we never seen her after that."

Carl put another stick of wood on the fire and lay with his head in Rinie's lap.

"Irine, you're a real pretty girl," he murmured sleepily.

She put her fingers in his hair. It looked almost orange in the firelight, a sort of burnt orange.

"Listen at that wind," said Ellie after a while. "Makes me think of a night once when I was a little girl. My grandpa'd come to visit from up in Wyoming. It was awful wild country up where he lived an' he told a story about a family that lived a way out in a little cabin. It was awful bad that winter an' one night, along toward mornin' when the fire was right low, a mountain lion come down their chimley, an' before they knowed what was happenin' an' the man could git his gun, it had killed one a their little girls."

Rinie shuddered.

"I don't hardly believe it now," Ellie said negligently, "but at the time, it like to a scared me to death. I couldn' git over bein' afraid a the dark for months. Course, grandpa was a great one for stories."

"You mean," asked Troy reprovingly, "that you doubt the word of your very own grandpa?"

"Well, it might a been true, but I don't hardly think a lion would git hisself in a tight place like a chimley, not with fire at the bottom an' people that clost."

Carl sat up, looking soberly thoughtful. "It might, if it was hungry enough."

"Jump down into fire?" scoffed Travis.

"Just coals," Carl said.

"And maybe they had fresh meat in there that it could smell," added Troy.

"Carl, what are you doing now?" asked Rinie laughingly.

He was on his hands and knees in front of the fireplace with his head turned to peer upward.

"Seein' if the chimley's big enough."

"Well, you're going to catch your hair on fire."

"Is it big enough?" asked Troy avidly.

"Hell, yes."

"I guess," said Travis, "if Santy Claus can, a lion can."

"You silly things!" marveled Ellie. "You beat all I ever seen for actin' the fool."

"But he might be out there right now, Ellie," said Carl ominously, brushing a spark out of his hair and withdrawing a little from the fire.

"Right now," agreed Troy with relish. "He might be slippin' up to that drift at the side a the house. It's just a little ways to the roof from the top a that."

"For a lion," nodded Travis.

"Oh, hush," said Rinie, half-frightened in spite of herself. They looked so serious.

"We ought to a gone to bed before," said Ellie wearily. "They git so outlandish when they been drinkin."

"We ought to be ready, in case he was to come," Carl said soberly.

"Yeah," breathed Troy. "I wonder if you can shoot a rifle up through there."

"You could a pistol," Travis said logically. "You'd burn yourself, tryin' to git a rifle fixed to shoot."

"No, it ought to be a rifle," said Carl with absolute finality. "It's not like you'd have to sight or anything."

179

"Yeah," Troy said. "You got to use a rifle on a big animal like that. It kills 'em better."

"Ah, you fool kids," snapped the eldest brother in disgust. "At close range like that, what the hell difference does it make?"

"Because it's straight up," Carl said reasonably, "an' what if you just wounded him?"

"You ain't makin' a bit of sense," said Travis, losing all patience.

"Well, you ain't makin' none yourself," snapped Ellie. "Come on to bed an' quit your foolishness."

"You're goin' to bed?" whispered Troy incredulously, "when there's a lion up there waitin' to come down an eat your kids? Lord love 'em."

"I can hear him now," Carl whispered. "—jingle—jingle—"

"No, dammit, that's Santy Claus."

"Oh, is he up there, too? Well, he dam' well better watch hisself."

Carl and Troy were in a state of near-collapse from controlling their hilarity and Travis suddenly went limp in his chair with helpless laughter. Ellie was trying unsuccessfully to stay truly serious, and Rinie's eyes were beginning to water with laughter.

"I wisht I'd never mentioned lions," choked Ellie.

"A lion," Troy explained carefully to his younger brother, "goes scratch an' claw an' like that."

Carl nodded and, moving catlike, took a rifle from the wall.

"Carl—" Rinie tried, but couldn't get any further for laughing.

Troy was up too, now, crouching and creeping to the fireplace.

"We got to be ready," he whispered. "Not that ole thing, Buck, a bolt action's too slow."

"You use what you want to," Carl said. "I always did like this ole .270."

Troy got his .30-30.

"You boys quit," ordered Ellie, " 'fore you shoot one another."

"We can tell each other from a lion," Troy said reassuringly. "Lions ain't redheaded."

Travis said stubbornly, "You can't git no rifle fixed to shoot up that chimley."

"Oh, Travis, hush about it an' come to bed."

"I don't think I ever saw a woman so anxious to go to bed," marveled Troy.

"I'm just tryin' to tell 'em they can't do it," said Travis logically.

"I dam' well can," said Carl, and, angling the rifle and then straightening it as much as he could with the butt in the coals, he fired up the chimney.

"Git 'im, Buck!" yelled Troy, letting loose all the pent-up hilarity.

The shot made a terrific noise and they were a little stunned, Carl, perhaps, more than any of the others. He tried to leap back, but couldn't get the gun free, and while the sound of the shot was still reverberating, they heard A. J.'s feet hit the floor.

"What is it?" he yelled, bursting into the room and grabbing another rifle. He was clad only in his "longhandlies," and he was wild with excitement.

"A lion, A. J.," began Troy desperately, "only—"

"Good God a-mighty!" bawled the old man gleefully and ran out the front door yelling, "Where is the sonofabitch? I'll git 'im, by Jesus!"

Helen and the boys came in, frightened and wondering.

"It ain't nothin'," said Ellie shortly, "Your uncles just got carried away. Git back to bed right now." And turning to the others, she demanded, "Do you know what you've done? That ole man with his rheumatiz?"

Troy was rolling on the floor and Travis was helpless in his chair, but Ellie's words sobered Rinie. Carl was trying to work the .270 out of the fireplace, cursing volubly. He hadn't even seen the old man go out, but he had heard him, and he was deadly sober.

The dogs came out of the shed where they slept and began baying in excitement.

"How come Granddaddy's runnin' around the house," wondered Kirby at the still-open front door. "He just passed agin an' his drawers ain't even buttoned."

"I told you to go to bed," said his mother in a menacing voice. "An' the rest a you better crawl up that chimley," she said, "before he finds out they ain't no lion."

"Oh, the poor thing," Rinie breathed.

Carl had got the rifle out. The stock was charred. He

laid it up in its place and backed away from it, looking frankly scared.

"Troy, my God! Why'd you have to say lion to 'im?"

"Well, Jesus Christ," said Troy, wiping his eyes and struggling weakly to his feet, "you're the one that shot the varmint." He made one leap, slammed the door of his room and shot the bolt, but his laughter came out to them in muffled shouts.

"Somebody's got to go and tell him," said Rinie indignantly. "He'll get really sick, running around like that."

"Travis will," said Carl, incredibly subdued. "He's the oldest. I better go to bed."

"The hell you will!" cried Travis, wiping his eyes.

And just then A J. came puffing across the porch.

"I didn't see no sign of 'im. Where was he at, Buck?"

"He was—he—he—" stammered Carl helplessly.

Travis had his face covered up, looking at the catalog at close range. Rinie brought a blanket.

"Here, A. J., you're gonna freeze," she said, putting it around his shoulders.

Ellie shut the front door.

"Well, hellfire! Why ain't you out after 'im? How come them dam' dogs didn' even rouse up till I come out? Where was he when you seen 'im? Or heard 'im? What the goddam' hell's the matter with you boys?"

"The boys had a little too much to drink, A. J.," said Ellie tentatively.

"Well, that ain't no excuse for not goin' after the bastard. Where's Bojack at? He surely went, I reckon."

"Yeah," Carl said grimly, "he did, the—"

"Troy went to bed," said Rinie with more boldness than she felt or would have imagined she could muster. "They—we were all acting silly, A. J.—talking about lions coming down chimneys and things, and—"

"And what?" demanded the old man slowly.

"An' I shot the rifle off," Carl said in a quick burst. There was an awful silence.

"There wasn' no lion?" A. J.'s face was brick red and his eyes bored coldly into Carl's.

Carl swallowed, looking at the floor. "No sir, there wasn't."

A. J. padded heavily over and put his rifle up.

"In all this time," he said, his eyes like blue flames, "you ain't learned as much as not to shoot off a gun in the house."

Heavily, he crossed the room and struck Carl viciously across the face.

Travis leapt to his feet, expecting trouble. Rinie gasped and Ellie put her hand to her mouth. Carl's face that had been pale, went scarlet and then white again, but he kept his hands stiffly at his sides and didn't raise his eyes.

After a terrible moment of absolute silence, A. J. turned and went into his room.

They went to bed in silence and lay very still for a long time, hearing the chinook wind moan around the house.

"Carl?"

"Just go to sleep."

"Carl, you're just wonderful, do you know that?"

"Rinie, don't—"

"Troy ran away and Travis wouldn't say anything and you let him—"

"It was my fault," he said shortly, "and I don't want to talk about it."

"But you didn't do any more than—oh, Carl, I'm so sorry that he hit you—and oh, sweetheart, I'm so proud of you for letting him."

"He had to hit somebody after a thing like that," Carl said bitterly. "He couldn' ever look any of us in the eye again if he hadn', the ole sonofabitch."

"Carl, I love you."

10

Spring came slowly, with an almost painful hesitance, to the West Fork country. There was the big thaw toward the middle of March, when the surface of all outdoors was water and mud and slush, but then it turned cold again and there was some snow just before Easter. After that, there was snow and melting and snow again many times through April and May.

Rinie was used to spring in Denver when there were almost always new leaves on the trees by May, and crocuses and tulips and daffodils in sheltered beds along house walls, and blossoms on fruit trees. Here, along Red Bear Creek, the willows budded, some of the birds came back and searched about busily for nesting places. Each time the snow melted, the grass emerged more vividly green, but the leaf-buds on the trees didn't unfold until almost June. The leaves would have been devastated by the heavy, wet, spring snows if they had unfurled sooner.

There were beautiful days, warm and soft to melt the heart, but always, underfoot, it was so heavy with mud and slush that one step on the ground robbed the day of some of its beauty.

"I guess it's not ever really spring here," said Carl a little apologetically. It was a Sunday afternoon. He was mending a saddle, sitting with Rinie in the sun on the porch. "I remember that used to bother my mother and she'd tell us what the spring was like back in Ohio when she was a girl. Here, it's winter—and then, it's summer."

"But when?" Rinie wondered.

She was riding old Jim to school every day now, and so tired of mud and dirty snow. No matter how she tried to keep clean and dry, she was always spattered with mud when she got there. She carried a dress in an oilskin bag, wearing a shirt and levis and changing when she got to school, but it didn't do much good. When she went outside with the children at morning recess, she got wet and muddy anyway.

Red Bear Creek ran over the ice of its winter level. The ice melted, and the water grew higher every day. Now Rinie understood the deep, rugged channel. She was afraid of the water, riding to school, but tried not to seem so. Kirby and Helen paid little attention to it. The lower ford seemed particularly treacherous, for the stream was deeper and swifter here than at the upper ford, and not far below roared the falls. But old Jim took it all quite casually and his calm gave Rinie confidence.

In the afternoon, Kirby always left the moment school was over, but Helen usually waited while Rinie did the things that were necessary to finish off that day or prepare for the next, and then the two of them proceeded home at a more leisurely pace and, fairly often, Carl would meet them somewhere around Red Bear Falls. It didn't come to Rinie until sometime later that he might be a little uneasy about the ford, too. If it had, she might not have crossed it any more with the water so high. The creek was always up more in the afternoon after a day of sun and melting. Carl wasn't really worried, but it made him feel good to watch old Jim with his own eyes, stepping easy and slow and sure across the dark, swift water.

Sitting on the porch now, drowsy in the sun, they could hear the creek. Usually, from here, it was just a murmur that you got used to and hardly noticed, and sometimes, in late summer and fall, you couldn't hear it at all unless everything else was very still. But now it was a great, low rumble, and under that, the muffled grinding of moving rocks, that made the porch, in the quiet warmth, seem more sheltered and secure.

The house was still. The children were out around the barns; Travis and Ellie and A. J. were taking naps as befitted a Sunday afternoon. Rinie did absolutely nothing. She felt a little strange about it because idleness was so rare, but she felt good, too, lying on an old blanket they had brought out, with the intense mountain sun boring into her back.

Carl wasn't getting much done with the saddle. His eyes were heavy and indolent, and they kept straying out across the flats or to Rinie.

"I guess I'll let this go," he said finally, laying down the tools. "Jeff's gittin' real good about fixin' tack. Maybe he'll finish it for me." He lay down beside her and she put her head on his shoulder and they were quiet, drowsing.

The dogs lay around in dry places soaking up the sun. Old Christmas seemed especially glad of it. A cow bawled somewhere. Magpies squabbled in the willows.

It was Sunday, a third Sunday, but no one from Red Bear had gone to church. There was no chance of getting the pickup or Model T out to Webber until the water went down and the mud dried. Carl and Rinie had gone riding before dinner, circling out across the flats and back up on the benchland. The new grass made a thick, green, water-soaked mat. The stock was taking advantage of the sun as the dogs were, by lying prone and absolutely still. It had frightened Rinie when she caught sight of the first horse lying like that. She thought it was dead.

They saw, from a distance, several new calves and two foals. They couldn't come up close to anything because the half-wild mothers moved their young away protectively. Up in the woods, Carl showed her elk antlers, shed with the spring and liberally gnawed by porcupines. They saw a porcupine later. It made Rinie laugh to see it shuffling along in a sort of lordly pomposity.

"He don't have to give a dam' about anything," Carl said, grinning.

The dark, tuft-eared squirrels were scampering and chattering up in the ponderosas, and chipmunks and ground squirrels and marmots sunned themselves on rocks by their burrows, waiting until the riders were very near before they bothered to take shelter. Some never bothered at all.

Carl showed her where a bear had rubbed and scratched himself and clawed high up on a pine. The horses snuffed and shied away from the tree and Rinie wondered if the bear was still around somewhere, but Carl said the mark had been made at least two days ago.

There were new birds in the woods, in addition to the magpies and jays and crows and juncos that had stayed the winter. It wasn't a country to support multitudes of birds, but now and then Rinie heard a new song. Carl didn't know the names of most of them but, from hearing them sing, he could tell her what they looked like and what sort of places they preferred for nesting.

Coming back down toward the house, they saw a pair of eagles, gliding high against the sun, over around the dark volcanic neck.

"They're just wonderful," Rinie said softly as they stopped the horses and sat watching the eagles. "I never dreamed there were so many things alive around here."

And he smiled, because the country was showing her its gentler side and he was proud of it.

But there was a sadness in the spring. Rinie had felt it as long as she could remember. Not a sadness that was a crushing misery, but the soft, wistful yearning over the past and the future that comes inevitably with nature's renewal of herself. She was so happy, quiet beside Carl while he slept. She thought that she could probably see the eagles again if only she turned over and looked, but it was too good, just lying still here. She loved and was loved by so many people that her heart seemed near breaking sometimes with the joy of it. Helping at school seemed almost too much because she enjoyed it so, only . . . she couldn't help wishing that instead of teaching she were waiting here at home, as almost every female thing in the world seemed to be doing, to give birth. Everything but me, she thought with a little, piquant smile, and drew closer to Carl. She tried not to worry, but she was becoming frightened as the months passed. What if . . . never . . . ?

"Carl?"

He mumbled that he was asleep.

"Carl, I want to plant something. . . . Honey?"

"What? What for, Rinie? There's stuff growin' all over." The words were all run together with drowsiness.

But then he woke up because the dogs got up and shook themselves and looked around the corner of the house as Troy came around on Brett, a handsome piebald gelding.

"God, ever'body's lazy," he said irritably, stopping by the porch.

"Where you goin'?" asked Carl, rubbing his eyes.

"Down to Webber or some goddam' place. I can't stand it around here. It seems like ever'body's dead. Do you want to come with me?"

Carl said he didn't.

"Buck, you're gonna be a ole man," Troy said peevishly. "You'll petrify."

Carl yawned. "When we can git the car out, le's go to Belford to a show or a dance or somethin'."

Troy looked no less glum. "It'll be the Fourth of July before I can git the car over this Christ-forsaken road. I know one thing. Next winter I'm gonna leave it at McLean's or some place where I can git it on the main road if I want to. Even if I do have to ride horseback all the way down there first."

Carl was making himself a cigarette. He said indolently,

"I guess you could leave it at the Keanes', that's closer'n McLean's."

Troy lifted one shoulder slightly.

"I guess that's where you're goin'."

"You just guess all you feel like. All you do any more's lay in the sun an' guess." Then he grinned. "God, no, I'm not goin' to the Keanes'. You think I want to set around all day an' listen to Sutter run off at the mouth? But, well, I might meet—no tellin' who-all at the store."

Carl didn't have any matches and Troy threw him a pack. Carl said, "Doxy's pretty young."

"Seventeen this summer. Old enough."

"Bo, you better—"

Troy's eyes flared. "Don't you start tellin' me what I better. You're gittin' to be as much of a ole fogey as Travis. I guess you never needed no advice an' counsel, did you? Do you remember that time up at Perryman's when you—"

"Got one hell of a lot of advice and counsel," Carl said dryly.

"Oh, hell, keep the matches." Troy waved them away.

"On top of ever'thing else, you're free-hearted," Carl said coolly.

Troy's eyes were full of anger and loneliness and frustration as he looked down on them—both of them—together.

"Bye, Rinie," he said and spurred Brett, so that the gelding leapt away, scattering a shower of water drops from the soaked ground.

Carl watched him out of sight, drawing on the cigarette, letting the smoke out slowly.

"Is something the matter?" she asked timidly. "I mean about Doxy and . . . ."

"Doxy's a little bitch," he said, biting the words.

"But Troy. . . ."

"I know." He threw the cigarette butt into the wet grass and looked at her. His eyes were troubled. "I guess he deserves her," he said impatiently, "only he's just bein' spiteful an' he's too stupid to see he's not spitin' anybody but himself—an' maybe her."

"I wish you didn't have to worry."

"Hell, I'm not," he said angrily.

There was a little silence. Someone was moving around inside the house.

"Carl? What happened that time up at Perryman's?"

"Which time was that?" He was looking out over the flats.

"You know which time. The time Troy was talking about."

"Oh. Well, Troy talks a lot."

"Carl?"

"Hmm?"

"Are you ever going to tell me about the things you did all those years?"

"When you're older."

"I'm old enough."

"What was that you woke me up for a while ago? Somethin' you wanted planted or somethin' . . ."

He was laughing because she was blushing, but she said stoutly, "I want to plant some flowers."

"There'll be wild flowers all over the place in a month or so."

"But I mean here around the house. Didn't your mother have a flowerbed right there along the porch?"

"Well, yes, an' it seems to me Ellie had flowers there, too, one time or another, but that's where A. J. fetches up his horse."

"But couldn't I try?"

"I guess you can, only you're not gonna like it when they git tromped on, an' they will. Anyway, it's still too early. They'd likely git froze."

"Carl, tell me about up at Perryman's."

"Be quiet. I want to look at you."

"I'll be quiet. You can talk and look at me at the same time."

He shook his head.

"Were you awfully bad?"

"About medium."

"Carl, please. I won't think . . . I'm not so childish as I used to be about things. I really want to know."

But just then, Helen launched herself off the porch rail onto her uncle's chest.

By fits and starts, the weather grew warmer. Two of Jeff's hens were brooding eggs. All the foals were born and most of the calves. The men worked from daylight till dark, having to do all the things that had been put off through the winter.

At the end of May, Carl went to break Corbett's horses. They lived just down the river from Webber, so that he came home to Red Bear at night, always riding one of the half-broken young horses. Sometimes he rode over to school and shared lunch with Rinie. He stopped that, though, because he said the children made his horse nervous, which was, without doubt, true, but mostly because he knew that the more she saw him riding the green broncs, the more she worried. He wished she wouldn't. It made him feel good to have her see that he could handle them—though these of Corbett's really required little handling—but she could never seem to relax and enjoy his prowess.

One day, standing down by the road and watching him ride away on a trim little black, Rinie realized that it was finally truly spring. There were tiny leaves on the trees and blossoms on the wild plum and currant and chokecherry along the river made the air redolent with a piquant sweetness. Even the smell of fruit blossoms was different here, she thought, lacking some of the heavy insipidity of tame town trees. Standing there in the warm, penetrating sun, watching Carl let the black out to a run, breathing the lovely air, hearing the rushing of the river and the voices of the children behind her, she felt a pride in the country, welling up so strongly that it brought tears to her eyes. The harshness and the barrenness and the loneliness were mostly hidden now, by the spring, but still it was a country different and distinctive in all its ways.

Travis had plowed up the garden spot by the time school was out, Ellie and Jeff had planted a good many things.

"It's not a awful lot a use," Ellie said. "The growin' season's short an' half the stuff's ruined by frost before it's near done bearin', but seems like I can't quit tryin'."

A. J. said they were getting more like farmers every year and Travis said he expected A. J. would be glad enough to eat the garden stuff.

Rinie got some seed packets at Putney's and planted flowers around the house, despite the dire predictions of their fate from all sides.

And then school was out and it was summer. The high water on the upper streams ran down and the trees were in full leaf. The young calves and colts, their legs strong and sure now, gamboled over the flats. The sow farrowed, the baby chicks hatched and scampered about in the sun on ground that was finally drying out.

Rinie was glad to be home again all the time. She and Ellie came down with a case of the cleans and had fairly good luck with getting things done as the men were away from the house almost constantly during the daylight hours. First they washed everything they could and dragged or carried what couldn't be washed outside to air.

"It's so good to have the doors open," Rinie said happily. "I didn't realize how long everything had been shut up."

"Helen," said Ellie, "you put all the longhandlies in that trunk with the blankets. We won't be needin' 'em for a while an' I'm right glad not to have to wash the things."

"Ellie," Rinie came to the door to look into the kitchen. She was washing the front-room windows and had the polishing cloth in her hand. "Why is it 'longhandlies'? I never heard underwear called that except by Stinsons."

Ellie smiled a little. "Ah, it's just one a them words that gits started in a family. A. J. always called 'em longhandles and they said one time when him an' Jenny first lived here through the winter Travis looked out an' seen the underwear froze stiff on the line an' he said somethin' about look at the longhandlies an' they always called 'em that. You know how that kind of thing gits carried on in a family."

Rinie went back to the windows happily. No, she had never been exposed to family words and such things shared by people through the years, but now she was becoming a part of the Stinson tradition.

In the kitchen, Helen said, "Mama, I don't see why I have to fold these clothes an' always stay in. Jeff an' Kirby don't."

"Well, when you git done foldin', you can go outside to the clothesline an' bring in them quilts," said the mother unsympathetically. "That'll give you some fresh air an' all."

When the house cleaning was done, Rinie made new curtains for the front room and kitchen. She would make them for other rooms as the materials became available. Carl had even conceded her curtains for their bedroom, but they had to be hung up so that they could be pushed back to expose the whole window, and when he was in the room, they were always open. At night now, they left their windows wide open, though it really wasn't all that warm at this altitude, and the green-smelling summer breeze could come and go at will.

"We'll have mosquitoes a little later," Carl said, "an' flies." But it was lovely while it lasted.

It was good, too, not to have to go to bed and get up in a frigid bedroom, and to have their own rooms warm enough to take a bath in, if they cared to carry water that far, rather than waiting for a propitious time to barricade the kitchen.

"W'y, them curtains makes this a whole new room," said Ellie, when Rinie had put up the new curtains in the front room.

She smiled. "I don't know what we'd do for material if your folks didn't have diary cattle."

"I been wonderin'," Ellie said hesitantly, "if there comes a few days this summer when the work eases up a little—well, I thought I might go an' see my folks for just a day or two."

"Oh, I hope you will," Rinie said eagerly. "There's not that much work. You go when you want to."

"Mama ain't been real well," Ellie said, half-apologetically, "an I'd like to go sometime when the kids ain't in school so they can go along."

The men seemed always exhausted. They didn't even complain much about misplaced things from the house cleaning. Doyle was home, but he said he should have known better. A. J. was able to ride some, enough to look into most everything that was being done and give advice. Troy and Kirby, Doyle and Carl, worked in teams on either side of the creek, trying to locate and look over all their stock in order to treat ailments, brand and count calves, head any that had strayed too far back toward the home range. Sometimes they were gone overnight.

One day when Troy went to Belford to replace some tools, Carl took Rinie with him, while Kirby and Doyle teamed up. They worked high up to the foot of the rock ridge and camped there. She had never before spent a night outdoors.

"I didn't know the sky was so beautiful," she said reverently.

They lay close and were mostly quiet as their small fire died out.

"What do you think," he said, "of a cattleman's life?"

She shivered and said defiantly, "This part is lovely, but I can't help it, Carl, I just can't stand to watch you brand those little calves."

He smiled in the darkness, thinking that those "little calves" could be dam' hard for a man to handle without help. Daylight was turning out well, though. A good horse was a lot of help, even if your working partner turned her back at crucial times.

"I wonder if Troy took Doxy with him to Belford," she said absently.

"Why?" he said a little tensely. This thing of the way Troy felt about Rinie was beginning to make him touchy.

"I—just wondered," she said, surprised by his tone. "He seems to be going around with her a lot."

She felt sad about Troy. Doxy was all right, maybe, but she seemed such an empty-headed little flirt. Why couldn't he go with someone like Vanda? Or Nell Tippitt? It was none of her business, but he seemed to be seeing so much of Doxy and if Carl was right and Troy was just being spiteful. . . . On the other hand, if Troy did marry, it would be better for all of them, only Doxy. . . .

Now Carl said carelessly, "He says he's not seein' her any more. She got talkin' a little too much about marriage an' all."

Rinie felt a combination of relief and uneasiness and she sensed that Carl felt the same, but this was a thing they couldn't talk about. It was best left alone, forgotten about if possible.

As they were drifting off to sleep, they heard a wolf howl, not a coyote, but a big wolf, Carl said. There were all kinds of animals up in the ridges. He wished they had time tomorrow to climb the rocks and look around. He'd like her to see some bighorn, but there wasn't much chance, this time of year, and, as she reminded him, she still hadn't looked at Utah.

The wolf howled again and she drew closer to him.

"I hope he keeps it up all night," he said contentedly.

At the end of June, Ellie took the children and went to visit her family. Troy drove them down and Ellie's brother would bring them home. Ellie had been so conscientious about "gittin' things done up" before she left, that Rinie was in need of a rest from trying to keep up with her.

She had a roast and potatoes in the oven for dinner; there was nothing to be done about that for a while. Carl was out at the corrals, shoeing horses. She thought she might go out there, but then decided not to, not just yet, anyway. It was a nice change, having the house to herself.

A. J. was on the porch, drowsing in an old rocker with his feet up. He said he couldn't enjoy the front room now because he couldn't find anything. In the course of their house cleaning, Rinie and Ellie had rearranged the furniture, the first complete rearrangement in ten years.

"I used to do it," Ellie had confided, "but he always complained so much, it didn't seem worth it. Course, now I know he just has to have his say about ever'thing, whether he means it or not, but I used to be bad to git my feelin's hurt an' that shore don't do around here."

This time, A. J.'s first opinion on the changed room

had been, "Huh! How is it you didn't move the fire-place?"

Rinie picked up an old magazine and lay down on the sofa. It was delicious to be lazy, with the warm breeze coming through the window, touching her skin with such a light, gentle caress. In a few minutes, she'd go out with Carl. She wished he'd come in instead. It was so lovely and quiet in here. She dozed briefly and was wakened by the dogs' barking.

"Howdy, Sutter," came A. J.'s voice, deep and a little gravelly from drowsing. "You dogs! Shut up! Nero! Git out! Come on up an' rest yourself, Sutter."

Rinie smiled, wondering if Sutter had smelled the roast. She got up and went to look at it and put more wood in the stove and came back to look for her sewing. Ellie was teaching her to piece quilts and she was making one in the wedding ring pattern, like the one Jenny had made so long ago and that now hung on the front room wall.

"Missy?" A. J. called. The window was open, but the curtains closed. "You in there? You got any coffee?"

"I'll bring some when it's hot," she answered.

She put cookies on a plate, too. Maybe Sutter wouldn't be staying for dinner. Anyway, the Stinsons thought this habit she had of offering food to guests along with coffee was "right refined," as Ellie put it, and they had come to expect it.

She took the things out and Sutter said, "Real nice day, ain't it, ma'am? An' you're lookin' pert."

"Thank you, Mr. Keane, and how are you?"

"Well, to tell you the truth, Miz Stinson, I have felt better, but when a man comes to our age, A. J., he can't expect real good health all the time, now can he?"

"I can," said A. J. staunchly. Sutter was at least ten years younger than he.

Rinie retired to the front room and her quilt pieces.

"Well, you're a man blessed by the Lord, then," said Sutter. "I ain't felt real good in a long time. Seems like it's the most I can do to keep my chores up that has to be done. I ain't even felt like gittin' no garden in this year. The women folks had had to do what's been done. Essie, she ain't never been what you'd call real stout, an' Supina, now, she's in the family way."

"Fixin' to be a granpa, huh," said A. J. jovially.

"Oh, yeah, yeah, but not for a while yet, sometime next winter."

Somehow Sutter's voice sounded stiff. Rinie thought she ought to move. She could just as well take her quilt pieces somewhere else, the kitchen or her own room, but she didn't. All those conversations around the kitchen table where everything was general knowledge were making shared information a habit. She had thought there was something strained about Sutter's face and now his voice sounded strained, too. She sat on near the window.

Sutter said plaintively, "I thought I'd be able to expect a little help out a Bob, Supina's husband, but that boy don't do a thing only hang around down at Putney's store an' suchlike. I tell you, A. J., one more mouth to feed is about more'n we can manage."

A. J. spat into the flowerbed. Rinie could imagine that he was making polite, sympathetic movements of his head.

"An'—uh—how's things up here at your place?" asked Sutter, after a little silence.

"Oh, pretty fair, I reckon, Sutter. We havin' a little trouble now keepin' ahead a the work, but I reckon we'll make it."

"You don't know, A. J., how well off you are to have your young 'uns all boys. Not that I don't love my girls, Lord bless 'em, they're the finest that walks the earth, but raisin' up girls is a worry an' a trouble."

"I expect," agreed A. J. disinterestedly. He was getting bored. It didn't take long with Sutter. He didn't find much of interest in a discussion of child rearing. It was a thing women talked about sometimes, he supposed. He'd never given it much thought and saw no reason to now.

"Yessir," said Sutter lugubriously, "a girl takes a lotta care an' trainin' an' prayin' over, where it seems like sometimes a feller with boys can just—let 'em grow—without much frettin'."

"Well," said A. J., shifting restlessly, "kids is what they are." And, having delivered himself of this all-encompassing bit of philosophy, he said more easily, "You want to walk out around the barns, Sutter? We got a right promisin'-lookin' litter a pigs."

"Well, no, A. J., I don't believe I will today. I got to go in a minute."

"We'll be havin' dinner here in a little bit. You might as well figger on stayin'," urged the host.

There was an awkward silence.

"A. J., the truth is, I come about—uh—Troy."

"Troy ain't here today, Sutter. He went to Belford this mornin' early."

"Well—yes, I seen 'im pass the house. To be honest with you, that's why I come up here today."

A. J. waited. Rinie started to get up and tiptoe away, but what if they heard her? A. J. wouldn't care, but Sutter would think she was terrible.

"You see—A. J.—my girl Doxy an' your Troy—they was sparkin' pretty heavy back there a little while. I guess you knowed it, did you?"

"I heard mention of it."

Sutter cleared his throat, was silent a moment, and then the words burst from him, "My young 'uns is good girls, A. J., ever' one of 'em. I'm a God-fearin' man, but I ain't got no intention of settin' back with my hands folded while ary one of 'em's done wrong."

Another silence. Rinie wished, sickly, that she hadn't listened, but now she couldn't seem to move. A. J. said easily, but very soberly, "All right, now, Sutter, why don't you just spit out what you come to say? I expect you'll feel easier about it if you quit beatin' around the bush. As ole man Arliss Butler used to say, just go ahead an' air your paunch."

Sutter cleared his throat. "My girl Doxy—she's in trouble."

Another silence that was dreadful to Rinie.

"An' she figgers it was Troy made the trouble," said A. J. matter-of-factly.

"Are you tryin' to say," cried Sutter, "that they might be doubt? That a girl a mine would have more than one—"

"Now just simmer down," said A. J. shortly. "All I'm doin' is tryin' to git the straight a this. How far gone is she?"

" 'Bout six weeks, I guess," Sutter was stiff and sullen with shame and broken pride.

"Well, you can't even be right certain, if that's all the time it is," said A. J. almost soothingly.

"Now you look a-here." Sutter was on his feet. "I'll lay you think he's a-gonna slide right out a this, but he ain't. W'y, Doxy ain't seventeen yet, an' he come hangin' 'round with all his big talk, leadin' her astray when she don't even know—"

"Goddam it! Quit yellin'!" yelled A. J.

Another silence.

"Well, what are you gonna do about it?" demanded Sutter.

Rinie felt sorry for him. He sounded ready to cry. It would take courage to face up to A. J. Stinson over a thing like this.

A. J. said tersely, "I'll talk to Bojack when he gits home."

"I aim to see right's done by my girl," Sutter said shakily.

"Troy's been of age some while now, Sutter. He'll have to work this out for hisself, but I'll talk to 'im."

"You mean you don't aim to try to influence him to the right? You always have let them boys—"

"I'll talk to 'im, Sutter."

"Well, when can I expect to hear somethin'?"

"I guess when you listen."

In her exasperation, Rinie all but ran out and shook A. J. by the shoulders. He had no right or reason to be flippant at a time like this.

Sutter was moving heavily toward the steps.

"If I ain't heard from you or the boy in a week, I'll be back. This ain't a thing to let drag on. I got a good name to keep up in this community. If this is took care of right away, they ain't no call for anybody else in the world to know about it."

He had a hard time getting his truck started and Rinie was on the verge of sympathetic tears.

A. J. didn't broach the subject when the others came in to dinner and Rinie was relieved. She shrank from the time when it should become a topic for family discussion. She wanted to tell Carl because she couldn't help the feeling that he could somehow ease the situation, but she knew that that was only an excuse. She wanted him to know so that he could, perhaps, make it easier for her somehow.

She felt loathing for Troy and Doxy. They had taken a beautiful thing and made it dirty, had even involved a child. Their love-making had become a thing for discussion by their fathers, and soon, by others, and she doubted that any real feeling of love had ever entered into

197

it. Unquestionably, Troy had no love for Doxy and Doxy seemed incapable of anything more than flirting and playing at sex.

After she had done the dishes, Rinie went out looking for wild greens for supper. She had to be out of the house.

The wild flowers hadn't reached their full summer glory, but they were spotting the meadows and hillsides with bright splashes of color. Ordinarily, she would have brought back a bouquet along with the greens, but today she didn't feel like flowers. She barely noticed them and the other beauties of the day, the warm soft air, a lovely butterfly, the eagles sailing against the blue sky.

Ellie had showed her which greens were good and they seemed at their best now. She kept picking and picking, deciding, without pleasure, that instead of just enough for supper, she'd get enough to can some.

She couldn't stop thinking of Sutter's visit, of Troy and Doxy, of A. J. and Heddie. How could they be so wonderful and yet so lacking in morals, this family of Carl's—of hers? Of course Troy must marry Doxy now; there was no doubt about that. But a marriage without love? No one, or very few couples, could have what she and Carl had surely, but marriage with no love at all! And with a little baby to be always in the middle . . . or left out entirely. . . .

Carl had said Troy was being spiteful and spiting no one but himself—and her, maybe. Had that been the day? That lovely, drowsy day in spring? But why did he have to be spiteful? Because he was jealous of her and Carl. She had felt sorry for Troy because he was lonely, left out, but she had also felt smug about their happiness. Perhaps both she and Carl had flaunted it sometimes; they couldn't seem to help it. But she had believed that whatever Troy's feeling for her, it wasn't of much consequence. It was as Carl had said, things looked better to Troy when someone else had them. His jealousy, envy, would pass, his attention shift to something, someone else. Only . . . what if he really did care about her? What if she was the reason . . . and she felt dirty and a partner in the guilt.

She cried a long time while she washed and cooked the greens, scrubbed the jars, and packed them for the pressure cooker. For reasons she couldn't name, she felt so desolate and lonely as if she were a part of this thing, not like Troy or Doxy, but more involved than A. J. or Sutter. She didn't try to understand her feelings. She wanted to forget them, but they wouldn't be put down. Her head began to ache terribly.

She made a shepherd's pie of the roast and potatoes left from dinner. That, with a huge bowl of greens and a platter heaped with cornbread, would be sufficient for the men's supper. There were two apple pies. That ought to be enough for dessert. They had rarely had dessert except for company or special occasions, until Rinie came to Red Bear, but now they had come to expect it in abundance. Ellie said Rinie spoiled them, but it made her feel needed, a vital part of the family, to have them like the things she did, only tonight she didn't care if there was enough dessert or not. She didn't even want to see them. Almost, she didn't want so see Carl, and that added unbearably to her misery.

While the men washed up on the back porch, she put the food on the table and said privately to Carl that she didn't feel well, didn't want supper, and was going to lie down.

She closed the door of their room and lay across the bed. The sun, low in the west, shone full upon her through the window with its curtains drawn back.

Carl opened the door when he had finished washing, and came hesitantly to the bed. She was pale and he thought she'd been crying.

"What's wrong?" he asked gently, touching her hair.

"Nothing—I—my head just aches. Go and eat, Carl."

"Did you take some aspirin? I could bring you some."

"Yes," she said. She hadn't, but if he didn't go, she'd be crying and she just couldn't talk about it now.

He pulled the curtains across the window. They shut out a good deal of light, but not much heat.

"God, it's hot in here," he said. "That won't be good for a headache. I'll leave the door open a crack to let some air through."

"Carl, don't—" she began, but he was gone, ravenously hungry, as usual.

They—all of them—ate and drank and swore and worked and—and made love with such lusty gusto. Rinie felt really ill.

"Ever'thing all right over at Ellie's folks?" Travis

199

asked as they filled their plates. Troy had got home just in time to wash for supper.

"Looked like it. They set a pretty good table at dinnertime."

"Where's missy at?" asked A. J.

Carl said, "She's not feelin' good. Didn' want to eat."

"Dairy cattle are really paying off for Ellie's people," mused Doyle.

"Well," said Travis, "livin' close to the railroad like they do, a lot of things might pay off."

"You don't have to have a railroad for sheep," mused Doyle. "They can be driven to market same as cattle."

"My God! Are you still on that sheep thing," said Troy incredulously.

"I just happened to think of it."

"Hunters," said Travis, "lost that skewball mare of theirs last week, her an' her colt. They figger that wild sorrel stud's at it agin."

Troy said, "When you gonna snap some more horses, Buck?"

"I ought to next week. I thought I'd go up to Perryman's."

"Whyn't you go to Fraser's? They got electricity. I seen 'em puttin' the line to the house when I went by today."

"I can't see that's got a hell of a lot to do with broncs."

"Well, in the ev'nin', when you're through an' restin' stuff, you could set around an' look at the light bulbs."

"They might even let you flip a switch or two," put in Doyle.

"An' if things was real dull, I could poke my finger in a socket."

"You oughtn't to go off yet, Carl, with all that's to be done," said Travis worriedly. "You ain't even broke our green ones yet."

"I'll handle them," said Troy. "Far as that goes, I could take care of Perryman's and Fraser's, too, only Carl don't seem to be able to think up any other way of making cash money."

"I don't want you to break ours," Carl said. "You ruined that little paint last year—"

"The hell I did."

"You roughed him up till he's not worth a hoot in hell an' you know it, Bo. If you'd broke him right—"

"Oh, for Chrissake don't start on that paint agin," said Travis impatiently. "You've hashed him over enough. Anyway, the thing is, one of you gone's the same as another. We need ever'body here now, till we git on top a some a this work."

"If you'd start paying wages," Doyle said, "you might have an easier time keeping your hands."

"You show me where there's anything to pay wages with, an' I'll divide it up—amongst all of us."

"You git bed an' board." A. J. spoke with unexpected severity. "This place belongs to all of you. Don't that count for nothin'? A man's got to work for what he gits. If any one of you don't like the way it is, he ain't got to stay."

They glanced at him and each other. Something was wrong, that was sure, but what? It wasn't like A. J. to be cryptic.

Travis plunked big wedges of apple pie onto their plates as they held them out to him. Troy said, grinning a little uncertainly, "Not many ranches has got a honest-to-God lawyer working' for 'em summers."

"He's even lost his blisters an' got calluses again," said Carl approvingly.

"Well, most places," Doyle amended, then he said thoughtfully, "don't want her supper, hmmm? You suppose that could mean anything?"

"He's a doctor, too," Troy observed.

"I guess," Carl said soberly, "when you go to college, you pick up a little bit of ever'thing."

"I just thought," Doyle said mildly, "that by the time I got home this spring, you and Rinie would have something to tell me."

"Well," said Carl, grinning, "what is it you need to know? I guess they don't teach you as much as I thought."

"What I think," said Troy judiciously, "is that Buck's rode too many broncs an' got hisself ruined someway."

A. J. said abruptly, "What about you, Bojack? You in good shape, are you?"

"Best you could think of," said Troy expansively, helping himself to more pie.

"An' I guess you was, say—two months or so back?"

201

"W'y sure, A. J. That was springtime when all the bulls was horny."

"Bring the pot while you're up, Siefog," said the old man soberly. "We'll all have us another cup."

When they had passed their cups to be filled, they waited, wondering at A. J.'s seriousness. Doyle, unobtrusively, took the last piece of apple pie.

"Sutter come up here today," A J. said finally

"I thought that was his truck I seen leavin'," said Travis. "I aimed to ask why he didn't stay for dinner but it slipped my mind."

"He had a thing to talk about that wasn' for the dinner table." A. J. was looking steadily at his second son, his blue eyes intent and probing. "Sutter says that back a while, about the time the bulls was horny, his girl Doxy got knocked up."

The kitchen was silent. Doyle held a forkful of pie and looked around the table with interest. Travis looked back and forth between his father and Troy, his face tense and harried. Carl, after one quick glance at his father and brother, looked across the room and out of the window, up to the ridge. The sun was out of sight, but had left behind a bright, jagged sword made of the topline of the spine of rock. Troy looked at his father and away and back again, his ruddy coloring heightened a little.

Solemnly, A. J. said, "She says you're the one, Bojack. . . . Well what you got to say?"

"I. . . ."

"I never would have believed Troy could be at a loss for words," Doyle marveled.

"Shut up," Troy burst out truculently, and to his father, "I dam' sure don't think much of havin' a thing like this brought up before ever'body this way."

"There's no women or children," Doyle pointed out, undaunted.

"All right," said A. J. with angry finality, "you keep your mouth shut if you ain't got somethin' to say worth listenin' at." And, turning to Troy, "You an' me coulda talked this over private, yes, but I don't see it woulda made no difference. These here's your brothers. We're all Stinsons together. I expect they'd be interested to hear what you got to say, like I would. You been havin' at the girl?"

"I have, some," Troy said sullenly, "but I ain't by no ways the only one."

"Well, you better figger what you're gonna do about this. Sutter wants to know in a week, an' he's got a right."

"I don't figger to do anything," said Troy, outraged. "Why the hell should I do anything?"

"Sutter pictures a weddin'."

Some of the color went out of Troy's face.

"Well, he can just goddam' sure picture hisself another groom."

There was another silence and A. J. said slowly, "We been through droughts and floods; we been broker'n hell; we had sickness an' death an' a lot of things an' we always talked about 'em. I'd be interested to hear what the rest of you thinks." He was looking at Travis.

Travis cleared his throat. "I reckon Troy's the only one can say if this is his responsibility—him an' the girl."

Troy snorted. "She'd say anything, the little bitch. There ain't nothin' hotter between here an' Denver. Sutter an' his Christ-Jesus religion! Ever'thing's got to be right, hell! You think he don't know what she is? He's got to git her the hell off his hands, is what."

He rolled himself a cigarette, spilling a few crumbs of tobacco, but his face showed a good deal less consternation.

"All right, Lawyer Stinson," said A. J., "you always got somethin' to say."

"If there were witnesses," Doyle said a little cautiously, "other men who'd say they'd had relations with her, nobody could prove a paternity case."

"What the hell—" began A. J., and Troy said, grinning. "I can git plenty of men that's related with her."

"But," amended Doyle, with grim pleasure, "even if you weren't in on the fact, the particular time when she conceived, it's evident that you were an accessory before and after—plenty, maybe—and, if you're the one they choose to be lucky, you may have a hard time getting out of it. They couldn't make you marry her, or maybe they could, she's a minor, but you might have a hell of a time getting out of child support. Actually, I don't know all that much about this kind of thing, but I could go to the law library—"

"Goddam' you!" cried Troy furiously, "this ain't no

trial an' there ain't gonna be no trial, so quit playin' lawyer."

"Just delivering an opinion."

"I ought to deliver you a fist in the mouth. Anyway, whose side are you supposed to be on? It's for dam' sure, nobody could tell from all that bull."

"The winner's," said Doyle placidly and finished the pie.

A. J. was looking at Carl, but Carl's eyes were still on the ridge. It's brightness had almost faded, but the sky above it was a soft gray-pink.

"Buck?"

He turned his eyes reluctantly.

"You got anything to say in this here meetin'?"

"Nossir."

Troy was angry, disappointed, hurt. Of all of them he had thought he could depend on Carl's staunch support.

"He's too goddam' high an' mighty lately," he said derisively, "to be bothered with other people's problems. Got his own woman an' all, don't give a dam' about nothin'. Next thing you know he'll be gittin' religion an' going down to hear Sutter preach. It's a goddam' shame he didn't marry one of the Keane girls."

"That'll do," A. J. said shortly.

"If I had, you'd want to," Carl said, his voice low, his eyes blazing golden.

"The hell I would." Troy half-rose to his feet.

"Both of you shut up," ordered the father and Travis said, "This sure as hell ain't the time to start fightin' amongst ourselves."

And Doyle drank his coffee.

11

Ellie's brother John and his wife brought Ellie and the children home to Red Bear two days later. Knowing when to expect them, Rinie had a big company dinner almost ready when they arrived and the house in as presentable a state as it might be with five grown men living in it.

Ellie was proud of her young sister-in-law. She had praised her a good deal to the folks. "Her a city girl, raised with all that modern stuff! W'y, when Carl brought her home, without a word, mind you, I was just sick. I couldn' help thinkin' it'd be just one more to wait on, but, my land, she's taken hold! W'y, you wouldn' hardly believe it."

And Ellie thought the girl had done herself proud with the dinner, but she noticed that Rinie seemed even more quiet and retiring than usual and she looked a little pale. She wondered . . . but then, the men seemed a little strange, too, quieter, like something bothered them somehow. They seemed subdued and thoughtful. Surely, they weren't impressed by John and Lucy, even if the farm was doing so well and they did drive a brand new GMC pickup. It took a lot to impress a Stinson; Ellie knew that. It was more like they might be having trouble among themselves or some such. What on earth? What now? A person couldn't go away from here a minute without something. . . .

John and Lucy couldn't stay long because they had to be back to help with the evening milking.

"The farm pretty much ties us all down," John said, and, trying not to sound like a braggart, he said that if things kept going as well as they had been, he and his father planned to install electric milking machines sometime next year.

"It seems to me like," said A. J., grinning, "that would be kind of shockin' to the cows."

The men sat on the porch and the children, happy to be home and to show their cousins around, went out around the barns. Jeff, tired from the trip, was more than content to sit unobtrusively in a corner of the porch, fondling Sport's ears.

Lucy wanted to help with the dishes but Rinie and Ellie insisted they be left till later since there was such a short time to visit. The two older women sat in the front room while Rinie cleared the table.

"She's a quiet little thing," observed Lucy in a lowered voice.

Ellie nodded. "She generally always is, but I don't believe she feels good."

"I thought she looked a little peaked," agreed Lucy. "Do you reckon she's. . . ."

The two women smiled softly and let the conjecture go.

When John and Lucy had gone, the men returned to their work and Rinie and Ellie were busy in the kitchen, Ellie sighed and said happily, "My, it was good to see them agin, an' mama an' daddy was so glad to see the kids, but it's always the best thing in the world to get home. . . . Rinie? The work ain't been too much for you, has it? I know what a mess this bunch can be. You don't look real good."

"The work hasn't been anything at all," she said, smiling. It was so good to have Ellie back that she felt like crying. Here was someone who would feel as she did—more or less—about this present crisis.

"Well, what's wrong then?" asked Ellie bluntly.

"Nothing—with me."

"Oh. I thought maybe you was in the fam'ly way."

"I wish I was," she said, feeling tears against her lids. It was all so cruel and unfair.

Ellie, smiling, made a little gesture of dismissal.

"Oh, that's what women always guesses about other women. But what is the matter? Somethin' feels odd around here."

"I—Travis can tell you," said Rinie unhappily.

"Travis? Well . . ." said Ellie, mystified. And as soon as they had the kitchen set to rights and Rinie had got the sewing machine out to do some patching, she went looking for her husband.

He was in one of the sheds, working on the decrepit

206

old mowing machine. He got up and, keeping his greasy hands away, kissed her warmly on the mouth.

"God, I'm glad you're back, hon."

"Why?" she said, going straight to the point.

"W'y, cause I kinda like you, an' I don't even object too much to the kids. I purely missed the bunch of you."

"That's good to know," she said, giving him a little, promising smile, "but what is it that's been happenin' while I been gone?"

When the week was up, Sutter came back and his son-in-law, Bob Fletcher, a short, thin boy with prominent brown eyes, was with him. It was the middle of the afternoon of a hot day. A. J. was resting on the porch and Carl happened to be there, repairing a window that Kirby had shattered in an enthusiastic demonstration of the fast draw. Kirby hadn't shot through the window— he was forbidden to practice with a loaded gun—it was just that the pistol had spun out of his hand. It was a front window or they would probably have let it go a while. Carl was carefully spreading putty along the final edge, thinking that he hadn't done a bad job of glass cutting, when A. J. called softly, "Buck, come 'ere."

He walked around the corner of the porch and A. J. swung his chin in the direction of the upper ford. A. J. had always claimed it was good to be able to see down the road a ways from the house.

"I've got to finish the window," Carl said uneasily.

"That's Sutter's pickup comin'."

"Yessir, I see it is."

"Where's Troy at?"

"Him an' Doyle are gone over on the mesa."

"Where's Travis?"

"He went to doctor Fancy. She's had that infection since she foaled—"

"You go in yonder an' tell Ellie that we don't need no kids or women out here."

"All right, A. J."

"An', Buck—"

"Yessir?"

"When you git done tellin' 'er, come on back out here."

"Well, I—I thought I ought to—"

"I don't give a goddam' what you thought you ought

to. The rest of 'em's managed to be gone, but I'll be damned for a dewlapped dog if I'll have this to myself. You think I been countin' on it? Waitin' for it? Now hurry up an' tell the women an' saddle your ass back out here."

The dogs were starting to bark and A. J. yelled and swore at them, loud. It relaxed the tension a little.

Carl brought back the coffee pot and cups and cream and sugar. Rinie had put the things quickly on an old battered tray when he went into the kitchen with his message.

He and Rinie hadn't discussed this situation of Troy's at all. He knew that she was aware of it and upset about it. He thought he knew most all of the reasons why it bothered her so much, but he was reluctant to try talking about it because he didn't think there was anything he could say to make her feel any better.

"I guess you know why we come," said Sutter on the steps. "No need nibblin' round the edges of it."

Sutter's son-in-law, Bob, wasn't anything to brag about, but Sutter felt more confident for having him along. Besides, Sutter had the certainty of right on his side and that was a great asset.

"I reckon you've talked with your boy Troy about this business."

"Well, yes, we've had some discussion. Have some coffee there, Bob, Sutter."

Carl poured it. How in hell had he been the one to get in on this? A. J. glanced up at him as he took a cup and Carl could have sworn there was a little, mocking twinkle in the old devil's eyes.

Sutter was encouraged by the hospitality. He was also glad Carl was there. The more people, the less likely there was to be trouble, at least he hoped that was how it was. It wasn't going to be so bad after all.

"I knowed you was a reasonable man, A. J., that I could depend on you to see that this was worked out friendly an' to ever'body's good."

"Looks like a good year," mused A. J. incongruously. "Plenty a water at the right-time. It's been a good long while since we've had grass this good."

Somehow, Carl thought, there was ambiguity in the musing, but he couldn't see just where it was.

"Yes, well, glad to hear it, but I'd like to git this other business took care of. I believe we'll all be easier when

208

things is settled. Is—uh—Troy around the house some-wheres?"

"Buck, where's Troy at?"

Carl looked at his father quizzically.

"He's up on the mesa. I told—"

"Well, no, Sutter, he ain't handy just now. He won't likely be back till suppertime."

Sutter was galled that they seemed to take this so lightly. They should have known he'd come today. The boy ought to be here. On the other hand, maybe it was better this way. Bob wouldn't be much support if he was needed and facing two Stinsons was easier than facing three. Carl was known for being mostly a quiet boy so long as he didn't get mad.

Sutter said, "I guess there ain't no help for it, though it'd be better if he was here, but I reckon we can settle things ourselves all right. We thought—that is, I an' Essie —that next time Reverend Turner comes up 'ud be soon enough for the weddin'. That way, it wouldn' seem so rushed into, like if they went down to Belford twict."

"Twict?" asked A. J.

Sutter nodded vigorously. "Onct for the blood tests 'an' all, an' agin for the weddin'."

"Blood tests," said A. J. "They didn' have no such stuff when I got married. Was you tested, Buck?"

Carl said he had been.

"Course, Buck, he got married over in Denver. You might expect nearly anything over there."

Sutter said nervously that he supposed that was true. "By next third Sunday," he went on, "that's over two weeks from now, Doxy'll be a good bit more'n two months gone, but it seems like the best time, less likely to cause talk an' all."

A.J. drank some coffee, cleared his throat, and spat in the flower bed. Missy's flowers were coming on right nice —they ought to, the way she fussed over them.

"Well, now, Sutter, I tell you, there's just one kinda hitch in these here plans a yours. They do sound good —I mean, as far as Doxy's concerned an' what folks might think an' all like that—but it looks like you may have to find yourself another boy."

Carl took a sip of his coffee and came near spitting it out. Why in hell had he put cream in it? He hated cream in coffee. Sutter's guant cheeks flushed and paled. Bob leaned forward. A. J. looked calm and formidable.

"What are you talkin' about?" asked Sutter tightly.

"It's a hard thing to mention, an' I don't fancy doin' it, but Troy claims that he ain't to blame for this. He says your girl's been a little—free with some a the other boys around the valley."

"W'y that dirty. . . ." Sutter's face flushed again and his lips moved wordlessly.

A. J. said, "It's a right bad fix. I'm real sorry about it."

"Sorry!" burst out Sutter, his voice breaking. "You set up here, raisin' up good-for-nothin' boys to turn loose on the valley! You don't know what sorry means! If you had a bit a decency, you'da set a halfway good example for 'em when they was young 'uns. 'Bring up a child in the way it should go.' You! Livin' here before your little childern with a woman married to somebody else! Gittin' a child on 'er! No wonder your boys turns out immoral. They come by it honest. But I'll lay this is is gonna be put right, A. J. Stinson, or as right as can be. No child a mine's gonna be vi'lated an' cast aside."

"All right, Sutter, quit yellin'," said A. J. forcefully. His face was stern and forbidding but not really angry. "Now. You want to git moral an' all. They's a commandment about adultery. Whatever you done or I done or my boys or anybody else done, your girl has broke it. You by God got more proof of that—or so you say—than you have about anything else that has to do with this business. Except for one case that we won't agree now, it always takes two in this kind a thing—"

But Sutter broke in shrilly, "That girl ain't no adult! She's a child under the law an' in the eyes a God. I'll go to law, A. J. I aim to have justice. She was led astray, seduced, vi'lated."

"Was, was she? Well, Sutter, it's a hard thing, but it seems like maybe she was led by more than one. Now I feel like right ought to be done, but I can't see exactly where right is."

He looked off toward the snag as if right might be up there somewhere, and Carl thought, you old sonofabitch, Doyle won't make a better lawyer than you would.

Sutter was greenish and Bob looked disconcerted and a little scared.

A. J. eased his swollen feet on the porch rail. He said, "It's like this, Troy was twenty-five back the early part of April. He ain't no way under my authority no more.

Whatever he might decide to do in a thing a this kind would have to be up to him, but I did talk to 'im after you was here before, an' his feelin' then, an' the last time this business was mentioned which was yesterday ev'nin,' as I remember, was that it ain't his doin'."

Sutter got up and Bob followed. Sutter was trembling.

"Well, we'll just see about whether or not it was his doin'. I tell you, I'll have justice for my girl an' her young 'un."

They got into the pickup and left.

There was silence on the porch when the sound of the loose old motor had died out down the valley. Carl was standing up—he didn't remember when he'd risen—gripping a porch post with one hand and his coffee cup with the other. The eagles were cruising the sky over by the edge of the mesa again. He threw the scarcely tasted coffee into the flower bed.

"Most likely," A. J. said, "coffee ain't good for missy's asters an' stuff."

He sounded tired. Carl turned. He looked tired, tired and old.

"When did you aim to go to Perryman's?"

"Sunday."

"For how long?"

"Two weeks, about."

"You reckon Charlie Perryman would care too much if Troy come instead of you?"

"Well, I—"

"Yes, he would," A. J. answered himself shortly. "Troy ain't got the way with horses you have, an' I wouldn' like it if I was in Charlie's place, but I was thinkin' that if he was up there a coupla weeks, Sutter an' the girl might settle on somebody else. . . . You could send Charlie word you couldn' make it for some reason."

"Bo asked me last night," Carl said, not looking at him.

"An' what'd you say?"

"I said all right."

There was a little silence and A. J. said tentatively, "I reckon it's so, what he says about the other boys she's been with?"

"I couldn' say."

"Oh, hell, don't git prissy. I know you ain't had 'er, but I know, too, you hear the other boys talk."

"A. J., I . . . this is not my business."

After a moment, the old man said quietly, "I know it ain't, Buck, nor it ain't mine neither, except that he's your brother an' my boy. We don't, neither of us, want to see him drug into somethin' that wasn' none a his doin'. Marryin' is a thing that lasts a long time an' is easy over done. On the other hand, if this kid is his'n . . . well, we can help him out this much an' that'll be all. Bojack always was handy about keepin' out a trouble he stirred up just by managin' not to be there when it come to a boil. This is a right ticklish business he's into here. I expect Sutter's girl got good enough reason to pick on 'im, but if they was others . . . well, after this next two weeks, the ole boy's on his own. I aim for him to understand that before he leaves for Perryman's. It ain't gonna be me that has no more talks with Sutter, I'll lay."

Every Fourth of July, Webber had a community gathering with a picnic in the afternoon and a fireworks display in the evening and patriotic speeches by some county officials who'd be coming up for election. This year, as an added attraction, there was to be an appearance by Mr. Everett Bell, the district representative to the state legislature, the man who was the uncle of the husband of Ellie's sister Bess. Bess and Larry were to be at Webber and, along with Everett and his wife, would spend the night at Red Bear before returning to Belford.

A. J. and Travis and Ellie and the children went down shortly after noon and wouldn't return with their guests until after the fireworks that night. Rinie and Carl stayed at the ranch. He would be going to Fraser's in a few days and it seemed they had scarcely been alone all summer. Troy was away up the West Fork at Perryman's and no one believed he would care to present himself at this particular community gathering. Doyle, who also elected to stay home, said, "I won't bother you two, wouldn't think of it, but I'd like a little quiet and peace myself. Just think, I can read for a whole afternoon without being interrupted once."

Carl and Rinie sat on the porch when the others were gone, enjoying the quiet. It was a hot day with a few puffy clouds moving rather aimlessly about a summer-blue sky. Rinie, in an old rocker that she still intended painting, was working with her quilt pieces. Carl had his straight

chair tilted back against the log wall with his feet, boot-
less for the moment, hooked around its front legs.

"Your flowers are doin' good," he said after a while
He wanted to see her smile. She looked sad too much of
the time lately. He knew it was this thing about Troy and
that it had brought all that business about Heddie to the
surface again. He knew, too, that she worried because
she wasn't pregnant. She hadn't mentioned it for a while
now, but that didn't mean she wasn't thinking about it.
Carl was even beginning to be a little concerned. He
wanted children. For himself, though, he was in no hurry.
He liked having Rinie to himself, as far as that was possible under the circumstances in which they lived, but if
not being pregnant was going to bother her. . . .

She said, about the flowers, "Maybe you were all wrong
and they'll get to bloom after all." Her eyes were warm
on his, but she didn't smile.

"You really rate," he said. "A. J. even gits on an' off
his horse at the steps when he thinks about it, carries his
saddle an' stuff all that way across the porch."

Carl had thought it would be good for Rinie to go to
the picnic today, but she hadn't wanted to. She was afraid
people might be talking about Doxy and Troy, and she
shrank from any discussion of the subject. It seemed to
her that they were all so mixed up in it, yet all of them,
the men, at least, treated it so casually. Ellie said, unequivocally, that it was a shameful mess and something
would have to be done, but she didn't say what. When
Rinie had timidly mentioned the men's attitude, Ellie
shrugged and said, "That's just how they are. You might
as well git used to it. Things that a woman can't git out
of her mind for a minute don't seem to faze a man one
bit, but you can't always tell, they may not be as easy
about it as you think. Anyway, actin' that way's born
into 'em, along with ever'thing, good an' bad, that makes
'em men—specially Stinsons."

In the beginning, from the first day Mr. Keane had
come up to Red Bear and she had heard the men discuss
his visit, she had felt a resentful bitterness toward them
all, even Carl, that they could treat a thing so serious as
the conception of an illegitimate child with such lightness,
even humor. No matter what Doxy was, regardless of
hers and Troy's feelings about each other and the child,
it seemed to Rinie there could be no possible question as
to what was to be done. They had to get married. But

213

they didn't, and it now seemed fairly likely that they never would. It was incredible, horrible, and even Carl was abetting Troy's procrastination and possible total evasion by giving over to him the job at Perryman's.

But, thank God, she thought fervently, Carl wasn't really like the others. Doyle observed all with a small cynical grin; Troy maligned the girl whose life he seemed intent on ruining; A. J. had said, with a grin of pride when Troy was gone up the valley, "I'd lay even money still that the slippery little devil comes out a this someway without a mark." But Carl didn't talk about it at all, not to Rinie, not to the others that she knew about, and he seemed to understand, without a word from her, how she felt about it which, she thought unhappily, was perhaps, more than she understood herself.

Her bitterness against him had lasted only a short time. It had existed in the first place only because he was a male. She did wish, though, that he had more of true, distinct conception of right and wrong. She knew he thought her something of a prude for some of her morals, but she couldn't help it—there was right, and there was wrong and he ought to know that this about Troy and Doxy. . . .

"I tell you what," he said now, enthusiastically, "when I git back from Fraser's—as soon as the work here slacks —le's take the money I make down there an' go to Belford an' have one hell of a time. Or maybe we could even go to Salt Lake. Neither one of us has been there. What do you think?"

"I—I wish you weren't going to Fraser's."

She felt frightened, not so much about the horses, she was beginning to get a little used to that. She had watched him break the few the Lazy S had ready during the past week. It had been terrifying for her, but she did it because she knew he liked having her watch. What frightened her most now was the thought of his not being there if something more developed about Troy and Doxy. Violent emotions in others affected her so intensely, and the Stinsons could be so violent. Without Carl—his calm, his humor, his understanding, his reassurance—she was truly afraid.

"I have to go," he said a little impatiently. "I told them I'd come before this. It won't be for long, Rinie . . . but what about when I come back? Le's do somethin' special. We never had any kind of honeymoon."

"A year next month," she said softly, and finally, she smiled. "Oh, Carl, it seems like I can't remember anything before then. There wasn't anything that really counted."

Letting his chair down, he said, "Put away your quilt pieces an' le's do somethin' now."

"What?"

He grinned. "We have been married a long time. A while back, you wouldn' have asked me what."

She blushed and they laughed and he picked up a little scrap of yellow cloth she had dropped and put it in the box.

In the middle of the afternoon, Carl suggested swimming. The boys had been several times, but Rinie hadn't gone yet, chiefly because she had had no bathing suit. Now Carl intimated she wouldn't need one, but she demurred because Doyle was somewhere around. Without his knowing, she had made herself a bathing suit, doing the best she could with materials at hand to copy one from a magazine photograph.

"My God!" he murmured when she modeled it for him. "Oh, Rinie, I—hell! You're the prettiest thing in the county, but don't go running around Webber or anywhere in that."

She laughed and said she hadn't intended to.

He sat on the bed and watched her deftly braiding her hair. When she stood like that, with her arms raised, he got the full benefit of her figure in the bathing suit. She wasn't what they called in books a "voluptuous woman," but, on the other hand, she wasn't exactly boyish either. Everything about her was small, her slender waist, her firm breasts, the full curve of her hips and buttocks, small and perfect. Her hands were small and quick, winding the heavy brown braids around her small pert head. Her face was small and oval, tanned now by the sun and wind, but the complexion smooth and flawless.

He got up and put his arms around her when she'd finished her hair, and the top of her head came just a little above the top of his shoulder, just right for leaning his cheek down against her hair. The only thing very big about her were her eyes, he thought as she drew back a little to look up at him. Those soft brown eyes were what had first attracted him to her when she was almost a little girl at his Aunt Minna's. Then they had been too big for her face but she had grown up to them, or almost. Sometimes, still, they made her seem so young and sensitive and vulnerable that he felt he ought to lock her away someplace where life and the world couldn't get at her.

It happened that the place Doyle had chosen for his afternoon of reading was the shade of a cottonwood beside the swimming hole. But he complained only mildly as a matter of principal, and they had been in the water less than five minutes when he marked his place, stripped to his shorts, and joined them.

The water was cold, shockingly so at first, but pleasant and refreshing once the body became accustomed to it. The creek here moved slowly. At the upper end of the pool, there was a wide shallow riffle over a gravel bar and then it deepened gradually until from about midway on to where it ended as the creek was split up by dark, mossy boulders, it was deep enough for good swimming except at times when the water was very low. Long ago, A. J. had built a diving board and, as the boys grew up, they made a second, higher one.

Carl offered to begin teaching Rinie to swim, but she was content to paddle around in the shallow water while he and Doyle swam and dived. She had come down to watch them before, and it was rather pleasant to think they put on these exhibitions for her, though she knew, smiling fondly, that they were probably more intent upon trying to impress one another. Neither Carl nor Doyle was as good in the water as Troy and both commented, during the course of the afternoon, on his swimming prowess. Carl said that after all, Troy had the advantage of more time for practice, being older, and Doyle said that Troy had webs between his toes and was so convincing that Rinie was almost ready to believe him when Carl overdid it a bit and said that Troy was so paddle-footed he could walk on the water.

When they were tired, they lay on Doyle's blanket, moving it out in the sun, because at this altitude, even in July, no one wanted shade just after coming out of the water.

Rinie noticed that both men were red from the sun. They were fair and burned easily. Carl's face and hands were always bronzed, but Doyle's still looked red-raw from so much exposure following all that time in town. Doyle was the true Carlisle of the Stinson family. Rinie supposed Jenny had given the name to Carl in case she had no more sons, but Doyle's face was shaped exactly like his mother's in the pictures and his hair was blond as Jenny's had been, with no trace of red. Jenny had been rather slight, though of average height for a woman of her day. None of her sons had inherited her slightness of build; on the other hand, none was quite as brawny as A. J. had been in his prime, though Troy came close. Doyle's shoulders were, perhaps, a little broader then Carl's though he wasn't quite as tall. His eyes were light brown as Jenny's had been, but without the golden tints that were peculiar only to Carl's eyes and made them so fascinating. Doyle's face was more handsome than Carl's, which was only regular and pleasant and fairly good-looking, but Doyle spoiled his good looks to some degree by the mask of cynicism he was so rarely without.

Doyle's handsome, Rinie thought as they lay in the sun, and reluctantly she thought that Troy was even more handsome, but Carl . . . Carl's red-blond hair was getting streaked from the sun again and it needed cutting. . . . Carl had that funny, endearing quirk of a grin at one corner of his mouth, the only one of the boys to inherit it from A. J. Carl had those strange wonderful eyes and the honest, open, boyish face. . . . Carl was tender and sensitive and perceptive, not cynical, not selfish. . . . Carl was hers.

Doyle said into their drowsiness, "Jeff's getting pretty good at swimming."

"It tires him," Carl said with concern. "It's a real effort."

"It's good for him, though," Doyle said staunchly. "That's what the doctor I talked to in Denver said, good therapy. It should have been started in the beginning. Probably too late now to do much real good."

"He always played around in the water."

"But not real exercise, Buck. Has Ellie said anything?"

"I guess she don't know the idea came from a doctor. Travis does, though. He says as long as Jeff's willin' an' it's not too hard on him. . . ."

There was another silence. Crows haggled raucously over toward the mesa. The sound of the creek was lulling. They all dozed a little. Doyle said after an intense yawn, "You know, this place is something else to come home to. I'm going to have to stop coming summers. This may be my last one."

"Why?" Carl asked surprised.

"Well, a year from this fall, I'll be starting law school.

217

I ought to stay in town and work somewhere, get to know people, make some connections."

"Sounds like Minna."

"Well, maybe it sounds like her, but they'll be connections of my own choosing. I hate to admit it, but I'll miss Red Bear. Most times, working, I think I'll be dam' glad, but times like this afternoon. . . ." He sat up and stretched and got his amused, cynical mask on straight again. "What time will the dignitaries arrive?"

"Not till around ten, I guess," answered Rinie, "with fireworks goin' off."

"You mean A. J.'s staying up that late?"

"Hell," said Carl, "you can't say it's really dark with fireworks goin' off."

"I'm kind of eager to meet this Mr. Bell," Doyle said, almost allowing himself to show enthusiasm. "It occurred to me I might work for him while the legislature's in session next winter. It would be dam' good experience."

Carl, from seeming half-asleep, sat up abruptly.

"Rinie, Irine, Miz Stinson, ma'am,"-his eyes were sparkling, "would you consider comin' away in the woods with me?"

She blushed. "Carl Stinson——"

"Oh, no, now, wait a minute," he said hurriedly, "don't git the wrong idea. W'y, I wouldn' have that happen for anything in the world. I'm not suggestin' anything illicit. Is that a good word, Lawyer?"

"Dam' good by the look of your face—and hers."

Carl shook his head vigorously and drops of water from his hair glinted in the sun.

'No, ma'am, not illicit at all—much. But why don't we go git dressed, pack us some stuff, an' camp somewhere tonight?"

"Oh, Carl," she said wistfully, "there's the company coming."

"Well, hell, they can have our bed. An' the fewer the people there are here, the better Doyle's chances of gittin' in good with Mr. Bell."

"But I ought to be here to help Ellie."

"We'll be back before dinnertime tomorrow if you want to, an' she'll have Bess to help her."

"Well. . . ."

He stood up and pulled her to her feet.

When they were at the corrals saddling up, he thought

218

with pleasure how much better her face looked, like she'd had a long rest or was recovering from sickness. And she thought how wonderful it was to be with him, really with him, again. Through the past, busy months they had seen each other but they hadn't been truly together often. She looked up at him and smiled.

"Do you know what I think?"

He didn't.

"I think you're running away from Ellie's sister Bess. Didn't everyone have you all paired up with her?"

He nodded carelessly and bent down to fasten a pack strap.

"Yeah, but this is Independence Day."

Rinie and Ellie were canning green beans. The vines, Ellie said, had borne better than she could remember. They had picked them in the early morning, right after breakfast, before the heat and the flies got bad, and when Travis came to the house for something a little later, Ellie got him to drive her down to the store. They needed more caps for the jars and some other things. Rinie and Jeff and Helen sat on the porch, breaking and stringing the beans, and Ellie joined them when she got back.

"Ever'body's talkin' about what a good year it is," said Ellie contentedly as she settled to work after changing clothes. "I expect cattle prices'll be low, though, with such a good crop, but you can't have ever'thing. At least we're gonna have plenty to eat this winter."

"Mama, I wish I could play," Helen said petulantly. "I just all the time have to work. It's worse'n school."

"Well, I guess you can go ahead for a while, you pore little thing. An', Jeff, you better go too, son, for I hear they've got some kinda bunch that looks into cases where children's bein' mistreated."

Jeff grinned. "I guess they'd have a hard time gettin' anywhere here at Red Bear," he said, "but I did want to go and look at my calf again."

Doyle had brought home a sick calf and Jeff was caring for it, teaching it to drink from a bucket, ministering to its ills.

"He really means it, I believe," Ellie said proudly when he had gone, "about bein' a veterinarian." She looked sad and a little guilty. "I know Carl an' Doyle have both been at Travis this summer to do somethin' about his schoolin'."

219

"It's hard, I know, Ellie," Rinie said shyly, "but he ought to be sent. With some children it wouldn't matter, but Jeff really wants it."

"I know he does," she said soberly, "an' deserves it, an' me an' Travis has talked of it ever' year, but we ain't had nobody we wanted him to stay with. Neither one of us could of stood to send him to Minna's. Jeff ain't tough like the other boys. The things she says would hurt him, make him mad, keep him tore up all the time—things about the folks, I mean. Oh, we know people in Belford, friends, good folks, that would be glad to let him stay with 'em, only it seems like we can always find one excuse or another why he oughtn't to, only now—" She looked pleased and near tears. "Well, Bess and Larry wants him to come to them."

"Oh, Ellie, that would be wonderful—wouldn't it?"

"Well, if we've got to let him go, I guess it's the best we could wish for. I ain't had no dealin's with grownup children of my own yet, Rinie, so I don't know how that part of it is, but I do believe the hardest thing in the world for a mama an' daddy is to turn a-loose. . . . Seein' your young 'uns hurt, one way an' another, is nearly past bearin', but it's a thing you're both part of, you an' them, an' sometimes you can help 'em over a hurt, or maybe ease it a little for 'em. But turnin' a-loose—that's somethin' the ole folks has got to stand by theirselves, 'cause mostly it's a happy thing for the kids, a thing they want."

Ellie looked off across the flats and was silent for a little, her hands working busily. She stopped a moment and blew her nose impatiently.

"Well, anyway, Bess mentioned it when me an' the kids went to visit the folks, an' Larry talked to Travis when they was up here. They offered for Kirby, too, but, Lord! Kirby'd have a ringtail fit if we mentioned more schoolin'. Larry's gone some, you know, travelin' for the newspaper to git stories an' all, an' Bess says she needs comp'ny." Ellie smiled. "It looks to me like, crowded up the way them houses are in town there where they live, she wouldn' have no chance to git lonesome, but she says she does."

"What does Jeff think about it?" Rinie asked eagerly.

Ellie looked uncomfortable. "We ain't said nothin' to 'im yet. Fact is, you're the first one a the folks here at Red Bear that I've mentioned it to. . . . We're gonna tell

220

Jeff right soon now an' let him make up his own mind. I —I guess we ain't got much doubt what he'll decide or we would a already told 'im."

They were quiet then, snapping the beans with rapid efficiency and dropping them into their pans. A humming bird, flashing, tiny, exquisite, buzzed the porch inquisitively and settled briefly on a phlox blossom, sipped, and was away.

"They're so wonderful," Rinie said softly. "I never saw them before this summer. I still can't believe anything so delicate can be so strong and energetic."

Ellie nodded appreciatively.

Old Christmas was lying on the cool shady ground in the flower bed. She stood up stiffly and looked down toward the ford. None of the other dogs was around the house.

"Must be somebody comin'," said Ellie. "Horseback, I reckon. I don't hear no engine."

Christmas gave one cracked bay and dropped down again, her head still raised alertly. It wasn't easy to see the road down along the creek, now that the trees were leafed out. Rinie said uneasily, "Maybe it's Troy."

"I expect it is," Ellie said shortly. "They been sayin' how he ought to be back the last three or four days."

A look of stubborn determination set Ellie's face for a moment, a look the likes of which Rinie had seen only once before, the time Ellie had insisted that Kirby go to school rather than on the cattle drive. But Ellie changed her expression quickly and said mildly, "You aimin'. to teach agin this year? My land! It ain't more'n a little over a month till time for school to start agin."

"They asked me to," Rinie said dubiously. "Mr. McLean on—on behalf of the school board."

"Well! Now ain't that somethin'." Ellie was tremendously proud and pleased.

"Just till June comes back," Rinie said quickly. "Her baby's due the first of October and she wants to be ready to teach again by Thanksgiving, but I don't know, Ellie, if I can do it."

"W'y, I don't see why not," Ellie said stoutly. "June's always sayin' how fine you done last spring."

"Yes, but without her there—well, I just don't know."

It was Troy riding up the valley. He grinned and waved to them and went on to the corrals.

The obstinate look passed over Ellie's face again as she watched him go.

Rinie said, "Now Carl will have to go to Fraser's."

"What does Carl think about you teachin' school?"

She smiled fondly. "Oh, you know how Carl is. He says it's my affair, not his."

Ellie nodded. "Carl's a good bit like Travis. I always did say so. They keep out a other folks's business mostly, but you let 'em git riled up about somethin'. . . . Well, anyway, I think you ought to teach if you want to. Time'll come when you'll have your own young'uns an' can't hardly set foot outside a the house, though runnin' around don't seem to draw you like it would most girls your age."

"Ellie—" she turned her face away because the tears came suddenly and wouldn't be held back.

"W'y, what in the world, honey! What's the matter?"

"Ellie, I—I want a baby so much."

"W'y, Rinie, you mustn' cry like that, child. W'y, here now, you ain't even got a handkerchief."

She gave her one and, surreptitiously, blew her own nose on her apron.

"It's been almost a year," Rinie said miserably.

"Well, that don't mean nothin'," Ellie said stoutly. "They's a couple lives neighbors to my folks was married fourteen years before they ever had a baby, an' now they got three."

Rinie said brokenly, "I—I think of Doxy. . . . I don't guess she wants a baby at all, and I'd give—almost anything to be having one."

"Course you would, an' you'll have one, plenty of 'em, I don't doubt, but don't worry over it. There's times I've wished me an' Travis had had more time together before Kirby come. Children is the most wonderful things, Rinie, but once they start comin', you can't never have back the times when they was just the two of you."

Rinie felt her face and neck flushing. She had wanted to ask the question for a long time.

"Ellie, is there—anything you know of that I could—do?"

Ellie said gently, "You got to quit worryin', that'd be the biggest help. Lots a people—even doctors, I been told —say that tryin' too hard, wantin' a baby too much, always thinkin' about it, can make it harder for a woman to git that way, an', Rinie, it's hard on Carl when you worry. A man can tell an' it seems like maybe it makes him feel like you think he ain't so much of a man."

"Oh, no!" she cried, shocked. "Carl—it's nothing to do with Carl. But—but, Ellie, aren't there things that women can do to—to help. A doctor—"

"Oh, honey, I wouldn't mess with no doctors. I have heard there's things a woman can take, certain times, an' all, but Heddie'd know more about that kind a thing than any doctor."

"Oh, I couldn't! I couldn't go to Heddie. I—I. . . ."

"All right now," Ellie said firmly. "I told you they's not a bit a use to worry this soon. Now you got to quit cryin' that-a-way. I'm goin' in an' put some a these beans on an' see about dinner. You come in when you feel better. W'y, you don't want Carl to see you red-eyed an' all."

"How come you took so long?" Carl asked immediately upon entering the kitchen and finding Troy there.

"Not ever'body's fast as you. Why?"

"Because I was supposed to of been at Fraser's two weeks back at least."

"Well, what's keepin' you?"

"You know dam' well we can't—"

"Quit fussin' an' eat," ordered Ellie curtly, but Travis said, "You had ought to know, Troy, that we can't hardly spare both of you at the same time."

"Maybe Troy ought to go to Fraser's, too," mused Doyle.

"Listen, Buck," said Troy eagerly, "you ought to see a buckskin gelding Perryman's got up there. I bet you that, next to Brett, that's gonna be the best goddam' all-round horse on the West Fork."

"Out of that little mare Marky?" Carl recalled.

Troy nodded. "They've brought him along like a pet puppy dog, spoiled him some that way to my way a thinkin' but he's one hell of a pony. Mr. Perryman's real choosy about who rides him, but he let me work him some, cutting out some calves he'd sold, a little ropin'."

"I can't abide a buckskin horse," said A. J. tersely.

"Well, you don't judge a horse by color," Troy said irritably. "Anybody knows that."

"I know that," answered his father, "but I can't abide 'em anyhow."

"I saw the gelding last year," Carl said soberly to Troy. "He'll never be the cuttin' horse Skeeter was."

"The hell he won't."

"No, he won't, Bo. He's not got the strength in his hindquarters."

"Well, hell, you can always make a claim like that. With Skeeter dead, nobody can hardly bet against you."

"I had 'er up there last spring. I seen 'em both work."

"Well, the buckskin ain't but five now."

"We ought to chase that wild bunch from the ridges," said Kirby. "Jess Corbett said they got sight of 'em when they was huntin' cattle 'way up on Snowball Creek last week."

"We ain't got time now for no wild horse chasin', son," Travis said wearily. "Hay'll be ready in not much more'n a week an' before that we got to—"

"I got to go to Fraser's," Carl said with finality. "Me an' Rinie ain't got more'n a few dollars between us, an' besides, I promised Mr. Fraser. I'll go late tonight if I can. If not, first thing in the mornin'."

"Well, listen, Buck, I sorta thought you might want me to do that for you, too. That is, if things here. . . ."

Ellie said, "You kids through with your dinner? Run on outside."

"I didn' eat my puddin'," said Helen.

"Take it with you," said her mother curtly.

"I don't want you to go to Fraser's," Carl said to Troy. "I seen Bud as I come home an' he said Doxy ain't, well, things ain't changed any, an' so I thought—"

"We need you here to work on some of the machinery," Travis told him. "We can't hardly keep that goddam' pickup runnin', no matter what. It's got to be fixed. An' the mowin' machine—"

"The rest of us lack your skill with things mechanical," said Doyle. "I even broke a shovel."

"An' besides," said Ellie abruptly, with the determined, set look on her face, "it's time you faced up to things."

There was a tense silence and Ellie spoke again. She spoke nervously as though she faced a group of strangers that could be expected to be hostile, but she knew she was right.

"While you was gone, Troy, up to Perryman's, we had the Fourth of July picnic an' all, an' Essie Keane asked me to talk private. Now you just hush your mouth till

I've had my say. Essie didn' bemean you like she could have, not half the way you have Doxy. I said you ain't to talk till I'm done. You ain't got no female blood relatives but your Aunt Minna an' I don't guess you want her in on' this an' it looks like somebody's got to do somethin'.

"Now today, me an' Travis was down at the store an' Essie was there. She asked me to stop by the house a minute. Travis waited outside an' they wasn' nobody there, but Doxy an' Essie an' me. They taken Doxy to Belford to the doctor the first of this week. He says this thing happened to Doxy the end of April or the first of May, an' Troy Dean, Doxy swears it's yours. Lord knows, I don't put much faith an' hope in Doxy, but this time I believe her."

"Well, hell, Ellie, that ain't bein' very loyal to your own," protested Troy, reddening.

"That child's to be my nephew or niece," said Ellie tartly. "I guess that's my own as much as any brother-in-law. Before long, it'll be three months on its way. I don't see no need for you to cause us or Keanes no more worry over it."

"She means—" began Doyle.

"I know goddam' well what she means, an' I won't do it. They can't prove a thing, not a goddam' thing. There's other guys that'll swear they was with her."

"But," said Travis, "was they really? Or will they just say it 'cause they're friends of yours?"

"Well, I'll say one thing, they're one hell of a better bunch of friends than is settin' here."

"Doxy says three times," Ellie proceeded relentlessly. "She can tell where an' when."

"I don't give a hoot in hell if she tells how!" cried Troy, banging his fist down so that the dishes rattled. "Nobody can make me marry 'er."

He looked around the table in the silence. Obviously, Ellie and Travis were against him. Rinie was crying without making any sound. Doyle was an interested observer. He looked longest at Carl and A. J. Their faces were sober, but that was all he could tell about the way they felt. Looking at his father he said defiantly, "Well, can they?"

A. J. shook his head slowly. "No, they can't."

Ellie said sharply, "Your mother would want you to do right."

"Oh, Ellie, for Chrissake, it's not your business."

"It is her business," Travis said hotly. "She lives here, cooks your food, cleans your house, puts up with you. She's got a right to her say."

Carl put his arm around Rinie. She was trying not to cry, though she couldn't stop trembling. She was so terribly shaken by the vehemence of the words and feelings around the table. She would have left the kitchen; it was what she wanted to do, but she couldn't bear to go alone and she couldn't bring herself to ask Carl to come with her.

"I'm a little past the age of bein' told what my mother would want," Troy said sullenly. "As far as that's concerned, we was doin' all right with Heddie here."

"Act your goddam' age then," said A. J. harshly, "an' watch your mouth. Why is it there's got to be all this Christ-awful fuss? If you're aimin' to marry, why can't you just—do it an' have it over, like Buck done?"

"Oh, hell, Buck always does right, don't he? An' I ain't aimin' to marry—not Doxy Keane or anybody. You can't any of you look me in the eye an' say you'd like to have that little bitch livin' here."

"They's some," Ellie said tartly, "feels like Stinsons ain't no bargain."

"Ellie," said Doyle with a grin of approbation, "you're a game lady."

"I better go to Fraser's, Carl," said Troy decisively. "Maybe I better go a few other places while I'm at it. It's so goddam' unfriendly around here."

"If you got nothin' to worry about," said A. J. heavily, "how come you feel like runnin'? That ain't never been our way."

Carl said tensely, "He never has said that he's not got anything to worry about. All he's said is that he's not got to marry her."

Troy stared at him and his eyes turned cold and steely.

"Theorn an' Bud will swear they—"

"I know what they'll swear," Carl said, "because they told me."

"They both had her," Troy was all but shouting.

"I know they did. Last week, they both told me when."

"You sonofabitch, you went around an'—"

"No, I didn', Troy. I went after horseshoes an' it happened I saw 'em both, separate. They said to say they was behind you all the way an' they'd say whatever you wanted said."

"Set down, Troy," A. J. said with authority. "We won't have no fightin' in the house."

"What did they say?" demanded Troy through his teeth, "about when they was with her?"

Carl said slowly, "What it amounted to was that neither of them was foolin' with Doxy the time Ellie said. I know that don't count, since they'll say they was, but I thought it might make a difference to you to know I know."

"An' you thought you ought to tell all the rest! An' you think I ought to marry the little whore."

"I think," Carl said, his voice rough with anger, "you've not got a hell of a lot of room to call her names. I don't give a good goddam' what you do about her, but I wish to Christ we wouldn' talk about it any more."

"*You* do!" Troy exploded. "You're through with it, are you? Now that—"

It was hard on a man to feel trapped and betrayed and deserted. A. J. said, almost gently, "Listen, Troy, Sutter tole me at the Fourth a July doin's that he aims to bring Reverend Turner up here after church third Sunday, the preacher an' Miz Keane an' Doxy, to talk about this business. Now it's got to be settled. The least you can do is give that much of your time."

"She can git rid of the bastard," cried Troy desperately. "I'll pay for that."

"You won't do it," said his father and the words dropped separately, heavily, like the big dark stones that washed over Red Bear falls. "Takin' life don't right nothin' . . . Keanes wouldn' hear of it an' we won't neither."

"I won't marry her."

"All right. That's up to you, but you can quit runnin' right now. Git on out yonder an' see if you can find out what's wrong with that goddam' ole truck, an' we won't have no more talk about this. We've all heard enough of it."

Carl and Rinie went to Belford the weekend of third Sunday. Bud Corbett lent them his almost new coupe. Carl had just finished at Fraser's and was in a mood to spend what he'd made. They stayed, for the two nights they had, in the Hayes Valley, the best of Belford's three hotels.

"What'll we do?" he asked expansively. "Go to shows? Dances? They say there's a band concert at the park." Suddenly he was a little crest-fallen. "There's not a hell of a lot to offer, compared with Denver. I wish we had more time, Rinie, so we could go to Salt Lake or some place, but the hay. . . ."

"I know," she said gently. "It doesn't matter. What counts is that you—you wanted to do something for me —with me. . . . Carl, we don't have to go much of anywhere as far as I'm concerned. Except for when we went camping, Fourth of July, it just seems like I haven't seen you all summer. I mean, we've been around each other, but you've been working so hard and—"

"Well," he said happily, "we could just stay right here an' be together. An' if that got monotonous, we could take a bath once in a while or watch the toilet flush."

She giggled. "You sound just like A. J."

"When did you ever watch a toilet flush with A. J., missy?"

They ate each meal at a different restaurant and on Saturday night they heard the band concert through their open window and then went to the late showing of a movie, the showing where all the couples necked.

"I feel like you shouldn't come in here with me," whispered Rinie in the corridor outside their room.

"Well, where'll I take a bath though?" he wondered.

On Sunday afternoon, they went to an impromptu rodeo at the fairgrounds. Privately, Rinie felt that Carl ought to get enough of that kind of thing at home, but he enjoyed it immensely except that he wished, to himself, that he were taking part.

They had to go back to Red Bear Monday morning so there was a kind of poignant sadness about Sunday night. They lay awake a long time, talking or being silent together.

"You'll be awfully tired to start haying," she said tenderly as they heard the courthouse clock strike again.

"I love you," he answered.

"Carl? Will he marry her?"

"Yes."

"How can you be so sure?"

They hadn't mentioned the subject since that frightful

day at the dinner table. No one had, to Rinie's knowledge.

"Because," Carl said slowly, "he knows what's right, an' he don't want to leave Red Bear."

"But would it come to that? I—I didn't know you felt so strongly about it."

"Not me," he said. "I'm sorry as hell for him, though he's got nobody to blame. But he does know what's right, an' besides, to stay at Red Bear, he's got to live with Ellie."

There was a silence and she said hesitantly, "It's the right thing—the only thing—for them to get married, but, oh, Carl, it would be so awful to marry without loving."

"They'll work it out, maybe," he said, but without much assurance. "Doxy's just a kid yet. They may be fine for each other after a while."

"But the baby, Carl . . . born without any love . . . the little baby. . . ."

She was crying and he drew her into his arms, holding her tenderly. She couldn't stop. All at once, when the tears began, she felt that her heart was breaking. For a time, he let her cry, holding her, lying very still, then he sat up and drew her up with him, into his arms.

"I'm sorry," she sobbed miserably, "to ruin this night of all times! Oh, Carl. . . ."

"You're not," he said quietly. "Nothin's ruined, little girl. How long have you been needin' to cry in somebody's arms?"

For a time, she couldn't speak, and then she said chokingly, "You always know."

"No. I wish I did. . . . What brought this on mostly is Doxy's baby, isn' it?"

"Oh, Carl please don't, I—"

"Rinie, you need to talk about it. You never do, an' it's a thing I know you can't help thinkin' about."

"Carl, they—they didn't want me." She tried to fling herself away from him, to bear the shame and misery alone as she always had, but he held her.

"But what's that got to do with you?"

"They didn't *want* me." She was becoming hysterical. Her fingers dug into his arms in a gesture that was half-clinging, half-repulsing.

"They said, at the orphanage, that you were a few

229

hours old when you were left there," he said gently. "Didn't they?"

She moved her head a little, miserably.

"Did you ever try to think what anybody could have against a few-hours'-old baby? Personally, I mean. What could there be about *you* they didn't want?"

"I—I—"

"Maybe he ran off and left her without bein' married. Maybe she died an' he didn't know what to do. Maybe they already had twenty-two kids, but Rinie, honey, can't you see that whatever their reasons, it would have been the same with any kid. It wasn't *you*. I know livin' with Minna didn' help to make you any more sure of yourself. I wish you hadn' had to go through that, but if you hadn't, it's likely we never would have known each other."

She lay against him, still sobbing, but the tension was going. A good deal of it had been in her as long as she could remember and now it was easing. She was ashamed of being deserted, unloved, unwanted, a foundling, perhaps she always would be, but Carl was right, it hadn't been her doing and having it said was what made the difference.

After a while, when she had almost stopped crying, he said, "Go wash your face, sweetheart, an' le's go to sleep."

"I want to be close to you," she said timidly when she came back.

"I want you to." His arms were around her.

"Carl, you're so good to me. Oh, I wish so much that I could do something for you, something that would really count. I love you so."

"That counts," he said, "more than anything I know."

She had never felt so utterly exhausted nor so contentedly relaxed as she did, falling asleep then.

12

"He shore is," said Travis, grinning broadly, "gonna join the married man's club an' all like that."

Rinie and Carl had arrived back at the ranch at dinnertime on Monday to find the whole family gay and complacent.

"When?" asked Carl, still dubious.

"Next Sunday," said Ellie proudly. "Reverend Turner's comin' back special. We'll have a big dinner after, maybe a barbecue. The day after that's A. J.'s birthday, you know."

Carl kept eying Troy covertly and finally decided it would be safe to speak to him directly.

"Haven't you got anything to say for yourself?" he asked, grinning tentatively.

"There's not been much chance," Troy said a little glumly. "I—I would like for you to stand up with me. Doxy wants Supina with her, I guess."

"Why has somebody got to stand up with 'em?" Helen wondered.

" 'Cause they ain't able by theirselves," replied her grandfather.

"What bothers me," said Doyle morosely, "is what am I supposed to do for a room after this week?"

"You could stay in Denver," Troy said ungraciously.

"We'll put up that cot in our room," said Ellie, "an' you can have Helen's room whenever you're home. That'll be fine, won't it, Helen?"

Helen didn't look pleased. She thought there must be a better way.

"Doxy could sleep with me an' then nobody wouldn' have to move."

"God," said Carl, "is this gonna come up ever' time?"

"By the time Doyle gits married," said Troy, "Helen'll have her own husband."

"But what'll I do with my books an' things?" worried Doyle.

"Oh, hell, Siefog, you're worse'n some ole lady," said his father. "You can put your dam' stuff in my room."

"Well," said Carl when he'd finished eating, "if you don't want to start on the hay till tomorrow, I'll go up an' look over the mares' fence. Bud was sayin' that dam' sorrel stud's still around close."

"Buck," said Troy a little stiffly, "if you'll—uh—wait just a minute till I find my spurs, I'll ride along with you."

"What was it!" cried Rinie, scarcely able to wait till they had the kitchen to themselves. "Ellie, what happened?"

Ellie threw out her hands in a gesture of helplessness.

"Lord, Rinie, I don't know. Well, you was here till Saturday mornin'. You know it hadn' been mentioned in over a week, not in my hearin' anyway, an' Travis said not in his. Reverend Turner an' Keanes come here yesterday an', Lord, you don't know how I dreaded it. In the first place, I expected Troy to hit out for far places. It ain't much in their nature, but the way he's been actin' lately—" She broke off, smiling softly.

"I was just rememberin' the first time Travis ever kissed me. It was in the ev'nin', after dark, an' we was on the porch. We lived where Barnharts lives now an' daddy an' the boys had put barbwire around the yard just that day to keep the stock out. Travis'd helped 'em. Anyway, he kissed me—just a little bashful peck, but we both thought it was somethin' awful special—an' it shook him up so, he says 'Night, Ellie,' real quick an' lit out runnin', but he forgot about the fence an' tore his pants and got his legs scratched up right bad. . . . He was the sweetest thing . . . still is, . . . but that wasn' what I's tellin', was it?

"Nossir, Troy never run. He was right here an' he behaved real well. Troy's always been a little spoilt. He's just exactly like A. J., stubborn as a mule an' used to havin' his own way if he just holds out long enough. They're ever'one stubborn like that, though. I think he thought A. J.'d egg him on to git out a this business, an' I know he never thought about Carl sayin' what he did about them other boys."

"Carl didn't ask them, they came to him. He didn't want anything to do with it," Rinie said and was a little surprised at herself. She had been proud of Carl, speaking out for the right as he had, but it had hurt him, alienating Troy like that, when Troy needed friends. He had told her, driving home today, how Theorn and Bud had come to offer help.

"Why couldn' they just say they'd been with her?" he had said unhappily. "I didn' give a dam' when or anything."

"Well, anyway," Ellie went on, "Reverend Turner was just as uneasy as the rest of us when they come in, an' I felt right sorry for Doxy. She was cryin'. Before anybody could start on whatever spiels they had ready, Troy went up to her, before we'd set down or anything, an' says, 'We'll git married, Doxy, when you want to.' Well, then nobody knowed what to say, an' Troy looked around kinda smart-alec, like, as A. J. says, he guessed he'd cut our water off. Then he says he had some work to do an' for us to make the plans an' he'd be willin', an' that's all they was to it. Course, he coulda stayed around, showed a little more interest, but he done so much better than I expected that I just simply didn't know what to think, still don't. Rinie, I swear, you just can't never say nothin' for sure about a Stinson.

"An' then, at suppertime, Troy come in an' asked what was decided an' we told 'im. It was his idea to have a big dinner or somethin' for all the community. Course, ever'body knows now that Doxy's in' trouble, with Sutter goin' around blatherin' about justice an' all the way he has been, but we might as well make the best of it."

She snapped a dish towel out the open window, ridding it of crumbs from the table.

"Do you know what I really think it is, though? I think it's the baby. I believe, after what the doctor said an' what them other boys told Carl, Troy decided it's actually his, an' he wants it. It wouldn't be natural for a Stinson not to claim his child."

Rinie felt a lift of gladness for the unborn baby, and she thought of the little grave up in the cemetery, Heddie's child, with A. J.'s name—all of it. She said, "Oh, I'm glad, Ellie! I'm so glad."

Ellie became dubious. "Well, it had to be this way, things bein' like they are, but, Rinie, I do dread Doxy bein' here all the time, don't you?"

Rinie had scarcely thought of daily living with Doxy,

233

of having her be another companion in the work, a part of the family.

Ellie sighed resignedly. "I guess women folks don't hardly look forward to no kind a change in their houses, even if it turns out to be for the better, but that pore little thing is purely empty-headed and useless, from what I've seen."

"Well, we'll just have to help her," Rinie said with a smile that was a little shaky. She felt worry for Doxy. "Sometimes, people that don't seem—worth very much just need—need to be loved."

Ellie looked out of the window and things out there misted up a little.

She said crossly, "I don't know how you come into a family like this, soft, gentle notions like you got, an' you still hang onto 'em."

Troy and Doxy were married after church that Sunday, the ceremony being followed by the exodus of a good part of the community to Red Bear where a beef was being barbecued in a pit near the swimming hole. Later in the evening, when Reverend Turner and most of the older people had gone home, it turned into quite a party, with dancing on the front porch to music that the Barnhart boys played on fiddle and guitar.

It was a beautiful night—Rinie thought the nicest she'd ever seen—warm enough so that sitting outdoors was pleasant, with a full moon so ripe and bright and beautiful that it was almost beyond bearing. The mosquitoes were bad this time of year, but mostly they were used to them and able to ignore them. The men had some bottled mosquito repellent to be taken internally, and they passed it around freely.

After a while, they went down to where the trestle tables were still set up, built up the fire and finished off the meat and the other leftover food.

Theorn threw the unwary Pup into the swimming hole and then the men decided that a swim would be a beneficial thing for a bridegroom just before retiring. Troy, obligingly, said they all ought to swim and most of the men decided they would. The women withdrew to the porch to talk and laugh quietly, while a great deal of mighty splashing and yelling and hilarious laughter carried up to them from the creek.

When the men came out, they were all of a bluish tint, and badly in need of something warming.

"Not coffee!" cried Bud Corbett in disgust, when the big pot was brought out.

They danced some more. Carl's hands were still cold and Rinie shivered and drew close to him at his touch through the thin blouse on her back.

"Don't dance with anybody else till their hands git warm," he told her.

"It's all so beautiful," she said softly. "After all the trouble and—and everything, surely no one could want a nicer wedding day."

It wouldn't have been this way in Denver, she thought; at least, not among any of the people she had known. Here everyone knew about Doxy and now it didn't seem to matter any more.

"I'm glad Doyle's paying some attention to Vanda," she whispered. "She looks so pretty tonight."

"I wish they'd all go home," muttered Carl ungraciously.

A. J. was still up. There was no use trying to sleep with all this racket going on. He sat on the porch, scarcely noticed by the young people as being different, and almost he could forget, amid the music and dancing, the talk and laughter, the drinking, the kisses in dark corners, that tomorrow was his sixty-ninth birthday.

During the afternoon and the early part of the evening, Doxy had been painfully concerned and uncertain about the propriety of things. Her childish face had been serious, at times mournful with the enormity of what was happening to her, but as she realized that people were paying her not much more attention than anyone else in the gathering, that she was not to be ostracized, nor need she behave like an elderly matron, she began to have a wonderful time.

It was well after midnight when Billy Barnhart put down his fiddle and said loudly, "God, Troy, you must be awful sleepy. It seems to me like you an' Doxy ought to be gittin' to bed."

"Yeah," agreed his brother Joe. "I've heard marryin's a tirin' business."

"In medieval times," proclaimed Doyle happily from the porch rail, "the guests at a wedding put the couple to bed."

"Yeah," said Theorn, "let's do like they done in them evil times."

Rinie was embarrassed and felt sorry for Doxy. Doxy's face was flushed, but she looked up at Troy and laughed as he came toward her, a little unsteadily.

Rinie looked around for Carl and found him standing behind her. He whispered exuberantly, "Jeff an' Kirby put a couple of frogs in their bed."

"Oh, Carl, that's mean," she said, shocked.

"No, it's not," he said reasonably. "I helped catch 'em."

The newlyweds went in, amid good wishes and sundry comments and speculations and laughter.

"We sewed the bottom of Doxy's gown together," Nell Tippitt whispered gleefully to Rinie as the guests were beginning to go home.

Well, they wouldn't do those things in Denver either, thought Rinie a little grimly, and she was glad that she and Carl had married without anyone's knowledge and had not spent their wedding night at Red Bear.

While the family still stood on the porch with the noisy old car motors sputtering away down the valley, there came a terrified scream from inside the house.

"My Lord!" breathed Ellie, and A. J., lifting his feet down off the porch rail said, in a voice full of suppressed laughter, "Ole Bojack's quite some boy."

Carl and Doyle, spluttering with laughter, said they guessed all Doxy'd found was a couple of frogs.

"Well," said Travis hilariously, "if that woke Helen up, you two boys can be the ones that explains to her what it was Doxy found."

Rinie was angry with them. She felt like crying with chagrin for Doxy's sake, but the next morning when Troy and Doxy got up late and came into the kitchen, looking tired and pleased with themselves, Doxy said peevishly, but with no embarrassment, "Somebody put some nasty ole frogs in our bed last night, an' I bet it was you, Carl Stinson."

All the men were still sitting around the table drinking coffee. There was plenty to be done, but it seemed hard to get started this morning. Carl said innocently, "W'y, Doxy, I wouldn't do a thing like that. There's a lot of frogs around an' they git in the house sometimes."

"Like hell," said Troy. "I guess it's about as likely for a couple of frogs to git in a bed around here as for a mountain lion to come down the chimley."

The mountain-lion episode had not been mentioned in the presence of the whole group until now and Carl, flushing, threw a quick look at his father, but the old man was laughing.

"What mountain lion?" asked Doxy, mystified.

"Well, as far as my part of it goes," said A. J., sobering, but with the corner of his mouth quirking, "I think I'd ruther you boys 'ud hunt frogs as lions—at times, that is."

Rinie fried bacon and eggs for the newlyweds while Ellie was finishing the dishes from the others' breakfasts. Doyle said solicitously, "But you slept all right? After the frogs?"

"No," said Doxy, unabashed. "Somebody sewed up my gown. I couldn' even git it on."

"An' that was a hell of a shame," murmured Troy complacently.

Ellie threw Rinie a look; raised eyebrows and a surprised grin, and when Rinie came over to get plates, Ellie murmured, "I did expect a little modesty from one of Sutter's girls."

And just then, Doxy was saying, soberly but tenderly, "Troy, you do cuss a lot. I—I do wish you wouldn' use them words so much."

"Cuss a lot last night, did he?" inquired A. J. very softly, and Carl choked a little on a swallow of coffee.

"What words is that, Dox?" asked Troy indulgently.

"Well, like—like hell an' goddam' an' all." She blushed. "That's blasphemin', an' it just ain't right."

"W'y, Jesus Christ," began her husband a little irritably, but Doyle said, "Well, now, Doxy, it's not necessarily blaspheming. It could just mean that people that call on God and all a lot are just closer, you know, on a first-name basis."

Doxy thought about it but looked unconvinced.

"I tell you," murmured Ellie, "this place won't never be the same. I don't know of nobody but Minna that ever had the gall to tell a Stinson not to cuss."

"Maybe a few new ideas won't hurt," whispered Rinie, and they giggled together as Ellie vigorously pumped water.

The summer was over so swiftly.

The first day of school was also Carl's and Rinie's first anniversary. She was disappointed that they couldn't spend the day together, and she was terribly nervous about teaching alone. She had so many plans and hopes. Together, she and June had been able to talk the school board into spending money for new books and Rinie was excited about them for the children's sake, and about all her own new ideas for the school year, but what if the children didn't think so much of her plans? What if she couldn't make things interesting and right for them?

Carl rode down with her, early. She had been to the school several times recently, and to Tippitts for conferences with June, trying to make sure she was ready as she could be. She would have twenty-one students among the eight grades. She yearned to know them, to teach them, to learn with them, and she was frightened of them. She wished Carl could stay with her today but that would be a little silly, of course, and she couldn't quite bring herself to ask him. He said proudly, "It all looks fine, Rinie, especially you. If they don't behave, just give 'em a couple a backhands. The school board'll go along with you."

"That's no way to teach," she said reprovingly.

"It works dam' fast though. It did with us anyway, but then, I guess you're not as strong as A. J. To be good, a backhand's got to have power behind it."

"Who was your teacher?" she asked. The Stinsons rarely talked about school.

"Well, we had about six as I remember. They don't last long. Either they can't take it an' leave, or they git married an' raise their own kids. Listen, that's an idea! We could git married, you an' me, an' raise all kinds a hell. What do you think?"

"Well—maybe—sometime—when I'm through with my career."

He drew her up from where she sat at her desk, arranging schedules for the various classes, and held her hard against him.

"If you ever need somebody," he said softly, his lips brushing her ear and making her shiver deliciously, "to erase your board or sharpen your pencils or anything at all, just let me know."

She put her head back to look up at him and he kissed her.

"I'm dam' proud of you, you know that? You're the prettiest teacher Webber ever had. Want me to meet you after school?"

She laughed. "How do you manage to make everything sound—sexy?"

"Nothin' to it. It's all in the way your mind runs. . . . Rinie. . . ." His eyes were eager and a little shy. "I'm goin' after the stallion today. That's why I brought along all that rope an' rode ole Dan. He's big an' fast an' can last a long time. I may not be back by the time school's out. It could be real late before I git home, but don't worry."

"But wouldn't it be better," she said uneasily, "if somebody went with you?"

"No. I want to git him by myself."

She felt a chill of fear.

"Carl. . . ." She was about to ask him to be careful and he knew it and frowned a little, so she said instead, "Bring him home for an anniversary present."

She didn't watch him ride away. Ellie said it was bad luck to watch people out of sight and she felt such an oppressive uneasiness about his going off alone after the wild horse. The children began to arrive at school then and Rinie had little time to think of anything but their affairs.

Carl was not there when Rinie and Helen got home, nor when the men came in for supper.

"Rinie, where's Carl at?" asked Travis peevishly. "I needed him today."

"Ah, Prunes, you need 'em all ever' day," said A. J. mildly. "You're worse'n any ramrod I ever seen."

Rinie knew that A. J. knew where Carl was. She wondered if Carl had told him or if he just knew. She said to Travis, "He went to look for the wild horses."

Travis frowned. "I don't see why it had to be today. I aimed for him to cut some corral poles."

"Did you ever think that that might be the reason he went?" asked Doyle sardonically.

"He's goddam' selfish about it," said Troy irritably. "I thought we'd go after that stud horse together."

Kirby said he'd wanted to go, too, and Helen wanted to know what color horse was a stud.

Doxy said, "I don't see what you need with another horse, anyway. They're all over the place."

"We got no stallion," Troy said candidly, "to breed our mares. This spring we had to use McLean's stud."

"Oh," said Helen to herself, "I guess he's talkin' about

239

ole Rip. He's a bay. I never did know that color was called stud, too."

Frowning at Ellie, Travis said, "Whyn't you talk to her? She's eight years old."

"I talk to her ever'day of her life," said Ellie shortly. "Why do you men have to talk about things like that at the table?"

"But why that ole wild thing?" insisted Doxy. "He won't never be no good for ridin' nor nothin', will he?"

"Oh, he'll be all right for a thing or two," said Troy, grinning, and she blushed and giggled.

"Carl can break him, maybe," said Jeff.

"I bet you he can't," asserted Kirby.

"Well, that don't matter a hell of a lot one way or the other," said A. J. " 'Cep' maybe to Buck, an' the horse. If he can git him, we'll have us free service for the mares. That's what counts about it."

"Service," mused Helen to herself. "Church service . . . funeral service. . . ."

"The talk at this table," stated Ellie, bringing forth a rice pudding from the oven, "gits more unfit ever' day I live."

When the dishes were done, Rinie went into her room to work on lessons for the next day. Ellie had urged her to go as soon as she finished supper, but Doxy wasn't much help with the work—she had got up from the table and followed Troy into the front room—and it wasn't fair for Ellie to have it all to do. Besides, Rinie didn't want to be alone. She was beginning to feel sick with apprehension. Why didn't he come? It was long past dark.

The others were all in the front room when he came and the radio was turned on loud—Doxy liked the radio —but Rinie heard his step and ran to meet him at the back door.

In the light of the single lamp, set on a shelf by the door, he looked exhausted. His hands were lacerated with rope burns and he tried to hide them from her. There was blood on his clothes.

"Carl . . .?"

She thought it was defeat in his eyes. He said quietly, "I got him, the sonofabitch. He's out there in the corral, though I wouldn' swear he'll be there in the mornin'. Ole Dan's nearly wore out. I'm worried about him. God, Rinie, that horse—"

But then Kirby, coming into the kitchen for an apple,

discovered him, and all of them came with questions. They took flashlights and went out to look at the stallion, but about all they could see were his wild, defiant eyes.

"Hey, Buck, there's two broncs, by God!" cried Troy. "What's this other?"

"A little filly," Carl said wearily. "She followed him. I thought Rinie might want her if she's any good."

While he ate, he told them how he had found the herd up near the head of Snowball Creek were they had seemed to spend most of this summer, and run them into a steep draw. The stallion had stood between him and the mares as they, with their colts, tried to scramble up out of the trap, and while he stood, rearing and screaming challenge, Carl had roped him.

"How many mares?" asked A. J.

"Looked like about eight, with several colts an' some yearlings. I didn't have much chance to look over anything but him."

"How in hell'd you git 'im home?" Travis asked. "I figgered if you caught 'im, you'd leave 'im tied someplace a while."

"I was afraid he'd git away," Carl said frankly, and then with admiration, "that ole Dan's one hell of a horse. All I could do was neck the stud right up against him with all the rope I had. He's been kicked an' bit an' stepped on an' I don't know what all."

"How could you ride," asked Doyle, "with them close together like that?"

Carl looked embarrassed. "I didn't. I walked an' took a quirt to the sonofabitch when Dan couldn' drag him any more."

A. J. grunted. "You're some horse catcher. Beat all I ever seen for walkin'."

"When you gonna ride him?" asked Kirby eagerly.

"I don't know. Not tonight, for dam' sure. You kids stay the hell away from him. I—I think I'll have a swim."

"It's cold," Doxy pointed out, but Troy and Doyle and Jeff and Kirby decided to go along, too, and Ellie said they might as well take some soap with them.

When Carl came back, Rinie was putting away her papers.

"How was school?" he asked, rubbing his cheek against hers.

"You're freezing," she said. "Get to bed."

"Yes, ma'am, I'm goin'. I can see you're already gittin'

241

bossy like a schoolmarm. Did you have any trouble?"

"Carl? What's that?"

There was a heavy red welt across his lower ribs on the left side. She touched it gently and he winced.

"I got too close once when I come up with the quirt," he said ruefully. "He just grazed me is all. It's not anything."

"That blood that was on your clothes—"

"Most of it's Dan's. I had another look at him just now. I guess he'll be all right. . . . What about school?"

While she got ready for bed and brushed her hair, she told him some of the things about her day, little things that were important only to her and perhaps to the children and, she was grateful to see, to him. She blew out the lamp and put back the curtains—mostly now she remembered to do it without being asked—and got into bed. She was very tired. The strain of this first day of school and of her worry about him had exhausted her.

"Carl, are you sure nothing's broken—your ribs?"

"It's a bruise, Rinie. When are you gonna quit frettin'?"

After a moment he said tentatively, by way of apology for his curtness, "The filly's a pretty little thing. She was two in the spring, I guess. Maybe you'll like her."

She laid her hand against his cheek.

"It's sweet," she said, "and sad that she'd follow him like that. I like her already."

There was a long silence. She thought he was falling asleep, but then he said slowly, "I've wanted him for three years. I've chased him an' dreamed about chasin' him, an' after—what happened with Skeeter, I've hated him, though that don't make any sense—but now I . . . when I put him in that little corral an' took the ropes to go after the filly, an' he run across there an' nearly crashed into the fence on the other side, I . . . I wished I hadn' caught him."

"You could let him go," she said very softly.

"No, I guess I wouldn' want to do that, either."

He drew a deep sigh and started involuntarily at the sharp pain in his ribs. She knew about the pain, but she made herself not mention it. She said, "What about the others—his harem?"

"His what? Oh, they'll be all right. Some young stud comin' on'll have 'em, or some ole boy'll have 'em in with his bunch. There's several wild bunches around yet, an' females are like that, they don't seem to care much who it is."

"Some do," she said defensively. "The one that followed him did."

"More likely, she was just curious or somethin'. Females are that, too."

"You're not a bit romantic, are you?" she said, pouting a little.

"Yes, I am, too, but horses ain't. You're mixin' me up with him."

"Oh," she said, "it seemed to me that you were mixing me up with her."

"No," he said, turning painfully and putting his arms around her. "I can tell the difference easy, even with it dark like this."

"Carl? A year ago tonight, I—I was pretty scared."

"Were you, Rinie?"

"Yes. Couldn't you tell?"

"Maybe some, but I guess I was too scared myself to notice much."

On Saturday, Travis and Ellie and the children went to Belford. They bought some things Jeff would need, going to school in town, stayed over night with the Treadwells, and came home—without Jeff.

"He was mostly so quiet," Carl said. "I didn't think about missin' him so much."

Ellie told Doxy and Rinie that Bess was to have a baby in the spring.

"Just ever'body's havin' 'em, seems like," said Doxy archly and she looked pointedly at Rinie. "I never thought of it till Troy mentioned it the other day, but our baby's due about Carl's birthday. Wouldn't it be somethin' if it was born then?"

Rinie thought she wouldn't like it and then she felt ashamed of her envy of Doxy's pregnancy. By way of atonement, she said, "Wouldn't you like to start making some things for your baby? I could teach you to knit if you want to."

"Well, that might be kinda fun, though I never did like to be still long enough to do hand work. But I guess I'll have to be still more now, with winter comin' an' the baby on the way. . . . Yes, I might learn to knit. I'd like to make a little pink sweater an' bonnet. I do hope it'll be

243

a girl. I want to name her Claudia Veronica. Ain't that pretty?"

"Listen, Doxy," said Ellie casually, "what's the thing you cook the best of all? I thought maybe you'd like to be the one to fix most a the supper one night soon. It'd make Troy real proud. A man likes to eat his wife's cookin' an' have other people eat it an' brag on it. What do you make best?"

Doxy's plump little face was perplexed. "Well . . . fudge, I guess. I'm gonna go tell Troy I want to learn to knit. Maybe we can go git some thread tomorrow."

Ellie sighed helplessly. "My Lord a-mercy! She's such a baby herself. I don't know how she's gonna take care of another one. Fudge! W'y, I wasn' as old as her when me an' Travis married an' I started doin' for this whole bunch. I can just see their bloomin' faces if they set down to a table full a fudge."

They both laughed and Rinie said, "I wonder, though, why her mother didn't teach her more things."

It seemed to Rinie that anyone with a mother should have so much; that anyone who was a mother should give so much.

"Well, Essie's a good woman an' all, but she ain't much of a hand to work. It wouldn' do if she was, I guess, Sutter lazy like he is, it'd drive her crazy. All of 'em down there does about as little as they can git by with. But don't you worry, I aim to bring Doxy along. It may be slow, but I'll do 'er. They won't no woman in this house spend all her time lookin' through magazines an' primpin' an' settin' on her man's lap; not while I'm up an' able. Fudge, my foot."

Two weeks after Jeff went to Belford, Doyle returned to Denver for his final year of college.

"Thinnin' out around here," observed A. J., looking around the table.

"The work ain't," said Travis, with the harried look that was always most marked in the fall.

"Don't worry, ole man," said Troy blithely, "we'll see you through."

Troy's face had a smooth complacence of late to replace the petulance that had been there so frequently during the past year.

They had their own cattle sorted and ready to ship and were holding them in the big corral for a few days until

244

all the ranchers in the area should be ready. For those few days, Carl and Troy hired out to help the others.

The last week in September, on a sweet, bright, poignant fall morning while Rinie sat on the school steps watching the children at recess time, Mrs. Putney, whose husband owned the store, came across to her with a troubled face.

"Did you hear about June?" she asked, her voice low under the clamorous noise of the children.

"No," Rinie said eagerly. "Has she had her baby?"

A dark-haired little first grader came hurrying up.

"Miz Stinson, will you tie my sash?"

"All right, Annie. There. Go play now."

Mrs. Putney said, "The baby was born dead—a little girl."

"Oh. Oh, no!" Rinie felt dizzy.

"It come in the night. She had a real bad time. Heddie was there an' all, but she said the baby was dead before June started to labor."

Having delivered herself of the news, Mrs. Putney returned to the store and Rinie sat there, shivering in the warm fall sun.

Poor June . . . Poor Alva . . . oh, poor little baby that never, never lived! Heddie was there. Heddie had been there when Ellie's baby didn't live, when Jenny died, when Heddie's own little boy died and still they had such faith in her! Why not a doctor? Oh, why not somebody who knew more than herbs and charms?

"Miz Stinson?" said Pearl Barnhart timidly.

Rinie hadn't realized she was crying.

"You look sick, Miz Stinson."

The other children were crowding around her.

"It's past time for recess to be over," said Jack McLean. "Maybe we better just go on home if teacher don't feel good."

"Did Miz Putney say somethin' mean to you?" demanded Helen fiercely.

"No," said Rinie quickly, trying to smile, her eyes goin over them quickly to make sure they were all there. "Where's Jerry? Oh, there you are.

"All of you come in now. We have a lot to do. Pearl, will you and Judy take the second and third graders and hear their arithmetic, please? I'll have my first graders up

245

here for reading and the rest of you may work on whatever you like for the next half hour."

There were only two first graders and their reading vocabulary, to date, was extremely limited, but, almost, they kept her from thinking of June and the baby for a little while.

She had to stay late at school, filling out some papers required by the district, and then she rode up to the Tippitts'. Alva's mother was red-eyed and haggard. She said June was sleeping and that Alva had gone out somewhere by himself for a little while. They would bury the baby tomorrow.

Starting home, Rinie looked wistfully up the road along the West Fork. Carl was up there, working for the Hunters'. How could she go home alone with this terrible sadness so heavy upon her? Without Carl?

Dispiritedly, she turned Jim down the road and before she came to the river's juncture with Red Bear Creek, she met Heddie. Heddie rode a rough-looking little bay horse and she was going to check on her patient. She made a little gesture of greeting, but Rinie could make no reply. Placidly, old Jim took the road along Red Bear Creek and it didn't really matter that Rinie couldn't see the way.

There was a little snow the night before they started the cattle drive. Rinie and Helen rode down early with Carl and Troy and Kirby to watch them start. The next to last thing Carl said to her as they sat their horses by the gate, was, "Don't forgit to see the wild ones git fed." The cattle streamed past, frisky in the early cold. The last thing he said, softly as he was about to take up a drag position was, "I love you, Rinie Stinson."

It was lonely at Red Bear, though Rinie didn't feel the desolation she had known last year. There was school all day, papers to grade and lessons to prepare in the evening and Doxy was there, chattering constantly.

A. J. was ill. There had been no talking to him about not working the roundup and now he suffered badly for all the riding and roping. If his pride had been a little less indomitable, he would have stayed in bed, but he spent most of his days on the sofa in the front room, complaining volubly of everything. Doxy was frightened of him and he sometimes made her cry. Ellie was not frightened of him and he often made her angry. Rinie, who conceded that she was, after all, away from the house all day, felt sorry for him.

"Did you ever think," A. J. asked Travis one night, dragging himself painfully up from the supper table, "that we'd ever be outnumbered by women at the Lazy Ass? Four to two. Jesus Christ."

Late that night, Rinie woke and went to the kitchen for a drink of water. The old man was standing there by the stove, a hulking shape in the darkness that frightened her for a moment.

"It's just me, missy," he said gruffly. "No need to shy."

"Are—are you all right?" It wasn't the question to ask a Stinson, but she couldn't seem to stop asking it.

"Can't seem to sleep," he said wearily. "I had a good bit to drink, but I keep turnin' over an' it don't do no good."

"If you go back to bed," she said timidly, "I could make you a toddy."

"Well," he said reluctantly, "that might be good, but go easy on the water an' lemon juice an' such. That extry stuff's easy overdone."

"All right," she said, lighting a lamp, "lots of whiskey and not much extras."

She went softly to his room, the small oil lamp in one hand, the big mug in the other and a book under her arm.

"What's that for?" he demanded, indicating the book.

"I thought you might like some company while you drink your toddy. I won't talk. I'll just sit here and read for a little while if it's all right. . . . Or I could read to you."

"Never cared much about readin'," he said gruffly.

She straightened his covers and spread an extra blanket over him. She did it without asking if he wanted it done, because, if she'd asked, he'd have said no. Then she sat down with her book.

He sipped the hot drink noisily.

"Little heavy with the water, wasn' you?"

She made no answer and after a little he said musingly, "Jenny used to read a good bit. She really took to it. She went to a fancy academy for young ladies back in Ohio. Not all them things Minnie says is lies. Their folks was fairly well off. . . . She used to read to the boys a good

247

bit. She taught Travis, mostly. They wasn' no school for some while after we come here." He was drowsy with the whiskey he had consumed earlier and with the toddy now. "You ever know me an' Jenny had a little girl?"

"Carl told me," she said softly.

"She didn't live but a little while. Caught pneumonia. . . . A man likes a daughter. Me an' Jenny always wished we'd have had another girl." He smiled and his tough old face was gentle and almost handsome again. "She was. so dead sure Buck was gonna be a girl. . . . God, that was a bad time—when he was born—end a January, colder'n hell, Troy not a year old an' Travis down with somethin' or other that kids gits, I disremember what." He sipped the whiskey. "There wasn't no way in the world I could leave 'em all an' go after Heddie or nobody."

"You—you mean she—you . . . ?"

"Times was different then," he said thoughtfully, "people, too.. Women wasn't used to havin' such a fuss made. After all, he was our fifth one. Jenny come through all right an' I can't tell it hurt the boy none." He laughed. Phlegm rattled in his throat and he spat into a delicately engraved brass urn he kept by the bed for a spittoon. "Course, I wasn' right strong there for a day or two after, but I made it."

"Was she sorry," Rinie asked quietly, "that Carl wasn't a girl?"

A. J.'s eyes were a little vague. He was drowsy, half-drunk, remembering.

"After it was all done with she laid there, lookin' at 'im, all wrapped up with just his face stickin' out of a pink blanket an' she said he looked like a fawn, hidin' in the woods, 'cause you couldn't hardly tell where the blanket ended an' the kid started in. I asked her if she was sorry it wasn' a doe fawn an' she said it come straight from heaven an' nobody had no right to question. She knowed where it come from better'n anybody, but Jenny liked to git fanciful that way, like a little kid. She never got over it. It was right nice sometimes, the way she'd talk. . . . She used to read a good bit to the boys, an' I'd listen some."

The book Rinie had picked up on her way through the front room was Rudyard Kipling's *Just So Stories*, a book she'd found in Jenny's box and was planning to take to school for a few days to read to the children. Not what A. J. would care for, she supposed. But maybe he felt as she had felt so often before she came here, lonely, ill, desperate for the sound of the voice of someone who cared, and the words didn't matter. She read very softly. There was such a charming, enticing, soothing rhythm in the words.

After a little, A. J. shifted with a slight groan. She took the empty mug from his stiff old fingers and went on reading, almost without breaking the rhythm. In a few moments, he was snoring lightly. After a little longer, she took the lamp and went back to bed. The rhythm, the words were running through her mind: "Old Man Kangaroo, he was gray and he was woolly and his pride was inordinate." She lay there in the darkness, smiling, with tears in her eyes. "Old Man Stinson, he was gray and he was woolly. . . ."

Carl hadn't ridden the stallion. It was over a month now since he'd caught him, and Troy was beginning to suggest rather often that Carl was afraid to try him. Carl didn't pay any attention to suggestions. Whenever the opportunity offered, he went close to the horse, to feed and water him, to clean the corral, just to pass by, but the stallion's reactions were always the same. He wouldn't go near food or water while anyone was watching and if Carl came too near he bared his teeth and sometimes struck out with his front hooves.

Carl had put the filly into an adjoining corral where they kept other horses and she was becoming gentle enought so that Rinie could take her oats in a bucket and she would come up close to eat them. Rinie thought she was the prettiest horse in the world, a rich, dark chestnut with a light star on her forehead. She was timid and gentle, but sometimes there was a gleam of irresponsible mischief in her eyes and Rinie had named her Sprite. Carl said she'd have to think of a name for the stallion, too. He couldn't seem to call him anything worthwhile.

The men were dragging logs on this Saturday morning in late October. They were about halfway down to the house when Carl said he guessed he'd quit after this and ride the stud.

"We ought to git all the wood we can while we can," said Travis worriedly.

"Ah, hell, daddy, le's lay off," protested Kirby. "We been workin' hard as anything."

"If you had any sense," Troy told his nephew, "you'd be in Belford goin' to school instead of up here workin' your rear off for a slave-drivin' ramrod."

When they got down, Kirby made an excuse to go in the house so he could be the one to tell his grandfather and the men that Carl was going to ride the wild one.

Troy and Travis were full of advice about how to get the bronc saddled, and what he was likely to do once mounted and before they had the logs stacked, A. J. was out there telling him how to do.

Carl had never liked breaking horses, really wild ones, in front of an audience. The idea was foolish, he guessed, but it seemed to him it was hard on a horse's pride, being watched like that, and made it necessary for it to behave worse than it might have otherwise. It didn't make things any easier on the rider either. Now that they were all so dam' eager about it, he wondered why he had thought he wanted to try the stallion today anyway. It was just that he was restless, tired of cutting wood, jumpy, the way the stock got sometimes before a storm and he wanted something to rid him of the feeling. All right, maybe the others felt that way, too.

He got old Buddy to go in and rope the stallion firm. He snubbed him to a post and got a hackamore on him. Troy, helping, was grazed on one hand by the fierce teeth. Carl had snubbed the horse once or twice before and handled him a little but had stopped because it was a waste of time. This was an animal nine or ten years old who was never going to be anything like tame, and if he was ever ridden at all, it would be for no other reason than the satisfaction of the rider's ego; it would never carry much weight with the horse.

By keeping him necked up to the post and tying up one hind foot, Troy and Carl got him saddled and by that time the women had come out.

Doxy was so excited she was all but jumping up and down. Ellie was grim. She never liked to watch a thing like this—cleaning up, patching up the things that sometimes resulted was bad enough—and she didn't think it was a thing Doxy ought to watch in her condition. She had said so to Doxy before they came outside, and when Troy went to get something from the barn, she said so to him, but they didn't pay any attention. Helen was flushed and excited. Rinie was pale and very still. Carl said shortly, "All of you go in one of the other corrals an' shut the gate."

"You aimin' to let him out?" asked Travis incredulously.

"Hell, yes. There's not room in here for him to git started."

"What if he gits away from you?" asked Kirby hopefully.

"I guess I'll just let 'im go."

"I mean with you on him."

"That's what I thought you meant."

Carl was getting excited. He thought the stallion was beautiful, always had thought so since the first time he'd seen him more than three years ago, way down on Deer Creek. But seeing him every day, penned here in this little corral, he had forgotten how beautiful he was. There was a lot of quarter horse in him, though he was bigger than the average quarter horse. He had the stocky strength of that breed, the indomitable stamina of the mustang, and the wonderful, adamant pride that could come only from a life of freedom. Carl guessed he was the colt of some mare stolen from a ranch by another wild stud. He was a light sorrel, gleaming in the sun, sweating from excitement and fear and whatever other feelings that were showing in his proud fierce eyes. He had a big white blaze that somehow made him look mean. Helen had suggested that Blaze would be a pretty name for him and it always made Carl laugh to think of calling him anything that tame. His ears were flat back and he threw his head as much as the snubbing post would allow. His nostrils flared and quivered and his teeth bared and he tried to strike at Carl as he come up to mount.

"I told you you ought to a used blinders," Travis called.

They're not fair, Carl thought, trying in the way he always instinctively had to communicate his thoughts to the horse. Blinders are cheating. Listen, I don't want to break you. I wouldn't want you much different than you are. Except—I wish we could be friends. It's just—I have to ride you, don't you see? The same way you have to fight me. You're going to be full of everything in heaven and hell after being shut up like this, aren't you? He said to Troy, "Stay on Buddy in case you have to go after him."

"You sound like you're fixin' to git throwed."

"I expect I am," Carl said matter-of-factly.

"Where's your spurs at, Buck?" A. J. yelled gleefully.

"Hell, spurs are the last thing I need."

As Troy untied the ropes with Buddy deftly evading teeth and hooves, Carl said to Rinie, "You got some coffee made? I'll be wantin' some in a little bit."

"It's ready," she said shakily, trying to smile back, but it didn't matter if the smile succeeded or not because the stallion was loose. For the first time, Rinie noticed that the horse's coat and Carl's hair were almost the same shade in the sun.

"Oh, that wild devil," breathed A. J. in admiration and not even he was sure if he referred to the boy or the horse.

Troy and Travis and Kirby and Doxy and Helen were all yelling at once, but Rinie didn't know what any of them said. She tried to watch Carl's face, but there was too much movement and too much dust, and then she just tried to watch, but she couldn't even do that for long at a time. It was more than she could bear.

Carl didn't try to do anything more than stay on. There wasn't anything else he could have done. He thought if he could do that long enough, the stallion would get tired and give over to some degree, but the stallion wouldn't tire. He pitched all over the area of the barns and corrals. He reared and screamed. He bolted down along the creek, twisting and writhing to rid himself of his burden. He ran under trees to scrape the rider off. After a while, Carl's vision was blurring badly and his ears ringing from all the jolting and he began to wonder if he could get off if he wanted to, or if this would just go on forever.

He decided a little foggily to make the stallion go back to the corral and that was a mistake because the stallion didn't want to go back and Carl had to make him, once he had decided.

The horse and rider were out of sight most of the time while they were down along the creek. Troy rode down and Kirby ran after him. A. J. climbed painfully up on the fence to try to see more and Travis lifted Helen up. Doxy was breathing rapidly and so flushed that Ellie felt frightened about her.

"He's gonna kill 'im!" she shrieked, and Ellie said, "No such of a thing, an' you better settle kown."

All Rinie could think was, if he's thrown down there, hurt, I won't be close to him, with him.

252

But he wasn't thrown down there. He finally got mad at the goddam' son-of-a-bitch because he wouldn't get tired, and made him come back up by the corrals. And then he was exhausted and lost a stirrup because the stallion seemed as fresh as when they started, and he finally was thrown, against the fence, almost at her feet.

When the stallion realized the man was on the ground, he whirled and came at him while Carl struggled to his feet, but Troy was there with Buddy and a rope.

The women had screamed—Doxy's had been a piercing shriek—and before Troy had the stallion fairly secured, Rinie dodged away from Travis's hand and ran to Carl.

He was standing up, hanging onto the fence, swaying, and she didn't have to ask, he told her voluntarily, with the words slurring together, that he was all right. She held onto the fence, too, trembling violently.

"I guess I'll take a turn," Troy said without enthusiasm. "Between the two of us, we ought to could wear him down."

"Oh, Troy, don't," Doxy pleaded a little hysterically.

Ellie said, "You come in the house with me, young lady, right now. We got to git dinner on."

"No, leave him alone," Carl said thickly to Troy. "I'll help you git the saddle in a minute."

Swiftly, waveringly, he walked off around the barn. Rinie was about to follow when A. J. dropped a hand on her shoulder.

"Got to puke," he said succinctly. "Used to do me the same way. Shakes a feller's insides up. He won't want you."

Carl wasn't very hungry at dinner and he was tired, but he felt good. Troy said, "Le's go to town or somethin', Buck."

"All right."

"Take our girls so they can see the elephants an' hear the owls hoot an' all like that," said Troy expansively.

Ellie decreed that Doxy must rest first, while the boys got their chores done, but they were ready to go by mid-afternoon and they had supper in the dining room of the Hayes Valley House.

Then they went to a movie. Doxy chose it. She was a great movie fan. It was about a girl who wanted an acting career more than anything in the world, or thought she did, and nearly ruined her life before she found out

253

what was good for her. Troy and Carl didn't think much of the story and they exchanged a lot of comments in loud whispers upon the progress of the plot. Doxy and Rinie both cried when the heroine and the hometown boy finally got together and Troy opined that the guy ought to have had her go ahead and act if she was so blamed good at it, because they'd have a lot more money and fun that way than from running a goddam' grocery store.

"He wouldn' have to work at all that way," Carl agreed. "He could just lay around the swimmin' pool all day an' save himself."

"For what?"

"Oh, you know, parties an' all that they have around Hollywood."

"I wouldn't mind savin' for her," said Troy heartily as they got to the car. "Goddam! Did you see her in that bathin' suit?"

"I couldn' hardly help it," Carl said dryly.

"Jeezus Christ," murmured Troy reminiscently.

"I wish you'd quit your cussin', Troy," Doxy said angrily, "an' I wish I wouldn' of picked that show if you're just gonna make fun an' talk about her figger. It ain't no better than mine—was."

She was nearly six months pregnant now, but not showing much and tonight it was not noticeable at all because of the full gathered skirt she wore.

"Ah, now, Dox," said Troy placatingly, "yours is better'n hers under normal conditions. You can't expect not to curve a little extra with my boy."

"It ain't a boy an' I wisht you wouldn' talk so free in front a people about it. You embarrass me."

"What people?" asked Troy, starting the car.

"Le's go somewhere an' dance," Carl said.

"Maybe Doxy's tired," suggested Rinie.

"Oh, Rinie, you're as bad a ole granny as Ellie. I ain't tired of nothin' but stayin' at home, an' I'm so sick of that I could spit."

"You could what?" asked Troy.

"Spit! An' I want to dance an' have some fun."

"But you used to tell me that dancin' was sinful."

"It is, an' you're a ole heathen," she said snuggling close to him. "Daddy was right about you ruinin' me."

"Love me?"

"You know I do."

"I feel old," Rinie whispered.

"Well, we'll just have to do the best we can with what we've got," Carl said. "What I feel is hungry."

"You see, you're not romantic at all. We are old, married all this time."

"I'll do better when I've had somethin' to eat."

Troy said, "I'm gonna git drunker'n seven hundred dollars, Buck. What about the Dark Lantern?"

"Well, all right," Carl said, "but they don't have very good food."

Rinie couldn't have a very good time at first because she was worried about Doxy, but none of the others worried, least of all Doxy. Carl made up for the meal he had missed at noon and both he and Troy drank a good deal. Rinie drank more than she ever had before, and after a while she stopped worrying about Doxy, too. Doxy said she didn't drink. It was obscene, she proclaimed, but she sipped so often from Troy's glass that he finally made her have one of her own.

They saw Bud Corbett with a girl from Belford that some—not Bud—said he was engaged to.

Two men went out in the alley to fight over a redhead, and Carl and Troy, along with every other male in the place, went to watch.

"Hell, it wasn' anything," Carl said, disappointed, and Troy explained, "When the cold air hit 'em, they about forgot what they come out for, an' when they remembered, they decided she wasn' worth it."

There was a good band and they danced until Rinie felt she couldn't stand up any more and she still wanted to dance. This was the first time she had danced with complete strangers and she didn't want to, only Carl said it was all right and he danced with a few other girls. She didn't like dancing with those other men, but she did like it with Troy. With the others, she thought about Carl. She looked for him over their shoulders if they weren't too tall, and smiled at him, but with Troy, she just danced, gave herself up to the music, the rhythm, the giddiness of alcohol, almost as much as she let go with Carl.

"Mmm, you feel good," Troy said softly, holding her close. "I can git closer to you than I can to Doxy now. Can't I?"

"Don't, Troy," she said, but not with nearly as much conviction as she should have.

He said exuberantly, "After Doxy has the baby, we ought to switch around some night. Wouldn' that be fun? I bet Buck would be willin'. I know she would. Hell, it's all in the family."

She jerked free and walked away from him and his soft laughter followed her.

Carl was talking with some people from Greenfield that he knew slightly, and he hadn't noticed anything. She went up and stood close to him, feeling small and apologetic and ashamed.

He introduced her to the people from Greenfield and then led her away and asked if something was wrong and she said no, so they danced some more.

They stayed until the place closed and then Troy and Carl came near fighting because neither wanted to drive home. Finally, gracelessly, they flipped a coin and Carl lost. He said sullenly that it was a crooked nickel, but Troy pointed out complacently that it had come from Carl's pocket.

From the back seat, above the noise of the motor, they could hear Troy's low urgent tones, Doxy's little moans and gasps.

Rinie sat close to Carl and his arm was around her. He said angrily, "This is not fair. It's not even my car."

"But we have to get home somehow," she said softly, leaning against him.

"Why do we?" he demanded suddenly. Then, loudly, "Bo, le's go back, to a hotel or someplace."

"What for?" came Troy's drowsy voice.

"Goddam dog in the manger," said Carl.

"I ain't in no manger a yours, Buck, but I wouldn' mind."

Carl didn't say anything. He didn't seem to get any angrier and it shocked Rinie and hurt her that he didn't seem to care if Troy talked like that.

After a while, he said quietly, "It'll be sunup when we git home."

She nodded against his shoulder, making herself think only of Carl, not of Troy or what Troy had said, or. . . .

"Remember the first time we came along here in Suter's truck?"

She nodded again.

"Rinie?"

"What, sweetheart?"

"I want to be at home an' make love to you when the

sun's comin' up, so I'm gonna have to drive faster an' use both hands, I guess."

"All right, Carl," she said and they laughed together, softly, for no particular reason.

13 _____

Rinie was very pleased that she was, for all practical purposes, breaking Sprite alone. Carl taught her the way a colt ought to be brought along, if one had the time, halter-breaking, hackamore, saddle blanket, saddle, a little extra weight on the back, finally a rider. She worked with the filly every afternoon she could. She enjoyed it and so did Sprite. It helped Rinie understand Carl, his feeling for horses, and it pleased him.

The filly was usually docile, eager to please but some-times—more often as the weather grew colder—she would show that she had a mind of her own. At first, Rinie just felt a little hurt by the filly's deliberate, wanton dis-obediences, but then one day Carl saw some slight mis-behavior and was a little angry with them both, Rinie, mostly.

"She's smart, but, God, honey, surely you're smarter than she is. Don't let her git away with that kind of thing. She's feelin' you out to see how far she can go. When you decide she's gonna do somethin', you by God be sure you make her do it."

"But, Carl, it wasn't that serious, was it? She just—"

"When she knows, without a doubt, that you're the boss when you feel like bein', that'll be the time for her to git away with an idea of her own once in a while, but you can't let her do it in the beginnin'. You don't want to be workin' a horse an' have it git the best of you some time when it don't know what the hell it's doin'."

Rinie was about to point out that she was really only interested in a saddle horse, not a cow horse, but he was so intensely serious that she let it go. She said later, "If

I keep working with her, and she keeps coming along, do you think we could help with the cattle next year?"

Carl grinned. "Sprite might, but you won't make much of hand till you can take one of those 'poor little calves,' brand it, castrate it, vaccinate it an' doctor it for screw-worms if it happens to have any."

"Oh, Carl, I just couldn't."

"Maybe you'll let me borrow your horse, then."

When Carl rode the filly the first time, there was nothing to it. Rinie stood by her head and when he mounted, Sprite gave a little start, rolled her eyes back at him, flattened her ears and then moved off, a little jerkily, to walk easily around the big corral.

The second time, Rinie wanted to ride her, but Carl said he'd better try her once or twice more. As she went past the corral where the stallion was, he reared and screamed and the filly, terrified, or spurred to defiance by the wildness, began to buck.

"An' she can dam' well turn it on," Carl said later.

"You can't never trust a wild one," Travis said.

They were at the supper table.

"She's all right," Carl said easily, glancing at Rinie, "away from him."

He was afraid the filly's exhibition of wildness might have frightened her, and it had, a little, but she smiled at him and said that she was going to ride Sprite next time, that they would take her away from the corrals somewhere and things would be fine.

Carl and the stallion had a sort of understanding now. Carl could go into his corral on foot without the horse's trying to strike or kick him but he couldn't touch him, and the stallion always bared his teeth at Carl's approach as a matter of principle. Carl would stand quite still at a respectful distance, and they would look at each other.

"In the spring," Carl said to him, "as soon as they begin to foal, I'll put you up with the mares. Maybe you'll be glad enough then you stayed." The horse flung his head and his eyes flicked from Carl away across the flats and his ears twitched as though he had heard something that interested him, off across there. "I'm tellin' you, things'll be better," Carl said, turning away. And when he went out of the corral gate, he came very near not sliding the bar.

At supper, A. J. said, "Van Forrester come up here today to see your stud horse."

Carl had been up on the mesa all afternoon.

"Van thought he might want to breed that white mare you like so much to the stallion."

"Jesus," murmured Carl sardonically, "what for?"

"A foal, I expect."

"Has he raced her?"

"Nobody can't ride her, but he thinks he might git one hell of a line started if he can find the right stud. Yours ain't him. Too stocky to suit Van."

Troy laughed. "How'd you like to step acrost a colt from them two? You'd have to tie your spurs an' ever'-thing else on. You ought to let him breed."

Carl shrugged. "I wouldn' care, but he don't want to. I ain't forcin' stud service on nobody."

The men thought that was funny and he laughed, too, reddening a little.

Ellie said, "Next week's Thanksgivin'. We got to make us some plans, girls."

"Goody!" said Helen. "Jeff'll be home, an' then it'll be nearly Christmas."

"We ain't cooked good stuff like we did last year, but I was thinkin' that when somebody goes after Jeff, we can send for some things an' start now. It ain't any ways too late. Last year, Doxy, we made cakes an' cookies an' candy an'—"

"Hid it," put in Troy.

"I thought we might have a turkey for Thanksgivin'," said Ellie.

"Me an' Troy's gonna git a deer," Kirby told her confidently.

"Well, that'll be all right, then, but you better git it got."

"What we ought to do is go after a bear," said Troy. "We ought to see if Pup's any good with 'em."

"Oh, bear meat ain't no good," said Travis.

"Well, that don't matter. I didn't 'specially want one to eat, just to hunt."

"Bear meat ain't all that bad," A. J. said staunchly. "We used to eat a good bit of it when we first come out here."

"Well, it just don't seem like bear's the thing for Thanksgivin'," said Ellie.

Carl said he guessed you could be just as goddam' thankful for a bear as anything else if you were hungry and A. J. said that was right.

"Did you ever eat any people, Granddaddy?" asked Helen.

"Oh, one or two, mostly little black-headed girls."

"I like punkin pie," she said, unimpressed.

"Yeah," agreed Troy, dropping an arm around the back of his wife's chair. "We all do. Whyn't you make us up a dozen, Dox?"

She looked startled. "Well, I never did know how to make pies."

"Ellie can teach you," said Troy blithely.

"I don't feel too good, Troy," she said plaintively. "The kitchen makes me sick sometimes."

"Well, you better git over it an' find out what you can about cookin' an' all, 'cause I been thinkin' that next spring I might start us a place of our own."

Doxy looked frightened. "I wouldn' know how to do, off by ourselves."

Later, Ellie said to Rinie, "I don't believe they's any reason for us to worry that they'll move out. Both of 'em's so used to bein' around people, they'd likely strangle each other if they had to be by theirselves. She did git right sick at butcherin' time last week, an' that shore ain't nothin' agin her in her condition, but she's gonna make them pies, Rinie, sure as I'm standin' here with this dishrag in my hand."

And she did, and they ate them for Thanksgiving dinner. Rinie and Ellie said how good they were, more than once, and Carl and Travis and Troy said so once, after meaningful looks. Ellie served seconds to the men and boys—they always wanted seconds on pie—and she let them know they were to eat them. Kirby whispered to Jeff that he wished he'd thought to bring in the hacksaw and they laughed some. The crust was a little like leather, but the flavor was good and Doxy's pleasure was a little pathetic. When dinner was finished, she said, "I could help with the dishes, Rinie. You ain't had much time off."

Rinie said she'd help, that it was time Ellie had a rest.

And Ellie said, a little complacently, "I think so, too. We'll just leave the kitchen for Doxy an' Helen."

Carl and Rinie walked a little way up in the woods and found a sheltered, sunny little spot, deep in pine needles. There had been snow several times, but all that was left now was in shady places; the sun was warm, the ground dry in the little clearing.

"That pie was a little much," Carl said, stretching on

the pine needles and putting a hand over his eyes. "Anyway, how can you enjoy eatin' anything when it's served up with a kind of looks Ellie was givin' us?"

"Well, Doxy tried and she's happy," Rinie said. "She has to start somewhere. Has Jeff said anything about how he likes it in Belford?"

"Not much, just about the library an' things like that. I guess he's been pretty lonesome but I believe he thinks it's worth it."

"It must be hard, goin' away from here," she said softly.

"Well, I guess you thought it wasn't any too easy *comin'* here, but to go away, when this place is all you've ever known about, God, it's a shock. . . . I guess it's better for Jeff, at Bess's, than it was for us at Minna's. I know it is. Bess is a different kind of person, an' I don't think Jeff would stay someplace like Minna's. He's got better sense."

They were silent a long time. The breeze made a soft, low-pitched sound in the trees. It was cool, coming down off the ridges, but the sun made them warm and drowsy.

"What are you thinkin' little girl?" he asked, turning his head a little to look at her. Her face was so serious.

"I was wondering," she said slowly, "what it would be like to live by ourselves."

"Would you like to?"

"Sometimes, I wish we did. I—I really wished it at first, before I knew all of them. I guess I'd miss everybody, but we might, sometime, don't you think?"

"We could have us a house," he said lazily, "up here in the woods some place. Or what about way on up the creek. There's some fine places up there."

"Where lions could come down the chimney?" she suggested and kissed him.

He grinned and then said thoughtfully, "Sometimes, I wish it was—oh, fifty years or so ago, don't you? When it was still fair fur country in here an' there wasn't hardly anybody around."

She said she wasn't sure she could wish that; it seemed wild enough to her as it was.

"I guess it would, growin' up in Denver . . . or maybe it's the Stinsons that make it seem so wild."

"But I like them," she said, smiling. "As A. J. would say, this taming business is easy overdone."

After a while, he asked, "You don't plan on goin' back to school, do you? Can't June go ahead by herself now?"

"She asked if I'd stay till Christmas."

"I'd like you to stay home."

"Why?"

"Because when I come in, I like to see you there. I don't give a dam' about Doxy or Ellie."

"Yes, but three women might get on each other's nerves, shut up together for the whole winter. If I kept on teaching till Christmas, I'd be something new—for a while."

"Doxy's baby'll be born in a couple of months an' you'll all be so busy makin' over it, you won't have time to git ringy."

"Carl?" She was so eager to tell him that it was hard to breathe, and yet she was reluctant to speak, half-afraid that talking about it might change things somehow. She lay still in his arms and he waited.

"Carl, I—I'm two weeks late."

"I know you are."

"You know?"

"Dam' right I know. Don't you think a man pays attention to things like that when they don't happen? Did you think I was gonna be the last to find out, like the men in those crappy magazine stories?"

"You read Doxy's magazines, do you?"

"No. . . . Well, a couple, tryin' to find out how women think, but I didn' git anywhere. They just make things harder to figger."

"But you didn't say anything, about. . . ."

"I did. I told you yesterday not to ride Sprite yet, an' just now I said I don't want you to teach any more. Besides, you hadn' said anything. I was beginnin' to think I'd have to tell you."

She laughed. "You silly old sweet thing. You really are kind of smart for a man, and kind of smart-alec, too. Carl?"

"What?"

"Sometimes—other things can cause a woman to skip, you know. It might not be a baby. Mostly, that's why I haven't said anything."

"It's a baby," he said with quiet assurance.

She smiled happily, lying there in his arms, and there were tears in her eyes. "You're supposed to be making a big fuss over me."

"I'm not much good with that kind of fussin', Rinie, but I do love you—both of you. Anyway, don't the man ever git any credit at all?"

He was grinning, but she said soberly, clinging to him, "Yes. Thank you, sweetheart."

"Ah, Rinie," his voice broke a little, "I was teasin'. You make me feel like a dam' fool. . . . Besides, it was my pleasure."

"Is that what they say in the stories?"

"Well, not in the ones I read, no. They're too prissy."

They agreed not to tell anyone for a while, just for the fun of keeping it to themselves, but the others knew before Christmas because by that time Rinie was dreadfully sick, almost constantly, and Carl was frightened.

"Doxy didn't do this," Rinie said miserably, guiltily, to Ellie.

"You don't know what Doxy done the first three months. I expect she'd be glad to tell you if you asked, but just never mind about that. Ever'body's different about this kind of thing. I expect you'll feel better in a few weeks."

"But Carl—"

"He'll feel better, too. I purely can't stand a man that has all the symptoms, though Travis was the same way when Kirby was comin'."

"But he doesn't have the symptoms," Rinie said defensively. "He's so good to me and sometimes I catch him looking so scared. He just won't believe it's supposed to be like this."

"If he ain't got the symptoms," snapped Ellie, "how is it he's off his feet? If he don't simmer down, it won't be long till he won't be able to manage nothin' but tea and toast."

Christmas was lovely, Rinie thought. Perhaps not as lively as some, but she had, despite her physical illness, such a feeling of belonging, of real importance and pride and worth to the world. Doxy was a little subdued by the contemplation of her approaching delivery, and Rinie couldn't manage to eat Christmas dinner, but the men brewed their hooch and were irrepressible and a little ribald, as usual.

Doyle told them proudly that he was going to work part-time as a leg man for Everett Bell's office when the legislature was in session. He also said, grinning, that he might stay in town and work next summer, especially since it seemed Red Bear would be full of babies.

"Why don't you just quit fightin' it," said Troy, "an' git married yourself. Really, Si, it's not half-bad. You don't have to go huntin' around. Your girl's always handy."

"I'm too young," Doyle said smugly.

"For what?" wondered A. J.

"I don't plan to marry for some while yet."

Travis said, "Hell, me an' Ellie'd been married two years when I was your age."

"Well, but I never have found anybody like Ellie."

"My land!" she said. "He's after somethin', sure."

"Well, I did bring home some dirty clothes," said Doyle apologetically. "I couldn't seem to get around to sending them to the laundry."

"I can iron," Helen told him proudly. "I expect I'll be able to do about ever'thing around the house before long."

"What the hell's a leg man?" Carl asked Troy.

"Well, I guess some guy that rubs ole man Bell's legs when they're tired, an' like that."

"I guess you'll marry some Denver girl," said Doxy.

"If it's that one sent him her picture last summer," said Travis, "I wouldn' mind bein' leg man to her."

"Judge's daughter," nodded Troy, "in a little bitty bathin' suit. Doyle'll be in chambers 'fore we know it."

"Chambers," said A. J. "No need to go to Denver for them."

"Judge Stinson," mused Travis and Carl said, "God, I hate to think he'd ever hear a case a mine."

"Case of your what?" asked Troy. "You got somethin' in cases?"

Doyle sighed. "It's a hard life, not to be appreciated among your own. Aren't you getting to feel that way, Jeff?"

"Well, not yet," said Jeff diffidently, "but I haven't been in school very long."

Troy was disappointed, vociferously so, about New Year's Eve. The community party was to be at McLean's and he felt that he and Carl should go, along with Doyle. Rinie wouldn't have minded much, but Doxy did.

"You ain't gonna go runnin' off, leavin' me this-a-way," she said querulously. "You might as well suffer a little. It's your young'un."

"All right. Hell, I thought we had that settled a good while back, but what's it got to do with anything? If I didn't feel good, do you think I'd expect you to do nothin' but set home with me, especially fussin' all the time?"

"Yes, you shore would, an' I tell you right now, if you go, I'm a-goin'."

"You'd go out to a party stickin' out that way?"

She burst into tears and ran into their room, slamming the door.

Cursing half under his breath, Troy went outside, letting the front door slam behind him.

"Slam somethin', Buck," A. J. said wearily. "Goddam', whyn't you an' missy fuss a little? Don't you feel left out or nothin'? Fuss is all them two's done fer a month or more."

"I think," said Carl, leaning back and putting his feet on the arm of another chair, "that I'm gettin' about ready to settle down, A. J. I git sleepy an' things a lot."

"You know who you look like?" said A. J. suddenly, "with that God-awful satisfied look on your face? My pappy, that's who. It's funny I never noticed in all this time, but, by God, you look like him. He was the meanest man in Texas an' he had them funny eyes like yours. He used to stay so drunk all the time he couldn' hit the ground with his hat, but it never stopped him from nothin'. Fight! Jee-zus Christ.

"He come out a the Civil War with nothin' but a ole, wore-out horse an' the clothes on his back—an' my mama, he picked her up somewhere along the way—but by Christ, he caught longhorns an' started him a ranch."

"How come you left?" asked Carl casually.

He got up to look for a match. He and A. J. were alone in the front room for the moment.

"W'y, ain't I never said how that was? Me an' my brother Troy had us a fallin' out—an' it wasn' no little, easy discussion—over a girl. He got 'er so I taken what cash there was for my share of things an' left. I got around some, seen some a the country, tried this an' that, finally wound up in Denver an' met your mama. . . . You boys probably got cousins down in there around Victoria that's richer'n hell. Some of you ought to go down there an' claim kin sometime."

Carl exhaled smoke slowly and looked at the back of Rinie's head. She was sitting at the kitchen table, marking off a pattern. A. J. couldn't see her from where he was, but Carl guessed the old man wouldn't care if she heard his reminiscences. A. J. said, "I don't know what got me started on that. I ain't thought about my folks in years—except you did put me in mind of ole Aaron James there for a minute. He was a heller, the one they patterned the others after: horses, women, fightin', God! It's a shame Minnie never knowed him."

"I'm not like that," Carl said mildly.

"But you have got them funny kind a eyes an' sometimes you can look so dam' pleased with yourself. Anyway, you growed up in a different kind a time from him. Besides, what I think is that this family's gettin' softer ever' generation."

Carl spat a shred of tobacco into the fire and said dryly, "It's all the easy livin'."

"Goddam' right," A. J. agreed. He sighed. "You know, Buck, I hate like hell to say it, but I'm gittin' old. It ain't a easy thing for a man to admit, but, feelin' the way I have been, an' then goin' back in the past I ain't thought of for so long, like I was just then. . . ."

Carl said quietly, "I don't think that, A. J. I think what it is is that you're just finally gittin' ready to settle down a little yourself."

"Hell," said the old man, sounding pleased, and Rinie started to cry.

As silently as she could, she left the kitchen and went to her room, where she lay on the bed, sobbing. She cried so easily lately. Often her tears made her angry and then she cried more. Ellie said that having a baby had that effect on some women and that it wasn't a thing to bother about, but Rinie hoped Carl didn't know she was crying now. He tried so hard, but he just never would be able to understand how painfully important things could get, things like burning the biscuits or having her hair tangled so that it hurt her to comb it and now she felt so sorry for A. J. that it was almost beyond bearing. Carl would be able to understand that well enough, but she knew he felt badly as it was without getting worried about her.

On the second Friday in January, Helen came home from school with a message that Doxy's sister Supina had given birth to a baby girl that morning.

"They said to say ever'body's all right," reported Helen

266

importantly, "an' they named the baby—le's see now, what was it?—oh, Claudia Veronica."

"W'y, that goddam' little bitch!" cried Doxy and then flushed fiery red and looked as though she were going to cry. "Oh, I—I—that was the name I had picked out an' she knew it."

"Well, Punkin," said A. J.—he'd given her the name after the Thanksgiving pies—"whyn't you change your mind an' have a boy?"

"She is," said Troy with conviction.

"I'd hate to think," said Doxy caustically to her husband, "that I'd ever be mother to one like you."

"Well, what the hell did I do now?"

"If you do have a boy," Ellie said placatingly, "it'd be your folks' first grandson. Don't you know they'd be proud?"

Doxy hadn't seemed to think of that before. She said slowly, "We could name it after daddy . . . only I've made that pink sweater an' all."

"No kid of mine," began Troy vehemently, but Travis said, "I just seen three snowflakes pass the window."

"I don't see how you stand it, Ellie," said Rinie, trying to smile, "with Doxy and me the way we are."

They were washing dishes after supper.

Ellie grunted. "I've about decided me an' Travis ought to have us another one. I felt kind of left out."

Doxy said petulantly, "I wisht I could have it at daddy's, but Troy says I've got to stay here. He says it might git real bad weather an' he couldn't git me an' the baby back up here till spring an' he won't stay down home for nothin'. I think he's mean an' hateful. Rinie, don't you wisht you had some folks a your own, a time like this?"

"I have, Doxy," she said and managed, by a great effort, not to cry.

Late in the night of the first of February, Bud Corbett came and said the mountain lion had killed a colt of Barnhart's. Several of the men in the community were going after it as soon as it got light. They needed a good lion dog. It was out of the question for old Christmas to try to run anything, she could scarcely walk now, but the men at Red Bear thought this might be Pup's big chance. They began busily getting their things ready while Rinie and Ellie cooked breakfast and got together some food for them to take along. A. J. was going and there was something in his face that made it impossible for anyone to suggest that he stay at home.

Ellie said, "Well, anyway, thank the Lord Doxy's still asleep. She'd set in for Troy not to go, an' if I have to live one more day without a rest housed up with them, fussin' like they are, I don't believe I can stand it."

"But the baby might come any day now," said Rinie apprehensively. She couldn't help feeling glad that Carl's birthday had passed safely. It was silly, but she didn't want this child of Doxy and Troy's to share that day with him.

Ellie said flatly, "We don't need no five men, nor even one, here for that."

It was bitterly cold, though there wasn't much snow on the ground just now. As they were leaving, the men's breath showed smoky and the new mustache that Troy was cultivating had ice crystals on it when he and Carl brought everyone's horses around to the porch.

"Be good," Carl said softly, kissing Rinie. The snow squealed under his boots as he stood on the step below her.

"Doxy might have the baby by the time you come home," she whispered.

He nodded. "That hasn' seem to come to Bo yet, or maybe he just doesn't want to have to make a choice. You go on in now where it's warm."

"A. J. looks bad," she said worriedly.

"I know he does," he said, frowning, "but nobody can ask him not to go. It'd be worse for him than it is for ole Christmas, shut up out there in the barn, 'cause he couldn't let loose an' howl like she is."

Doxy's labor began in mid-morning. She was crying and furiously angry with Troy for not being there.

"Now listen," Ellie said aside to Rinie, "I'm gonna saddle a horse an' go git Heddie. Nothin' won't happen for hours. Will you be all right?"

Rinie nodded, biting her lips. She was terribly frightened.

Ellie was back in not much more than an hour, with Heddie, but by that time Rinie was on the verge of hysteria. Doxy screamed and writhed and begged somebody to help her at each pain. At first, Rinie had tried to talk to her about something, anything, but even in the lapses between pains, which were terrifyingly short, Doxy whimpered and cried and wouldn't be distracted from her terror.

After a cursory examination of the patient, Heddie looked piercingly at Rinie and said curtly to Ellie, "Take her out of here."

Ellie took Rinie firmly by the arm and led her into the kitchen. The girl was shaking violently. Ellie tried to be casual.

"I stopped by the Keanes'. Essie's comin' up too, right away. Now what I want you to do is go to bed."

"Oh, no, I can't! I—"

"I oughtn't to have left you that-a-way, but my land! I didn't dream she'd carry on like that."

"Ellie, she's—"

"Go on in your room an' git in bed to warm up. You're shakin' like I don't know what. I got to git some stuff together for Heddie. Go on now."

Numbly, Rinie went in and huddled under the covers. She kept thinking of that night they had taken Skeeter's foal. She covered her head with a pillow, but nothing would shut out Doxy's screams. She thought she would hear them for the rest of her life. Oh, Carl . . . if only he were here with her. She wasn't aware that she was sobbing wildly. She didn't know when Ellie came in until the pillow was gently pulled away.

The look of the girl scared Ellie. "Now, Irine, you just stop that right now."

"Oh, Ellie, she's dying. She's—"

Ellie slapped her stingingly. "Now you just straighten up, young lady."

She snapped away from the hysteria and she was only crying, exhausted.

"She ain't dyin'," Ellie said with quiet firmness. "She's havin' one of the easiest times Heddie says she's ever seen with a first baby. Doxy's a baby herself an' she can't help hollerin'. Some women just does that. It's their nature. All that beggin' for help an' stuff, she don't know what she's sayin'. She's just got to say somethin' an' it don't matter what. It won't be more'n a hour now till it's all over an' she likely won't even remember the way she's acted. Now then, can you drink some coffee?"

"Ellie, I know she's going to die," Rinie said dully,

hopelessly. If birth was like this, no wonder people left their children on the steps of orphanages. Only her baby, Carl's, could she bear it? Surely her own mother must have died giving her life. She didn't want to die, to leave Carl. It was all so mixed up with Doxy and the past and the future. Hysteria was getting hold of her again. And Doxy shrieked.

"Now, Rinie, she ain't no such of a thing. You quit that cryin'. You got to think about your own baby's health."

"I am," she sobbed hopelessly.

Ellie was becoming desperately worried. She must do something. "What if Carl was to come home right now an' walk in that door? W'y, you'd have him half-scared to death, goin' on this way."

Rinie began making a real effort to pull herself together then, but it was nearly impossible with Doxy's screams filling the house.

Ellie brought her coffee, but the smell of it was nauseating.

"I'm so ashamed," she sobbed. "I'm more trouble than she is."

"Heddie an' Essie's with her," said Ellie calmly. "I'll just set down in here a while an' drink me some coffee. I bet you anything she has a boy. I've thought that for some time, the way she was carryin' it, but I wouldn' of said so to her for the world, the way she's had her heart set on a girl. Which do you want, Rinie? I never have heard you say?"

"A boy," she said, scarcely audibly, trying desperately not to cry. "A boy that looks like Carl."

"An' what about Carl? What's he say?"

"He just says that whatever Troy and Doxy have, we ought to have the opposite so it won't lack for attention. Ellie, I'm starting to show so much sooner than Doxy did. Does that mean anything, do you think?"

"Means you're littler. Doxy's plump, wide in the hips. That's why it wasn't noticeable with her so soon."

There was a horrible, rending scream and then dead silence. Ellie held her cup halfway to her lips. Rinie couldn't breathe . . . and then they heard the baby cry.

"Oh," she whispered and her own tears seemed replenished but they didn't frighten Ellie now. Soon, she knew, the girl would wear herself out and have to sleep and that was the best thing she could do.

Carl came home just at dark. He had A. J.'s horse tied up close to his own. It took both his hands to support the old man in the saddle.

Ellie saw them coming. She called Heddie and went to get A. J.'s bed ready. It was nearly impossible for Carl to lift his father down alone, but then Heddie was beside him, her short, strong arms lending support. A. J. was conscious, in a way. He just couldn't seem to talk or move or feel or think much.

"You got a good stout grandson," Heddie told him as they got him to bed, and they could tell by his eyes that A. J. understood. Heddie felt a little encouraged. "Got hair like his papa's, like yours used to be. Real good-lookin' Stinson."

"Where's Rinie?" asked Carl, coming into the kitchen after putting the horses up. "I wish she wouldn' have to know till. . . ."

"She's sleepin, Carl. Don't go in there now," Ellie said. She hadn't thought he could be more pale, but he whitened. "What's wrong?"

"Nothin' now, I think. She got awful worried about Doxy. Wore herself out. An' you're shore right that she don't need to start in worryin' on your daddy. She's got to rest is all an' she'll be fine."

"Ellie, you wouldn't just say . . . are you sure—"

Heddie came in then, soundlessly, as was her way. "He's cold," she said simply.

"I'll heat some rocks an' fix the hot-water bottle," Ellie said quickly.

Carl carried in wood and built a roaring fire in the fireplace. Some of the heat from that would go into A. J.'s room.

"What is it, Heddie?" he asked as she passed through the room. He begged her with his eyes to say it wasn't as serious as he feared.

"Stroke," she said laconically. "How long he been that way?"

"Just a little while. I'd have stopped somewhere if it had happened sooner. He got tired. The lion's way to hell an' gone up the West Fork, but the dogs was trackin' good an' most of the men wanted to go on after him. I asked A. J. if he wanted to come home, an' he told me well, he said no, but then, in a little while, he said if I still felt like comin' home, he'd ride along with me. He was all right—I mean, you could tell he was havin' a lot of

271

pain, but I thought it was the same trouble, in his joints —an' then, just this side of the lower ford, he said, 'Buck my head hurts so bad, I believe I'm fixin' to die,' an' he— he just went limp an' nearly fell, an' I . . ." He put his hands over his face.

"You go rest some," said Heddie. "I stay by him."

Ellie was ladling up stew for him. She and Heddie and Essie had eaten a little earlier, she said.

He went softly to the door of his and Rinie's room. Her face was turned away and about all he could see in the dimness was the dark of her hair against the white of the pillow, but it made him feel a little easier somehow.

While he was trying to eat, Essie brought the baby for him to see. He looked at it and said how was Doxy? Essie said fine; she'd been able to eat a little and was sleeping again. Essie asked him plaintively if it hadn't occurred to Troy at all that he might be needed. Carl felt so jumpy and apprehensive that he said he didn't know what might have occurred to his brother, then, more kindly, he said the baby looked like Troy, though, in truth, it didn't look like much of anything to him, and he was relieved when she took it away finally.

"Do you know where the others might be stayin' at tonight?" asked Ellie.

"Perryman's maybe. Butler's. Do you think I ought to git 'em?"

"Le's wait a little while an' see what Heddie thinks. Try to eat somethin', Carl."

Troy Dean Stinson, Jr., was a big, healthy baby who did everything ahead of schedule and was the pride of his family, most particularly of his father. After the birth of her son there was, for a time, a sort of muted contentment about Doxy. She felt no need to strive and clamor. Her new role as Dean's mother gave her a favored place in the heart of her husband and of his family.

Very slowly, A. J. grew better. His joints pained him relentlessly, but this other thing, this thing that had left him virtually speechless and unable to move his limbs, seemed to loosen its hold with slow reluctance. Perhaps the only reason it was overcome to any degree at all was the old man's obstinate determination not to be fed and dressed and cared for in many of the same ways that his grandson was.

Rinie begged them to send for a doctor when she knew how ill he was, and Carl would have gone, despite the feelings of the others, except that he knew how angry it would make A. J. During the first few days, Carl felt a dull, heavy certainty that his father couldn't live and he couldn't bear making the old man's last hours more unpleasant with the presence of a doctor. Sometimes, in those first, difficult weeks, as Carl helped his father as casually and unobtrusively as he could, it seemed he could see in the old man's still-clear, sharp eyes, the wish that he had died, rather than have his body humiliate him in all these ways.

By the end of six weeks, A. J. was able to do for himself pretty well with his arms and hands, though his legs were still almost unmanageable and he could barely walk with help. The left side of his face was a little drawn, though they came not to notice that. He had regained the ability to speak quickly, though sometimes it was impossible for him to articulate precisely what he wanted to say, and, with all else he had to bear, he found this a little too much.

"It's kind of strange," Travis said harriedly, "he has so much trouble gittin' out somethin' like 'hand me a spoon,' but he don't have no trouble at all sayin' 'Give me the goddam' sonofabitchin' bastard'."

A. J. seemed to prefer having Rinie help with his food and such things and, after the initial shock of how the illness had ravaged him, she was glad to be of what help she could. Sometimes, she read to him and he would lie quietly, his stubborn struggle taking respite.

Rinie herself never felt well now. As her pregnancy passed through its fifth month, she still had frequent attacks of nausea and a great deal of back pain. Ellie asked her more than once if she was absolutely certain she wasn't farther along toward her time.

"I'm getting so big," she lamented to Carl, trying to smile. "I hate to think what I'll look like before this is over."

She did her share of the work and, when the weather was not too severe, she went for walks and spent time outdoors, but Carl was not the only one who was concerned about her. Ellie didn't like the look of her. Her skin was pale and blotchy and she was not gaining weight as she should have been. She lacked the bloom of health and contentment that so often marked the middle months of pregnancy.

Since the day of Dean's birth and A. J.'s stroke she had been depressed by a terrible, premonitory fatalism. It seemed to her, with a sort of vague, ghastly justice, that in this country, for every good thing there must be something bad, a sort of retribution for happiness. Dean was thriving and happy and, in the room next to where the baby slept, A. J. was old and miserable and fighting for every move he was able to make . . . she and Carl had been so happy now, for all these months that it frightened her. What sort of payment would they have to make?

She couldn't talk to Carl about her fears. They were horrible but vague. She didn't think she would be able to explain them to him if she tried, and, if he should understand, then, surely he, too, must sink into this terrible depression.

She tried to be gay. She made things for her child, but there was no pleasure in that because she felt with a dull fatalism that the child would never be there to wear them.

Sometimes she dreamed of her mother—a vague woman with dim features—but she knew it was her mother, who died, horribly, in giving birth to a girl child. She thought that perhaps she, Rinie, would die, but it made her only a little sad. Nothing seemed to matter. She couldn't feel really close to Carl now. She was in the grip of this terrible depression and he couldn't come to her.

"Ellie, somethin's got to be done," Carl said desperately one night after Rinie and almost everyone else in the house had gone to bed. "She wanted a baby, we both did, but now—I don't know if she's happy about it or not."

"Bein' here, the way Doxy was, scared her," Ellie said, trying to reassure him. "She'll be all right, an' happy enough when it gits here, you can bet on that."

He didn't look at her. "It's—it's like she's—gone away. She's just partly here, talkin' to us, listenin' to things. It scares me, Ellie. I wish she'd git mad an' yell an' throw things the way Doxy did toward the end. She don't even cry any more. She just. . . ."

"Ever' woman is different with ever' child she bears," said Ellie. "Some draw into theirselves an' you can't follow. All these months is a long time to wait. No matter how she tries, there ain't much she can think about but

274

waitin'. She can tell you're frettin', Carl, an' that don't help her. Rinie ain't the kind that wants ever'body else to feel bad just because she does."

He was silent for a while, watching Ellie set the bread dough, and then he said slowly, "If I can borrow Troy's car, I'm gonna to take her to Belford tomorrow. We may stay three or four days if she wants to."

Ellie nodded. "That'd be real good for her, I expect, just to be some place different for a while."

Carl didn't say that his chief purpose in taking her to Belford was to have Rinie see a doctor. He knew that, to Ellie, for a woman to see a doctor was immodest almost to the point of wantonness, but he wasn't going to argue, he had made up his mind, and there was no point in upsetting Rinie with discussion.

After they had checked in at the Hayes Valley and were settled in a room, he said casually, "Larry Treadwell's been tellin' me about this doctor Bess sees. He's kind of new in town, from some big medical school back East. Supposed to be real up-to-date. I thought maybe you'd want to have him take a look at you."

"But I'm all right—" she began and stopped. She was not at all certain that she was all right. Perhaps if she saw a doctor and he should be reassuring, some of these sick, morbid feelings. . . .

Dr. Baird was a young man, quick and efficient and perceptive. He had bought the practice of an old doctor in Belford because he had always yearned after the West. He was not going to get rich for some little time here, and the practice was picking up quite slowly because people mistrusted a stranger, particularly when he was from Vermont, but he'd have been a little disappointed if they hadn't. When he had finished examining Rinie, he said briskly, "I don't have to tell you, of course, that you're pregnant. Is there a history of twins in your family?"

"I—I don't know anything about my people," she said diffidently.

"Well, I'd be willing to bet that you've got twins. How would you feel about that?"

"I—I don't know."

"Mrs. Stinson, do you want children?"

"Oh, oh, yes."

"Yet, you seem very depressed. Can you tell me what it is that's worrying you?"

She began to cry and couldn't speak.

"You really have nothing to worry about," he said matter-of-factly. "I'm sure you're very uncomfortable. I think you should try to eat more, get a lot of rest. After all, you're going to need a good bit of strength, caring for the two of them."

While she dressed, he went to talk with Carl. Carl was awed at the prospect of twins. He stood and stared rapturously past the little doctor for a moment, then he said fearfully, "But Rinie? Is she all right?"

"Physically, she's reasonably well, but something's troubling her. It would be a good thing if she could get it out of her system. I'm afraid I'm not equipped for that kind of thing, but perhaps you could try and find out what it is that troubles her and perhaps do something to help. . . . Now, Mr. Stinson, I am a little concerned about her delivery. She's small. Twins have a way of coming early and being small babies, so perhaps there'll be no problem. I'd like to see her deliver in the hospital here, but I realize that's not practical. Is there a good midwife in your community?"

Carl nodded and said hesitantly, "If—if we could git word to you, would you come?"

"Well, I could try," said the doctor slowly. "It's a long way, but, yes, if you could come or send word when her labor begins, I think I could get there in time. It would be my first delivery of twins since I've been in private practice."

That night they went to the Treadwells' for supper and afterward Jeff and Larry took Carl to see Jeff's school.

"I don't know what we did without Jeff," Bess said to Rinie as they sat alone in the living room of the nice little house in a good part of town. "He's the best boy and I'd be so lonesome without him, times when Larry's away. He reminds me of Carl. Don't you think they're alike?"

Rinie said she had thought so ever since she'd come to Red Bear.

Bess laughed a little. She looked a lot like Ellie when she smiled.

"I had an awful crush on Carl once. I suppose Ellie told you that."

"She—mentioned something once."

"Well, Ellie talks a lot. It was just one of those passing things, but it did take it a good bit to pass. Next to

Larry, I still think he's the finest, kindest man I know. I guess you won't mind my saying so after all this time."

Back at the hotel, Rinie sat on the bed and was silent. She kept watching Carl, smiling faintly sometimes. He was fine and kind and a lot of other wonderful things Bess hadn't mentioned and shouldn't know about, and she, Rinie, had all but forgotten him during the past few months.

"Carl?"

He turned from the window and let the drape fall closed.

"You—you need a haircut."

He walked across the room, slowly. There was something in her eyes, warm, almost a twinkle, trying to show through the unhappiness that had been there lately.

"I'll get one tomorrow."

"Carl, I love you."

He sat on the bed beside her and took her hands.

"I've been so scared." The words came unbidden. She didn't even think of how scared she had been before they were out, perhaps she didn't really know.

"Of what, Rinie?" Gently, he turned her face so that she had to look at him and his eyes cared so much. "Please try to tell me."

She took his hand that held her face, and turned away a little. "Of—of having something happen. It seems as if there's always something that—that's going to hurt us."

He was silent, sitting completely still beside her, his face concerned and concentrating.

"Things will hurt us," he said finally, very gently. "We're not that special that we can go through life without ever being hurt. . . . But things can make us happy, too, can't they? Maybe there are some people that don't get too much hurt from living—maybe somebody like Aunt Minna—but they don't get too much happy either. . . . Look, it—it seems to me like if you're gonna go swimmin' in the creek at home an' the water's cold. Some people jump in, an' some just put in their feet an' don't ever get any farther. The ones that jump get the shock over and have fun swimmin'. The ones that fool around the edges don't ever get used to the cold an' bein' afraid. They're in the water—sort of—but, hell, it's no good to 'em. Does that make any sense?"

"Yes." Her voice was a whisper.

"People like Aunt Minna stay around the edges an' fret an' bitch an' never ever know about the good things. . . . Remember you said once that maybe there was some time in her life when things could have turned out different?"

"She didn't jump," Rinie whispered and began to cry. "But, Carl, lately I've noticed this awful—balance that you can't get away from. For any happiness, there's got to be misery. . . ."

"Maybe it is like that, some, honey. I couldn' say. I don't know of anybody that could. I expect preachers would have somethin' to say, but . . . what do you mean —exactly?"

"Since I saw it, it's in everything," she said miserably. "All the little things like the weasel that killed the two chickens and then was killed in Kirby's trap; the way the milk cow was so sick after she got into the grain . . . but the big thing is that on the very day that Dean was born, A. J. . . ."

"Rinie, I couldn' give you any answers about things like that. Just God might know an' he don't tell."

"Do you believe in God, Carl?"

"Yes."

"It's strange I never knew you did. I always thought you didn't. You don't go to church or—"

"I look at the sky," he said softly, "at the leaves on the trees, at the birds comin' back every year, a thing like the stallion, a little new thing like Dean that's so perfect, at you, at us—together. What could a church do?"

She turned to him and he drew her into his arms. Her head lay on his breast and she was very still, hearing his heart beat. She felt peace, like a thing with substance, soft and comforting, all around them.

After a long silence he said gently, "Don't be afraid any more, little girl. If you're always busy bein' scared of the bad, the good'll never be worth a dam' to you."

"Carl, when are we going home?"

"I'd thought the day after tomorrow. Why?"

"Would it be all right if we go tomorrow? I'll have to get so much more ready for twins."

14

The winter had been cold and dry and open, the spring was warm and wet. There was more rain than snow in April and in May, there was rain almost every day. It made the outside work heavy and dirty but it was a real spring and Rinie liked it. There were April showers instead of blizzards and they truly did bring May flowers. Everyone kept saying how the warm weather couldn't hold; there'd have to be more cold before summer, the flowers and leaves would all be ruined, but they weren't. The bulbs Rinie had planted in the fall sent up shoots so green and tender that she wept a few tears of pure joy when no one was looking.

When a lovely, big, full hyacinth was ready to begin opening, she took a deep crock—she couldn't find a flowerpot that wasn't broken—and very tenderly digging around it to get plenty of the soft wet earth with it, she took up the plant and gently put it in the bowl and carried it in to A. J.'s dresser.

"Twins, huh?" was his greeting. His speech was still a little garbled at times, but he didn't have much trouble making himself understood.

She nodded, stepping back a little to admire the plant and its reflection in the cloudy old mirror.

"Well, what are you bringin' me flowers for? I never had nothin' to do with it."

She was getting quite self-conscious about the shape of her body by this time, but she said stoutly, "I thought you'd like to look at them and smell them, and you did have something to do with the twins, at least you had something to do with Carl."

"You're gittin' right sassy lately," he said approvingly, the corner of his mouth quirking a little.

The left side of his face—his whole left side—was still difficult to control, but Rinie thought that if there had to be after-effects from the stroke, she was glad it was his right side that seemed fully recovered. It was the right side of his mouth, like Carl's, that always gave him away, indicating his true feelings.

The calves were being born and all the little wild things, and now Rinie was part of it all. A pair of blue birds began building a nest in the box Jeff had made and Carl had hung from the eaves outside his and Rinie's window. While the female did most of the work, the male sat on the edge of the roof or the clothesline pole nearby and sang to her, masterfully, mellifluously, possessively.

"Oh, he's just wonderful!" Rinie whispered raptly as they lay in bed one morning at sunup, watching the female flitting assiduously back and forth, listening to the male sing.

"She's not so dam' bad," Carl observed, "doin' all the work like that while he just sings. If I could sing like that, would you build a house for our kids to be born in?"

"Yes."

"You're a little crazy, Irine. You know that? This thing of twins is effectin' your mind."

She laughed. "We'd better get up."

"Wouldn' it be something," he said, stretching, "if they were born on A. J.'s birthday, the end of July?"

"I don't think they'll wait that long," she said dubiously.

"But that's about when they're due. Why do you say that? Do you feel bad?"

She did. Her back ached constantly and she never felt really well, but it didn't matter. It was just a part of this pregnancy for her and it didn't frighten her any more. But she tried not to let Carl know because, as Ellie said, "Some men are such ole women."

She said now, "Well, you know Dr. Baird said twins usually come early, and I'm so big and oh, Carl, they kick so much. It's getting so I can't sleep."

"Little devils," he said, grinning proudly. He threw off the covers and leapt out of bed.

Toward the end of a bright, muddy May afternoon, when he was riding down from the ridges, Carl saw the first foal up in the mares' pasture. "All right," he said to Daylight, whom he was riding, "I guess the stallion may as well go on up there."

There was no one around the barns and corrals. The

rest of the men were out on the flats. Carl sat Daylight for a minute looking speculatively at the stallion. The sorrel bared his teeth. Carl rode into the corral and snubbed him to a post.

"Just stand easy, goddam' it. I'm gonna take you up to the mares, but I'll be dammed for a dewlapped dog if I'll lead you, you Chrissakin' ole bastard. . . . Now listen, nobody's gonna watch this time, just you an' me."

At suppertime, when the men came in, Carl was not with them.

Travis was helping his father to the table. He said quietly so the women wouldn't hear, "He left where we was to go up toward the ridge 'bout the middle of the afternoon, an' that goddam' stallion ain't in the corral now."

"Mares started to foal, have they?" asked the old man knowingly.

"Not that I know of, but—"

"Carl!" Rinie cried. He was standing at the back door, looking in a little sheepishly, covered with mud.

"Good Lord a-mercy." said Ellie impatiently. "Where in the world have you been?"

"Did you ride him, Buck?" asked A. J., trying to control a snort of laughter, "or just waller around with him?"

"I rode him, by God, A. J., an' then—well, wallered around some."

When he had washed and put on clean clothes and sat at the table he didn't look so bad, only a few scratches and minor bruises showed.

"How come you to ride 'im by yourself?" asked Troy. "I swear, you're not right in the head."

"Brownie foaled," Carl said, ladling gravy, "a nice filly, so I thought he might as well go on up there."

"Did you ever think," asked Rinie a little shakily, "of just putting a rope on him?"

"Well, hell, honey, I was ridin' Daylight. Daylight ain't Dan. I couldn' of led that sonofabitch with Daylight."

"You're not makin' any sense," Travis complained. "You sure you didn' hit your head on somethin'? Ole Dan's right out yonder in the big corral, was all day since dinnertime."

Carl glanced around at them defiantly. "I wanted to ride him," he said with simple exuberance. "It's springtime an' I felt like it. Besides, he's gittin' a dam' sight better deal now than shut up in that corral like he has been all winter."

"He's got more room," agreed Helen practically, "and other horses to be friends with."

Kirby snickered and turned a little red.

"An' you told him what a good deal he'd be gittin'," said Troy sardonically, "an' he said how he appreciated all you was doin' for him."

"How many times he throw you?" asked A. J., getting down to the meat of the matter.

"Twice."

"An' he didn't git away? How come?"

"Well—the first time I held onto the reins."

"An' he didn't stomp you to death!" cried Ellie.

"He stepped on my hand," Carl admitted unwillingly, "before I could git up, but it was in a mudhole an' didn't hurt nothin'."

"Good God!" breathed Troy. "An' what about the next time?"

"Well, he did git away then, but by that time we was in the pasture. I had to catch ole Curry an' go after him to git my saddle an' stuff."

"Carl, you didn' catch that sonofabitch on ole Curry. She can't hardly git as fast as a trot."

Carl said deprecatingly, "I know, but he was pretty tired by that time."

"Carl, you're crazy," stated Ellie, "ridin' that ole wild thing by yourself, w'y nobody even knowed where you was at."

"You could have been hurt—" Rinie began and stopped herself. He hadn't been and he looked so happy.

"It's this twin business," said Troy solemnly. "He ain't been normal since they come back from Belford after they seen that doctor."

Old Christmas died that spring. She went away into the woods she had hunted for nearly fifteen years to meet death alone. Kirby found her by accident while looking for calves. He buried her up there and when he came home and told Travis about it, he couldn't help crying again.

A. J. didn't cry. He sat silently in the front room after supper and, finally, in the midst of some other conversation, he said, "She was the best huntin' dog on the West Fork in her time. I got 'er from ole man Arliss Butler. Ole Arliss was a sonofabitch hisself an' he knowed dogs. She was just a pup an' I won her on a bet. Arliss had him a walleyed fit when he seen I was goin' to make him pay off. . . . Most ever' hunter in the valley's got a dog that's some kin of hers. A gover'ment hunter seen 'er go after a lion one time, offered me two hundred fifty dollars for her. . . . Likely you boys'd got that lion last winter if she'd been able to go along. She's better now, though. She never knowed nothin' but huntin' an' when she got to where she couldn' do that no more. . . ." His voice broke a little and he turned and spat noisily into the fire.

In the silence that followed, Doxy, her son having finished his meal, buttoned her blouse and carried the baby to where the old man sat.

"Dean wants to tell Granddaddy good night," she said timidly and put the husky, drowsy three-month-old child into the old man's arms.

"W'y bless her heart," Ellie murmured to Travis, "an' here I keep thinkin' she ain't got a lick of sense."

Sprite dropped a fine, light sorrel colt on the third of June, Rinie's twentieth birthday.

"Just for me," Rinie said softly, standing in the mud by the corral, watching the young one wobble on his unsteady legs. There was something pretentious about him, even in this awkward state and she and Carl laughed and Sprite looked around at them with pride.

"Look," Rinie said, "he's got a blaze like Sultan."

"Who?"

"His father. You told me to think of a name. You can't just always go on calling him the goddam' sonofabitch. A sultan is someone with a harem."

"Well, he's that, all right. You ought to see him studdin' around up there. Troy an' Travis say he'll break the fence an' run off the mares, but he don't show no sign of thinkin' about that kind of thing."

"Do you think I can do as well as Sprite? You know, produce true to the line and all those things you talk about when you get started talking about breeding horses and cattle?"

"That's a funny thing to say," he said, looking at her quizzically.

"Why? You're always lumping all the females in the world together, including me."

"Well, you are pretty dam' female," he said, his eyes darkening.

The rains went on. Red Bear Creek was a rushing torrent and the road down to Webber was impassable to any vehicle. The river was over the Belford road in several places and no one could go for Jeff, though school had been out over a week. Doxy's sister Becky was to be married to one of the Hunter boys on the third Sunday, provided Reverend Turner could get through to Webber, and they hoped that if the minister did come, he would bring Jeff. Fearing that the water might get even higher and make the canyon impassable, Doxy took Dean on Friday and rode down to her folks' so as not to miss the wedding. Troy went along to see them safely to the Keanes' Place, but he came straight back to Red Bear. Sutter had tried to talk him into fixing the leaky roof.

Toward noon on Saturday, there was a terrific storm with flashing lances of lightning and great, sharp, incisive crashes of thunder and, even watching the lightning, knowing the thunder would come, it was hard not to flinch.

The men were out around the barns, but Carl ran to the house in the opening moments of the downpour and rushed into the kitchen, drenched to the skin.

"Where's Rinie?"

"Take them spurs off. She's layin' down to rest a few minutes."

Rinie got up heavily and they stood by the window watching, their fingers clasped together.

"You're soaked," she said, her voice all but drowned by the pouring rain.

"I wanted to see it with you," he said.

"It's beautiful, Carl. Oh, it's so scary and so beautiful."

"Do you really think that, Rinie?" Not long ago, he thought, she wouldn't have been able to see the beauty, only the scariness.

"Yes," she said stoutly when a gigiantic peal of thunder would let her be heard.

"I guess maybe you'll do," he said proudly.

The storm was a long time moving off, but finally the rain slackened enough so that they heard Travis and Troy and Kirby come into the kitchen.

"Over an inch a water out a that little shower," Travis announced, stamping vigorously at the back door. "The creek'll be hell-roarin'."

"What's for dinner?" asked Carl, watching a patch of clear sky grow bigger.

"A meat loaf," she said, "and Ellie was going to fix scalloped potatoes and things. Carl?"

"What?"

He was finally changing his wet shirt. She didn't say anything so he turned to look at her. Rinie felt small and shy and frightened, and at the same time tremendously powerful and important.

"I—I think maybe it's started."

He stared and she couldn't help laughing a little.

"Now you look like one of those fathers that's the last to know."

"Well, I—I better go git the doctor."

"No, wait. It would be awful to make him come all the way up here for nothing. It could be a false alarm."

"You've been readin' too many books."

"Why? Don't your other female things have false alarms? Just go and eat your dinner and, if—by then—" The shadow of pain crossed her face. She tried not to let it show.

"Honey, I can't eat," he said helplessly. "I'm gonna tell Ellie."

"Can't anything be a secret around here, just for a little while," she said plaintively, but he was gone into the kitchen.

"All right," said Ellie casually. "You just set down an' eat your dinner. I'll go in in a minute."

"I don't want any dam' dinner," he said angrily. How could women treat a thing like this with such nonchalance? "I'm goin' after the doctor."

"You can't git no doctor, Carl," Travis said reasonably. "The road's flooded."

"I'll take a horse for him."

"Clear to Belford?"

"I don't have time to talk about how an' all that. I promised Rinie the doctor. She's figgerin' on him bein' here."

Troy came to him at the corral where he was saddling Dan.

"Let me go, Buck," he said almost shyly. "You'll want to be with her. She's already askin' where you are. I'll git ole Juber here an' it'll be fine."

Carl barely glanced up, but Troy saw the gratitude and relief in his eyes.

"I can git a car to Fraser's," Troy said, pulling the cinch tight. "They've got a phone now if the line's not down."

"That's what I was thinkin' of doin'," Carl said grimly.

"If it wasn' for this last goddam' storm, I think he could of got to Webber all right."

"Yeah, well, I'll leave the horses at Doxy's folks or someplace, grab somebody's car an' go to Fraser's, an' what'll I tell 'im if I can git 'im on the phone?"

"Tell 'im to git the hell up here."

Troy grinned. "I guess I can probably remember that. If ever'thing goes all right, we ought to be back in five, six hours. Buck? It didn' hardly take that long for Dean to be born. I better stop at Heddie's, just in case, don't you think?"

"I guess. Bo?"

Troy had swung up on Juber, Dan's reins in his hand. He looked down, waiting.

"That lower ford's gonna be meaner'n a bitch bear."

"I can swim."

"Yeah, but I don't know if the doctor can—or ride either."

"Well, if Dan can bring in that stud horse I guess he can git the doctor up here, one way or another."

In the house Ellie said, "You ought to lay down, Rinie. You look pale all at once."

"I'm cold," she said a little apologetically. "I was all right till I told Carl and now I can't stop shaking."

"That storm was somethin' to make anybody shaky."

"Do you think it made me start? Carl says cows and mares start laboring sometimes because of a storm."

"Cows an' mares," grunted Ellie, brusquely arranging the bed. "Men is the most useless things, times like this. They're about done eatin' in there now. Somebody can help A. J. back to his room an' the rest can go on off somewheres."

"Ellie? Please don't make Carl go."

"Well, I won't if you say so, but it may be that later on you'll want him to. You just tell me if you change your mind." She didn't mention that Carl had said he was going for the doctor. Maybe Troy had been able to dissuade him. No use worrying Rinie with that till she knew herself.

Travis helped his father back to bed and then he and Kirby went back out around the barns. Ellie was a little relieved when Carl came into the kitchen. She said, keeping her voice low so Rinie wouldn't hear, "Carl, you know that doctor can't git through. They's no use goin' any farther than Heddie's."

"I promised her there'd be a doctor," he said, stubbornly, "that time we went to Belford an' she saw him. Troy's gone after him. He'll do as much as I could, an' he said he'd stop at Heddie's, just in case."

Ellie felt better. "Well, they better be somebody, for I don't know about this twin business. I don't know why it is Rinie feels the way she does about midwives, but when the time comes, she won't care if it's a doctor or Heddie or who, I know that. Now you go in there an' set with 'er if you want to, but don't you worry 'er. I'll git this kitchen straightened up. Ain't nothin' likely to happen for a good while."

"I wisht I was twins," said Helen from behind them at the table.

"Lord a-mercy, I forgot about you," said her mother, starting nervously.

"Well, I'm just fixin' to wash these dishes," stated Helen, stacking busily, "but I was thinkin', if I'da been twins, I'da had somebody to sleep with."

Rinie was smocking the yoke of a tiny white dress. She had had to stop for a while because her hands shook so badly, but now she was all right again. She wasn't afraid, she told herself firmly, not with Carl here, and Ellie, and Dr. Baird coming. The pains were not so bad, they didn't last forever and, for now, there was a long time between them. She had been thinking of this time for so long and she wondered nervously why its onset should be such a shock as to cause her to shiver as she had, uncontrollably for such a long while. She wanted to be sensible and brave about all of it and yet she had given way like that right at the beginning.

"Don't you want to go to bed?" Carl asked uneasily as she picked up the dress again. She, what was happening to her, awed him.

"Sometimes," she said calmly, "they make women walk around, even at the last, to hurry things along. If there weren't so many people around who'd think it was immodest of me, I'd walk around. I'd like to. I'd go down and look at the creek. Just listen to it roar."

He heard it all too clearly. He couldn't just sit there. He kept looking out the window and opening a dresser drawer now and then, feeling awkward and completely helpless.

"Want to read my book that the doctor gave me?" she offered gently.

"I've read your book."

"Well, I think you ought to read it again because you look pale."

"I've never done this before," he said and then felt foolish because she was the one it was happening to, and she hadn't done it before either, and she had all of it to go through, while he just stood around, doing nothing. He came to her almost timidly and put his hand on her hair.

"Carl . . . by this time tomorrow, there'll be somebody, some little person that the world is all new to, to wear this dress. I hope I can get it done."

He smiled back at her and sat on the edge of the bed. "It'll be kind of sissyish for either of the boys, don't you think?"

"Don't be selfish."

"But if it's two boys, I can teach 'em ever'thing at once, not have to go over stuff twice, an' by the time they they're say fifteen, sixteen, you an' me can—Rinie?"

"It's all right," she gasped, her eyes pleading with him not to make a fuss. "What can we do?"

"We—we can run around an' leave the work to the kids."

"But if there's a girl," she said, relaxing, "she can take care of the younger ones."

"Oh, well, yeah, maybe. . . . Honey, please go to bed. I'm gonna git Ellie. She can help you better than I can."

"Carl?"

He turned.

"Don't—don't go far."

He walked distractedly into A. J.'s room. The old man was propped up in bed, looking out at a drizzle that had begun to fall some time ago.

"How's she doin?"

"All right, I guess." Through the other window, Carl looked out at the wild roily creek.

"You figger that doctor'll make it?"

"If he got up the river before this last water piled up too much, but I don't see how he could."

"I thought Ellie said Bojack was gonna send Heddie."

"Maybe she's waitin' for him to git back from Fraser's an' come with 'er."

A. J. snorted. "Heddie ain't one to be afraid of a little water. If she was home when Troy went by, she'da been here. Buck?"

"Yessir?"

"It's a worryin' time for a man if he gives a dam'. Don't never git easier, I guess."

"If I could just help someway," Carl burst out, his face still to the window.

"That's the hell of it. You can't, not one goddam' bit."

"Ellie—Ellie says I oughtn' to stay, that it'd be easier for her not to have to have to put on any kind of act or anything."

"An' what't missy say?"

"She says 'Don't go far,' things like that."

"You stay," A. J. said firmly. "She wants you. It's hard, but it don't hurt for a man to know how it is. You want a drink?"

"No. That—it seems like it'd be cheatin'."

Rinie lay in bed and he sat beside her. It was getting bad now, the pains coming harder and closer together, but she wouldn't scream the way Doxy had, not ever, not as long as Carl was with her.

"Carl? One has to have your name. Please. I know you don't like it, but it's something to be proud of."

"What if they're both girls?"

"I'd like to name a little girl for your mother. . . . Is it raining?"

"A little."

"Do you think the doctor can come? It's been a long time."

"He could be here any minute."

He got up and lit a lamp. She was so pale and sweat stood out on her forehead, though she shivered from time to time.

"Carl—if he doesn't come. . . ."

"Please don't worry, honey."

"A. J. and your mother didn't have anyone when you were born."

Ellie, standing in the doorway, said, "There's some supper on the table, Carl. You eat. You never did have no dinner."

He went out for a little while, but he didn't eat. He just walked around the house. It was cold, cold like the fall instead of past the middle of June, dark and dreary at six o'clock.

"I'd like to see her deliver in the hospital," the doctor had said. Carl thought of going to look for Heddie. Troy, with or without the doctor, should have been back by now. Carl thought half-formed, half-hysterical thoughts of many things. He had been witness, even assistant, at the birth of many animals, but the only one he seemed to be able to think about now was when Skeeter's colt had had to be cut to pieces unborn, and even that hadn't been enough to save her. He was sick, standing outside in the drizzle, listening to the creek roar.

Kirby and Helen went to bed after supper. Travis and A. J. were in the front room, A. J. on the sofa with an old wool blanket over him. They talked desultorily in low voices. There was a good fire going to keep off the damp, and they had a bottle of whiskey that they exchanged from time to time.

Ellie was becoming distraught. She had little doubt about her ability to assist at the birth of a child, even of two, but she was uneasy about Rinie, the way she had felt so bad all along, the way the labor seemed to be going more slowly than it ought to. If only they hadn't been so set on having a doctor since they came back from Belford that time, Heddie could have been alerted and probably would be here now. Well, Ellie thought grimly as she checked mentally through her list of supplies, this is liable to be quite some night.

She kept a big fire in the kitchen stove and the door to Rinie's room open so it would be warm in there. She went softly in and out, and even when everything she could think of had been prepared, she still couldn't seem to sit down and be still for any length of time at all. Having Carl there made her nervous, though she had to admit it was what Rinie wanted and she didn't suppose she, Ellie, could have made him leave if she'd tried, but it was no time or place for a man and that's all there was to it.

Rinie was crying and whimpering and writhing. She didn't know it. All she knew was the pain that kept coming and coming, and making her gasp and bite at the pillow and try to struggle away from it. It was the whole world.

"Everything," she gasped, "everything in me wants to get out."

"That's how it is," Ellie said gently.

Carl stood up. "Hold my hands and push, Rinie." He tried to sound sure and steady. "It won't be long now."

But it went on and on. Carl's hands bled where she dug her nails into them and he was almost as pale as she was.

Ellie pushed the hair gently back from Rinie's forehead, moistened her lips, wiped her face with a cool, damp cloth.

"We'll have to do somethin'," she said finally. "She can't stand this much longer."

Rinie couldn't hear them.

"What?" he said fiercely. "What'll we do? What's wrong?"

"She's just got to this place an' can't seem to go no farther. Oh, Lord, I'd give anything if Heddie was here."

"Is the doctor coming?" Rinie begged weakly.

"Yes," Carl said through his teeth as her nails bit into his lacerated hands.

"Carl, Carl! I'm afraid! Oh, don't let the babies be hurt. . . ."

"It'll be all right soon, Rinie," he said shakily. Tears were running down his cheeks and he had no free hand to wipe them away, but she didn't see them. "What'll we do?" he cried desperately. "For God's sake, Ellie . . . somethin'. . . ."

Ellie had got as far as the door to the kitchen when the dogs began a great clamor.

Carl would have laughed at the first sight he had of Dr. Baird that night if he had not been so frantic and so relieved. The little doctor had come in soaked to the skin and they had given him some clothes of Travis's to put on. He had taken several turns in the sleeves and the pants' legs, but that did nothing to remedy the bagginess. His shoe heels scuffed along the floor as he tried to move about with professional briskness. He made Carl leave the room while he performed a quick examination and Carl was so distracted that it came near requiring force on the part of the doctor and Ellie to make him go.

Tory was in the front room, on the floor in front of the fire, exhausted. He had stripped off his wet clothes and was wrapped in a blanket eating from a plate of food someone had got him.

"By God, we kep' his bag dry," he was saying triumphantly when Carl came in. "Hell, I thought it'd be all over by the time we got here. It's nearly midnight." He took a long pull at the bottle Travis had passed him. "That's a dam' game little guy."

"How'd he git here?" Travis asked.

They were paying no attention to Carl, standing there with desperation in his eyes, not hearing much of what

291

they said. It was easier for all of them if they just didn't notice.

"Well, they didn' have much a that big, hard rain up the West Fork," Troy said. "So the river wasn' bad for a while. I waited for 'im at Fraser's an' by the time he got there, it was risin' fast, so we left the cars an' borryed horses from them. He'd already been stuck twice between there an' Belford. With horses, we could git back from the river, not stick to the road where it was bad. It was all right till we hit Red Bear Canyon. We had ole Dan an' Juber by then, an' I'd borryed a flashlight, though I lost the dam' thing."

He drank again and went on. "I never seen the water like it is! Jesus! I took the doc's bag when we was fixin' to cross the lower ford, an' I says, 'Can you swim?' an' he said 'Would it make any difference?'" Troy grinned wearily. "He's pretty goddam' plucky for somebody from Vermont. Buck? You want a drink?"

Carl took the proffered bottle, looked at it for a moment, and gave it back.

"It's a kinda funny thing about Heddie, though," Troy said thoughtfully. "When I stopped by an' told her, she said, 'If you don't git the doctor or he says he can't come, you come right back an' tell me. If he can come, I'll stay out of it.' You reckon she's jealous, about the doctor?"

Carl went back to the bedroom. They had said they would call him and they hadn't.

"He's fixin' to give her ether," Ellie whispered, terrified. "You oughtn' let 'im."

"Carl," Rinie's voice was small and plaintive. "Carl, please, I can't. . . ."

He was beside her, holding her hands. "The doctor's come, Rinie. It'll be all right in just a little while, sweetheart."

She didn't know what he said, but she heard his voice, felt his hands on hers. He was there.

After a moment of breathing the ether, she lay almost inert, moaning a little, murmuring wordlessly.

"The things I asked you to sterilize when I first got here," the doctor said brusquely to Ellie. "Will you bring them, please? Still in the pan of water."

When she had gone, he said quietly to Carl, "Your children are both trying to get into the world at once. It can't be done."

292

Carl was dizzy from the ether, and sick. Rinie's hands were limp in his. She was so frail and still.

"Now," said Dr. Baird when Ellie had placed the large pan of steaming water on a chair near him, "we'll get this thing done with."

Ellie gasped "What—what's that?"

"Obstetrical forceps, Mrs. Stinson," said the doctor calmly. "One of these youngsters is going to be among us soon. Do you have everything ready for him?"

"Carl!" Ellie's voice registered terror, protest, outrage, but Carl couldn't think. He felt faint and dropped to his knees beside Rinie, biting his lip so that he wouldn't lose all contact with the room, what was going on.

Rinie stirred, rousing, crying out.

"She mustn't have any more ether just now," said the doctor to Carl, who lifted his eyes dazedly. "We'll need her help. Can you stay here? She seems to want you. Can you talk to her?"

Carl never knew what he said, neither did any of the others. It didn't matter. He spoke softly to Rinie and she heard, though the words meant nothing. He didn't watch the doctor's ministrations, but Ellie did, with the sharp eyes of distrust.

Rinie's fingers dug into Carl's hands more painfully than ever and her breath came in rending gasps, but she didn't scream. The little reality that reached her now came through the thick haze of the terrible pain but she never let go of the determination not to let Cark hear her scream.

And then there was respite, abrupt, unbelievable release. She still gasped for breath and tears came hot down her face.

"Rinie, there—there's a little girl," Carl said dizzily.

"She's not crying," Rinie murmured dimly, but before her weary nerves could register concern, the little girl was crying, making her first protest at the demands of living.

The boy was born less than an hour later, without forceps, and with less noise at being made to breathe. Ellie had a bed ready for them by the kitchen stove, "like a litter of pups," A. J. commented, grinning proudly, when the men came in to look.

Carl went outside. He couldn't seem to realize it was over. Rinie couldn't either. Even when it was all finished, exhausted as she was, she had kept asking for reassurance that the babies were all right and crying nervously until Dr. Baird had given her some sort of injection.

"She's lost a good deal of blood," he told Carl soberly. "The hemorrhaging has almost stopped now, but she must be absolutely quiet for a few hours at the very least."

And when she finally slept, Carl had come outside. It wasn't raining, though the sky was still heavy with clouds. It must be around three, he thought.

"Buck, you want a cigarette?" Troy stood beside him and gave him the smoke, already made and lit.

"That doc's in there havin' hisself a drink. Says he's goin' to bed soon if Rinie's still doin' all right."

"I thought you'd be asleep," Carl said. His voice didn't sound right. It seemed to come from somewhere else to his ears. He dragged the smoke deep. It made him cough and that sounded more natural.

"I'm goin'," Troy said, "right now, an' you ought to, too. You look like you been drug through a knothole. What do you think a your kids?"

"Not much," Carl said, and then felt a little shocked and ashamed of his frankness.

When Rinie woke, he was beside her. It was morning and the bluebird was singing.

"The eggs ought to hatch soon," she murmured groggily, and then, "Oh, Carl, you look awful! Haven't you been asleep?"

"For a while. I'm fine. How about you, missy?"

"I feel so tired," she said drowsily, "but not a bad kind of tired. I want to see my babies."

"In a while," he said. "You don't want 'em waked up. They just got to sleep again. They're the reason I'm awake. They're pretty loud, the two of 'em together."

"But they're hungry," she said, moving as if she would sit up.

Quickly, gently, he put his hands on her shoulders. "You have to keep quiet today. I mean really still. All right?"

"Why?"

"Bceause the doctor says so, an' he also says you're not to feed the babies—for a while, at least."

"But, Carl, I—"

"Now listen. We're not gonna bring a doctor that can't swim all the way up here through a flood an' then, when he gits here, ignore what he says. All right?"

"Yes," she said meekly. Then, after a little, "But you're sure they're all right?"

"Yes, I'm sure." He laid his cheek against hers. "Are you satisfied, little girl? You've done a thing no Stinson woman in A. J.'s recollection has ever done, produced 'em two at a time, an' you've made Helen's life worth livin' because now there's another girl, an' Ellie thinks she's died an' gone to heaven—now that she's got over the shock of havin' a doctor in the house—an' I—God, Rinie, I don't know what I feel like, now that it's finally beginnin' to soak in."

"Oh, Carl, I love you," she whispered. "And, yes, I'm satisfied, and happy and everything else good."

"Do you want to try an' eat somethin'? The doctor said you ought to, an' Ellie says she's got some broth or tea or some kind of God-awful stuff that's just wonderful good for you."

"In a little while," she said drowsily. "Right now I think I want to sleep some more. Carl?"

"What, sweetheart?"

"How soon will it be now till I can ride Sprite?"

15

With July, the weather turned from cool and wet to hot and dry. Abruptly, there was no more rain. Winds came over from the Utah desert, and it was incredible how quickly life was sucked from the vegetation. Ellie's garden things, so green with promise, turned dry and sere before they had had a chance to come to full fruit. Rinie watered her flowers with a bucket, when she was able, and Jeff helped, but the wind, like the breath from a furnace, dried them to husks. The creek, in the course of a month, dropped from a raging, fearsome torrent to a muddy thread, moving listlessly among its dark boulders. The well got low; the water came from the pump, muddy and grayish. The forage dried up and the hay in the upper meadows dried on the stem, lush, but short and difficult to handle.

The only things that seemed to thrive were the insects. They had had a good start in the spring and now they were a constant torment to the stock. The cattle and horses sought shade and stood in it through the day, breathing heavily, stamping and swishing their tails and looking as if they might go mad sometimes with the constant torture of the flies. There was sickness among the cattle and several young calves died. Reluctantly, the men decided to dip. It was no easy operation. It amounted to an extra roundup, and then to driving the assembled cattle through the chute and the vat, making sure that each was completely wet down with the dipping solution.

A. J. made them put him on a horse so that he could go out and watch a few hours of the dipping process. He rather enjoyed it. It was almost his first contact with the work since his stroke, even though he could do no more than watch from a camp stool in the shade, but the others, working in the blistering sun and choking dust to force wild cattle to go into a chute and jump into a vat of foul-smelling water, found it one of the most tiring, disagreeable jobs they had ever had to perform.

Doyle had stayed in Denver to work through the summer, and if Kirby, big and strong at fourteen, had not been able to do a man's share of the work, they would have been hard-put to keep up with all that had to be done. Certainly, there was no money to hire help.

The men said that the calves they had lost were the greater part of the year's profit, even if prices were good, but they only mentioned it once or twice and they weren't complaining, just saying how things were, shaking their heads a little, spitting dust and going on. That's how things went. Some years were good, others not so good.

Troy was hurt while they were dipping. He had roped a big cow and had her in the chute, but as he tried to free his rope before driving her into the vat, his right shoulder was badly, painfully wrenched. It was over a month before he could throw a rope again, or do much else that required the use of his right arm.

"Think how much easier this would of been with

296

sheep," he said at the house after the accident, his face grim and white.

The babies were fretful with the heat. Dean, beginning to crawl and teethe, was not content anywhere and Helen spent a good deal of her time trying to entertain him. Doxy seemed to lose interest in her son as a child might as the newness wore off a toy. She, too, was fretful and restless, and after Troy was hurt and he was around the house a good deal, they argued and quarreled almost constantly.

Rinie's recovery was, to her, exasperatingly slow. She had to stay in bed a good part of the time for several weeks, but she had the twins' bed brought in beside hers, over Ellie's protests, so that at least she could do the greater part of caring for them. It bothered her that she wasn't doing her share of the work around the house; there was so much to be done, but she found great satisfaction in sitting propped up in bed, watching her children sleep and eat and make the beautiful, unknowing sounds and movements of infancy. While she was still not allowed to spend much time out of bed, the baby bluebirds hatched, were fed and cared for and taught to fly, and she watched their progress with pleasure and awe, sitting very still while her own babies slept. How terrible to have them grow up so quickly, she thought, and felt sorry for the bluebird parents.

During this time, she learned that, as well as his father's thick, red-blond hair and even, exuberant temperament, James Carlisle also had inherited Carl's "funny eyes," as A. J. called them. Virginia Irine, on the other hand, had the dark red Stinson hair, the dark blue, incisive Stinson eyes, and the truculent, imperious, endearing Stinson temperament. The baby girl was small-boned and slight and Carl insisted that her features were like Rinie's, but the grandfather said unequivocally that she "wasn' nothin' but Stinson."

Rinie was happy with the feeling that she knew her children completely from the beginning of their lives, a knowledge she would have been unable to obtain had her health been better. It was so terribly important to her to know them, understand them, be close to them. She couldn't help thinking often of herself as an infant, treated with the best possible care, but with only the small amount of love and tenderness that the overworked

297

women at the orphanage had had the time and the strength to give to each individual child. When she had known she was going to have twins, she had worried a little that maybe one at a time would have been better, because perhaps she wouldn't be able to love and care for two so well as she wanted to. But now she found that love was an expanding thing, capable of suiting itself to any situation.

She missed Carl in those weeks. She wasn't lonely with the twins to watch and care for and with all that went on around the house, but she missed sharing things with him. Often, the men took lunches with them when they went out to work in the morning, and it was after dark when they come in to supper. She wanted to tell Carl about the little things the babies had done—how Jamie had smiled, or seemed to, how Ginger had flatly refused to drink water—that sort of thing. He listened and smiled at her and at them, but he never said much. He was so tired he could hardly keep his eyes open and often fell asleep before she blew out the lamp. Then, well before daylight, A. J., who was now able to walk with the help of a stout stick, roused the house for breakfast—he could at least do that much to help keep things going.

Rinie understood Carl's exhaustion. She knew that besides the physical tiredness, he, all of them, had the nervous strain of worrying about the stock, the feed for winter, money to pay the bills, but she couldn't help feeling hurt at his lack of interest in his children. When she came to think of it, Troy had essentially the same attitude toward Dean until very recently when Dean had begun to be more of an individual than an infant, a husky, imperious little boy who wanted his daddy when he saw him and had already been taken swimming and on horseback. But Rinie had expected that Carl would be different, more perceptive, that he would see the personalities of his children developing as she did, without having to wait for the obvious indications that even a stranger would see. For the first time, she felt disappointment in him, and there was a vague coolness, a little distance between them, because he was not sharing all the wonderful things.

While Troy was unable to do much work because of his shoulder, Doxy persuaded him that he should teach her to drive. He said these lessons were harder on his shoulder than working would have been, not to mention the stress on his nerves, but she became fairly competent and it was an outlet for some of her restlessness. Carl suggested that she should drive Rinie and the twins to Belford as soon as Rinie was able to make the trip. Dr. Baird had impressed upon him the importance of a post-natal examination for Rinie. Before he had left Red Bear on that dreary Sunday afternoon following the twins' birth, he had said privately to Carl, "It would be a little silly of me to say so this early, before things have had an opportunity to get back to normal, but it seems likely to me that she shouldn't have any more children. In fact, I believe she may be unable to conceive again. However, that is something I can tell more about later."

Rinie felt the trip was unnecessary. She was, at last, strong enough to be of some use around the house, and it seemed a waste to take a whole day for a trip to Belford, not to mention the addition of her unpaid doctor's bills. But Doxy thought it was a wonderful idea. Becky and Bill had moved to Belford after their marriage and she hadn't seen them since. Even Ellie was mildly enthusiastic about the trip. It wasn't any too early to start laying in supplies for the winter, she said, and there were some things for which a man simply couldn't be trusted to shop. Also, she longed to see Bess's baby girl, born on the Fourth of July. She didn't mention that she thought Rinie should see the doctor. That would have been giving in—or seemed like it—and Ellie still didn't hold with doctors, though to herself she did admit that without Dr. Baird, one or both of the twins, possibly even Rinie, might not be alive. Rinie's slow recovery of strength worried Ellie and she felt that she ought to see and talk with someone who knew more about such things than she, Ellie, did.

And so they went, and Dr. Baird said to Rinie after his examination, "I'm sorry Carl couldn't come. I would have liked to talk with you both."

She paled. "Is something wrong? The babies—"

"You have two of the healthiest youngsters in Bell County," he assured her, smiling, "and you're doing well yourself now. What I feel should be told to both you and Carl is that it looks as if there are not likely to be any other children."

"Oh." She felt numbed.

"That shouldn't be any sort of blow," said the doctor heartily. "You've presented the family with twins, which is no small accomplishment. Two children make a lovely family. Now, I want you to tell Carl about this, won't you?" And he carefully explained the physical reasons why she was not likely ever to conceive again. "You will tell him? It's only fair to both of you that he know."

She was very quiet on the drive home. To have no more children because you agreed there were enough was one thing, if you could manage it, but to be unable to have more was something entirely different. It made her feel ashamed, as though she were only half a woman. Carl would pity her, perhaps in time come to resent her. They had never really discussed it, but she supposed he envisioned a large family as she always had. Things kept misting up as she looked out of the car window, not hearing Ellie's and Doxy's talk, and she held Jamie, sleeping in her arms, with infinite tenderness. To the twins, at least, perhaps this failure in her would not matter.

Before leaving Red Bear, Dr. Baird had given Carl a prescription for some pills for A. J. He said that perhaps they wouldn't help, but they might relieve the rheumatic pains to some degree and make it easier for the old man to move about. Carl said that his father wouldn't likely take them and the doctor said wryly, "Try them anyway. Have the prescription filled when someone goes to town. They should be practically tasteless dissolved in whiskey."

Carl sent the prescription to be filled when the women went to town, but he disliked deception. To give the medicine to A. J. without his knowledge made it seem as if the old man was senile, so he said simply, "We got you these pills."

"What fer?"

"Whatever ails you."

"Where'd you git 'em?"

"Drugstore."

"Who told you to?"

"Dr. Baird."

"Humpf."

"He said they might ease your joints some."

"I ain't takin' nothin' from no doctor fer females. Christ knows what might come of it."

"He's in general practice, not a doctor for females."

"A foreigner."

"Vermont's been in the union quite a while now."

"I ain't takin' no pills. All the good that medicine does is in a feller's head."

"I'll just put 'em on your dresser."

"Well, you might as will put 'em somewheres else, fer I ain't takin' 'em."

Carl, at the door, turned and caught the old man's eye sternly.

"A. J., I don't give a dam' if you take 'em or not."

"Meanest man in Texas," muttered the old man resentfully as his son walked out of hearing. That night he began taking the medicine. When the pills got low in the bottle, the prescription was refilled and it wasn't mentioned again.

People came to see A. J. that summer, old people who had been friends and acquaintances since the West Fork country was settled. They sat on the porch in the hot afternoons talking about the weather and cattle; about how things had been or might have been. A. J., with renewed interest, became a little carried away on the subject of silver.

"Next thing you know," Troy said, "he'll be at us to start minin' an' freightin' ore."

"Well, it might not be such a bad idea," said Travis wearily, "considerin' what we ain't gonna make off of cattle this fall."

A. J.'s friends wanted to see his twin grandchildren, because twins were a novelty, but, once looked at, they were far less impressed with them than with young Dean, who was usually on a pallet quilt on the porch and could hold his share of attention in any gathering. All the men agreed that the little girl twin was "shore a Stinson," but their eyes kept going to Dean who they said was A. J.'s spit'n image, and they'd grin and say how the men in the valley'd have to lock up their women folks when that one come up.

Some old friend told A. J. about the rodeo at Belford on the Labor Day weekend, and A. J. told the family at supper.

"Big doin's. Belford's been a town fifty years. Some feller from up in Wyomin's bringin' in a bunch of stock for the rodeo. Got one bronc he claims can't be rode."

Carl looked up from his plate. "Does, does he?"

"What'll he pay?" asked Troy.

"Who?" inquired A. J. innocently.

"The man with the bronc."

"For what?" The corner of the old man's mouth quirked in spite of him.

"Goddam' it, what kind of money will he lay down on this bronc he says can't be rode?"

"Oh, him..Hundred dollars."

Carl and Troy exchanged glances and began to grin.

"How's your shoulder, Bo?"

"Mendin'. You ride him first."

"You think this man from Wyomin'll stand still for that?"

"Well, hell, if he's bettin', he's bettin'. If guys pay their entry fees to ride the bronc, I don't see it makes no difference what order they do it in."

"Not much," said Travis dryly.

"Van Forrester," A. J. said casually, " 'ud like to race his mare."

Carl groaned.

"He tole me to ask you," said the father, seemingly disinterested. "He figgers to make one hell of a lot of money, seein' she ain't raced before."

Carl couldn't help grinning, but he said, "I'm not a jockey."

"Good Christ, he don't want no little bitty jockey. Can't you see one a them squirts flyin' through the air, first jump she made? What Van's after is a feller can stay on her, make her run instead of pitch an' go over backwards. He'd pay you a percentage of what he made off the race. He ain't so much interested in the money—don't have to be—he just wants to see the ole thing run."

"We goin'?" asked Kirby breathlessly, and Jeff said hopefully, "That's when I have to go back to school, right after Labor Day. Maybe everybody could go down that weekend."

Helen said wistfully, "I ain't been to Belford but ten times in my whole life an' I'll be ten years old this winter."

"Well, I'm goin'," stated Doxy. "I can't stand stayin' around here without never doin' nothin' fun. I want to see all that celebratin'."

"Seems to me," said Troy, "it's time we all had a little time off."

One of the twins began to cry and Rinie left the table. Later, when Carl came to their room after a swim, he said eagerly, "There's a dance Saturday night, Rinie, at that big open pavilion they've built at the fair grounds this summer, an' a barbecue for the whole county Sunday, an' rodeos Sunday an' Monday both. Rinie?"

"Carl, you have to have money to enter the rodeo. It would take every cent we've got."

"Don't you think I could win it back? And more besides?"

"Yes, but. . . ."

"Well, what then?"

"You—you've got a family to think about. What if you—were hurt?"

"Rinie, I've got to make us some cash money. We need it, not just you an' me, the whole family, an' we'll need it a hell of a lot more before the winter's over. I don't know many ways I can make money. I've got to do what I can."

He tried to regain the exuberance he had felt outside with the others.

"Doxy and Troy's gonna stay at Becky's. Ellie says she's sure we could stay with Bess and Larry. I wish it could be the Hayes Valley again, but we just can't afford it this time."

"Oh, Carl, we couldn't expect Bess to take us in with her baby and both of ours and Jeff just moving back there. It would be too much."

He was silent a moment and then said tentatively, "Ellie said she'd keep all the babies here at Red Bear."

"Oh, no. I couldn't. . . ."

"Rinie, for two nights? Rinie, I. . . ." His jaw set a little. She saw the muscles tense and looked away. He said wearily, "I want that money if I can get it. It'll pay Dr. Baird. Do you want the lamp out?"

"Yes."

They lay silent for a long time and then she said tensely,

"Carl, do—do you wish we didn't have the twins?"

"My God, Rinie! What kind of question is that?"

"Shh! You'll wake them. I know you're worried about all the other things, but sometimes. . . ." She was trying hard not to cry.

He felt he was being unfairly, unreasonably criticized. He had tried hard to take into account her ill health for all that long time, but now she seemed to feel well enough, only things between them were not the same. Whatever he did, he got the feeling that, to her, there was always something a little wrong with it.

"I love the kids," he said a little defensively, "and I love you. I'd like like hell to have you to myself for those two nights—one night, one hour, really just us together."

"You do resent them," she gasped, hurt and incredulous.

"All right then, sometimes I do, a little, but that dam' well doesn' mean that I wish we didn' have them."

"But when people have children, they—they have to give up things for them, sometimes."

"I guess I'm just not much of a sacrificer," he said caustically.

There was another silence in the room. Coyotes yapped frantically up toward the ridge.

He said slowly, "Because of what happened to you, you don't have to be a—a slave to your own kids, give up any kind of life of your own—of mine—for 'em. It won't make 'em happier or better off in any way. About all it'll do is make 'em a couple of spoiled brats—"

"Is. that what you think they are?" she cried angrily.

"Rinie, can't we even talk any more?" he pleaded. "They're all you think about an' that's fine I guess, but I . . . you're like a bobcat or somethin', spittin' 'cause you've got kittens. I don't want to eat 'em. I love 'em, but we're still us. There's still a world. . . . Listen, your folks, whatever it was caused them to give you away, has got nothin' to do with Ginger and Jamie. You don't have to make up to them for that because it didn' happen to them, an' you can't use them to make it up to yourself, honey. You had nothin' to do with it, no blame, no credit. It happened an' you've got to have done with it."

"I don't want to talk about it, Carl. Anyway, you're imagining a lot of things that were never in my mind."

"Rinie, what did Dr. Baird say to you?"

"I told you."

"You told me what he said about the twins and that you were fine, but was that all?"

"Yes. What else would there be?"

"When he was here," Carl said slowly, "he said he thought you—we might not have any more children."

Her voice was stifled. "He doesn't think I can." And then, uncontrolllably, the hurt and shame and humiliation she had been feeling turned to fierce anger against Carl. "Oh, it doesn't matter if you make love to me, if that's what you're trying to ask. That's got nothing to do with it. It's all my fault and what you do doesn't make any difference. Now I've told you. What do you think?"

"Rinie, honey, for God's sake—" He reached out to her, but she pushed his hands away.

"I can't breed you any more Stinsons. I'm really not quite a whole woman so leave me alone."

He sat up and looked down at her in the dim moonlight. Her face was tormented.

"Rinie, when we were married, I didn' have you checked out to see if you could breed Stinsons. I love *you*. You were the one that was so worried when there wasn't a baby right away—"

"Then you don't care about them," she cried viciously. She knew it was all so unreasonable, that if only she would let him he would hold her, talk to her rationally, make her feel better, love her, but somehow she couldn't let him. She felt an actual need to hurt him and she couldn't stop herself.

One of the twins began to fret and she got up to change a diaper before they should both awake. When she came back to bed, he lay very still but she knew he wasn't sleeping. They had never really quarreled before and now it had to be over the babies. She had been unreasonable, yes, but he had to realize that parents owed their children so much, simply for having caused them to come into the world. They must never, never feel unloved, unwanted. Oh, Carl, please understand, these are all I can have, we can have, and babies, children, people, need so much love.

He counted the yaps of five different coyotes. He listened to her breathing, stifled and uneven. She was crying. His body ached to hold her against him, but he couldn't bear the thought of having her push him away again. He didn't want to quarrel any more.

He thought he might go and talk to Dr. Baird while he was in Belford, but what was there to say? "She doesn't want me to make love to her?" That was what it really boiled down to, wasn't it? And how could you say that to anyone else? He had thought that perhaps he shouldn't because having another child would be dangerous for her, but if she was telling him the truth, that she was unable or very unlikely to conceive, then . . . of course, she was telling the truth. She couldn't lie if she tried, but why did it make her hate him—herself—this way? They had Ginger and Jamie. It wasn't as if they were childless.

He had heard or read somewhere that women were often disinterested in sex for a time after childbirth. God knows, she had suffered enough to make her disinterested and enough to make him not want to have her pregnant again . . . but maybe her chief interests all along had been in getting a baby, and now that that was done and there couldn't be any more . . . no, he couldn't believe that, not when he thought back to the way things had been between them so often before the twins were born.

She was sleeping now and he looked at her again in the dimness. She was still too pale and thin and she looked tired all the time. If only she would come away from the babies, think of something else for just a little while. . . . Rinie. He drew his hand back before it quite touched her.

He counted six different coyotes now. Had she remembered at all that today was their second anniversary?

Ellie and Rinie and A. J. stayed at home with the babies. Rinie thought, without much conviction, that they ought to clean house, but Ellie said she just wanted to be quiet awhile. A. J. wondered how anybody could just be quiet with three babies in the house, but it was surprisingly peaceful. When they slept, nobody slammed doors or yelled for clean socks and woke them up.

Rinie went out to visit Sprite and the colt. She had hardly been as far as the corrals since the twins were born. Carl kept the mare and colt down, hoping she'd take an interest in them again. Travis was irritated with him for not putting them up in the pasture. It was a waste of feed, but Rinie didn't know about any of that.

"He's handsome," she told Sprite, rubbing the mare's nose. "And he knows it, too, doesn't he? They've got big plans for him, you know, if he turns out as well as he looks like he will. He seems to know that, too. He's a very proud young man. That's what we could call him: Pride. Do you think Carl would like that?"

And then she started to cry. Carl had gone away— what? Angry? Hurt? Certainly unhappy, quiet, scarcely looking at her. What if he got hurt? Being around horses made him so wild. . . . But he wasn't being fair, because what he had done, really, was to ask her to choose between him and the twins. They were so tiny still, not

306

much past two months. What if one of them got sick and she was away? Why Ellie could hardly even have gone for help because there was no other grownup there but A. J., and he was barely able to take care of himself. She'd make it up to Carl. It was strange that she was being so much more mature about it than he, and he was all that much older, but men were like that, she supposed, when it came to things like that. He'd come to understand, though, how things had to be a little different when there were children.

As she walked slowly back toward the house the dogs began barking and she saw Heddie riding around toward the front on her shaggy little bay. Rinie went in by the back door.

"Heddie's come," said Ellie. "I was fixin' 'em some coffee to take out there. We got any cookies left?"

Rinie put some on a plate.

"Isn't she coming in here?"

"W'y, I don't reckon. She come to see A. J. like so many of his friends has been doin' here lately. She sent word by Carl a while back that she'd be up. It's good of 'em to come an' it does A. J. good. Here, hon, you take this out. I got to git these jars washed before the jelly's ready."

Rinie didn't want to take the tray out to the porch. She knew she was being silly, but it irritated her that Carl was still going to Heddie's and that he never mentioned it to her. Also, she felt shy of seeing Heddie because she had no idea what Heddie felt about their not having her when the twins were born. It didn't really matter, Rinie told herself, but she still felt uneasy.

She saw them through the window, A. J. and Heddie, sitting there on the porch, not talking, not looking at each other, like a couple who had been together so long, knew each other so well, they didn't need words or even looks any more. But it was the same porch, perhaps A. J. sat in the same chair, where Carl remembered him telling Jenny she was the proudest thing he'd ever seen. Rinie let the screen door bang unnecessarily because she felt embarrassed and like an intruder, and they should know she was coming.

"Well," said A. J. impatiently when the two women had barely spoken to each other, "take 'er in an' show 'er the young'uns. The coffee can wait a minute."

"They're all asleep," Rinie said, but that seemed to sound rude and she said, "but do come in."

Looking at Dean, Heddie said, "Like Troy. Not a bit of a Keane."

It seemed to Rinie she stood a long time looking at the twins and, unreasonably, Rinie didn't like her looking at them. It made her feel a little afraid.

"The boy's like Carl—just like, an' the girl like you."

Rinie was surprised. "But her hair . . . and she has blue eyes."

"She's like you," Heddie said. "She be a real pretty little girl."

Somehow, the words seemed ambiguous, but Rinie couldn't see why and supposed she was just picking at things.

Heddie stood in the kitchen a moment, talking with Ellie.

"This place gittin' pretty lively again, A. J. says."

Ellie smiled. "Yes, it is, an' it's kinda nice."

"Well, I go back out an' set with him a while. He lookin' better. I got to go to Hunter's tomorrow. It's the tenth this time."

"I heard," said Ellie. "My land, Ethel Hunter must think the earth needs replinished."

Rinie stirred the mixture of wild plum juice and sugar to keep it from boiling over. Helen and one of Doxy's little sisters had gone way up the creek to a wild plum thicket that the men told them had a lot of fruit and hadn't been killed off by the drought and hot winds. This was just about the only jelly they'd made this year and there wasn't a great deal of it.

Ellie said, "Seems kinda funny in this kitchen any more without Helen. She's come to be a right smart help."

"Somebody had to help, with all the work you've had on your hands."

"Well, she had worked an' I was right glad Travis said she could go to Belford with 'em. She ought to git to do somethin' a little special here with Jeff leavin' an' school startin' an' all."

"You should have gone, too, Ellie, to see Bess and your folks."

"Shoot, I was glad not to go. Oh, I'd like to see the folks an' all, but Lord, it's so peaceful. I don't know what it is about this summer, but I been real jumpy. Well, the men's part of it, worried like they been, but we've had

308

years like this before—worse ones. I ain't in the fam'ly way, an' I'm too young for the change—at least, I hope I am."

"It could have something to do with three little babies in the house."

Ellie shook her head vigorously. "Them babies don't bother me. As far as I'm concerned, there could be twict as many. The twins is too little to do anything bothersome, an' Jeff an' Helen both been real good about seein' after Dean when Doxy don't. . . . Rinie, I worry about Doxy. I honestly believe that's what's got me to feelin' so nervous. Travis says I'm makin' mountains out a molehills, but he always says that when he ain't the one's doin' it."

Ellie began to strain the jelly into the glasses and Rinie got the melted paraffin ready to seal the tops.

"Doxy's different, some ways, since Dean was born. She's a good little mother when it suits her to be an' she can take hold with the housework, though a good bit a what she does has to be done over, or ought to be, but sometimes, it seems like she's honestly tryin' to learn. The thing is—since Troy let her learn to drive an' since he's been able to work again, well, you know yourself, she ain't here much more'n he is."

"But she's at her folks," Rinie said slowly.

"No," Ellie said heavily, "she ain't. I'd been wonderin', if she went to 'er folks, why she never taken Dean, them thinkin' he's the grandest thing ever lived even if he does look like a Stinson, an' the other day at church, Sutter says to me 'If you people is havin' such a bad year, how is it you keep sendin' Doxy to Belford two, three times a week after stuff? W'y, she don't hardly have time to stop by our place an' say howdy'."

"Belford," Rinie said thoughtfully. "Do you think she goes to Becky's?"

"Irine Stinson! For the Lord's sake! Her an' Becky fusses like sore-tail cats when they ain't been together ten minutes. You been married two years, got two young'uns, ought to know a little somethin' about folks. Now you look a-here at me an' tell me if you think she goes to Becky's two, three times a week. . . . Set the coffeepot on. I need some."

"You—you think she's seeing some man?"

"I shorely do, an' if Troy finds out, he'll kill him an' her an' I don't know what all."

"Oh, Ellie—"

"Rinie, you ain't hardly seen these boys mad. You think you have, but you ain't. If they's one certain thing that'll git their goat, it's for their woman to fool around. Troy was goin' with that Hunter girl—she's married a Fraser now—but this was about four years ago. A lot of folks thought they was promised. Troy thought it hisself, I guess. But one time at a dance at the schoolhouse, he caught her out with Theorn an' he like to a killed him— Theorn that's always been his an' Carl's best friend, an' when they got him off a Theorn, w'y he taken out after her. Her daddy come close to callin' the sheriff but A. J. an' Travis finally talked 'im out of it. Course she never had no more to do with 'im. She was scared to death of 'im.

"I wouldn' even venture to guess how Troy an' Doxy feels about each other. When they first married, I thought things might settle down an' be all right, an' maybe they do care about one another. Some folks always fusses, it's just their way, but she's his wife an' that's all he'd think of if she's foolin' around. Troy's settled down a good bit the last year an' he's just a plain fool over that baby. That don't mean he might not flirt around some, bein' A. J.'s boy, an' it don't mean that he'd care much if she flirted, a little, with him there, but if he found out she's seein' somebody—well, I wouldn' want to answer."

Rinie poured the coffee and they sat at the table. The smell of the jelly still filled the kitchen, bittersweet and heavy in the hot air.

"We could go out on the porch," Ellie suggested, "but I guess if they'd a wanted to be with us, they'd a come in here."

"Ellie, what happened when you and Travis married? I mean—about Heddie?"

"W'y, nothin' happened. Why?"

"Well, I thought—Carl said that Travis didn't like her being here. . . ."

"Oh, well, no, he never, at first. He was sixteen when his mama died an' had a head full a notions like all kids a that age, that he knowed what was best for the whole world. When he was wantin' to marry me, he was still kind a prissy about it an', truth to tell, I was, too. Him an' A. J. talked some, had some pretty good fusses, I expect, fer Travis is as stubborn as any a the rest when he sets his

310

head, an' course, Heddie couldn' help hearin' 'em. She said when Travis an' me was ready to marry, she'd leave, that if there was somebody here to see after the boys. A. J. could come to her place when he needed to."

Rinie was deeply shocked. She could feel herself flushing.

"W'y, Rinie, that's the way people are made," said Ellie, incredulous at the girl's dismay. "It seems hard, yes, the way it happened, her bein' here when Jenny died, an' then just stayin', but, Lord knows, the boys had to have somebody."

"But he—he kept on seeing her and you—didn't mind?"

"Well, my land! When she didn' live here no more, it wasn' no affair a mine. Course he kep' on seein' 'er. Is it that—the two of 'em—that's bothered you so about Heddie all this time? Honey, men an' women got needs. You know that. If somethin' was to happen to you, you can think it, but can you honestly believe—foolish as he is over you—that Carl wouldn' ever touch another woman?"

Rinie burst into tears.

"Now I didn' go to upset you," Ellie said impatiently. "I'm just tryin' to git you to see that people's people."

"Raised in a family like this," Rinie said angrily through her tears, "I don't guess he'd wait a day." She stood up and then stopped and said contritely, "Oh, Ellie —I—I'm sorry. . . ."

"Don't tell me you're sorry," said Ellie without rancor. "You're as much a part a this fam'ly as the rest of us, an' I expect you're as much of a normal human being. I know you been touchy about Heddie all this time, an' what you believe's right an' wrong ain't be business, but what other folks believes ain't neither. I know you an' Carl ain't gittin' along just right now, but my land! Child, you can't fall to pieces ever' time that happens. If a man an' a woman don't never talk an' fuss an' git mad, how'll they ever git to know one another? It does seem to me like what'd be good is if you was to jump in an' make yourself a new dress to wear when he comes home. Carl's one to notice things like that, where some men wouldn' see a thing. He'd be right pleased, I expect."

The babies were asleep and A. J. had gone to bed before they heard the pickup laboring up the road on Monday night.

"My land, what do you reckon they're drivin' around to the back for?" wondered Ellie. "Do you reckon they're that drunk? An' on a Monday night?"

"Mama! Rinie!" cried Helen, bursting in at the back door. "We got somethin' but I ain't to tell you what it is, an' you ain't to come out till it's unloaded. It's just me an' Kirby an' Carl an' daddy. Troy an' Doxy ain't comin' till tomorrow."

She rushed out again.

"If it's a horse," said Ellie with slow deliberation, "or a bull, I'll kill Travis Stinson, I swear I will."

But it wasn't anything alive. They listened and wondered through a lot of scraping and bumping, and then there was the sound of a hammer knocking boards apart.

Helen jerked open the door.

"Come on! Hurry!"

It was a gasoline-powered washing machine, gleaming on the back porch in the lights from the truck.

"Well, my land!" breathed Ellie blissfully.

"Carl an' Troy won money at the rodeo," Travis said proudly. "An' Carl rode Fraser's mare an' won the race. Now you gals can wash your di'pers an' stuff just like downtown."

"Look at the wringer, ma," urged Kirby.

"I told you an' told you not call me ma," said Ellie absently, entranced with the wringer.

"Oh, Carl, it'll be so nice to have," Rinie said softly.

"I paid the doctor, too." he said, shyly taking her hand. "You made a new dress, didn' you? It looks fine."

"Le's wash somethin'," urged Helen. "There must be lots of dirty stuff. I want to see it work. Can I put stuff in an' run it through the wringer, mama?"

"Well, not hardly tonight," said Travis. "It's nearly ten o'clock."

"First thing in the mornin'," said Ellie, almost as eager as her daughter, "we'll put in an' wash ever'thing in the house."

When Carl was undressing for bed, Rinie saw the scrapes and bruises and some of them were not minor. There were tears in her eyes. He had to do that to himself for a washing machine.

"That Wyoming bronc was pretty mean," he said casually, catching her eyes on him.

"Carl—Carl, I'm so sorry . . . those things I said. . . ."

"Rinie," his breath came hard. "It don't matter. That

312

was before. Now it's now, an' you're standin' there with your hair down an' the moon shinin' through that silly, thin gown, an' you're drivin' me wild."

When he was asleep and she had begun to doze, the babies both woke hungry. She fed them and changed them and crept close to Carl again. She was wonderfully relaxed and contented, but it wasn't the way it used to be. There was a kind of poignant sadness mixed with the happiness, a disillusionment that came from the loss of some of the dreams and the innocence.

Maybe, she thought wistfully, this is what they mean when they talk about the honeymoon being over. They lived happily ever after isn't true, of course, except in fairy tales, where anything may be, but maybe, when the first kind of happiness begins to wear a little, there's another kind, an even better kind if we only know it when it comes and appreciate it.

She moved a little against Carl, just to feel the warm strength of him and, in his sleep, he put his arms around her. Her very own family was all right here in this room where she could hear their breathing and the little movements they made in sleep, but she yearned over the things that had been, the way she had felt on their wedding night, the comfort and release she had known when Carl understood what it was that bothered her so terribly about Troy and Doxy's baby—for the deep, utter peace that had surrounded them that last night they had spent together in Belford.

We just have to grow up, she told herself firmly. Most people probably never have times together quite that wonderful. I can't expect them to go on and on. It's been two years. We're parents now. People can find happiness in all kinds of ways. And then, she remembered their anniversary and she turned her face away from him and cried bitterly because she had forgotten the day and she felt so sure he had not. It was a long time before she slept.

16 _____

When the stock was shipped in the fall, there wasn't
enough money to pay the bills the ranch had accumu-
lated. Troy and Carl both found extra work. The man
Becky's husband worked for offered Troy a job as a
truck driver, mostly between Belford and Salt Lake City,
and he took it. At first, he rather enjoyed it; it was different, going somewhere, seeing new things, new people.
They shared a little house with Bill and Becky and after
the first few days, it was worth driving the truck to him
just to get away from Doxy and Becky, quarreling and
arguing. He would have moved his family to an apart-
ment of their own, but he frankly admitted to himself
that he didn't trust his wife, times when he was away
overnight. It was a humiliating admission. What he would
have liked would be to send her and Dean back to Red
Bear, but he didn't think she'd stay and then things
would be even worse. At least, this way, the family
didn't have to know of his suspicions. Together, he and
Doxy spent all the money he made, but at least they
weren't costing the Lazy S anything.

Carl broke horses. He was getting a reputation all over
the western part of the state and sometimes he was away
from the ranch for several weeks at a time. He was
offered a permanent job by a quarter-horse breeder over
along the East Fork. The man wanted him for a trainer.
Carl would have liked the work, but not for someone
else. He didn't even mention the offer to anyone at Red
Bear. There was tension between him and Rinie, though
they both tried to pretend it wasn't there. To him it
seemed she was so touchy about the children; everything
he said or did that had to do with them was wrong somehow, though she seldom said so. She knew the necessity
of his working away from the ranch, but she couldn't
help a suspicion that he was a little glad to go away, a little hesitant to come home. He felt that perhaps she was

relieved to have him gone. Unhappiness lay between them and both were hurt and worried, but they couldn't talk about it. That night before he went to the rodeo, Carl had told Rinie what seemed to him to be the problem, basically. Until she told him different, or wanted to talk to him, there was no need bringing it up again. For Rinie's part, she kept trying to convince herself that no real problem existed, simply that they were older now, the parents of children, with a different kind of life to share and that when they had made the necessary adjustments, things would be right again.

The winter began dry and open. "Looks like we ain't even gonna have no snow," Travis fretted, worrying already about the spring's grass.

At Thanksgiving, Nell Tippitt and Bud Corbett were married and less than two weeks later June and Alva had a fine, healthy baby boy. Vanda had been in Denver through the autumn and, at Christmas, she brought a young man home to meet her family.

"I'm a little sorry about that," Ellie said thoughtfully. "She woulda been right good for Doyle, I believe, though I never did think he'd marry her. He mighta got around to it someday, when he was certain where he's goin'. She woulda been a help to him if he coulda kep' her off a horse long enough, but a girl can't wait forever. Vanda's —le's see twenty-two now I guess."

Somehow, that last statement made Rinie feel old and sad. She, herself, was not twenty-one yet, the mother of two children, left here in this isolated place while Carl . . . She was ashamed of herself for the feelings. She wanted to be here in the heart of this family; she wanted her children. Carl was working—hard, dangerous work —to support them all. And yet, she wondered guiltily what it was like to be someone like Vanda, secure in her family and yet free, grownup, spending time in Denver, going places, meeting people. . . .

She had a difficult time sleeping that night because she couldn't stop crying. She was so lonely and despondent and, despite all she had, almost everything she had ever longed for, she felt dismally that she had missed something in life; in many ways, she had missed childhood and youth. Well, at least she could see that it didn't happen to her children. They would have a secure family-life basis upon which to build and they would enjoy all the good things that life had.

The family was all together at Christmas time. Carl and Troy and Kirby and Doyle went after a bear and got one. Pup came off well in the hunt and the men were proud of him, but a little regretful that it looked as if he was going to be a better dog after bear than lion. There wasn't a really good lion dog in the valley now, unless you counted Sheba who, Travis maintained, would come into her own, given time.

They had a big Christmas tree and Jeff and Helen, with some slightly sheepish help from Kirby, had done more decorating than the house had known before. Jeff had got a lot of new ideas at school about things that could be made at home and both he and Helen were showing something of an artistic flair. Ellie just couldn't get over what could be done with paper and crayons and bits of wire and pieces of cloth and all the things you'd never think of using to make something pretty.

The women worked in the kitchen and Doxy, in the beginning at least, was happy, a little superior to the others because she had been living in town. Dean was to have a tricycle from Santa. Rinie couldn't help feeling a little resentful and the resentment was directed toward Carl. The twins were receiving small gifts by comparison. She knew they were too young to care, but she couldn't help resenting the money Carl had spent on a good used mowing machine that he had found at a fair price. In the long run, of course, the mowing machine would, as he had said, benefit them all, but. . . .

On Christmas Eve, the men brewed their hooch and got into a horrendous, hilarious argument over putting Dean's tricycle together. By the time it was finally assembled, they had succeeded in waking Dean and he was brought out to enjoy his gift at one in the morning, which pleased him as much as it did his male relations.

It was a happy time, but there was an undercurrent of sadness because things were changed. A. J., watching his grandchildren, felt the change, perhaps more strongly than anyone. After all, he thought a little grimly, there wasn't much for him to do nowadays, but think about how things had been and weren't any more.

Kirby was fifteen now, a little more sober and quiet than his looks implied to most who knew Stinsons, but he was a fine, strong boy and he had shot his first elk that fall. They were going to have elk steak for Christmas dinner. Kirby, shaping up the way he was, would be a good man to take charge of the Lazy S someday and that was the way it ought to be, the oldest grandson, as he was.

Jeff, growing tall now, was twelve, a serious boy whose brown eyes missed nothing. It didn't seem to bother him much now that he limped and couldn't do a good many things other boys did. He was finding confidence and a great deal else that he wanted just now in books. A. J. had never inclined to think much of education, but for Jeff, he was proud. They had put the boy a year ahead of his age group in school at Belford.

Helen was ten a few days after Christmas. A little to everyone's surprise, she was becoming quite adept and serious about housework and she could care for the babies almost as well as their mothers.

Dean was walking now and at every opportunity he made a dash for the big Christmas tree, straight to the trunk, seemingly oblivious to the prickling of the lower branches, and laying hold with both hands, shook it with all the strength of his husky little body. The tree was large and well-anchored and Dean was shaken more than it was, though his attacks always brought down at least a few ornaments. A. J. waited with more eagerness than Dean for the unguarded moment when another assault might be feasible and was known to have suggested more than one to the little boy. Dean gave A. J. great hope for the generation.

The twins, at six months, were becoming true individuals. Ginger could scoot around after what she wanted, and Jamie would raise himself on knees and elbows and look very complacent, though he didn't go much of anywhere as yet. Because she was that rare thing, a Stinson girl and a twin besides, and because she demanded it, Ginger drew by far the greater part of everyone's active attention, but it was Jamie, quiet, content to watch something as simple and wonderful as the movements of his own hands for longer than anyone would have expected of a baby so young, that they all smiled on, perhaps only in passing, but always smiled.

A. J. was deriving a lot of pride and pleasure from watching his grandchildren, now that he had all this time, but it was in his boys that he saw the change that bothered and saddened him. It was funny, he thought, how a man liked to have the grandchildren come along and grow before his eyes, and at the same time regretted almost painfully seeing his own children getting older and settling down.

There wasn't much change in Travis, hadn't been since the day he was born except that he'd grown some. He was thirty-six now and his brown hair was graying rapidly. He had his own family, getting close to being grownup, to be proud of and to worry about and that made A. J. feel he was more his equal than he used to when Travis was a kid, but that was about all that was different.

And Doyle, well, Doyle was about what you'd expect of a boy Minna'd had so much to do with. He was a good enough boy, in his way, who always seemed to like coming home to Red Bear, despite all his complaining about privies and limited hot water and the rest of it, and despite the bad times he was so often given by his brothers. He arrived nattily dressed in sports coat and slacks, his blond hair freshly cut, but as quickly as possible, he hunted up his boots and levis and changed to them, and his baby niece, who went to him willingly after a quick scrutiny with her intense blue eyes, made short work of disarranging his smooth, shining hair. Doyle, A. J. thought, got to look more like Jenny's people all the time, but he had the inner strength and determination of a Stinson. He was getting what he wanted out of life—A. J. would never understand why he wanted it—but he had gone after it all these years and he was getting it. He would always do the sensible thing, which was not typically Stinson, but Doyle was all right.

A. J. wondered about Troy and felt uneasy. Troy had a temper, always had had, nothing wrong with that, but Doxy had one, too, and they seemed always at cross-purposes. Dean was about all they seemed to have in common and they fought over him, too. A. J. still felt sorry that Troy had had to marry the girl. He could have done so much better. Van Forrester's girl, for instance, she would have been a match for old Bojack. But it wasn't as if the thing had happened when Troy was a real young kid, he ought to have known better, and A. J. was glad of Dean, and maybe, if you got down to brass tacks with Troy and Doxy, they'd say the little boy made all the rest of it worthwhile.

And Carl . . . it was strange about him and missy.

A. J. couldn't exactly say that they weren't getting along, but things were different someway. They didn't look at each other the way they used to. The boy didn't run in and grab her and kiss her, the first thing when he got in the house, and she didn't watch him and follow him around with her eyes the way she had. They were old married folks now, A. J. guessed, feeling the responsibility of parenthood and all, but why did it have to be such a burden, if that's what was bothering them? Kids made out all right if you just mostly let 'em be—backhand 'em once in a while for something really wrong or bothersome, praise 'em a little sometimes if it didn't give 'em the big head—and they came along just as well or better than they did with all this new-fangled worrying and fretting over them. He guessed missy had picked that up from Minna or out of some book—she was always reading something—it surely didn't seem like a thing Buck would change overnight, worrying about. A. J. had liked the way the two of them used to act about each other. Sometimes it had come close to making him angry with envy—the yearning to be young again—but this difference between them made him sad.

On Christmas night as the women did up the kitchen, Ellie remarked that all a holiday meant to this family was an excuse "to never quit eatin'." Though they had just finished a heavy snack of leftovers from dinner, Kirby and Jeff were still eating cookies as they played dominoes at the old scarred center table. In a corner of the kitchen, Helen, eating an apple, was rocking Ginger who hadn't the least intention of going to sleep.

In the front room, the men sat or lay about comfortably, talking lazily. Carl held Jamie in one arm and rolled a cigarette with his free hand. Fleetingly, he observed that he was smoking a lot more lately and wondered why.

"You know," Doyle said indolently, "just from looks, I'd almost swear that kid is yours."

"They do favor," agreed A. J., "'bout as much as them other two."

Troy lay on the floor in front of the fire with Dean clambering over him. He said, "When did you figger to go to Harris's, Buck?"

"Not till next week."

"I thought you might want a ride with us when we go back to Belford tomorrow." He pried Dean's fingers loose from his nose and frowned. "I hate like hell to go back. I'm gonna tell Kingsley I won't be drivin' much longer. Work ought to start pickin' up around here before long."

"It ain't never slacked off that I've noticed," said Travis, "an' now that dam' stallion's broke the fence an' took off all the mares an' foals. I wish to God we'da known sooner'n two or three days after it happened."

"We'll go after him tomorrow," Carl said easily.

"It's fixin' to snow," predicted A. J.

"I don't think he's gone far," Carl said.

"Think you've tamed him, do you?" asked Travis caustically.

"He don't have reason to go far. He's out of fence an' he's got his mares. Why travel?"

"You know," Troy said thoughtfully, "Buck could easy make a lot of money so the rest of us wouldn' have to hunt town jobs an' all. He ought to rodeo."

"I don't want to," Carl said, but just for a moment, he thought how it might be if he made the really big-time. He had thought of it before, when he was a kid, but it always came to a choice between rodeoing and Red Bear and there was really nothing to choose. Now, though, maybe Rinie would be happier if they had more money, if they didn't live here. She wouldn't like his making money that way, but it was the only way he could. . . .

"Why don't you want to? Hell, you're doin' it now, only you're just gittin' bronc-snappin' pay instead of prize money."

"I'm too old."

They all protested and Troy said derisively, "Twenty-six next month! That ain't too old."

"But you ought to start a thing like that when you're a kid."

"You never rode a bronc till you was old enough to vote, did you?" inquired his father. "I remember knockin' you halfway acrost this room one time when you wasn't much older'n Jeff for ridin' one I'd told you to stay off of. You recollect that?"

"Yes, It was a black gelding that that government hunter brought up here to be broke an' I rode him."

"An' I told you not to," insisted A. J. "No, you never started when you was a kid, did you?"

"But I'm talkin' about professional rodeoin'. You've got to break in young now, with all the associations an'

320

stuff they got. Anyway, Bojack, if it's got so dam' much appeal, why don't you do it?"

"I got stuff I don't want busted," said Troy, disentangling Dean's hands from his hair. Doxy looked in from the kitchen and he said, "Whyn't you come put this boy to bed?"

"If you want him put to bed, put him," she said curtly. "I'm a good bit busier'n you are."

Doyle said smugly, "What you both mean about rodeoing is that your wives wouldn't let you. That's what comes of getting married; two world's champion rodeoers nipped in the bud."

"Well, you've not been nipped," Carl said, "so you can be the one to make the big money to send home for years like last year."

"I might at that," Doyle said seriously. "Mr. Bell's going to run for governor next election and he wants me to be his aide. I'll be through with school just in time for the campaign."

"God, I didn' figger you'd git through school, ever," Troy said.

"What you gonna aid him with?" asked Travis.

"Oh, all sorts of things. Really, it's like being a sort of glorified office boy, but it gives you a lot of inside stuff on politics. I've been thinking, I may decide to go into politics myself, after I've passed the bar and all."

"Which bar is that?" asked Travis, grinning a little.

"All this law education," mused A. J.; "an' now you're thinkin' about goin' into politics. What's Minnie say about that?"

"I haven't asked her," Doyle said, "don't intend to, but don't you think a politician ought to be educated? Know what's going on in the world?"

"Might ought to, but they mostly don't, that I know of."

"You'd do better not to pass any bars if you're goin' political," Troy told him. "Politicians pick up the most part a their votes in saloons."

"When you git there," A. J. said, "to the legislature or wherever it is that you're a-goin' when you git by the bar, have 'em put the railroad on up the West Fork."

"What in hell for?" asked Doyle.

"W'y, the goddam' silver."

"A. J.," Doyle began patiently, but Carl said, "What's

the good of havin' relatives in politics if it's not gonna git us anything?"

"Yeah," agreed Troy, "an' see if you can git 'em to put us in a couple a bridges. We got stuck in that dam' upper ford comin' home, an' it ain't but a little bitty stream a water half-froze."

"We ought to move that ford," Carl mused, shifting his son who was falling asleep. . .

"An' remind 'em," said Travis, "that there's a depression."

"Oh, hell, that's all but over," said Doyle with a gesture of dismissal. "The way things are looking in Europe, this country stands to make a lot of money in the next few years and really get back on its feet."

"It ain't over at Red Bear," said Travis, "not so's you'd notice, not with cattle prices what they was last fall, an' Europe won't help us none."

"Oh, you might be surprised. They're going to be wanting to buy a lot of beef over there."

"Well, then, tell 'em we're upgradin'," said A. J., his mouth quirking.

"But we don't have any sheep," said Troy. "Be sure and make that clear."

Doyle frowned. Usually, it didn't bother him, but just now and then he'd like to carry on a serious discussion. It could be done all right, talking to them one at a time, but when they were all together like this, they always seemed to feel the need to be so damned clever.

Rinie came and took Jamie to put him to bed.

"You're pretty good at that," she said softly to Carl. "Do you want to have a try with your daughter? I can't just put her to bed now because she'll wake Jamie." She was pleased because he had picked his son up and held him all this time without having it suggested.

Carl went to the kitchen and took Ginger from Helen, who was tired of sitting still, and Troy immediately told her to put Dean to bed.

She had done so and was playing a game of darts with the boys, their board hung on the front room wall, when A. J. suggested a drink before going to bed.

"You're gittin' so generous," said Troy approvingly.

"He can afford to be," said Doyle, "all that bonded stuff I brought him for Christmas."

"We never used to have a dart board," recalled Troy,

holding his glass in one hand and throwing darts with the other. "We just marked off targets on the wall."

"Place is gittin' too full a women," observed A. J. without rancor. They were through in the kitchen now.

"They stick better in a board," said Travis. "You'd never git these things to stick in the logs."

"Hell, we never had these little straight-pin things," said Carl. It was difficult for him to take a turn holding Ginger. She jumped around so much.

"What did you have?" Jeff asked.

"Knives, mostly."

"Gosh," said Kirby, "We ought to try—"

"Not while I'm up an' able," said his mother shortly.

Doxy wound the phonograph and put on one of the new records they had bought. Troy was having another turn at darts so she asked Doyle to dance with her.

"There's just not a thing to do around here for fun," she fretted. "I didn't know how dull it was till we started livin' in town. I sure will be glad to go back tomorrow. I don't see how you can stand it after Denver. If I ever got that far, I wouldn' never come back."

Rinie took Ginger so Carl would have a decent turn at the dart board and when he had finished, Doxy wanted to dance with him.

"Twins ain't so special some ways," she observed, "seems like one or another is always needin' attention."

Carl had been drinking rapidly. He felt like getting drunk. He hadn't been drunk in a long time. Doxy danced warm and close. She said, "Rinie kind of spoils 'em, don't she? Dean, now, we just put him to bed. He don't have to be helt an' rocked an'all that."

Ellie and Travis were dancing and A. J. said, "Sal, you don't look no more'n sixteen."

"W'y, you ole thing," said Ellie, pleased. "Here, I'll even pour you another drink for that."

A. J. grinned. He had hoped she would do something like that. He couldn't quite reach the bottle without getting up and that was hard to do.

"You better give me that young'un, missy, so you can dance, too."

As soon as Rinie put Ginger into her grandfather's arms, Doyle was there to dance and it was fun, dancing with him. He danced differently, more smoothly, than the others.

Doxy didn't want to dance with Travis. She didn't want

to dance with Troy either—she was a little afraid of Troy lately—but he was preferable to Travis. With Travis, you never got the feeling you were doing anything to him. He just wasn't the least bit sexy, but she supposed, with his age and all, he couldn't help it. Doyle was all right. He was almost like someone new, he had been around so little during the time she and Troy had been married. The things he said were strange sometimes, but he was different and fun. And tonight, Carl seemed different somehow. He had never paid much attention to her before, treating her more like one of the kids than a grown woman, but he finally seemed to be noticing. He didn't say much; in fact, he wouldn't quite look at her, but she could feel it.

She sipped from Troy's drink, sitting on his lap for a minute while Doyle changed the record.

"For New Year's Eve," she said, loud enough for the others to hear, "let's go to the Dark Lantern. They're gonna have a band there from Denver for that night."

He frowned. "I'm supposed to be drivin' New Year's Eve. You know that. That's how I got off extra time for Christmas. Listen, Dox, I'm gonna tell Kingsley I'm quittin' soon as we can move back home."

"Oh, shoot, Troy," she said fiercely. "I ain't movin' back here. I like it in Belford. You don't make much, but at least it's ours."

"Where's the party this year?" Troy asked, not seeming to have heard his wife.

"Corbett's," supplied Carl.

"You gonna go, Si, an' see what your rival looks like?" asked Troy. "Don't they say he's at Forrester's with Vanda till after then?"

Doxy got up angrily and danced with Travis anyway. Doyle was dancing with Rinie and Carl was pouring himself another drink.

"I'd like to see what he looks like myself," Troy went on. "What is he? A banker's son, or somethin'? Vanda was smart to wait. Maybe I'll go ahead an' quit now, go back to Belford tomorrow an' git our stuff an' go tell Kingsley to stick his truck up his ass."

Doxy was stiff with anger in Travis's arms.

"I'm gettin' drunk," Carl said soberly to Rinie, "or at least I'm workin' on it. Why don't you, with me?"

"Maybe a little," she said, smiling dreamily. In spite of all there was to keep her busy now and in spite of the unhappiness between them, she did miss him sadly when he was away and she was so glad he was home. "It feels good in your arms."

His eyes darkened, looking down at her while she snuggled her face against his shoulder.

Jeff and Kirby and Helen went to bed. You couldn't throw darts with people dancing in the way all the time. Ginger, unintentionally, fell asleep on her grandfather's chest and Rinie took her to put her to bed. While she was gone, Carl danced with Doxy again. She pressed close and he held her.

"You don't think Tory means it," she asked, "about movin' back here, do you?"

"I guess he does. He sounded like it."

"Oh, I just can't stand it," she whispered miserably. "You ought to know how it is. You been goin' around quite a bit lately. When you've been other places a little, Webber just ain't nothin', an' to live up here at the ranch all winter, housed up. . . ." She was about to cry.

"Well, it seems all right to me," Carl said and she thought he meant now, this moment, dancing with her, and pressed closer.

"That's my girl, Buck," said Troy, cutting in rather roughly.

Ellie didn't like the looks on Carl's and Troy's faces. They hadn't fought for a long time.

When Rinie came back, Doxy was dancing with Doyle and Carl with Ellie. Troy took her in his arms. He said a little viciously, "I think Buck's about ready for that trade we talked about. How about you?"

"What—" she began, and then remembered, her face turning crimson.

He laughed. "The way's all clear now, no kids on the way or nothin'. I'm dam' sure Doxy'd be agreeable. Look at her, dancin' with him again, plastered up against him. The dam' little bitch. I ought to beat hell out of her—both of 'em." He pulled Rinie close.

"Don't," she said. "You're being silly."

"About beatin' or tradin'?"

"Troy—"

"Tradin' don't seem silly at all to me. Like I said before, it's all in the family."

Doxy was saying softly to Carl, "I always did wonder how you kiss."

325

Carl said, grinning a little, "Well, if it really bothers you, I guess I could put your mind at ease."

"Not here," she said impatiently. "Somewheres by ourselves."

He laughed a little sardonically. Being drunk was making him more morose than gay. Doxy was such a baby. He said with a touch of bitterness, "I can't even be alone with my own wife."

"I know," she said tenderly. "I feel sorry for a man when his wife always puts the kids before him."

Carl said angrily, "I feel sorrier for a man when his wife puts other men first. Don't you think things get around, Doxy? You better straighten out before Bo finds out or—"

"What are you talkin' about?" she demanded, going rigid with anger and fear. What if Troy found out? What if . . .

"Oh, go to hell," said Carl. "I want to dance with Rinie."

"Carl wants to sleep with me," Doxy whispered to Troy. She was frightened and furious and something had to be done. "We can't come back here to live if he's gonna act like that, can we?"

"You can stay down at your folks', then, if you're afraid of him," said Troy. His face darkened. Doxy hoped they'd fight. It would serve them right, both of them, and Rinie, too.

Rinie said, "Carl, don't drink any more."

"All right," he said, holding her close. "Let's go to bed."

Tears stung her eyes. For a few moments the evening had seemed to hold such promise of things being the way they used to be. Then Troy had said those things and she had seen the way Carl was looking at Doxy—the same way he was looking at her now—and it was all ruined.

"Maybe you'd rather go with Doxy," she said, her voice low, shaking with hurt and disappointment and anger.

"Rinie for Chrissake, I didn'—"

"With you Stinsons, it doesn't really matter much who the woman is, does it? Let me go, Carl. I don't want to dance any more."

Troy was angry with Carl, but he was still reasonable enough to realize that it wasn't very fair of him to be. After all, what Doxy said Carl had suggested to her was

326

the same thing he had been suggesting to Rinie at the same time, but the point was that Rinie wouldn't and Doxy would and Carl damn well knew it. But Troy couldn't get quite mad enough to fight Carl. They never talked about it, but each knew the other was having problems. No, he didn't really want to fight Buck, but he wanted to do something and he saw his chance.

Doxy was dancing with Doyle now, close and sexy. She danced the same with anybody, and Doyle, smiling, bent down and kissed her.

"All right," Troy said angrily, "that's it." He jerked Doxy out of the way.

"What the hell!" cried Doyle, surprised. "It was just a brotherly—"

"Didn' look nothin' brotherly about it to me," snarled Troy. "You want to go outside or do you want me to knock hell out a you right here?"

"Turn loose a my arm, Troy," cried Doxy shrilly. "You're hurtin' me."

"You don't know what hurtin' you is," he said fiercely.

A. J. had been dozing, but now he was wide awake. Carl took the needle off the record and turned off the machine. Rinie had already gone to their room, crying. He wouldn't mind fighting someone himself.

Ellie said warily, 'Now they won't be no fightin'."

And Travis said, "We've all had a little bit much to drink. Le's git to bed an' forget about this."

"I don't think Doxy's decided who she's gonna sleep with," said Troy. "It's hard for her when there's several to pick from."

She screamed something wordless and ran into the bedroom, slamming the door.

Doyle said soberly, "Listen, Bo, I really didn't mean anything. I—I just—"

"Oh, just shut your goddam' mouth," Troy said dully. Abruptly, he was very tired.

Doyle went to bed. Travis and Ellie followed. A. J. got up with the help of his stick. Things were different, all right, he thought sadly as he stumped off to his room.

Carl sat on the floor and stared at the fire. Maybe Rinie wouldn't want him to come to bed. If she didn't, he didn't think he could bear lying there so close to her all through the night.

"Buck?" Troy had stood silent a long time, staring out of the side window.

Carl looked up at his back, not answering. Troy felt him looking.

"If you'll wait till the day after tomorrow to go after the horses, I'll go with you. Tomorrow, we're goin' after our stuff to move back home. I can't take Belford any more. I'll find some other way to earn some cash."

"Maybe we can snap broncs together," Carl said after a silence. "Harris, anyway, has got quite a bunch."

"That sounds good," Troy said. "Do you want another drink?"

"No." Carl got up. It was funny how fast the liquor had worn off, or maybe he had never been drunk at all. He just wanted to be. For a few moments there, he could have been drunk with happiness over how things seemed to be going. Only they weren't better, drunk or sober. Hell, they were worse.

He said, "The moon's bright as anything, Bo. Le's go hunt the horses now."

"The fence all fixed?"

Troy thought about it. "Hell, yeah, lets go. You're prob'ly right an' they ain't gone far."

They blew out the lamps, all but one that they took with them to the kitchen to get their jackets.

"We could have some coffee first," Carl said.

"Hell, le's don't take time for that. You know, Buck, I feel like havin' a go at that stud. I hope it don't take long to find the sonofabitch."

Rinie heard them go. She had heard their words in the kitchen and she didn't sleep.

What's wrong? She kept trying to think it out and all she did was cry. She wanted Carl there with her, wanted him so desperately that it was a physical pain, yet she realized that if he hadn't gone out, there would have likely been the tension between them. There were so few right moments now. They both tried to pretend that everything was all right. Maybe pretending was a part of the trouble; they needed to talk about it, but there was nothing to talk about, really, all the little things that didn't count kept going wrong and adding up to tormenting unhappiness.

I'm the one, she thought dismally, that almost always says the mean things, like tonight, but he makes me. And she cried again.

Mostly, the twins slept through the night now, but toward morning of this night, Jamie woke hungry. Rinie took him into her bed so he wouldn't wake Ginger and went to heat a bottle, glad of something to do. The tears came again as she gave him the bottle, looking down at him in the lamplight. He looked more like Carl every day.

Someone else was moving around in the house. She heard steps in the front room, the closing of the front door and, after a moment, the sound of Troy's car being started. It must be Doxy, but what was she doing? Mad at Troy, Rinie supposed, taking Dean and going to her folks' or maybe back to Belford.

Half through with the milk, Jamie let go the nipple, his hands relaxing on the bottle, and looked up at her drowsily, with those brown-gold eyes, and for just an instant, as she smiled tremulously at him, the right corner of his mouth seemed to quirk. Rinie thought her heart must break.

Rinie and Ellie had dinner about ready to put on the table when Carl and Troy got home.

"Find 'em?" A. J. asked.

"They're just up around the beaver meadows," Carl said. "There's plenty of shelter and the grass is better up there than in the pasture."

"You reckon they'll stay?"

"Unless it gits real bad, an' then they'll come back this way."

"You think that ole stud horse'll stand for that?"

"After bein' fed hay an grain all last winter, I think he will. . . . Bo rode him."

"Did, did you, Bojack? How was he?"

Troy grinned. He was holding Dean who had run to him as soon as he entered the kitchen.

"He wasn' so bad—what time I was on 'im."

As they were ready to sit down to dinner, Troy said reluctantly, "Where's Doxy at?"

The others waited uncomfortably for someone to speak. Helen did.

"She left this mornin' before we got up."

Troy frowned, embarrassed and angry. "Left?"

"In your car," supplied Helen.

After a moment, Troy said coldly, "I guess she went to her folks."

The meal was eaten in comparative silence. When it

329

was over and the children were occupied with other things Travis said quietly, "Troy, Doxy taken what clothes she had here, Ellie says. She didn't say nothin' to nobody, but do you reckon she went back to Belford?"

Troy flushed and walked out of the house. A little later, he came to Carl where he was filling the wood box. The woodpile was at the back of the house and there was a window just above the wood box. All that need be done was open the window and toss in the wood. Troy threw in a few sticks and then stood back, waiting uneasily, till Carl was through.

"Buck, I wish you'd come with me to bring the pickup back if you're not too sleepy. Doxy may be at her folks', but I got a good suspicion she's not. I'm supposed to be at work tonight. I—I think I'll just leave Dean here, for I plan on bein' back soon."

Carl went with him and neither had returned by nightfall. Obviously, Doxy hadn't been at the Keanes' place.

"I wisht we knowed somethin'," said Ellie worriedly, when they had agreed with A. J. that there was nothing to be gained from everyone's staying up all night. "I feel just plain sick, I'm so worried."

"Now, hon," Travis tried to comfort her. "They may of just had trouble with that ole pickup. You know what a shape the thing's in."

"How much money we got?" A. J. said heavily.

". Less'n fifty dollars cash right now," said Travis.

"Hell, that ain't enough for bail for anything, is it. Siefog?"

"Oh, for Godsake, A. J.," Doyle said tensely. He felt partially responsible for whatever might be happening because of that damn kiss last night. He wished, in a way, that he had felt welcome to go with Troy and Carl. At least he'd know now what was going on. But, as always, it was the two of them, while he either stayed out entirely or was tolerated as a tagalong kid brother. The poor little baby brother's feeling sorry for himself again, he thought angrily and went to bed.

Rinie was asleep when Carl came in. He had a lamp in his hand and she was about to caution him automatically not to wake the twins, when she saw his face.

"Oh, Carl! What is it? What's wrong?"

He put the lamp on the dresser and sat down on the bed, moving slowly, dazedly.

330

"Doxy's dead."

"Oh, *no!*" she gasped, and, after a moment, as the shock ran through her rendingly, "Carl, Troy . . . didn't—"

"Sometime," he said dully, "around noon today, Doxy and a man went off a curve in Troy's car . . . about fifteen miles east of Belford . . . into the river. They haven't found his body yet, but they know who he was."

Rinie lay utterly still, horrified, sick.

"He worked for Lovelaces," Carl went on woodenly, "that big ranch north of town. She's been runnin' around with him, among others, since last summer when she learned to drive."

"Oh," Rinie breathed.

"Did you know anything about it? You or Ellie?"

"No! Well, Ellie—mentioned when you went to the rodeo at Belford that time—that she was worrried about Doxy, but. . . ."

"She ought to have told Troy," he said angrily. "I ought to have told him."

"You knew!"

"Some men were talkin' at the last place I worked, but I . . . he could have put a stop to her runnin' around fast enough. He wouldn't have let her live in Belford at all if Ellie'd told him, an' this wouldn' have happened. Oh, hell, she wasn' ever worth a dam' anyway." He felt as if he were going to be sick.

Rinie said angrily, "Maybe she wasn't, but you don't have to say that now. You men always have to be so tough. Why didn't Troy ever try treating her like some thing more than a not-very-bright whore he kept?"

"That's about what she was," Carl said bitterly. "An' how do you know he never tried treatin' her better ways? Maybe she wouldn' let him."

He was talking about them now and they both knew it. After a silence, he went on talking. Something was driving him to tell her about it—all of it—though he knew how upset she would be. He was exhausted and upset and for the first time in his life he wanted to hurt her. He didn't try to think why. He didn't want to think—about anything.

"There's not much water in the East Fork either, enough to wash his body downstream somewhere, there were the car went off, but Doxy never got to the water. The car turned over twice and they were both thrown out. . . . It rolled over her."

"Oh, Carl!" She put her hand to her mouth, sick with horror, and began to cry.

"He had to go and identify her."

"You went with him?"

"Yes."

"Where is he now?"

"He's in his room asleep. Drunk . . . I wish I was."

After a little, she said timidly, still crying, "Carl, let me get you some coffee or a drink if you want it."

"I've had some drinks, Rinie. I don't want any coffee."

"Did—did you tell the others?"

"Travis got up. I told him." He was tugging exhaustedly at his boots.

"What—about her folks?"

"We didn't stop tonight. Bo was passed out already, or just about. It can't make any difference if they don't know till mornin'."

They didn't say any more. He undressed, blew out the lamp, and lay down. She put her hand in his and after a while he fell asleep. He hadn't slept at all the night before and not much on Christmas Eve. This day, in retrospect, always seemed to him horribly, unendurably long.

Very quietly, Rinie got out of bed. When she opened the door to the kitchen, Ellie was there already, putting wood in the stove with as little noise as possible, the coffeepot ready to set on. Travis was sitting by the table.

Ellie got some mending and Rinie took up the snow suit she was knitting for Ginger. Travis smoked, read bits from a week-old newspaper. They sat there through what was left of the night, the three of them, saying almost nothing.

17 _____

Carl and Troy were at the Harris ranch through January and a part of February. The weather was bitterly cold and there was wind almost without ceasing, but still very little snow.

Troy came home for a while because he was sick with a bad cold. Travis caught the cold and it developed into pneumonia. He was dangerously ill for several days and Heddie stayed at the ranch two days and nights. When Travis was recovering, Helen came down with the measles, caught at school, and shortly after, Dean, who to Helen's joy had become her bed fellow, began breaking out too.

Rinie was terrified that the twins would catch something. She supposed, wearily, that Carl would say she was just borrowing trouble and that, anyway, they had to have all those things sometime, but they were still so small it would be dangerous. And why wasn't he here to say that? To say anything at all? To help when she was so worried and tired? He was over in Utah breaking a bunch of wild ones somebody had caught.

"Any snow where Buck is?" Troy asked. He had been to Webber and someone else had been to Belford and brought up the mail. There was a note from Carl.

"He doesn't say, so I guess not," Rinie said.

They were momentarily alone in the kitchen. She was stirring pie filling on the stove.

"Want some coffee?" he asked standing by the cup rack.

She shook her head. "Not right now."

He spooned sugar into his cup. "Dean's rash or whatever you call it's about dried up," he said. "I guess I'm not much good at talkin' like a daddy, but it's a dam' relief to see him feelin' good again. I guess enough time's passed so you can be pretty sure the twins won't git measles."

"I think so. Ellie does, too. I hope so. They're so little."

"Yeah, it might be hard on 'em."

Somehow, she was grateful to him for saying that. Carl wouldn't have said it. He would have said something about how she could stop worrying now, but having a man admit that she had had something to worry about, made her feel better somehow.

Troy said, "They were sayin' at the store that Sutter an' Essie's littlest girl, Mary, that Helen plays with, is real bad with measles. They're afraid it's goin' to damage her eyes."

"Oh," Rinie said sympathetically. "I hadn't heard that."

"I thought about stoppin' by there," he said, "but, hell, Sutter don't talk to Stinsons any more, an' it would of just made things harder on Essie." He sipped coffee. "I guess Sutter would be comical—he always used to be—if he wasn't so dam' serious an' pitiful about havin' it in for all of us. . . . He told me, that mornin' at the funeral, that I—ruined Doxy, made her like she was. Do you believe that, Rinie? Ah, hell, that's not a fair question to ask anybody—only it matters to me what you think. I guess what you think matters more than just about anything."

"Troy. . . ." She wanted him not to talk like this and yet he looked so lonely and sad. Without question, he had been shaken and changed by Doxy's death; he was quieter, less boastful and boisterous, and he looked older. Thinking back, it seemed to Rinie that he hadn't appeared to grow any older for four or five years, and then, during the year and a half he had been married to Doxy, and most markedly, in the few days after her death, his face had aged, from looking younger than Doyle until now he might be taken for a few years older then he actually was. The maturity hadn't harmed his looks; in fact, it had made him more handsome. His face was often grave now, his blue eyes pensive and sometimes sad.

"I didn't love her," he went on now, begging her with his eyes to listen, "But most times I thought I tried to treat her right. Lookin' back, I can see a lot of ways I didn't, and when she was alive, sometimes I knew I was bein' dam' mean to her, but mostly, I tried. With Dean—we both loved Dean, an' I thought maybe things might be all right, but she never could quit bein' a bitch. Hell, I knew what she was doin'. I wouldn't admit that I knew, even to myself, but I did. When Buck an' me went to Becky's an' they said the sheriff had been there an' what had happened, I—I was halfway glad. About the only clear thought I can remember havin' was now I don't have to be married to her any more; now I can have Dean without Doxy. An' then we had to go and identify the body an' I remembered how she looked, cute, sort of, like a little kid, an' I remembered what I'd thought an' it made me sick."

Very carefully, she poured the chocolate filling into the pieshells on the work table taking unnecessary care to make them all very equal. Finally, she turned and stood across the big table from him, gripping the back of a chair. His face was full of misery and torment.

"I never said that to anybody else," he said, flushing a little and looking away. He stood up. "Rinie, I can say it to you because you ought to understand. I don't mean to blame you, it was all because I was such a dam' stupid kid, but what happened with Doxy was because of —of the way I feel about you. I mean, that was the reason I fooled around with her in the first place. I'd see you an' Buck together an' I—couldn't take it."

Rinie was thinking of standing by the fence around the orphanage play-ground, watching other children going along the street outside, going home. The look on Troy's face and the loneliness she herself was feeling made her remember that.

He came quickly around the table and she was in his arms, crying for his loneliness and for hers, for all the unhappiness that had come to them.

"Rinie, I know it's not so good with you an' Buck now an' I'm sorry about him, but I can't help hopin' a little that you might care about me. You know how I've always felt about you."

"Oh, Troy, no! It's not right." Yet she stood there and didn't push away his arms.

"Rinie, I want you so much! I want you to love me an' look at me the way. . . ."

She scarcely knew what he said. She forgot her children and herself and her husband for a moment and leaned against him, his arms warm and strong, his heart beating wildly against her. He cared about her. He was lonely. He wanted her. There was no tension between them.

"You do care about me," he said pleading, his cheek laid against her hair.

Someone was walking through the front room toward the kitchen door. Tory's arms dropped and he stepped back quickly. Rinie ran into her room, crying.

Finally then, in mid-March, it began to snow and everyone felt a little better. Now at least there would be some water for the grass. The first day, there were only a few flurries, but it was relatively warm and the gray clouds piled up like dirty fleeces in the northwest. A. J. was gleeful saying it would snow for a month. Travis, still looking thin and haggard, grinned and said he hoped, for once, the old man knew what he was talking about.

The next morning, when they got up, it was snowing continuously and Carl came in in time for breakfast. He had met Theorn in Belford last night and got a ride to Webber but it was after midnight when they got to McLean's, so he had stayed over and borrowed a horse at daylight. Rinie was buttering bread for toast when he came in. He kissed her and held her fiercely for a moment. She leaned against him and then she began to cry, feeling that he ought to hate her because she had felt so nearly the same things for his brother that she was feeling for him now.

"Rinie?"

But she went away into their room, crying he thought. All the others were there and he didn't know what to do.

"Set down an' eat," Ellie said briskly. "She's tired an' not expectin' to see you an' all today. She'll be better left to herself a minute. I expect she's wrote you quite a bit's been goin' on around here since you been gone."

When they were about finished eating, Travis said that if it was going to keep on snowing, somebody ought to go and try to get old Brownie. She was due to foal any day now and she "oughtn't to do it in no month's worth a snow."

"I'll go," Kirby said, but Carl said he would.

"That stud's liable to chase you clear up the ridge, Ringtail," A. J. advised the boy.

"Hell, I wouldn' be afraid of him when I'm on horseback," Kirby said.

"You better let Carl go, if he don't mind," said Travis.

Carl went in to see his children. They were awake and playing in their crib which was moved to the front room during the day for warmth.

"God, they grow fast," he said to Rinie, smiling at the

336

twins. She liked the way he looked at them. She was glad Jamie didn't cry or turn away. He had grown very shy of strangers lately and, after all, Carl had spent very little time at home the past months. He turned his eyes to her, questioning, pleading, full of love and she felt that everything inside her was melting, all the hurt and imagined hurt, the bitterness, the loneliness—leaving only love for him. But no, there was guilt besides the love and she couldn't be easy and free with him the way she yearned to be.

Carl went and got Brownie. He put her into a stall where she had no desire to go, being more than half-wild, and she promptly kicked a hole in the rotten old boards of the dividing wall. While he was repairing the hole, she kicked him, knocking him sharply against the jagged edge of the broken boards and giving him a bad cut on his upper arm. He walked into the kitchen with an old piece of horse blanket catching the blood.

"Set down quick," ordered Ellie matter-of-factly at sight of him. "Put your head on the table. You're a-fixin' to pass out."

"No, I'm not," he said foggily, "I never did." But he did as he was told.

"Oh, Carl!" Rinie breathed dizzily. She had been kneading bread dough on the work table and she came to stand by him where he sat, her floury hand touching his hair.

"Git my kit," Ellie told her brusquely, washing her own hands. "That's gonna need sewin'. You've ruined a shirt an' jacket, Carl. I swear, I don't hardly know what else can happen to this bunch in one year."

"Somebody could ruin their pants," Carl muttered caustically.

"Oh, hush up. You always git so smart-mouthed when you're hurt or sick. What is it you're a-tryin' to prove?"

Kirby, who had been in the barn with Carl, had gone to the machinery shed for Troy and now they came in together.

"Think it needs a tourniquet?" Troy asked, looking worried.

"I don't think so," said Ellie. "It's got to be cleaned out though. I see three splinters right now. Carl, I'm gonna pour in alcohol. Do you want to lay down?"

"No, but can't blood be enough to clean it?"

"Set down, Rinie," Troy said gently, drawing out a chair for her. "You're whiter'n he is. You want some whiskey, Buck?"

"I couldn'," muttered Carl.

There was a moment, as Ellie poured in alcohol to wash the wound, that things went sick and dark, but then he was feeling again, all too clearly, though his ears rang and there were bright points of light, even with his eyes closed. Rinie's fingers were pressing his.

"I'm all right," he mumbled automatically so she wouldn't ask.

"Did Brownie hurt you, where she kicked?" Troy asked him.

"No. She barely touched me. I was gittin' out of her way an' I stumbled."

"Did you ever think of fixin' the hole from the other side?"

"Dam' it, did you ever think that there was ends of nails stickin' out a them ole boards that had to be bent down?"

"Leave him alone," Rinie said fiercely. "Why do you have to keep making him talk?"

"Don't be like that, sweetheart," Carl said, a little surprised. It was always better to keep talking at a time like this, but he guessed she wouldn't know.

With tweezers and a needle, as gently as she could, Ellie removed the splinters, washed the wound again, and gradually the bleeding stopped.

"It's gonna need several stitches, hon. I think you better lay down while I do that." She didn't like his color, or lack of it. He had bled quite a lot.

He stood up, swaying. Troy took his right arm.

"I—we better go someplace besides our room," Carl said giddily. "The kids are asleep in there, I guess."

"Use my bed," croaked Kirby from near the back door.

Ellie said, "Son, you better go outside an' breathe some snowflakes. You're a little bit greenish."

As Ellie took her careful stitches, waves of dizziness and nausea swept over Rinie, but Carl watched the procedure with detachment.

"It don't hurt," he said as the needle went through his skin.

"That's how it is sometimes," Ellie said calmly. "It gits numb for a while around a bad cut."

When she had almost finished bandaging, he began to shake violently from the shock. Troy helped him get his boots and levis off and Rinie turned back the covers and then put them gently around him. She sat beside him when the others had gone and after a while he stopped shaking enough to talk without his voice trembling.

"Rinie, there's somethin' I want to say to you, not to scare you, because I'm fine now, but it's a thing I've thought about, bein' away so much. If—if anything was to ever happen to me, I wouldn' like mournin', you know. An' sometime, when you could, I'd want you to marry somebody else. The twins would need somebody, you would, too. Honey, please don't cry. It's just a thing I've thought of, not a thing that's goin' to happen."

In a moment he was asleep, breathing deeply and evenly, but his face was still so white it frightened her. It was such a fine face, so young and kind and all things good. Oh, how had he come to say a thing like that about finding somebody else? She supposed the cut had made him think of it, but it was almost as if he knew about her and Troy.

Troy was alone in the kitchen when she finally left Carl. She shook her head at his offer of coffee, trying not to retch. She had been terribly shaken by Carl's being hurt like that.

"Buck asleep?"

"Yes, but he's still so white."

"You're not exactly rosy-cheeked yourself. Why not sit down a minute an' have some coffee?"

"I—think I'll feel better if I do something." She washed her hands and went back to the dough, shaping it into loaves.

"Ellie went out to milk," he said. "She said it's because it'll be dark by the time Helen gits home, an' that's true, cloudy as it is, but the real reason is that Ellie's not as tough as she lets on. I think she just needed to git outside for a while."

"I wish he could see a doctor," Rinie said worriedly.

"Rinie, people like us gits through a hell of a lot without a doctor. Buck'd be the first to tell you he's not hurt near as much as it looks like."

"I know he would. He always does."

She was beginning to think now of other things besides Carl's white face and the frightening thing he had said, and she felt nervous and uncomfortable there alone with Troy. She carried the big pan with the bread loaves to a warm place beside the oven to rise.

"Rinie," Troy began slowly, "I want to talk to you. Please, sit somewhere an' listen for just a minute."

Without looking at him, she went out of the back door, then she ran around the house and down along the creek in the thick-falling snow.

I did want Troy, she thought with burning shame, I always have. It wasn't just that one time last week. Oh, my God! I'm worse than Doxy or Heddie or anybody. It's cleaner to be open and frank than to be a smug little married bitch. I've been so unreasonable with Carl about the children, about us, and if Troy had told me to, the other day, I would have. . . .

She stopped, turning impulsively. She would go straight to Carl and tell him, beg him to forgive her . . . then she remembered what Ellie had said about the temper of the Stinson men where their women were concerned. She mustn't be the cause of serious trouble between Carl and Troy. There had been trouble enough already because of her.

She walked on a long time, her cheeks stingingly cold because of the tears, her mind a frightening turmoil. Finally, she thought again of Carl lying on Kirby's bed, so pale and still, saying, "If anything ever was to happen to me. . . ." She turned and began running toward the house. Carl, Carl, I love you. Oh, please, please, be all right.

He was sitting at the table, drinking coffee with A. J., and Ellie was sliding the loaves into the oven. There was something so warm and commonplace and comforting about everything connected with the kitchen that she almost burst into fresh tears. She hadn't been noticing those wonderful things about home lately.

"Oh, Carl!" She ran to him and put her arms around him. "Are—are you all right?"

"Well, yes," he said, looking up at her, smiling a little uncertainly. "You're soakin' wet, you little girl, an' your hair's turned white. What have you been doin', outside all this time without a coat?"

"I—I went for a walk," she said, trying to keep her mouth from trembling.

"Well, your kids are awake an' hungry."

Carl didn't want any supper. His arm was paining him badly now and he went to bed again after a little while.

Rinie ate very little. The twins were beginning to eat some table foods and she hoped no one would notice her lack of appetite because she was so busy feeding them. She didn't look directly at Troy and the only words he spoke were those necessitated by direct questions. Was he angry with her? Would he do something? Say something to Carl?

When they were washing the dishes, Ellie said, "Whyn't we put the crib in our room before you put the twins to bed? They might wake in the night and bother Carl. He needs his rest."

Rinie agreed. Excepting the night they were born, this would be the first time in their lives that her children had spent a night in a room away from her, and she was surprised and a little ashamed at the relief she felt at not having to think of them along with all the other thoughts that circled frantically, almost hysterically, in her mind.

As soon as she was sure the twins were asleep, she went softly into her and Carl's room. He was sleeping, but he woke when she got into bed.

"Still snowin'?"

"Yes. A. J. says this storm will last three days and there'll be more for a month, one right after another."

"He's got it all figgered, has he?"

"Yes. I'm sorry I woke you. Does it hurt awfully?"

"Not so bad now. Kids asleep?"

"Yes, they—they're in Ellie's room for tonight."

"They are? Why?"

"Because I—because you need rest. Your arm. . . ."

"They don't even wake me up," he said slowly.

"Oh, Carl, if you're teasing, please don't. If—if your arm doesn't hurt too much, please, please hold me."

"Oh, Rinie!" He drew a quick harsh breath and pulled her hard against him. She could feel the wildness of his desire and she felt shy of him and deeply, painfully thrilled at the touch of his hands.

"I've been such a fool," she said unevenly.

"Don't talk."

"Please, I have to."

"No, not now. Forget you know any words. Forget everything—everything. . . ."

A long time later, he said gently, "Do you still want to talk?"

She began to cry. "You were right about what I was trying to do with the twins—making up to myself for things I missed. Remember the first time we ever really talked about a baby, that day after you got home from the cattle drive, that first year we were married? I said it wouldn't make any difference in our love, except to make it bigger? Only I wouldn't let it. I've been treating you like —as if you were my parents and thinking of myself as one of the babies. Oh, sweetheart, I don't know if that makes any sense to you, but I think it's what I've been doing, sort of, and it's so unfair."

"I've not been exactly unselfish," he said. Apologies came hard to him, but if they were going to talk about this, as he thought they ought to, then he had to do his part, too. "I had the idea that we—the two of us—could always be just the way we were before, and still have the kids and all the good things that go with having them."

She lay in his arms and cried. They were so close now, released from the tensions that parenthood had put upon them, but there was still her terrible guilt about Troy and Carl and even Doxy, and she couldn't get it out of her mind, no matter how close she was to him and how tenderly he sheltered her in his arms.

"Can't you tell me the rest of it, Rinie?" he said finally, worriedly.

But that was what she couldn't do, must never do, what made it all so terribly hard to bear.

"Is is because there won't be any more kids?"

"No," she said brokenly. "I see now that that was just an excuse, mostly, to be mad at you and—and make you keep away, because you saw through what I was trying to do with the twins and I didn't want to see it. I'm so glad we've got them."

But her tears wouldn't stop. She tried desperately not to cry. He was ill and needed sleep and he could be so perceptive that she was terrified of his guessing.

"Rinie, as soon as there's time, when the heavist part of the spring work's done, would you like it if we started

342

buildin' our own house? Maybe up in that clearing where we first talked about your bein' pregnant."

"Oh," she said softly. She had supposed he had forgotten that talk about a house of their own.

"I think," he said, trying to make her smile, "that livin' with so many Stinsons could get to be a strain, especially the way things have been goin' lately. Only, you know, I don't recall things bein' so hectic around here before you came."

But that was the wrong thing to say somehow, because she was crying desperately again.

"Carl, it's so silly to cry like this," she gasped. "I feel so close to you again and it's so wonderful, but I just can't seem to stop. . . ."

"Well, you've got to," he said firmly. "You're gonna make yourself sick. All this wasn't brought on by that cut I got today. It's not anything—"

"No," she said, disengaging herself gently, blowing her nose, "but I guess it did start me thinking with some sense about you—about us. Carl, what you said . . .about something happening to you . . . I—I want you to know that I feel the same way and I—I understand now about A. J. and Heddie—pretty well. I'll try to be more mature about things like that after this. You're right to call me little girl. I certainly act like one. Does it hurt?"

"Not much. It was worth what happened a little while ago. Anything would be. Rinie, I've been God-awful lonesome. Bunkhouses are dreary places to sleep, an' dam' cold sometimes."

"You've got a fever, Carl," she said, laying her cheek against his. "Oh, I'm so sorry I've been acting like this, worrying you, keeping you awake. I'm going to get you some aspirin."

He took them and lay down again and she came into his arms.

An owl was hooting desultorily up in the woods.

"What would be out for him to catch on a night like this?" Rinie wondered.

"Most of the things that are out on a clear night. They all have to keep trying to live."

After a while, she said timidly, "Are you going away again?"

"No. Not till after shipping this fall. Not then unless I have to."

After another long silence, his arms tightened and he said drowsily, "I hope A. J.'s right. I hope it snows forever."

18

The snow had stopped in the morning, but the sky was leaden and heavy and A. J. assured them it wasn't near through. Helen begged not to go to school.

"If it's gonna snow as much as Granddaddy says, it might fill up the canyon an' I couldn't git home."

"I don't hardly think it'll snow that much," said her mother, "an' it ain't cold, even."

"It will be," stated A. J., "colder'n a well-digger's butt when this here clears out."

"Ah, let 'er stay at home, hon," urged Travis. "We ain't had this much snow at one time this whole winter. It's somethin' to celebrate."

"I'm goin' huntin'," announced Kirby, helping himself to more ham and biscuits. "Who all's comin'?"

"I will," Troy said, "if you don't rush me. We'll need to drink a lot of coffee first."

"You didn't use to fool around about goin' huntin'," said the nephew impatiently.

"Well, when you git to be his age," Travis said, "you begin to study things over pretty careful before you make any moves."

Troy said, "You comin' with us, Buck?"

"I don't know. Maybe."

Carl was feeding oatmeal to his daughter and it took some concentration on his part. She sat on his lap and with his left forearm, he tried to keep her hands out of the way without letting her know she was being restrained, while with his right hand he fed her very fast.

344

"You're gonna choke that child, shovelin' food into 'er that way," Ellie said, smiling.

"It's the only way to keep her from goin' after it herself," Carl said, without looking away from what he was doing.

Rinie was feeding Jamie. He was easier, but Carl had had his choice. Jamie liked to eat in a more leisurely fashion, pausing now and then to look around the table with serious, still-sleepy eyes. Rinie smiled, watching Carl with Ginger. How could she have been so dispassionate about him all that long time? Seeing him this morning was almost like seeing him that first morning they'd been at Red Bear. Only this was even better because now they had their children, and the four of them were warm and secure in love.

Carl's face looked tired. She knew he hadn't slept well, but the fever seemed to be gone.

Rinie didn't want to look at Troy. Two or three times, their glances crossed and his eyes were intent with— what? She didn't know. She didn't want to think. What had happened between them the week before, what she had felt for those few moments, was like a dream and she wished she could believe that that was what it had been. During the night, unable to sleep, she had made herself admit that the kind of feelings she had had for Troy might come again from time to time. He was attractive, a man, and she a woman. There was nothing so shameful about the way she handled the feelings. Now she was confident that she could handle them casually, as they merited, but she was afraid of what Troy might do. They must never talk about it again. He might get angry with her and Carl might find out. If that should happen, her whole world could fall apart.

Carl and Troy and Kirby went hunting. A. J. sat by the kitchen table with his feet on a chair and advised Ellie on the dressing she was making to go with the stewed hen they were having for dinner.

The babies played on the floor. Dean, at fourteen months, seemed to have a condescending attitude toward his younger cousins. He managed to open a cabinet door to get at some pots and pans and, in his magnanimity, he brought a single lid and dropped it on the quilt where the twins were. Both wanted it and there was a tug of war. Jamie let go abruptly and Ginger fell over backward. She got red in the face with fury.

"Good God!" murmured A. J., smiling. "That one's gonna be a holy terror."

"She's spoiled," Rinie said flatly.

She was at the sink, washing diapers, and hardly gave her angry daughter a glance.

Ellie threw Rinie a sharp look and felt relieved. It was a good thing Rinie was coming to see that. These tempestuous ones had to be handled with a firm hand right from the start or they got completely beyond reason.

"Ah, now, missy," said A. J. placatingly. "She's got to take up for herself amongst all these boys."

Rinie didn't answer, but Ellie liked the confident look on her face. She was going to do all right with her children, her and Carl.

"You can't hang them diapers out," she said. "It's startin' to snow again."

Rinie smiled a little grimly. "Never mind. I'll just drape them around the front room so the men'll have something to talk about when they get back."

"Just exactly like Buck an' Bojack," mused A. J. happily, watching his two grandsons as Dean now tried to reclaim the lid and Jamie hung on with all his strength. "Two chestnuts an' a sorrel, them little ones is. That light hair's kind a funny, sort of a mixture a me an' Jenny, I guess but it's funny it'd breed so true in Carl's young'un. You wouldn' hardly expect it to show up that-a-way in one out of two when it just come up in one out a six of our kids."

"Carl says it's a recessive gene and I've got it, too," Rinie said.

"A what?"

"Recessive gene."

"Good Lord! If he told me the stock had that, I'd say vaccinate as quick as you can. He's been readin' again."

"Well, yes, and he wants to buy another bull in the fall if we can."

Ellie was glad to hear her talking like that, too. She had got the feeling lately that Rinie was beginning to resent the ranch, not that she could blame her much, with Carl having to be gone all the time, the only one contributing any cash money.

"Mama, is it all right if I slap Deanie's hands?" asked Helen at the end of her patience. "He keeps runnin' by an' grabbin' my paper dolls an' tearin' 'em up an' I can't make him quit."

"Yes," agreed Ellie, "but not hard."

Dean was outraged. He lay down on the floor and banged his head.

"Dean Stinson!" Ellie stood over him and spoke in a terrible voice. "You git up from there right now an' quit that or I'll wear you out."

He looked at her belligerently and then, in quick flicks, his eyes went around the room to see if there was help. His grandfather had a hand up, hiding his mouth, but Dean wasn't yet old enough to know the meaning of that, so his eyes, looking up again at his Aunt Ellie, grew blithe and innocent, and he held up his arms and she set him on his feet.

"Cookie?" he ventured.

"Here's you a biscuit. Now you behave yourself." And to Rinie, she said, "It's just hard to believe how young they start learnin' how far they can go."

Rinie knew it was a hint for her as well as a comment about Dean, and she took it kindly. Even as late as yesterday, she would have felt defensively that Ellie was meddling.

They had dinner ready before the men got back. Travis paced the floor like a hungry bear, peering under pot lids and complaining that he was starving to death. Rinie and Ellie and Helen fed the babies and put them down for their naps.

"We got nine rabbits," Kirby announced happily as they came trooping in the back door after a lot of stamping on the porch. "I shot four of 'em."

"Well, it's good we got somebody to keep meat on the table," said his mother. "We'll have some of 'em for supper."

"That mare out in the barn dropped a right nice-lookin' bay filly this mornin'," said Travis. "I may be wrong, but I got me a feelin' it's fixin to be a good year."

"How's your arm, Carl?" asked Ellie.

"Stiff, but not bad."

"I notice he can still reach across the table," said Troy.

"What chicken is this?" inquired A. J.

"What chicken?" asked Ellie, mystified. "What do you mean, what chicken? It's a ole hen that I think had quit layin'. Why?"

"Hell, I was hopin' it was that bastard of a rooster. He wakes me up ever' mornin' of the world."

"Old Early!" cried Helen. "We couldn' eat him. Jeff would have a fit."

"The hens wouldn't like it much either," Carl said.

"That's the reason I never hear that rooster crow," Troy said. "He wakes you up, an' there's so dam' much noise of that club of a walkin' stick poundin' on doors, nobody else gits to hear the rooster."

"Well, if you're hankerin' to hear him," said A. J., "I could wake you up earlier sometime."

"We been talkin' 'bout makin' a change in the house," said Travis. "Kirby an' Troy figgers they can stand each other to sleep with, an' we aim to cut a door between these two back rooms here so the twins can sleep in a room to theirselves an' still be handy to take care of."

"W'y, that's a real good idea," said Ellie, without the slightest indication that she had suggested last night that Travis should make such a proposal to the others.

"What have them two little bitty things got to have a room to theirselves for?" asked A. J. innocently. "I ain't heard of them complainin'."

"Kirby's got to be careful spendin' a lot of time around Troy," Carl said "He'll fall into evil ways."

Troy shook his head. "All I ask is that he be quiet an' don't wake me up when he comes in late."

"Late from what?" wondered Kirby.

"W'y, from bein' out on dates," Troy said.

Kirby's ruddy complexion grew a little more ruddy and he looked at his plate.

"He got a girl, has he?" asked the grandfather with interest.

"More like five or six, the way I hear it."

"Aw, Troy, you never heard no such a thing," protested the boy.

"Why, they're talkin' all up an' down the valley," Carl said.

"Aw, quit," said Kirby, snickering a little and flushing more deeply.

"One a these times, say in another five years," said Travis meditatively, "Me an' Ellie could be grandpa and granma, an' A. J. a great-granddaddy."

"That's what they call long-range plannin'," said Carl.

"Well, yeah, but you might as well figger on these things, for they're bound to happen."

"He better not git married," said Helen with her customary practical candor, "till somebody moves out or dies. We're short of beds as it is, times when Jeff an' Doyle are home."

The others laughed and Rinie and Carl exchanged a look, thinking of the house they might build, vacating rooms for younger couples that would come to Red Bear.

"Helen," Troy said, "When you're grown, you ought to run a hotel. You've always been such a good hand for plannin' sleepin' arrangements."

"Well, Rinie," Travis said, "is it all right with you, about puttin' in that door?"

"Yes," she said softly. "I think it would be fine."

"There's a ole door out there in the shed," he said, "that we can scrape down an' paint, an' when the kids wakes up, we can knock out a place for it."

"My God, this man's got energy," said Troy.

"It's the snow," Carl said. "Its' kind of drove him wild an' he's got to do things, you know, like a old gander that's got to fly south or somethin'. You can scrape a door if you want to, Travis, out there in the cold, an' I do appreciate the thought, but I'm gonna take a nap by the fire before I do one more dam' thing."

"There's di'pers dryin' in there," Kirby warned.

"I'm too sleepy to care."

"You better let me look at that arm," said Ellie.

"What for? You just like to have me take my shirt off."

"Oh, don't be fresh an' think so highly a yourself."

"I'm not. You are."

"She just wants to admire her stitchin'," Troy said.

"I looked at it this morning," Carl said, "an' Rinie did, too. It was fine, wasn't it, hon?"

"It was awful," she said. "It was red and swollen and feverish, but he told me it was all right."

A. J. said, with his mouth almost straight, "Now just a minute. Is this still his arm we're talkin' about?"

The others laughed and Rinie blushed deeply.

"I always did like a woman that blushes," said the old man with gusto. "It makes most ever' thing a hell of a lot more fun."

A. J. felt good. Things were coming right again. It

349

was kind of funny that a good snow could make all that difference.

The next day, with snow still falling intermittently, they got out the sleds and toboggan and snowshoes and couldn't decide what to do first.

Dressed in snowsuits and mittens Rinie had made, Dean and the twins were brought outside. In most places, the snow was deeper than Dean was tall, but he went plowing around with happy shrieks, looking like a weak swimmer in heavy water. Ginger, after getting snow on her face, wanted no more part of it, but Jamie, carried by his father, kept grabbing for handfuls and eating it greedily. Carl took him down an easy sled run and at the bottom the baby was laughing joyously and he reached for the sled when he was taken off.

"Carl," Rinie said softly, "the two of you—together—are just beautiful."

"That's a hell of a thing to say to two men, isn' it, Jim? Besides, what about the two of us separately? Here, le's trade an I'll take Miss Gingersnap for a ride."

While she stood there with Jamie, Troy came down the run with Dean, who was yelling with lusty joy and battering his father's head with snowy gloves. Troy looked up at her, laughing, and then his face sobered. He got off the sled.

"Rinie—"

She turned away.

"Rinie, don't be such a baby. Give me half a chance to be decent, will you? I've been tryin' to say just a few words to you for a week."

"Troy, I don't want to talk—"

"I do. I want to have this straightened out. The—the kind of thing that happened the other day—it won't ever happen again, not from me. I swear it, Rinie. Can't we be friends, all of us?"

Carl came back down then, with Ginger clinging to him, wide-eyed and solemn with fear, and Carl was pale.

"What's wrong?" cried Rinie, seeing his face.

"Take her a minute, can you, Bo?" Carl said, prying the little gril's hands loose from his arm.

"She hurt you," Rinie said. "Is it bleeding or—"

"No, it's all right. She just grabbed hold an' I couldn't git her loose an' handle the sled." He smiled wryly. "She's got quite a grip for a lady."

350

"Well, at least she don't like snow in the face," said Troy, having some difficulty holding his son and Ginger. "That's pretty ladylike, I guess."

When they were back in the house and had changed the twins' clothes and removed their own heavy outer garments, Rinie made Carl show her his arm. All around the wound the flesh was red and swollen hard.

"Carl, it's infected. We've got to do something."

"It'll be all right."

But she was calling Ellie.

"You know, I believe there's a splinter still in there that I missed," Ellie said judiciously, studying the arm. "If that ain't better tomorrow, I guess I ought to take them stitches out an' let it drain."

Carl had put his shirt back on. "I wish you'd both quit fussin' over it," he said curtly and went out.

"That's a-hurtin' him," Ellie said crossly. "I wisht they wasn' so bloomin' stubborn about saying so."

The next day was sunny. Ellie and Rinie started up the machine and got the washing done. The clothes froze on the lines, but they were clean and not hanging in the house to dry.

Carl and Troy and Kirby went out on snowshoes to see how the stock was faring.

"It only snowed two days," Troy mentioned casually as they sat in the front room that night. "Seems to me somebody said it'd be three."

"I never said three days in a row," A. J. pointed out a little defensively. "Day after tomorrow's first of April."

"What's that got to do with anything?" asked Travis.

"April Fool," said Carl dryly.

"Three days before my birthday," guessed Troy.

"We're apt to have a God-awful blizzard," said A. J., ignoring them. "Snow this much, this late, gittin' colder the way it is, wind's likely to come up an' there'll be hell to pay."

"Oh, for Chrissake," said Travis unhappily, "you would have to predict somethin' like that when half the cows is ready to calve."

"Well," said the old man smugly, "I never had nothin' to do with the weather or with when the cows calve neither. I'm just tellin' you what it's likely to do."

"From all his years of experience," added Carl.

"I think it's like Christmas," said Helen. "I feel just like Christmas."

351

"I feel like lookin' at Carl's arm," said Ellie.

Carl looked scared. "Ellie, can't you think about anything else?"

"I reckon I can. I ain't mentioned it since the middle of yesterday."

"She likes to look at men's bare arms," said Travis. "It's apt to git 'er all het up."

"My Lord!" said Ellie, laughing, though she tried not to.

"Take your shirt off Buck," urged Troy, "an le's see what happens."

"You take off yours," Carl said. "I don't believe I could trust myself with 'er, even right here in front a God an' ever'body, if she was to git all het up."

"Ah, have a little faith in yourself."

"I wish you'd all forgit the dam' thing," he said sullenly. "I'm cold an' I don't want to be fooled with."

"You're layin' right in front a the fire," said Travis mildly.

"An' I ain't gonna fool with you," snapped Ellie. "Not so's you'd notice."

"He's got a fever," Rinie said, and he threw her an angry look as though she had betrayed him.

"Let 'er see, Buck," said A. J. "Whenever'n a woman gits it into her head she's gonna take care of you, there aint a goddam' thing you can do about it."

"Oh, Carl, for the Lord's sake!" said Ellie, shocked, when she saw the wound.

His whole upper arm was swollen and the side where the cut was was an angry purple-red, with streaks radiating to elbow and shoulder. The wound itself was badly festered and swollen hard around the stitches.

"It's a lot worse than this morning," Rinie breathed, looking away.

"An' you been out runnin' around on snowshoes this whole day," Ellie scolded him.

"What you gonna do, hon?" Travis asked her.

"Well, I got to git them stitches out before I have to cut skin to do it. Maybe then it'll drain an' git all right. Helen, git my kit an' some clean rags."

"Ellie," Carl pleaded, "just leave it alone, will you? It'll be better by mornin'. It hurts so much, I. . . ." He hadn't meant to say that. He turned his eyes to the fire, feeling sick.

352

"Git 'im some whiskey." A. J. told Troy, "an' some for the rest of us, too."

With a pair of thin-pointed scissors, Ellie took out the stitches, sitting on the floor beside Carl, while he strained his hands together, trying not to move. A sickly yellowish pus drained sluggishly from the wound. Carl drew his breath in between gritting teeth and held it a long time, his face draining of color. After a little, the pus changed to a small flow of blood.

"Now maybe it's out," said Ellie shakily. "I didn' see nothin', but it coulda been just a little bitty splinter. They can cause a lot a misery." She washed the wound and bandaged it, leaving it open to drain. "It'll leave a worse scar this way, but you ain't gonna worry about that."

Carl drank again from the bottle Troy handed him. He drank as much as he could without drawing breath and his throat felt scalded by the strong whiskey.

"Go to bed now," Rinie urged him gently.

"No, I'm cold." He put his head in her lap and lay close to the fire. There was sweat on his forehead and he shivered.

"There was a feller I knowed once down home in Texas," A. J. said, talking to relieve his own concern, "that got a hurt somethin' similar to that, only in his leg, about halfway between his hip an' his knee. How he got it, they was a tornado come through down there an' they was a splintery end of a board got stuck in this feller's leg—Joe Farley, his name was. It swole an' festered an'all, and it ended up, they had to take his leg off. . . ."

They were all staring at him belligerently, except Carl, whose eyes were closed. Hell, that wasn't the best story he could have told, A. J. thought, too late, a little dismayed but it didn't have anything to do with Buck. It had just come to mind was all.

Helen said, "Tell about tornadoes, Granddaddy?"

Well, that ought to be safe enough to talk about, he thought, looking at the others defiantly, and he proceeded to detail ravages, miraculous escapes, and other phenomena connected with tornadoes in South Texas.

Carl raised his head to drink again and Rinie held it tenderly. The pain was just about more than he could stand now. Since sometime yesterday it had been a gradually increasing, sickening, dull, bone-deep ache, but

353

now it was sharp and violent. He could hardly restrain himself from twisting about to try to escape it, or at least relieve it. The whiskey didn't seem to help and Ellie was coming back.

She brought Rinie the thermometer.

"It's over 102," Rinie said aside to Ellie after a while. Carl heard the words as though they were echoes, bouncing back and forth off the walls of a cave. They didn't make any sense, and they wouldn't stop reverberating. He drank again.

Sometime later Troy said, "You better go to bed, Buck rabbit," and took him by his shoulder, the one that wasn't hurt, and dragged him to his feet. He tried to say that he didn't want to go to bed, but they didn't pay any attention. Maybe they couldn't hear him any more.

In the night he woke. Rinie had got up to do something for the twins. He wasn't drunk any more and his whole body ached almost unbearably.

"Carl? Are you all right?"

"What time is it?"

"About four. Honey, you're burning up. Is your arm bad?"

"I don't know. My head is. My throat hurts. My bones all ache."

"I'll get some aspirin."

"What's wrong with the kids?" he said when she got back into bed.

"I just went to see if they were covered up all right. It's getting colder I think. They seem so—far away, in there."

"We could bring 'em back."

"No," she said softly. "I like being here by ourselves. Honey, you're shaking."

"The wind," he said groggily. "It must be turning colder."

She put her arms around him. His skin was burning hot. She hadn't heard any wind.

"What kind of house will we build?" he said, turning his head restlessly.

"Just a little house," she said tenderly, "for four people to love each other in."

"That year that I lived at Minna's, I—I had that back bedroom upstairs. You know?"

354

"Yes."

"Not the one you had. Across the hall."

"Yes, Carl, I know."

"From the window you could see the mountains, but the house next door was what I was gonna tell you about, only I can't remember. . . ."

"The little green house?"

He was relieved. "Yes, with a white trellis and roses on the back porch. Do you think you could grow roses here?"

"I could try." She was becoming more frightened by the moment. He seemed so listless and it wasn't like him to talk about roses at four o'clock in the morning. And it wasn't like him to admit to having all that pain. She sat up.

"I want to light the lamp and see how your arm looks."

He shuddered violently as she moved the covers.

"Do you think," he asked between chattering teeth, "that Ginger would like to be courted on a back porch like that? With roses?"

His arm made her sick. Ellie had bandaged it loosely, but it had swollen and bulged around the bandage. The wound was almost swelled together, its edges dry and dark, like the thin lips of a cruel, puckered mouth. He cringed away from her hands as she put on another bandage. She wanted to call Ellie but in two hours or less the whole house would be awake. She would wait.

"I think it's flu," Carl muttered, not seeming to think of his arm any more. "I had it a couple of times. It makes you ache—all over. Did you have it?"

"Yes, once. Carl, don't talk. Try to sleep. The aspirin will make you feel better soon."

"I want to talk," he said petulantly. "An' I don't want you to catch anything from me. . . . We had all kinds of stuff when we were kids, measles, mumps, whoopin' cough, all like that . . . scarlet fever, Troy had an' we had diphtheria when Aaron died. He was such a cute little kid. . . . Rinie?"

"What, sweetheart?"

"I'm glad you wanted to name the kids after mother an' A. J. He's as pleased as anything, A. J. is. I don't know why none of us was named for him . . . except Aaron, an' he died."

She shuddered.

"Are you cold, little girl?"

"No, I'm fine. Are you warmer now?"

"Mm-hmm."

"And sleepy?"

"Rinie? Rinie, stay close, will you?"

"I am, Carl, I will."

He slept fitfully. His temperature was lowered by the aspirin and he began to push restlessly at the covers.

"Goddam' hot," he mumbled once, "flies an' dust an' this Christforsaken sun. . . . Nothin' smells as bad as stock dip."

As soon as she heard someone in the kitchen, Rinie went in. For once, A. J. hadn't gotten up first; it was Ellie.

"W'y, what's the matter?" she asked, looking at Rinie sharply.

"Ellie, he's so sick. He even says he is."

Ellie took up a lamp and they went into the bedroom. On each of Carl's cheeks, there was a fiery red fever blotch. He looked at the women almost as if he didn't see them.

"Git the thermometer," Ellie said brusquely.

As Rinie was looking for it, a gust of wind hit the house, like the heavy shaking of a giant's hand.

Carl's temperature was almost 104. They gave him more aspirin.

"He said it feels like flu," Rinie said, following Ellie distractedly back into the kitchen.

"It could be somethin' like that."

"But did you look at his arm again? With—with all those streaks and—"

"Yes, Rinie, I looked at it," she said quietly. "It's about the worst infection I've ever seen."

"What can we do?" Rinie said pleadingly.

"Well, right now, there's breakfast to be got, an' I want you to be sure an' eat, an' when them aspirins has had time to do some good, I want you to git Carl to eat. He needs the strength."

Rinie helped with breakfast, trying to keep hold of herself. When the twins woke, she got them up and dressed them, tiptoeing in to look at Carl every few minutes.

More gusts of wind buffeted the house, coming at closer and closer intervals until, by the time the men

356

came in from their morning chores, it was an almost solid force against the back of the house. It howled eerily around the corner of the bedroom.

"This is it," A. J. said triumphantly. "I told you they was comin' a blizzard. What's the matter, gals? Scared of a little blowin'?"

They told him about Carl. He went into the bedroom, walking as quietly as the stick would allow.

"He been talkin' out of his head, has he?" he asked, coming back.

"He was talking," Rinie said slowly, "but not. . . ."

"Buck gits odd with fever. Always has."

Travis and Troy and Kirby tugged at the back door and then fought to keep it from slamming too hard behind them.

"Christ! You can't tell if the snow's comin' from the ground or the sky," said Travis, still a little breathless. "Keeps up like this, we'll have to run a rope to the barn to keep from gittin' lost. You can't hardly see your hand before your face."

Carl drank some of the broth, sitting up, propped against pillows Rinie brought. The world was a strange, frightening place, the room swayed vaguely and the wind was a great roaring.

She said, "Can you drink some coffee?" Her voice was hollow and terrifying.

He said, "I want to look at the ridge." They were trying to shut him up here in this strange room, with only a lamp for light. He wanted to see out.

"You can't see even a few feet out there now, sweetheart," she said. "It's the blizzard A. J. predicted. I closed the curtains because you can't see anything and I thought it might be a little warmer with them closed."

"Don't close them," he said a little frantically. "I want to see out."

She opened them. The world was a blur and he felt more frightened than ever.

He drank a little of the coffee she brought because he couldn't think of the words to say he didn't want it, and after a little while, he began to vomit. He kept retching until he was trembling with weakness and exhaustion. Then he couldn't keep aspirin down any more. He was

357

unbearably thirsty but water made him vomit and retch long after there was nothing to vomit and they finally stopped giving it to him.

Each time they took it, his temperature was higher. By mid-afternoon, it was 105 and he shook with constant chills, rolling his head from side to side, mumbling incoherently.

Rinie stayed with him, frantic and helpless. Always, always before, he had been with her when anything was really wrong. If she were sick, or one of the babies, he would be there for her to lean on, but now he was the one; she couldn't help him and there was no one to stand between her and terror. She remembered when the twins were born, how he had stayed with her, and how she had been really frightened only when he was out of the room. Now she couldn't tell if he even knew she was with him or not.

Ellie and the others came in and out, their eyes concerned, their voices low and worried, but Rinie had never felt so alone if her life. Oh, God! Just when I was beginning to learn to grow up, to know what love really is! Oh, please, please, don't let anything happen to him.

"Ellie. . . ."

"Rinie, honey, I just don't know no more to do."

"The doctor. . . ."

"Honey, this wind, this snow, nobody can git anywhere. Now Carl's strong. He may can fight out of this."

"May!" she gasped and began to cry.

"You've got to hold up now," Ellie said firmly. "Times when he comes to hisself, you don't want him to see you a-cryin'. An' there's the babies to think about. . . ."

She patted Rinie's shoulder awkwardly and went to see about supper which was scarcely touched by anyone but the babies.

Troy came in and stood silent by the bed a long time. "Rinie, I—I don't know what the hell I feel like. I'm not tryin' to say it's as bad for me as it is for you, but I swear to God, I don't know how I ever come to think of taking —anything away from him. Buck means—to me he's about—goddam'! I wish I could pray."

"Bo. . . ."

They were startled. Carl's voice was weak and grating. "Buck?" Troy bent over him.

"What—what A. J. was talkin' about—the man in the tornado—I can't live without my arm. . . ."

"Your arm'll be all right," Troy said shakily. "Do you want anything?"

"I'm thirsty."

Troy looked at Rinie and she shook her head, crying. Carl said fretfully, "I want to see the ridge."

Troy stood up, beckoning Rinie to the door.

"I'm goin' after Heddie." His eyes dared her to defy him. "I—I know you don't like her, but maybe she can do somethin'. . . . Rinie, *I've* got to do somethin'."

"Oh, Troy, the storm. . . ."

"Don't worry about the dam' storm. I'll take a good horse that can come home without any help. . . . I wouldn't do this, Rinie, knowin' how you feel about Heddie, only it seems like he. . . ."

"I just pray you can get there and she's home and you both get back safely, and that Carl. . . ."

"He's a tough kid," Troy said, turning to the rack where the coats were hung. "Stay close to him, He'll be all right."

19

Rinie went back and sat by the bed. Carl was more restless now. It was hard to keep him covered and he mumbled monotonously, almost constantly. His breathing was quick and shallow and his heart beat rapidly and, she thought with sickening horror, irregularly. The fever no longer showed itself in red blotches on his cheeks, his whole face was flushed darkly. Sometimes he opened his eyes fully and they were strange and wild, seeing things other than his present surroundings. He asked for water often.

"Dam', I can't work dry like this. I've got to have water. It's so dusty. My throat. . . ."

"You can't tame a horse like that," he said, later, angrily. "Bein' mean may break him, but it won't ever make him tame."

And after a while, "Rinie, there's somethin' wrong with the toboggan. For God's sake, jump off."

He sat up. He had seemed so weak but she found, trying to make him lie down again, that he still had strength. If she talked to him, maybe he would listen, at least a little, and lie more quietly.

"Carl . . . I think the wind's slacked off some. . . . Troy's gone to get Heddie."

He said, "Bo didn' say a word all the way to Belford. He never was that quiet that long in his life. I thought he'd kill 'er, but she was already dead. . . . The car rolled over her, she—"

"Carl," she took one of his hands that kept picking restlessly at the covers. "Carl, please know I'm here. Oh, sweetheart, I love you so."

"Rinie. . . ."

She laid her cheek against his.

"You're cold, Rinie. All the way home, I was thinkin' how warm you'd be. . . . Skeeter'll be all right, I guess, just a strained tendon. . . ."

She drew the covers around him again.

"A. J.," he said suddenly, loudly, out of mumbling. "Oh, my God, what's wrong?"

He was sitting up, flinging the covers off, and she couldn't stop him. Ellie, looking in, called Travis and he came quickly. The three of them forced Carl back on the bed.

"Goddam' it, he's hurt. He thinks he's gonna die. He can't stay on his horse," he cried hoarsely, fighting them.

"A. J.'s all right, Carl," Travis kept telling him. "He's right in there in the front room, all right."

"We've got to try some more aspirins," Ellie said. "This fever's just simply too high."

But he knocked the glass of water out of her hand, gasping in agony when the cold liquid touched his burning skin.

For a little while he was more quiet, gritting his teeth and mumbling incoherently, but not fighting to get up. Then he said, "Rinie?"

She knelt by the bed, her hand passing gently over his

face and neck, feeling the hard-swollen glands beneath his jaw bone.

"I can't do anything," he said pleadingly. "I'd give anything if you didn' have to go through this."

"But, Carl, I'm all right, I—"

"I don't think the doctor can get here. . . . I don't know what's best to do. Rinie, if anything happened to you, I . . . it's my fault. I waited too long. I. . . ."

"Carl, I'm all right," she said desperately. "Jamie and Ginger are safe asleep. Carl, sweetheart, please lie still."

"My throat hurts so bad, Heddie. Aaron an' Doyle don't ever stop cryin', but it hurts to cry."

A. J. came stumping in. His face was like a hardened mask. He was determined to hold up.

"He's talkin' about that time they had diphtheria, all of 'em together—the time Aaron died. They all would of, if it hadn' been for Heddie. They ain't no tellin' how many nights she went without sleep, an' then, the one died was hers. You recollect that time, I guess, Travis."

Travis nodded. Carl was fighting to get up and Travis, as gently as he could, was forcing him back on the bed while Rinie retrieved the covers from the floor.

"He was like this then," Travis said worriedly. "Little kid younger'n Helen is now an' it was all I could do to keep him in bed. Troy laid quiet, mostly, but it seemed like Carl was . . . afraid to."

"He always was like this with any fever atall," A. J. said. "Remembers ever'thing that ever happened. You tried talkin' to 'em, missy, to keep him quiet?"

"He—he doesn't hear, A. J."

Ellie said, "I don't know. Maybe it's somethin' more than the infection in his arm. He's said several tir s, things about his throat an' head."

"Buck," A. J. said loudly, his voice a little shaky, "the wind's let up an' it's snowin' like hell out there. How much you figger we'll git?"

Carl's eyes opened wide for a moment and he seemed to look at his father, to see him. He said slowly, "I didn't mean him to be hurt like that, A. J. We both fell an' he hit his head. Doyle run off the horses an' we was fightin', but I didn't mean Bo to be hurt bad."

A. J. left as hurriedly as he could, his mask shattered.

To Rinie, it seemed this terrible time had been going on forever. The eternal torment people talked about in church could be no worse than this. For Carl, there was the pain, the fever, the tortures of delirious dreams; for her, the choking fear, the utter, maddening helplessness. It was incredible to think that not much more than twenty-four hours ago he had been taking off his snowshoes at the porch, coming in to supper, feeding Jamie, lying in front of the fire. Looking back into that terribly distant past, she remembered that he had eaten little and been very quiet. She had known he was feverish and they had all seen how bad his arm was. We could have sent for the doctor last night, she thought miserably. He could have got here then. . . . Oh, God, please send him help. . . . Please! Soon.

Ellie said tremulously, "I can't help feelin' like if I'da left his arm alone, this might not of happened."

"You done the right thing, hon," Travis said gently. "Anybody would think, the first thing to drain a wound like that."

"Well, then, I didn' go far enough with it," she said brokenly. "There must still be somethin' in it."

Their voices were vague, their words almost as meaningless to Rinie as to Carl. She thought of twice when he had talked about quick death being good, once when he told her about their stallion being struck by lightning before she had come to live at Red Bear, and again when A. J. had shot the deer from the porch. Then she wasn't thinking much any more, just kneeling there by the bed as she had been for ever, trying to keep the covers drawn up around his shoulders . . . trying to keep him warm . . . trying to keep him.

"It's hot," he muttered petulantly. "I don't like bein' hot. Why don't we all go swimmin'? You could wear that sexy bathing suit."

"Maybe his fever's breakin'," Ellie said hopefully, but he wasn't sweating.

Gradually, he became quieter. Travis didn't have to push him back on the bed any more and he left the covers alone. His hands moved restlessly, but only small listless movements. He breathed with his mouth a little open, rapidly, hoarsely, and his lips were cracked with the fever. Rinie kept moistening them with a damp cloth.

His eyelids fluttered a little sometimes and they were never quite closed, but neither did they open fully. He didn't talk now; he only moaned a little sometimes and moved his head painfully.

"Oh, God, how long has Troy been gone?" asked Rinie in a muffled cry. This quietness was worse—so much worse than the talking and tossing and fighting. She felt she must go mad. She couldn't bear it any longer. "How long?" she all but screamed, looking up, wild-eyed, at Ellie.

"Five or six hours," Ellie said reluctantly. "It's after eleven now."

Rinie bit her lip until the blood ran down. The pain made her feel a little more sane. She mustn't begin to cry. If she did, she was lost and Carl might wake and know.

"Whyn't you just walk around the house a little, Rinie," Travis said gently. "We'll be here with him."

She went and stood by the window. Ellie had wanted to close the curtains at nightfall, but Rinie wouldn't let her. He wanted them open. He always wanted it so he could see the ridge or the sky or the trees or . . . what was he seeing now?

"Do you think," she said woodenly, her back to them, "that Heddie wouldn't come because—because of me?"

"Oh, no!" they both said together, shocked, and Ellie said, "Heddie ain't that kind of a person. She ain't got nothin' against you, an' even if she did, it wouldn' stop her from comin' to help where there's sickness. Heddie's funny some ways, I guess it's the Indian in her, but she loves Carl like he was her own. I remember one time when he was about sixteen, he got throwed off a horse an' broke some ribs. He couldn' hardly breathe an' come near havin' pneumonia. She set up with him, wouldn't let me do a thing. . . . I—I'm afraid she wasn' home, but maybe Troy can git somethin' at the store. Mr. Putney knows a little somethin' about medicine an' keeps a fair supply."

Forty miles to a doctor, thought Rinie desperately. And the snow was a thick curtain outside the windows. No telephones, not even a real drugstore. A road that wouldn't be plowed until they were sure the storm was over because the county road crews had little reason to do extra work on the West Fork road. The harsh, pitiless, uncaring, indomitable country that he loved so much! It was killing him. Almost anywhere else, he could have been taken to a hospital. But not here, oh, God, not here! She put up her hand to draw the curtains and she saw a light.

"Someone," she choked and she couldn't say any more. She buried her face in her hands, fighting not to cry. Carl mustn't find her crying.

Heddie came into the kitchen white with snow, bulky and shapeless in a heavily padded sheepskin coat. She took off her gloves, put her battered old drawstring leather bag on the table, took some things from it and dropped them into a pan of water simmering on the stove, before she took off her coat and scarf.

"How is he?"

"Bad," said Ellie, her lips forming the word soundlessly as she looked around from putting wood in the stove.

Heddie stood there to warm her hands, the short, stubby fingers spread to the heat.

"I was at the Watresses," she said. "She had a baby this mornin'. I was gonna stay the night with the weather like this. . . . Troy's like somethin' wild. I never knowed him to be scared before. . . . How long since he got hurt?"

"Somethin' over four days."

Heddie went to her bag and took out a packet. "You make up some tea out of this. Use about four cups of water. Boil it till it's real strong."

"Heddie, he can't keep nothin' down. We've—"

"You make it anyway."

She went into the bedroom and, without speaking to Rinie or Travis, almost without a glance at them, made her examination.

"We thought," Travis said uneasily, "he might have somethin' besides the infection in his arm. He ain't breathin' right, an' he's complained some of his head an' throat."

Troy had come in from putting up the horses. He stood by the bedroom door, shaking from the cold and from the hours of tension he had been under.

Heddie looked at Carl's arm and noted that the lymph glands all over his body were hard, bulging knots. She said, "It's the infection. That makes him hurt all over, makes the fever. Fever makes him breathe this way." To Troy, she said, "You git warm. I need you." And then she looked at Rinie, standing forlornly, helplessly by the foot of the bed. "You go out for a while. Lay down. You look sick."

"No," Rinie said steadily. "No, Heddie, I won't leave him."

They looked at each other for a long moment and the room was still except for Carl's quick, shallow breathing. In Heddie's sharp black eyes, Rinie saw worry, fear, and, overlaying that, a sizing-up, an estimating of Rinie herself. But she saw no malice, no resentment. In the girl's eyes, Heddie saw, desperation, pleading, terror, love for the man, but no distrust, no contempt for Heddie.

"You stay, you don't argue with what I do. You argue, you go."

Rinnie nodded with a feeling of deference and respect, and went to the side of the bed opposite her.

Heddie ordered alcohol and clean cloths.

"Where's A. J.?" Troy asked, his voice low.

"He went to sleep on the sofa a little bit ago," Ellie said. "He'd had some to drink. I don't think he's li'ble to wake up for a while."

Heddie went to the kitchen and took from the pan of boiling water, a small knife with a thin, razor-sharp blade.

"Oh, God!" Rinie whispered, looking away from it.

"You hold this arm," Heddie said to Troy, "an' see he don't move it. Travis, you hold the other one. Ellie, you take these rags when I hand 'em an' look at 'em good to see if there's splinter or anything. Can you hold the lamp close?"

"Yes," Rinie said numbly.

Carl cried out once, hoarsely, and then lost consciousness. Heddie probed the wound meticulously. It was impossible to see anything in the viscous pus. She put her short, strong hands around the worst part of the swelling and squeezed with a gentle, increasing pressure. The fluid came from the wound in a thick, sullen stream. Troy retched, holding the arm firmly, and Travis mumbled something incoherent.

Rinie didn't look. She hadn't looked since the first glimpse of the knife. She stood like an automaton, gripping the lamp with white-knuckled hands, not seeing or hearing, scarcely feeling anything any more.

"There's a splinter," Ellie said finally, dizzily, "Lord, I don't see how I missed it. It's half a inch long."

365

"Down in," said Heddie succinctly, "maybe against the bone." And she kept up her pressure on the wound.

"Heddie, it's just blood now," Troy said a little faintly. "All that other stuff must be out."

"Blood clean it," she said. "Got to be sure."

"I'll have to git some more rags," Ellie said and went out hurriedly.

"But, Heddie," Troy said desperately, angrily, "he's too weak to lose blood like that. They quit bleedin' people a long time ago."

"You know more about this than me?"

"No, ma'am but—"

"Then you be still."

Rinie didn't know what they said. She just stood there, holding the lamp.

Finally, Heddie released the pressure on the area around the wound and the bleeding slowed gradually. When it had almost stopped, she made a poultice with some of the tea she had instructed Ellie to brew, laid it on the wound and bandaged it loosely. She looked at Carl's face. She had kept glancing at it all along, but now she studied it closely. It was completely drained of color, though his skin burned with raging fever. His breathing was slow and rough and irregular. She laid her hand over his heart and felt it thudding heavily, slowly, irregularly.

"See how much fever he got," she said into the silent room. "If it ain't started down soon, we make it go."

Troy came and took the lamp from Rinie. He had to draw her fingers away from it one by one.

"Come out for a minute," he said gently.

She heard him. "No."

"Just for a minute. You'll feel better."

He put his arm around her and opened the new door into the twins' room. A little light came in from the other room and she looked down at the babies, sleeping, and feeling came back into her with a terrible pain. She began to tremble violently.

"Come in the front room for a little bit," Troy said, opening the other door. "There's a good fire. Come on. they're with him."

"He might wake up. I—"

"Not for a while, Rinie."

He half-carried her to a chair by the fire and pushed her gently into it.

"Troy!" she gasped in sudden terror. "I—I couldn't look at him. I couldn't see him, or—or anything—in there. Oh God! Carl's not dead!"

"No," he said quickly, turning from putting wood on the fire. He knelt by her chair and looked straight into her terror-filled eyes so she'd know he was telling the truth.

On the sofa, A. J. coughed, stirred and opened his eyes.

"Bojack?"

"Yessir?"

"How is he?"

"He's not too good, A. J., but Heddie's come. She's with him now."

The old man sat up, grunting with the pain in his joints.

"Missy's plumb wore out."

"She's all right," Troy said firmly. He was afraid to think what might happen if she began to cry.

There was a silence. A log fell apart in the fire. Rinie felt as if she were asleep, hearing things that went on around her, but not able to wake up. She must go back to Carl, but she couldn't move. She felt that her body was infinitely heavy and might never move again.

A. J. said, "He was talkin', a while ago, 'bout that time you an' him fell at the falls an' you hit your head. You recollect that?"

Troy nodded.

"Seemed like he was thinkin' 'bout how I whupped him before you come to that time," the old man said brokenly.

"Buck always talks with a fever," Troy said, clearing his throat.

"I beat the blood out of 'im," A. J. said miserably. "I oughtn't to of done it. He was hurt already an' you hittin' your head wasn' no way his fault." He put his hands over his face and his stooped old shoulders shook.

Troy stood up. "I'm gonna git us all some coffee."

Ellie was already pouring the coffee. Troy asked her with his eyes.

She said, "He's just layin' there, white as paper, not hardly breathin'. Troy, I just don't believe he can. . . ."

"She oughtn't to of let him bleed like that," he said fiercely. "She ought to've been at home when I went to git 'er, goddam' her to hell."

367

"Troy Dean Stinson!"

But he had gone, with the coffee.

"Rinie," he said gently, "drink this. It'll help."

"She's asleep," A. J. said. "Leave 'er be."

"She's not asleep," he said steadily. "Are you?"

She raised her heavy, heavy hand and took the cup. It was hot, burning her fingers. It made her feel alive. She drank some of the coffee and got up and went into the kitchen. Heddie was at the table with a cup in her hand. Travis was with Carl.

"He looks so—thin," Rinie said shakily, "like he's been sick a long time."

"That's how it is sometimes," said Travis, feeling awkward and useless. She spoke with a sort of calm detachment that made him look closely at her face. She was pale and exhausted and there was something haunted about her eyes and he felt uneasy. It wouldn't be any wonder if her mind failed her under a strain like this.

Carl stirred, moving his hand weakly.

"Rinie?" His voice was weak and hoarse.

"I'm here, Carl," she said tenderly, taking his burning hand in both of hers.

"It hurts so much," he whispered. "I wish I wouldn' wake up."

"Oh, Carl. . . ."

"Thirsty," he mumbled. "We never had a year that made the creek dry up before."

Heddie had come back and Troy and A. J. stood by the door. Ellie was looking after one of the twins who had begun to whimper.

"Can we give him water now, do you think?" Rinie asked Heddie.

Heddie said to Troy, "Git a bowl of snow." Holding Carl's chin gently, she put the thermometer into his mouth. When she had waited and looked at it, she said to Ellie, who had just come into the room, "Git a pan of water—cool water—an' a washrag."

Heddie took the blankets and quilts off the bed, laying them across a chair, until only one blanket and the sheet remained, covering Carl.

"He's shivering," Rinie protested.

Heddie said, "A. J. there's too many people. You men drink coffee or somethin'."

A. J. and Travis withdrew, but Troy stayed. He had got the bowl of snow and put it on the dresser. Heddie said impatiently, as if he should have known, "A spoon."

Ellie brought the pan of water and put it on a chair.

Carl's teeth were chattering and the bed was shaken by his chill. Troy reached for a blanket.

"Leave that alone," Heddie said curtly. "It ain't cover that'll make a difference. He's cold because his fever's 106. I don't know why fever makes chill, but it does, an' cover won't help. The fever got to come out of him, quick." She looked at Rinie. "You want to wash him, or will I do it?"

"Wash him?" Rinie repeated distractedly.

"To cool him."

"Oh, Heddie," said Ellie, "he can't stand this cool water, hot like he is."

"It take the heat from his skin," Heddie said adamantly. "A person can't stand a fever that high for long. It break his mind if it don't kill him."

Rinie remembered at the orphanage hospital when she had been there with flu, a girl in another bed with a high temperature, and the nurse bathing her with alcohol, saying gently, "The doctor says, Ruth. Something cool to bring your fever down."

With trembling hands, Rinie dipped the cloth into the cool water and wrung it out. Carl gasped when it touched his cheek. Gently, she bathed his face and arms and neck and hands. It took only an instant of touching his skin before the washcloth grew hot to her touch. She folded back the covers and laid the cloth on his chest.

"No," he cried hoarsely. "Please! Please don't!"

"Oh, Carl," she whispered, praying that he didn't know it was she who tortured him like this. But she had to be the one to do it, not Heddie. It might help and she had to do something. Keeping him partially covered, she bathed him all over and the water in the pan was almost hot when she had done.

"Carl," said Heddie strongly.

He moaned a little as though he tried to answer, shaking in the grip of violent chills.

"You thirsty, boy?"

"The pump," he said thickly. "I guess it's broke."

"I give you somethin' so you won't be so thirsty." She held a spoonful of snow, just touching his lips. "You just let this lay in your mouth. It'll feel good."

"No, Heddie, it's cold. The whold goddam' world is—"

But she had slipped it into his mouth and he choked a little. Heddie spooned snow into the pan of water to cool it again.

"Keep on," she said to Rinie.

"You're killin' him!" Troy cried hoarsely.

"You git out or keep your mouth shut," said Heddie laconically. "Sick room's no place for men no-how."

This time, Carl knew it was Rinie who ran the cool cloth of torment over his body, and Heddie and Ellie had to hold his hands. Troy hadn't left the room, but he would have no part in what they were doing now.

"Oh, God, Rinie, please," Carl begged weakly, pathetically, "I'm so cold! Please, honey, don't."

She was crying, but she went on with it, on and on. And Heddie kept forcing spoonsful of snow into his mouth as he pled with them. Troy had gone away and Ellie was crying.

Heddie said, "You got a thermometer like for babies?"

"Yes. It's in the dresser drawer," Rinie said through her tears.

"We can't take his fever from his mouth after he's had the snow," Heddie explained, looking in the drawer.

She showed them the reading and said with a trace of satisfaction in her taciturn voice, "Down four degrees since we been doin' this. Stop from washin', Rinie. Let him rest a little."

She went into the kitchen as Rinie tenderly, thankfully, drew the covers close around Carl's shoulders. His breathing was easier now, more normal, but he still shuddered violently.

"I believe it's cleared up outside," said Ellie, standing at the window. She felt as if she were finally rousing from a horrible, seemingly endless nightmare and her voice sounded strange in her own ears. "It'll be daylight right away now."

Heddie came back with a cup half-full of the strong, dark tea from which she had made the poultices. She spooned in snow until the cup was full and stirred until the snow had melted.

"Carl," she said and he opened his eyes and saw her. "I got some tea for you to take."

370

All the men had come to stand by the door. Kirby had got up and he was there, too.

Rinie raised Carl's head a little and Heddie gave him a spoonful of the cold tea.

"Christ, Heddie," he protested weakly, "it tastes like horse piss."

The other laughed and cried in relief and A. J. said gruffly, "You tasted quite a lot of that, have you, son?"

"Maybe it is," said Heddie stolidly, holding another spoonful at his lips. "No way of tellin' what a witch might use. Open your mouth."

Ellie and Helen fixed breakfast and all of them but Rinie ate. She said she would eat when the others finished. She wanted to be with Carl. She still felt frightened of what might happen if she left him.

He lay utterly exhausted and so weak he could scarcely raise a hand, not asleep and not quite awake either. He hadn't vomited the tea and they had given him some aspirin. Heddie said the herbs in the tea were far better for getting a fever down to normal than aspirin, and Rinie didn't doubt it now, but she said timidly that it couldn't hurt to use both.

"All right," Heddie had said with a flicker of a smile. "After the way you've behaved this night, I guess I don't argue with you."

Carl's fever was still dropping, more slowly now, and whenever he roused, she gave him a spoonful of snow.

"Not that," he said petulantly. "Water. A whole jugful."

"Not yet," she said softly. "Heddie says not much for a while yet."

He dozed again and her eyes went to the window. The world was too dazzling to contemplate for long, the sun on all that snow. Her eyes moved up to the ridge, and there it was, bare and dark against the morning sky, the rock spine swept free of snow by the wind. It surprised her to see it like that, standing in its proud, dark sameness in the midst of all the billowing whiteness, and her heart felt a little lift of pleasure and awe and pride. She realized that in her nearly three years at Red Bear, this was the first time she had looked at the ridge with only gladness and respect. Always before there had been dread, fear, resentment. But this morning, oh, this morning, she was glad of everything and even the ridge was beautiful in its

371

own special, peculiar way. And then she stood up in surprise at what she saw nearer to the house.

"Carl?"

He raised his eyelids slowly, wearily. She shouldn't wake him, but she knew he would want to see. She slipped her arms under his head and shoulders and lifted him a little. Sultan, gleaming and magnificent in the sun and snow light, was leading his mares and foals toward the barn. While they watched, he flung up his head and threw a defiant, demanding, challenging scream at the house.

Carl lay back, smiling wanly. "The ole sonofabitch got hungry," he murmured with satisfaction.

Rinie gave him more snow and he dozed. Heddie came and told her to eat. Rinie wasn't hungry, but she ate some anyway. She didn't even feel tired now, though she and everything around her seemed vaguely unreal, a little more intense and vivid than reality. She watched the twins and held them in her arms with a deeper joy than she had known before. He was all right! Oh, thank God for the morning and the ridge and the horses and the children and that he was all right!

"You've got to git you some sleep," Ellie said sternly.

Troy and Travis and Kirby had gone out to give hay to the horses and do the other morning chores. It was like any other morning at Red Bear except that they had been through hell in the night and they were all seeing things fresh and new and beautiful.

Helen said, "Do you think that old stallion knew Carl was sick?" and A. J. said, very softly, "It nearly seems that way, don't it, Puss?"

Heddie changed the bandage and renewed the poultice. There was no stain of blood this time.

She said to Rinie, "I make somethin' now to give him strength. You sleep some. I stay by him. He be all right now."

"All right," she said quietly. "I'll go in a little while. Heddie . . . thank you." She put her arms around the sturdy shoulders and kissed the older woman's dark, smooth cheek.

For the briefest moment, Heddie laid a hand on the girl's thin shoulder, then, not looking at her, she went into the kitchen.

· Carl was breathing easily now and a tinge of healthy color was beginning to show in his cheeks that had grown so hollow overnight. Rinie's own eyes were half-closed when he said, "Hello, tired little girl."

She touched his dry cracked lips with her own and laid her cheek against his. She couldn't say anything. His skin was almost as cool as hers now.

"What, exactly, happened to me?" he asked slowly.

"You got a splinter in your arm," she said, fighting tears.

"Well, I'm God-awful tired from it."

"Then rest."

He said quizzically, "The last thing I remember for sure was Ellie cuttin' the stitches out."

"That was night before last, honey. Don't worry about it. Just rest. It's all right now."

"Night before last?" He looked a little frightened. "Is Heddie here? Or did I dream that, too?"

"She's here."

He said dazedly, "I had such a bunch of dreams or nightmares or—"

"Don't think about it," she said tenderly. "Just go to sleep now and rest."

"I'm so thirsty. Snow?"

"Heddie says, for a while."

"Are the kids all right?"

"Yes."

"And are you?"

"Yes, Carl. Everyone's all right."

"I thought . . . I dreamed . . . anyway you don't look it."

"Well, I am, and that's really not very complimentary, is it? Will you stop talking, please?" She kissed him again.

"Rinie . . . was it a dream that Sultan brought the mares down?"

"No, it wasn't. They're out there eating now while he stands guard. . . . Carl, I was thinking about our house, if we ever built it. It can't be up there where we talked about."

"Why not?" he said drowsily.

"Because we can't see the ridge from there at all."

"Does that matter to you?"

"Yes. I want to be able to look at it any time I want to."

"It's really got you," he said contentedly, looking into her eyes. "I knew it would, sooner or later. Nobody can tell anybody else about this country, or make 'em know, but it always gets to you, eventually, if you give it time. . . . Did you know I knew words like eventually?"

"I don't see why you shouldn't."

"I read a lot, nights when I was away. . . . If I wasn't so dam' tired, I'd try to think of some right words to tell you how I feel about you."

"Go to sleep," she said, gently touching his eyelids, "and so will I. We've got a lot of time. You can tell me, and I'll try to tell you—eventually."

INTRODUCING
THE RAKEHELL DYNASTY

BOOK ONE: THE BOOK OF JONATHAN RAKEHELL
by Michael William Scott

(D30-308, $3.50)
(Available August 1982)

BOOK TWO: CHINA BRIDE
by Michael William Scott

(D30-309, $3.50)
(Available August 1982)

BOOK THREE: ORIENT AFFAIR
by Michael William Scott

(D90-238, $3.50)
(August, 1982 publication)

The bold, sweeping, passionate story of a great New England shipping family caught up in the winds of change— and of the one man who would dare to sail his dream ship to the frightening, beautiful land of China. He was Jonathan Rakehell, and his destiny would change the course of history.

THE RAKEHELL DYNASTY—
THE GRAND SAGA OF THE GREAT CLIPPER SHIPS
AND OF THE MEN WHO BUILT THEM
TO CONQUER THE SEAS AND CHALLENGE THE WORLD!

Jonathan Rakehell—who staked his reputation and his place in the family on the clipper's amazing speed.

Lai-Tse Lu—the beautiful, independent daughter of a Chinese merchant. She could not know that Jonathan's proud clipper ship carried a cargo of love and pain, joy and tragedy for her.

Louise Graves—Jonathan's wife-to-be, who waits at home in New London keeping a secret of her own.

Bradford Walker—Jonathan's scheming brother-in-law who scoffs at the clipper and plots to replace Jonathan as heir to the Rakehell shipping line.

You'll want to read the best by Frances Casey Kerns...

__CANA AND WINE
by Frances Casey Kerns   (A81-951, $2.50)
A vast novel of the Magnessen family, respected and loved,
until the past's dark horror is exposed in the brilliant Idaho
sun. Was Viktor Magnessen the collaborator who had parti-
cipated in savage Nazi experiments and then changed his
name, his country, his identity, and his morals? The only
possible end for the family is disaster.

__THE WINTER HEART
by Frances Casey Kerns   (D81-431, $2.50)
Two young Scotsmen stand at the ship's rail on the eve of
their arrival in America. They yearn for power and wealth—
and a new land free from the fetters of the past. They jour-
ney to Colorado and there they part, caught up in the brutal
present. Their goals change under the realities of the harsh
land. And, finally, each looks for the only succor—a
woman.

__SAVAGE
by Frances Casey Kerns   (A95-603, $2.75)
Roger Savage was their beautiful mother's darling—a
scholar with a taste for violence and a hunger for respect
from the father who ignored him, the wife who never loved
him, and the brother he loved, envied and must now
destroy. And Nolan Savage, battered as a child by mother
and stepfather—and now destined for greatness in the
world of folk music and tragedy in the realm of the heart.

BEST OF BESTSELLERS
FROM WARNER BOOKS

THE CARDINAL SINS
by Andrew M. Greeley (A90-913, $3.95)
From the humblest parish to the inner councils of the Vatican, Father Greeley reveals the hierarchy of the Catholic Church as it really is, and its priests as the men they really are. This book follows the lives of two Irish boys who grow up on the West Side of Chicago and enter the priesthood. We share their triumphs as well as their tragedies and temptations.

THE OFFICERS' WIVES
by Thomas Fleming (A90-920, $3.95)
This is a book you will never forget. It is about the U.S. Army, the huge unwieldy organism on which much of the nation's survival depends. It is about Americans trying to live personal lives, to cling to touchstones of faith and hope in the grip of the blind, blunderous history of the last 25 years. It is about marriage, the illusions and hopes that people bring to it, the struggle to maintain and renew commitment.

To order, use the coupon below. If you prefer to use your own stationery, please include complete title as well as book number and price. Allow 4 weeks for delivery.

WARNER BOOKS
P.O. Box 690
New York, N.Y. 10019

Please send me the books I have checked. I enclose a check or money order (not cash), plus 50¢ per order and 50¢ per copy to cover postage and handling.*

_____ Please send me your free mail order catalog. (If ordering only the catalog, include a large self-addressed, stamped envelope.)

Name _____

Address _____

City _____

State _____ Zip _____
*N.Y. State and California residents add applicable sales tax